PUPPETS

PUPPETS

A NOVEL

DANIEL HECHT

BLOOMSBURY

Published by Bloomsbury Publishing, New York and London
Distributed to the trade by Holtzbrinck Publishers

All papers used by Bloomsbury Publishing are natural, recyclable products
made from wood grown in well-managed forests. The
manufacturing processes conform to the environmental
regulations of the country of origin.

Cataloging-in-Publication Data is available from the Library of Congress.

ISBN 1-58234-495-7
ISBN-13 978-1-58234-495-9

First published in the United Kingdom by Pocket Books in 2001
First U.S. Edition 2005

1 3 5 7 9 10 8 6 4 2

Typeset by Hewer Text Ltd, Edinburgh
Printed in the United States of America
by Quebecor World Fairfield

1

M O SPOTTED THE VAN, just by accident, as he and Mike St. Pierre drove past the parking garage on Wilber Street. It was up on the second level of the three-story ramp, a burgundy Ford Aerostar just pulling up to the concrete barrier wall. Only the top half was visible, license plate out of view, could be somebody else's van. The driver's-side door opened, but then they rolled on past and Mo couldn't see who got out. For a couple of days his pulse had been goosed by every burgundy Ford Aerostar, it was surprising how many there were, but for some reason this one got him jumpier than usual.

"Think we should check it out?" St. Pierre asked. He slowed down and was craning his neck to keep looking at the van in the side mirror.

"Yeah," Mo said.

They had just been talking to neighbors around the supposed residence of Willard Baker, a strong suspect for the serial rapist who had practically shut down the campuses of all the colleges in southern Westchester County. He was a particularly brutal guy who had left seven victims half-dead, and the psych profilers they'd asked in from Albany said it was only a matter of time until he started leaving them all the way dead. They'd gotten Willard's name from Motor Vehicles after witnesses at two crime scenes reported seeing the Aerostar nearby. It made sense, since the rapes occurred in a vehicle, and vans, particularly reddish or purple vans, seemed to be the vehicle of choice for serious crimes against persons, taking over from the Volkswagen buses that had been in vogue among the murder and rape set twenty years earlier. Working backward from all Aerostars with New York plates to those with two *D*'s on the license, it hadn't taken long to zero in on Willard, whose appearance matched victims' descriptions. Neither Willard nor his van had shown up at his home, but Mo kept having a feeling about this parking ramp, only four blocks from his address.

"So, what?" St. Pierre said. "We drive up in there, see if it's even the right van. Then what—call White Plains, they can wait for Big Willie to come back?" Willard had earned the nickname because according to his Motor Vehicles records, he was big, six-six and about three hundred pounds. It'd be easy enough to see at a glance if it was Willie: white guy, bald, that size, hard to mistake him for someone else. St. Pierre's tone suggested he wouldn't mind leaving this to the local police.

True, here in town it really was White Plains PD's job, not theirs. But Mo said, "Take too long. If it is Willie, maybe he's not going home. Maybe he's going to do his thing again. Maybe he's got somebody in the van right now."

St. Pierre sighed, unenthusiastic but expecting it: He was new to the State Police Major Crimes Unit, but had already observed Mo's preference for the direct approach. "Okay."

The problem was that the van was parked halfway between the stairwells, two four-story, concrete-and-glass towers over half a block apart. No way to tell which one Willard, if it was Willard, would come down. So they divvied them up. St. Pierre dropped Mo off at the south tower—"Talk to me, Mike," Mo said, meaning stay close on the two-way—and then made a U, cruised back past the north tower, and pulled over at the corner of Second Avenue.

It was almost eight o'clock, half-dark, Wilbur Street was deserted, and Mo didn't much like the stairway tower. The ramp was recently built, Bauhaus-influenced modernesque, and the towers had tall, narrow windows above each flight of stairs. Heavy concrete planters

2

ribbed each floor, now filled with dead vegetation and trash. As Mo approached the door, he saw movement in one of the windows, someone coming quickly down, and not wanting to run into a big guy like Willard without some equalization, he drew his Glock.

He had barely stepped into the ground-level doorway when something hit him like an anvil dropping from above. It drove him into the left-hand wall, knocked his head hard on the concrete. Willard, it was Willard, was like a wall himself, the biggest human being Mo had ever been this close to, three hundred pounds of marbled beef, muscle and fat. Stunned, Mo lost the Glock as he fell, and though he leapt up only an instant later, Willard had gotten the gun and was pointing it at him. In the small space, the explosion hurt his ears worse than the bullet hurt his shoulder, where it tore through the shoulder pad of his jacket before taking out a chunk of the wall. Willard bounded up the stairs again, a huge bald guy with Mo's gun gripped in a fist the size of a head of cabbage.

Talk about losing the element of surprise, Mo thought vaguely.

It was funny how your mind worked at moments like this. He looked down at his jacket shoulder, seeing his skin through the shreds of fabric and padding, hardly any blood there, just a scratch. He felt irrationally angry at Willard for wrecking this suit, which was new and represented a considerable investment on a cop's salary. Homicide investigators were famous for their lousy taste in clothes, a running joke, grown men dressing like clowns in mixed plaids and checks, lime-green shirts, ties made of vomit-patterned upholstery fabric chosen because it hid the soup stains. In one of the homicide workshops Mo had taken, an instructor had told them to get a grip on their couture, to dress for success: dark gray suits, white shirts, power ties. This guy had a Ph.D. in social psychology and had memorized statistics from RAND Corporation apparel studies and chided the class, "You guys, the only way you know you're ready for a new suit is when the ass of your trousers gets so shiny your partner asks you to bend over so he can shave in it." That got an uncomfortable laugh.

Mo had taken it to heart and had kept up with his clothes. He had bought this suit only two weeks ago for four hundred dollars, and now Big Willie had ruined it.

His two-way crackled and made tinny noises that would be St. Pierre talking, but Mo was afraid to answer, Willard would hear what he was saying. His ears were still ringing from the shot, but he thought he heard the scrape of a shoe on concrete above him. Which meant that Big Willie was still up there, probably crouched on the second-floor landing, wondering whether to run for the van or try some other way out. From that position, Willie would have a good view of the street in both directions and the choice of going up or down or out into the ramp itself. Good for him, bad for Mo: no way for Mo to leave without being seen.

The element of surprise, Mo thought. Hard to tell what St. Pierre would be doing, going up in the other tower and wondering why Mo wasn't answering. Mo had only worked with him for a few weeks, not long enough to anticipate how he made decisions. So he unclipped the two-way from his belt and set it on the floor in the far corner of the stairwell foyer. Then he eased just far enough out the door to look up the outside wall of the stairwell tower, the planters at each level, the windows already lit from inside by mercury-vapor lights even though it was still pretty light outside. At the end of the second-floor window, he briefly saw a big shadow move.

Mo took off his shoes and set them next to the door—shoes would make too much noise on the stuccoed concrete. He climbed up on a wall-mounted hydrant and from there leapt up to catch the first planter. He pulled himself over the saw-toothed lip, scraping his hands and chest and trying to tell himself not to worry, the suit was fucked anyway. He stood and perched on the planter for a moment, catching his breath and listening. Presumably Big Willie would also be pretty deaf from the gunshot, but hopefully not so deaf he wouldn't hear the crackle of St. Pierre's voice on the two-way in the foyer below, and think that Mo was still with the radio. The element of surprise.

Up one more planter and now it was getting scary, balancing on a two-foot-wide shelf, sixteen feet off the ground. One more, another grueling kip and scrape over the stuccoed rim to land face-first in dead plants and litter, then getting on his feet on the third level. He edged sideways along the planter to the wall of the ramp, then vaulted up and over the third-floor railing. Only a couple of cars scattered on the slanted slab, the sky going dark now, the door to the stairwell throwing a rectangle of light on the asphalt. Mo crept to the open door and crouched just inside, listening.

For a moment he didn't hear anything but the distant crackle of the two-way echoing up, St. Pierre over in the other tower or at the van and wondering what the hell. Then he heard the little shift, somebody large moving slightly, waiting. Big Willie was still undecided, hesitating in the second-floor landing.

Mo edged forward until he could see down the stairs: blue, tube-steel banister railing going down a short flight and turning to the right at the halfway landing and then down another short flight to the second level. Where he could just see the shoulder and hip of Big Willie, a massive mound of pink skin in a white wife-beater T-shirt, black jeans over a thigh like a tree trunk. Directly below. Also crouched at the railing and looking down to the first floor.

There were other options, Mo reminded himself. Run in his stockinged feet down to the other tower, find the car, call in backup. Or stay here on the assumption that Willard thought Mo was still waiting on the first floor and figured someone else would be on the second floor where the van was, in which case he might come up here to get away. But Mo didn't like the idea of leaving Willard there—someone could come at any moment, some hapless parking garage customer walking blithely up the stairwell until Willard shot him dead. Or St. Pierre could come down the ramp to find out what was going on and walk right in on big, mean, scared

Willie, already primed for action and carrying a nine-millimeter automatic.

Mo didn't really have to think about it. He looked down at the uneasy mass of Big Willie's body, then unbuckled his belt. A new belt, too, thirty bucks' worth of prime cowhide, double-stitched, quality work but a little too long for a thirty-three waist. He pulled it slowly out of his pants and looped it through the buckle again, then doubled the other end around his fist. Keeping well away from the railing, he crept down the left wall of the stairs. When he got as far down as he could without being seen, he stepped quickly to the railing, leaned over, dropped the noose around Big Willie's bald head, and yanked.

It worked perfectly for half a second, until Willard felt it and reared back and nearly jerked Mo's arm out of its socket. He held on, trying to get a leg around the lower rail, until Big Willie fell back so hard he pulled Mo between the railings, down right onto three hundred pounds of angry bull bucking and wheeling in the concrete box of the landing. Mo cracked both shins on the second-floor banister, then fell on his side, an elbow smashing the floor. But the fall was broken mainly by Willard, and he'd been lucky enough to end up behind him. They were both down on the concrete now. Big Willie had lost the gun, and Mo's one thought was to keep the pressure on the belt, the taut band of leather between his hands and Willard's neck. Cut off carotid flow until he blacked out, maybe twenty seconds. Willard whaled backward a couple of times with one thick arm, and the elbow caught Mo's jaw, but still he held on, using the momentary slack to double the belt around his other hand. Then Big Willie made the mistake of groping at his own neck, giving in to the primal instinct to loosen the constriction there. The big body writhed and rolled, but Mo was able to bring his knees up against the slab of back and arch away, increasing the tension. Like wrestling a refrigerator. Within seconds Willie stopped fighting. For a moment he just clawed at the belt sunk in the meat of his neck. Then he went still.

Mo waited another few seconds, then let the tension off. He pried the belt loose and watched for the color to change on Big Willie's hairless face. But it stayed a blackish purple. Mo got up achingly, wondering what the fuck was going on. The big body didn't move, no breath, and when he put his hand on the neck he couldn't feel a pulse. He slapped the loose cheeks, rolled the head back and forth on the limp neck, moved the jaw up and down. Willie's weight shifted hugely and he rolled onto his back like a big sack of potatoes, but he still didn't breathe. Still dazed from the fall, Mo stared at him, trying to figure what was going on.

"Hey, Willie," Mo called. "Hey, come on. Willard!" He prodded him with his stockinged foot, got no response. It took him another half minute to notice the glint of gold in one of the creases on Willard's neck, and he dug in his fingers to find a heavy chain buried there, a necklace that had gotten snarled in the fight and that had stayed tight far too long.

He had clawed it loose and was kneeling on the floor giving Willard mouth-to-mouth when Mike St. Pierre burst through the second-floor doorway, his gun leveled.

"Jesus," Mike said, taking in the situation. Then he said, "I didn't mean to intrude," thinking he was funny.

Mo took his mouth off Willie's. "Ambulance," he panted. And then back to the sour, hammy taste of Willie's slack lips.

St. Pierre called in, but then he hunkered down next to Mo to put two fingers on Willard's neck. "You might as well quit, Mo. Guy's gone. Jesus, what happened here? You look like you got hit by a truck." He frowned and added, "How come you're not wearing your shoes?"

Three ambulances and an array of White Plains and State Police cars came, lighting up the parking ramp and the street with flashers of different colors. Like a giant mirrored disco ball, only nobody was dancing. Gawkers stopped their cars and came out of apartments to look at the show from the street. Mo's boss at Major Crimes, Senior Investigator Marsden, came from the Bureau of Criminal Investigation, along with a lieutenant and a captain all the way from Poughkeepsie and a sallow-looking jerk from Internal Affairs. Even Richard K. Flannery, Westchester County's super-officious DA, put in an appearance. Flannery's attendance at this gala made it good odds it was going to turn into a shit heap. The whole sequence of events was hard to explain. When Mo told it, the episode seemed stranger than it had been at the time, when everything was happening so fast and it all fell into place with the inevitable logic of necessity. His shoes still stood side by side next to the ground-floor entrance, that was great, he'd never realized what a psychological disadvantage you're at when you're wearing only socks outside in the city at night. Flannery gave him ugly looks, told him to keep his mouth shut, and made some perfunctory statement to the press, a big, square-shouldered, cue-ball-bald guy hogging the cameras and pretending he didn't enjoy it. A News3 helicopter thumped away overhead, bathing the whole area in a searing white spotlight and making so much noise that after Mo had retrieved his gun from the stairwell he was tempted to shoot it.

Every bone, every muscle, every inch of skin, *everything* hurt. He would have been sore just from that first short scrap with Willard on the ground floor, but being pulled through the railing and having to wrestle with the guy had just about done him in. His shinbones felt broken, he'd sprained muscles in both shoulders, his elbow needed an X-ray, his head was covered with bumps, it felt as if he'd pulled a ligament in his groin. His suit was in rags and he was wearing only socks. His belt had been bagged as evidence. He was exhausted but he knew there'd be hours of incident reports and debriefings to go through before he could go home, and there'd be all kinds of departmental repercussions. It was the shits.

And then to have St. Pierre come up to him and ask him for his gun.

."My gun? You want my *gun*."

St. Pierre toughed it out: "Hey, Mo, regs. Apprehension of suspect, death resulting." He couldn't really look at Mo.

"I didn't *shoot* the guy! I *strangled* the—"

"Mo, come on, *regs*. 'When a firearm is involved.' It was 'involved,' okay?" St. Pierre tried to look reasonable, standing there outside the second-floor doorway, hand outstretched, trying for an *I'm your buddy* grin, not really making it.

"You have got to be shitting me! Right? You're putting me on?" Flannery and Marsden and the Troop K and White Plains brass were down at street level, but a couple of patrolmen were watching and they seemed to be trying to suppress grins.

"Marsden's orders," St. Pierre said regretfully. The hand still out.

Mo handed it over, immediately missing the weight of it under his arm and thinking again, *This is the shits.*

He got back to the house at half past midnight. Coming home to the big house was no great relief. Carla and he weren't lovers anymore, just uneasy roommates in the house they rented from her mother, one of several she owned on the west side. It had seemed like a good idea at the time, moving into one of Mom's extra houses with the understanding that they'd do some painting and wallpapering in exchange for cheap rent. Nice yard overhung by big oaks, a neighborhood on the outskirts of town, good for walks and jogs. The place was in good shape and would be great if you were happily married and had kids and dogs and Volvos, but as things stood, it was far too much space. Moving from a three-room apartment, they hadn't had enough furniture to inhabit more than the back end of the ground floor, leaving the front of the house and the whole upstairs empty. Lots of big rooms with glistening, bare oak floors, tall, curtainless windows that let in stark sun during the day and too much blue streetlight glow at night. They'd solved the problem by setting up the kitchen, converting a small rear study to a bedroom, and calling the former dining room their living room. Kind of like a three-room apartment.

Mo unlocked the front door, stepped into the echoing front hall, aching and thinking that the mostly empty house, the temporary and unfinished feel of it, was a pretty close metaphor for their relationship.

The lights were still on in the back rooms, meaning Carla was still awake, and she had Chopin playing quietly on the stereo. He heard water running in the bathroom sink, no doubt Carla taking her lenses out and brushing her teeth and putting on some specialized fruit-based facial cream before bed, and he called out, "It's me," before heading into the kitchen to get a beer. He yanked the top and dropped hard onto one of the chairs in the former dining room and then slugged back some beer. It tasted metallic, and he wondered why he always bought cans instead of bottles. *Easier to recycle,* he answered himself. Still, it was nice. He took another swallow. The bathroom pipes squeaked as Carla turned off the water.

"How was your day?" she called, only marginally interested. "Anything new and exciting?"

"Not really," he called back. He rearranged himself on the chair with difficulty, trying to find a position that didn't cause some body part to hurt and then giving up. He held the cold can against one of the bruises on his forehead. "Just the usual," he said.

2

B UT WHEN SHE CAME in and saw him, her eyebrows jumped. Carla was small and dark, and the colorful silk shirts and scarves she often wore made her look a little like a gypsy. It helped in her client relations and public image, she said, meaning that as a fortune-teller and astrologist a somewhat exotic appearance didn't hurt. The observation was typical, a combination of the esoteric and the pragmatic, from a woman who had almost gotten a master's degree in psychology before her largely accidental career had taken off. Now she had a daily astrology bit that was aired on three radio stations, a daily column in the *Journal News,* a growing private clientele. She had started writing a book about "contemporary predictive consultation" and was researching everything from psychic hotlines to voodoo ceremonies, but Mo could never tell just how seriously she took herself. Certainly she put a lot of work into her sessions and believed she did some good for people, but she'd never claimed to have real supernatural talents. Instead she talked about beneficial transference, the placebo effect, neurolinguistic suggestion, constructive catharsis. She was pretty insightful, and he figured she saw herself more as a kind of psychotherapist for those who needed a sense of a link to "the beyond," to universal truths. "So tell me about you and me," Mo had asked her a couple of months ago. They'd had another fight, things had already been difficult for a while. "Read our future. Are we going to make it?" She had looked at him deadpan, seeing it for what it was, more of a provocation than a question. "That's not how it works," she'd answered. Meaning how her predictive processes operated or how Mo should probe her intentions, he wasn't sure.

But it was nice that she was sympathetic now. Mo's whole body called out for some kind of comfort. She came to him and touched his bruised face with her fingertips, eyes full of concern. "Wow. You want to tell me about it? You've been to the hospital, right?" She scanned him up and down. "Oh, God—and your new suit!"

It was nice that she understood about the suit, too. So he told her about the run-in with Big Willie. Then about how pissed Marsden had been at him for killing another suspect, and in such a creative way, and about the likelihood of problems with the DA's office. He told her he was okay, though: At the hospital, they'd x-rayed his legs and elbows and found no breaks, and the shoulder wound was truly just a scrape, not even requiring stitches.

Carla knelt beside him, arms on his thigh, listening. When he was done and had sucked the last of his beer, she said, "You're feeling bad about this. You're kind of in shock, aren't you?"

"Well, it's not so unusual—"

"You don't have to be defensive. Of course you're upset. You should be."

"I mean, the guy, what he did to those women, maybe he deserved it. But it's another thing when you're right there? When you take somebody's life with your own hands? I was right there, I didn't even know he was dying right in front of my eyes. Didn't even know it."

Sitting there, Mo could still feel the bucking of Big Willie's massive torso against his own chest and knees, a body-memory replaying itself, what Carla called "kinesthesic perseveration." When he'd been down on the floor, he'd felt it as Big Willie's fighting *him,* resisting arrest or something. But now his body knew it as Big Willie's fighting for something much more basic, some rudimentary animal prerogative: life itself. How easily you could take that away from somebody. How it could go out of a living person and from two feet away you couldn't even tell. How unmomentous a change. Made everything seem pathetic and sad. He wondered how long he'd have dreams of Big Willie's final moments.

He couldn't express it, but Carla seemed to understand, maybe this was what her clients needed, what they got from her. "Yeah," she said. "Yeah." She rubbed his thigh sympathetically, looking up at his face. Carla had dark brown eyes with flecks of gold around the iris, the whites so clear they were almost blue, alert eyes that still fascinated him. He loved being this close to her, having her undivided attention, basking in the warmth of her sympathy. Like when they made love, their bodies joined and their faces this close, and it seemed he could see every movement, every sensation, mirrored instantly in her eyes—

But now she was up again, tossing her hair over her shoulders as she headed toward the kitchen in her blue silk robe. "I'm going to get you another beer. Then I'm going to run you a hot bath. It'll help loosen up your muscles. Anyway, you should always have a ritual cleansing after something like that. You know what I'm saying?" She was still being solicitous, but he couldn't help but think she'd seen him falling toward her and had deliberately interposed some distance.

Oh well, he thought. He was too tired and sore to worry about it. And yes, another beer would be nice.

Friday he had a meeting with Marsden in the senior investigator's office. The *Journal News* had put the story just below the fold on page one, and News3 and Cable Ten had both played footage of the scene on the ten-o'clock and the morning news. Serial rapist suspect killed in parking garage. District attorney to investigate rapist's death, killer cop. Unusual circumstances in apprehension of rape suspect. Cop in parking garage incident has prior history of violent arrests.

The last was untrue, the plural part anyway. Mo had only killed one other suspect, one other person, in his life, and that was in a shoot-out where he'd had no choice, a situation where Inspection had raked him over the coals but had ultimately deemed his actions entirely reasonable. Flannery had grudgingly accepted the determination, but had publicly stated that the DA's office intended to closely monitor State Police arrest procedures. At his press conference back then, Flannery had pointedly mentioned Mo's name, a little warning that Mo had come up on his personal radar. DAs, Mo learned, hate issues where they're caught between supporting the police and pandering to the constituencies that elected them.

Mo had felt pretty bad after that one, too, even though in retrospect it was emotionally much easier to kill a guy from fifty feet away than lying against him with a belt around his neck. But any time a death resulted during police work it had to be looked at closely: Most cops went through a whole career without killing anyone, many without even taking their gun out in the line of duty. Mo had been an investigator for eight years and had already killed two people. It didn't look good, went against the law of averages. Plus the belt and the no shoes thing.

Mo didn't look forward to his meeting with Marsden. On the bright side, this would probably mean a thirty-day suspension. Even if it was without pay, that didn't sound too bad.

Marsden had been a highway patrolman, moved up to investigator, showed talent, moved up to senior investigator of Major Crimes through grit and endurance. He was in his mid-fifties now, a tired-looking guy with jowls and suspicious slit eyes and thinning dark brown hair combed against his head. A chronic skin condition, eczema or something, flared red on one side of his nose and itched and made him irritable. He could make you hurt if your mistakes impaired the effectiveness of the unit. At the same time, he knew what you were up against and had some sympathy for the vicissitudes of the job.

Mo knocked on the door frame of Marsden's office at the far end of the MCU's "back room" at the State Police White Plains barracks building. Marsden beckoned him in, gestured for him to sit, tossed aside a folder he'd been studying. Mo took the chair in front of the desk.

For a full minute, Marsden just stared at him through his slit eyes, pouting, chin on his clasped hands. Finally he said, "You know, I gotta say, I admire you. I admire the hell out of you."

Mo didn't answer. It wasn't an auspicious beginning.

"I admire you because you can pull the craziest shit, so help me, where even a guy like me, thirty years as a cop and police administrator, has to go back to the procedural manual and try to figure if what you did was right or not. Consult with counsel, the whole nine yards. You'd think by now I'd have seen everything. But no. Not with Mo Ford. So, I hand it to you. Really." Marsden tugged at his lower lip, exposing the purple-veined inner surface.

"Doesn't sound like I'm supposed to say 'thank you' for the compliment," Mo hazarded.

"I also admire that every time you get yourself in hot water, you get lucky, you get the right guy. We sent photos of your dead buddy around to the victims. Positive ID. Fibers from the van carpet are a match with the ones we've picked up from victims. So it looks like you killed the actual perpetrator."

That was some relief.

"And, one more thing, this is what's really slick—I admire that every time you get us in trouble with some constituency, you manage to give everybody conflicted emotions that take wind out of their sails. On this one, here in the State Police, you got half the guys pissed at you for loose procedure and half practically starting up a fan club for your ingenuity and balls. The White Plains guys, half of them are steamed because you acted in their jurisdiction, but half are jumping up and clicking their heels because you got Big Willie out of their hair. In the community, you've got the suspects'-rights, police-brutality types mad that you killed a guy without knowing for sure he was the perpetrator. But he was *white,* with maybe a skinhead connection, so you shook off criticism from the African-American

15

community! Plus you've got the feminists, who're usually part of that same police-brutality constituency, secretly feeling, hey, this guy really deserved it. Bottom line, nobody wants to raise too big of a stink for us. We don't have to publicly self-cannibalize or even make a ritual sacrifice out of you. So I admire you—I really do." Marsden tossed his hand at the file, which Mo could see was the beginning of the File 3, the internal report on Mo's dance with Big Willie.

Marsden's buildup of his deep admiration was scary, but so far the news was not bad.

"So—"

"So we're not gonna suspend you pending the outcome of the internal investigation. I can't make promises about what Flannery might do, but for now you get to go back to work."

Mo found he was leaning to the right and rolling his pelvis forward, a way of keeping weight off the groin pull. "I got kind of banged up. I was thinking maybe I could have a couple days of sick leave—"

"I'd recommend it," Marsden snarled.

"You going to tell me what the problem is?" Mo was stiff and still tired. Another reason for a couple of days off would be to spend time with Carla, maybe sort something out. At this point, it all added up to he didn't much care what it cost to be out front with Marsden.

"The problem? What problem? You mean Flannery? You mean the DA on my ass about I can't control my people? That Flannery wants to stick his nose in this to show what a take-charge guy he is, and that I need you on the job so badly that I gotta be your umbrella here? You mean between our caseload and red tape I got a rock and a hard place? Hey—forget about it. Nah. It's nothin', really. But Ford"—and here his so-what act slipped, a dark glint flashed in his slit eyes—"not again. No problems for me. Nothing that gets press attention. Or I make problems for you. I hear they're shorthanded on highway patrol out in Oswego." Marsden commanded him out of his chair with his fingers. "Now get outta here, I got work to do."

Mo went out to the floor and back to his desk. He felt a mix of relief and disappointment. Part of him really didn't care if he stayed on this job. He was tired and sore and depressed, and half of his problems with Carla were related to the job, his coming home from work with ugly pictures in his head, the risks he had to take, the jocks and ex-service types who were his colleagues. There were other things besides being a homicide detective. Any glamour it had had—when was that?—had long since worn off. Maybe this was one of those times when you really retrenched. Maybe he should go back to school, take psychology or history or something. Carla would like that, maybe it would make the difference for them.

Or maybe not. With relationships, maybe the external stuff people blamed for their problems was just camouflage for a deeper disconnect, the absence of fire or magic or chemistry, or the lack of real common ground, or the fear of real intimacy. The mostly empty house, the bare, unused rooms—harder stuff to face up to. Maybe that's where he and Carla were at. Maybe she saw that better than he did, and that's why she seemed more willing to let go.

He was still thinking about it when he got back to his desk and found Mike St. Pierre waiting.

"I've been looking for you," St. Pierre said. "We're up. Got a call, there's a body down on Maple Brook Road."

"Why do they want us in there?" White Plains had a good detective bureau, didn't usually ask for help from the State Police.

St. Pierre shrugged. "Didn't say."

Mo thought about telling him about his plan to take a few days' sick leave, about his acute desire to go home and fall into bed and let it all slip for a day or two. Maybe this one could go to Valsangiacomo, or Estey. But St. Pierre looked so eager, a big puppy, he couldn't bear to disappoint him. Mike was still new enough to be caught up in the mystique, to want to do battle with evil. A big, sandy-haired young guy, good-humored, should have been a pro baseball player or something else more wholesome and sunny. St. Pierre hadn't yet noticed how far it was from White Plains to Hollywood, or from the BCI Major Crimes offices to his house in the burbs, his wife and kids.

"Oh—here's this," St. Pierre added, handing him his gun. "Marsden says you can have it back."

"Big of him," Mo said.

3

THE MURDER HOUSE WAS the left half of a two-story duplex in a middle-income residential neighborhood of aluminum-sided singles and duplexes built in the sixties and seventies. It was another area where the old elm trees that had once given the street some grace had died and the city had planted little lollipop maples in their place, leaving the sidewalks and houses looking naked. On the other hand, the cars parked along the curbs were new, the lawns well-kept and set off with flower gardens. In front of 1431 were a couple of ambulances, three squad cars, several unmarked White Plains cars. They'd already strung tape around the house and yard. Even though it was a nice May afternoon, sunny, robins popping on the lawns, nobody seemed to be outside. People hovered in door-ways and windows, looking on from a distance, parents keeping their hands on their kids. Word had already gone around the neighbor-hood, and it was the kind of word that scared people.

Mo and St. Pierre greeted the cops at the door and went in to meet the White Plains investigator in charge. They found Jim Melrose in the living room, standing in front of a big home-entertainment center. Melrose had a long, gray face at the best of times, and now he looked particularly not good. Mo recognized the look: a man with bad pictures in his head.

"Hey," Mo said. They shook hands and Mo felt a pang of sympathy. Sometimes you could joke about it, act tough and jaded, and sometimes you couldn't. "How are you doing?"

"I was supposed to be on vacation this week," Melrose said. "Then we changed the schedule around so we could go to my sister's wedding? So I ended up being here for this."

He gave them the story. Neighbor kid was playing in the yard next door, threw a Frisbee into the back yard of 1431, came to get it, saw something through the window, went home crying. Mother took a peek, went home crying, too, called 911. From her glimpse through the window, the mother next door identified the corpse as Daniel O'Connor, owner of the house.

"So how come you want us here, Jim?" Mo asked.

Melrose just gestured with his chin and led them back through the house. Nice place, Mo decided, furnished with wicker chairs and Durie rugs and natural wood tables from Pier 1 and the Pottery Barn. As always, he had the uncomfortable sensation of being a voyeur, the little kinky charge that came from walking around uninvited in a stranger's house. Looking so closely. Seeing the way other people lived, so much like the way you lived yet so different. Different food smells, different body odors, unfamiliar faces in photos, the kind of books you'd never read. Maybe for burglars this kind of trespass was more fun, but in a death house everything seemed frozen in time, abandoned. Bad things had happened here, nightmarish things that still echoed in the quiet rooms.

"It's freezing in here," St. Pierre complained. And Mo realized he was right, it was midseventies outside and was barely in the low sixties in here.

"Yah," Melrose said. "I noticed it, too. There's a thermostat in the living room, central air, set as low as it can go."

Which would be good for preserving the corpse, Mo thought. But it was only mid-May, not yet that hot, so why would O'Connor have wanted it so cold? Or had the killer set it?

From the living room they went into a central hallway and glanced into a cheerful kitchen: black-and-white tile floor, little round table with an open newspaper and a coffee cup. They passed a small bathroom and then at the back of the house went into a large room that made up the rest of the ground floor. Low-pile, green carpeting, a StairMaster, a little weight rack, a bicycle and kayak up on hooks on the right wall, a television, a computer desk and CD player. Obviously O'Connor had used this as a combination exercise-utility-office room. Brightly lit by a pair of big windows and a louvered glass door that led out into the backyard. A couple of other White Plains guys were there. Mo didn't see the body until Melrose gestured for him to turn around.

Yes, it was one you weren't likely to forget.

O'Connor had red-blond hair, a boyish face and freckled arms and shoulders, a good build. He was naked and suspended upright by some kind of cord that was tied to his ankles and knees, elbows and wrists and neck, and ran up to nine steel eyelets sunk into the wall. In addition to the poly line, a disposable-type nylon handcuff hung from each wrist. His head and shoulders lolled forward and his weight was equally supported by his arms, up at head height, and his legs, with the ankles drawn up and knees bent sharply. A marionette on strings. His skin was a sick, purplish white except for where the cord had trapped blood and where postmortem lividity had stained the lower surfaces of his body bright, mottled red. Aside from the coloration changes and ligature indentations, the body seemed at first unmarked. Then Mo spotted two small wounds in O'Connor's hair, one just above each ear. Dried blood, not much, had run and clotted below the wounds, crisping the short blond curls.

Mo scanned the room, looked back to O'Connor, looked around the room again, trying to map things in his head before it got any crazier here. Within minutes, the White Plains CSU van would come, Marsden and others from the BCI would show up, there'd be photographers and forensic technicians and the medical examiner's people. There'd be photo flashes and vacuums running and people dusting for prints, and all the activity would change the way the room looked and felt. Patterns that might register subconsciously would be lost, the overview smothered in details.

He sniffed delicately in the direction of the corpse and caught only the faintest odor of ripe meat. When he pushed the head gently, it resisted, suggesting that the body retained rigor. The air-conditioning would have arrested decay somewhat, but taken together both were signs O'Connor hadn't been dead that long. From this close, he could see that the line used to suspend the body was not a heavy poly fishline, as he'd first thought, but the sharp-edged, serrated cord used for weed-whackers.

Melrose was keeping his distance, as if what had killed O'Connor might be catching. Mike St. Pierre stood well back, too, not so enthusiastic now.

With the big windows directly opposite the corpse on the wall, the drapes pulled all the way apart and the ceiling lights on, it was clear the body had deliberately been displayed—a spectacle just waiting for someone to find it. Mo took a turn through the room, but he already knew what he'd find. On a side table he saw an arrangement of objects organized in geometric patterns: a pair of folded sunglasses, bracketed by two gardening gloves. Above them, a collection of pens arranged in a neat zigzag line with coins placed in each angle. A couple of stacks of music CDs, perfectly squared with the edge of the table, with an empty Gatorade bottle on top of each stack. At the computer desk, diskettes had been lined up side by side all the way around the keyboard, and a cork bulletin board had been arranged with similar precision, postcards and cartoons and jotted notes arrayed down the center in a symmetrical pattern surrounded by triangles outlined in colored thumbtacks. A compulsive symmetry. Once you noticed it, the arrangement of all the room's little things took on an eerie subliminal geometry, scary, like seeing the diamonds on a rattlesnake down in the grass, or the hourglass on a black widow spider.

"You like the designs?" Melrose asked. "Bedroom's the same way."

Mo's head had begun to ache again, and he could feel all the muscle pulls and bruises distinctly. He was thinking, *If only I had made it to the desk and had signed out for sick leave. Just like two or three minutes head start, and somebody else would have gotten this.*

"You recognize this, Mike?" he asked St. Pierre.

"Looks just like that guy, what do they call him, the control freak—"

"Yeah." Mo wondered if Mike understood what that meant.

The New Jersey State Police had begun calling him Howdy Doody, after the famous TV puppet of the 1950s. The first murders with the distinctive signature of strings tied to limbs and ritualized arrangements of objects had begun early in 1999. Three people killed in northern New Jersey, then three in Manhattan and another in the Bronx in a thirteen-month period, the remorselessly accelerating rhythm of kills typical of serial murderers. Mo knew Ty Boggs, who'd headed up the Bronx end of the investigation and was part of the interjurisdictional task force, and they'd talked a little about the crimes. But Ty had been stingy with details. As with every serial spree, the police and FBI had kept many specifics of the crimes out of general knowledge. This had the several goals of discouraging the killer from changing his habits and maybe camouflaging his style, of being able to weed out bogus confessions, and of being able to differentiate between murders by the original artiste and future copycat crimes.

Serial murder was the most horrendous and most difficult kind to solve. It was horrible because the habits of the killer, the repetition of certain types of torment or mutilation, spoke of some unfathomable sickness in the psyche, of a mind infested by demons that demanded a specific ritual. As did the motivation: The act of killing itself was the killer's objective, not particularly the end result.

If you thought about that, it could mess you up inside.

The difficulty in catching serial killers arose from the fact that unlike with most crimes the victims were not linked to the murderer by a web of interpersonal contacts, normal motivation, or cause and effect. Serial killers came from outside their victims' social spheres, so you couldn't nail them by establishing links between people with typical motives like jealousy or greed or revenge. Usually, the only connection was to be found in the psychology of the murderer, the compulsions or delusions or fears or hungers that drove him to kill. You had to inspect the psychological implications of each death, explore the symbolic narratives in excruciating detail.

Getting that far into the mind of multiple murderers was not healthy, either.

And all that aside, Mo thought, from a strictly professional standpoint there were other things that made this one a prospective nightmare. The administrative complexity of tying your work to an ongoing investigation by the FBI and other police agencies, the interjurisdictional task forces and the resulting increase in paperwork, conflicts of authority, and rivalry for leads and evidence and glory. The DA would want in on this, big time. There'd be publicity and publicity-seeking and political pressure, and scapegoating when things didn't go well.

And one other problem as well, Mo reminded himself.

Melrose brought it up before he said it: "Yeah, the control nut, the Howdy Doody killer. But they caught that guy, three-four months ago. Down in the city."

Mo looked at O'Connor, dead and grotesquely serene on the wall like the limp Jesus of the pietà.

Then he heard people in the hall, and there was Angelo Antonelli, the deputy medical examiner. Behind him came Marsden, and then a jumpsuited woman carrying a big aluminum equipment case, and a couple of other evidence techs. And then it was just time to rock and roll.

4

"Yo, mo," ANGELO SAID brightly. "Hey, I was just looking at your pal, what'd you guys call him—Big Willie. They gonna give you grief or what?" He winked at Marsden and said for his benefit, "Tell you what I'll do, I'll sign off it was accidental death. Hit his head in the tub or something."

"Not funny," Marsden said. "Don't even joke about that." The irritated skin next to his nose was bright red and looked painful.

Mo saw Angelo once in a while over drinks over at The Edge, and before his relationship with Carla had turned into a minefield they'd even gotten together a couple of times with Angelo and his girlfriend as a foursome. He was small and wiry, dark-haired, with the luscious big eyes and long, dark lashes of a stereotypical Italian Renaissance lover. His job was slicing up people who'd been killed by all kinds of gruesome means; he worked in a labyrinth of gray tile floors with drains in them, brushed-chrome refrigerators, and savage-looking medical equipment. You'd expect him to be ghoulish, secretive, but in fact Angelo loved his job, loved his customers and his colleagues, maintained a relentlessly cheerful disposition. He was an avid whistler and often peeled off cheerful ditties as he burrowed into the abdominal cavities or braincases of murder and accident victims.

When he saw O'Connor, Angelo's face registered a look of surprise and gleeful anticipation. By his seriously nasty look, Marsden recognized the Howdy Doody MO and the problems this would entail.

Angelo and his assistant looked over the body. Angelo was a stickler for detail, using a handheld tape recorder to record his observations here just as he would dictate what he saw and did back at the morgue when he got around to cutting. They took an air temperature reading and a basal body reading, tested the degree of rigor, measured the area of lividity patches, picked at spots of dried blood and saved it in glassine envelopes, went over every inch of skin with an illuminated magnifier, bagging up hairs, fibers, dandruff, dirt.

At last they put paper bags over the hands and with Mo's help cut the body down and lowered it onto a gurney. The assistant bagged the cut-off lines and nylon handcuffs as they came free. It was an awkward process, figuring how to keep O'Connor in place until all the cords were cut and then manhandling an inert, 170-pound, naked adult male who was frozen in such a position. The neck cord was really slicing into the creased skin there. Angelo supervised as the three of them leaned and strained: "There . . . Hold it! . . . Wait— there, now push a little. Lift . . . Lemme just get—no, hold it!" Mo had felt the curiously heavy, pliant stiffness of corpses before, but this was particularly unsettling. Dancing with a dead man. When they cut the wires holding the wrists, the arms dropped forward a few inches and bobbed on the remaining elasticity of their sinews, like some-body playing monster to scare some kid. When they laid him on his back on the gurney, he kept that same position, head still forward and held well off the pad, arms up at head height, and worst of all, legs up at the spread knees and heels not quite touching the pad. They put a sheet over him, but the contorted, clutching tented shape was in some ways worse.

Photographers began to shoot the scene, still and video, a sketch artist mapped the room, and the trace techs went at the surfaces. St. Pierre went out to talk to the uniforms and the neighbors, and as the techs continued their work, Marsden took Mo aside. They went into the kitchen, where the geometric arrangements were in evidence on all the counters. Mo put on a fresh pair of gloves and poked cautiously around in drawers and cabinets. Marsden stood glowering out the window over the sink.

"So we've got a copycat," Marsden said. "Starting up here in White Plains."

"Looks that way."

"Your sick leave is canceled."

"I figured." Mo opened the refrigerator, looked at plastic-wrapped cold cuts, a bag of carrots, bottles of Heineken, milk, OJ. Typical stuff. The killer had not done his hypercompulsive arranging in the fridge.

Marsden said, "I know Biedermann a little, he's the FBI's guy running the Howdy Doody investigation. Manhattan field office. You'll need to get in touch with him. Also the other members of the first task force, see what they can tell you about the original. I understand the feds called in an outside consultant to work with Behavioral Sciences, a shrink in Manhattan, you might want to consult with him."

Mo used his pen to lift the edge of a pot holder, peered underneath. "Maybe they've got the wrong person, we're dealing with the original here?"

"Caught him red-handed, the way I heard it." Marsden watched Mo for a moment, standing with his arms crossed and resting on his big belly. "Why's it so cold in here?" he complained.

"Central air-conditioning. Somebody turned it all the way down. Not bad for our purposes, but I'm wondering why." Mo opened another drawer, found the kitchen utensils, and bent close to stir his pen through potato peelers, knives, kitchen shears. Probably the killer had brought his own gear, but it would be good to bag up every likely tool in the house, look for residues of the plastic line, prints, maybe some DNA.

"The bitch is," Marsden said, "that the first guy got into a rhythm of about once a month toward the end. We don't know how the new guy will do it. But if we've got something like this to deal with once a month, it's going to be a shitty summer." The SI's voice had gotten thoughtful, almost sad-sounding. "There's another thing for me, I haven't mentioned this to anybody, I've been having this heart stuff. Took a stress test last week, where they put you on a treadmill? Flunked it, I've got a congestive problem in the coronary arteries, they're gonna do an angiogram on me, end of the month. But if I have to get a bypass, I'll miss a lot of time or maybe even get moved to some other department. Plus in the meantime I've got to avoid stress, anxiety, overwork, that shit. Like that's a possibility. Supposed to lose weight, quit smoking, too."

Mo looked at Marsden. This was an unprecedented level of intimacy, and he wondered what the senior investigator was leading up to. "Jesus. I'm sorry, Frank. I have to say, you've been hiding it well. I mean, you look good—"

"Bullshit."

"Okay. You don't look any worse than usual."

Marsden grinned sourly. "I've been thinking who's gonna stand in for me as unit coordinator. St. Pierre's out, too new. Paderewski's okay, but she doesn't get along with half the guys. Benoit, he's dumb as a stump, I don't know how he ever got in here, and Estey and Valsangiacomo just like guns and cars, they're not good with paper or people. Then there's Mo Ford, he's the smartest of the bunch, got the best solve rate, but can't stay out of trouble and he's earned some enemies. Maybe his commitment to a career isn't what it has to be for unit coordinator, maybe he doesn't have the patience to do things by the book. Maybe his personal life gets in the way? So you can see what I'm up against." Marsden gestured toward the door, the back of the house where O'Connor's body had hung. "And then this . . . thing . . . has to come up, just to put more pressure on."

Mo heard the backhanded flattery, surprised at how good it felt, impressed by Marsden's insight about his personal life, which Mo had made a point of never mentioning. He was thinking of a way to answer when Marsden gestured with his chin to the window.

Outside, a pair of dark cars had pulled up, and Mo recognized the big form of District Attorney Flannery getting out with a couple of his investigative assistants.

Marsden heaved himself away from the edge of the counter. "Getting on four, I gotta go talk to Biedermann about how they handled public relations on the Howdy Doody kills, then talk to the mayor. I'll leave you and Flannery to have a tête-à-tête. What's your next step?"

"I'll finish up here, talk to the White Plains people about getting a canvass going in the neighborhood. Then I'll pull up the files on Howdy Doody. I want to see just how close this guy is to the original, how they profiled him, what resources are online for a related crime. Then I'll see if I can get Angelo to expedite the autopsy."

"Yeah," Marsden said dejectedly. "Okay. Give me an update on Monday." He went to the living room door, scratching unconsciously at the raging skin next to his nose and watching the techs at work. "The first guy got seven before they caught him. Seven." He caught Mo's eye meaningfully. "Town the size of White Plains, this new guy could depopulate the place. Have to change the population figures on the city-limits signs, huh?" A weary attempt at humor. Also a plea: *Mo, do this right for once. And catch the son of a bitch soon.*

When the DA came into the murder room, his eyebrows went up and his blue eyes took on a look as he saw the Howdy Doody MO and his wheels started to turn. Everybody liked to be on hand for something "with hair on it," a significant murder scene, but political animals saw it through a different lens, did different calculations.

Flannery spent some time talking to the White Plains investigators, then came over to Mo. Mo told him his take on it so far and about the next steps he and Marsden had discussed. Flannery nodded thoughtfully, his eyes never leaving the body of Daniel O'Connor, which Angelo had uncovered at his request. When Mo was done,

Flannery tipped his head toward the backyard. "How about we have a chat outside, Detective."

They went through the back door and stood a few yards away from the house, looking around. The yards were fully greened up already, and a little apple tree next door was shedding pink blossoms in a slight breeze. Flannery was several inches taller than Mo, a big guy in his mid-fifties who had learned to cover his sadistic side with a glad-handing, smiling, bearish charm that he exploited well. His premature baldness didn't hide his muscular body, another personal characteristic he'd learned to use to his advantage—sometimes he liked to talk to the press while working out on the treadmill he kept in his office, good for the image of prosecutorial vigor. Or maybe he wasn't actually bald, Mo thought, just shaved to look like Jesse Ventura or somebody. Now he crossed his arms and stood staring down at Mo with a speculative look.

"Detective Morgan Ford. You really catch the goodies, don't you."

"Seems that way," Mo agreed.

Flannery looked around the neighborhood in an appreciative way. "Frank Marsden—I really admire that guy. In fact, I'd call him a good friend." He paused, but when Mo just waited for the bullshit to continue, he frowned. "I bring it up because Marsden's word on your behalf is what's allowing you to keep your badge for the moment. Your stunt in the parking garage may go down okay with some people, but you should know my office will conduct a thorough investigation. This being the second time for you. I won't have it said I condone or turn a blind eye to bad police procedure in Westchester County."

"Go ahead. Please. Tell Marsden to take me off." Mo pointed his thumb at the house. "You saw what was in there. You really think I want any piece of it?"

Flannery's eyes narrowed, and he smiled slightly. He put his arm around Mo's shoulder and steered him down the sidewalk that bisected the backyard. Two guys having a friendly, confidential chat. This was Flannery's idea of political suavity. Mo hated the controlling pressure of the big arm but avoided showing it.

"Take you off? When you're perfect for the job?" Flannery said. "You kidding? Let's be frank, Detective, I think you deserve to know where things stand. A, you're good, my good friend Senior Investigator Marsden says you're the best he's got. B, you're the perfect fall guy if anything fucks up—we can all blame the rash, impetuous cop who is already under scrutiny for his past sins. You're my cover! Best of all, C—" Flannery coughed self-depreciatingly. "Well. Those are reasons enough, aren't they?"

"C," Mo said for him, "with the Big Willie thing, you have something you can jerk me around with whenever you like. I'll do things the way your office wants." He was grudgingly impressed: Flannery had been here for only ten minutes and already he'd seen all these angles.

"You *are* smart!" Flannery clapped him on the back. "But that's a little blunt. I'd put it, oh, I'd say that it's always good for an investigation when the various police agencies keep the interests of the district attorney's office in mind. We're the ones who'll prosecute this in the end. We're the ones who need to look forward to the overarching legal strategy we need to put this guy away. Right?"

The Westchester DA's office maintained a powerful investigative and prosecutorial staff, but was always complaining of being short-handed on the investigative side. Flannery holding Big Willie over Mo, pulling his strings, would be almost like getting another employee without having to pay his salary. Better, because Mo would co-opt some State Police resources, and Flannery would have a scapegoat outside his own shop. And if they caught the copycat, he could use Mo to make sure the credit flowed to the DA's office and to himself personally.

"Right," Mo said.

Flannery walloped him on the back as they turned and strolled back toward the house.

"There we go. It's nice to think we're on the same page here!" When he saw Mo wasn't sharing his enthusiasm, he said, "Hey, don't take it so hard. Think of this as part of your political education. You'd do the same thing in my shoes. Wouldn't you? Honestly, now—wouldn't you?" Flannery saw it as a rhetorical question. His big grin was completely sincere.

5

S T. PIERRE HELPED WITH the first neighborhood canvass, then got a ride back to the barracks with one of the uniforms. Mo got out of there at eight o'clock, after sundown, one of the last to leave. The neighborhood's nine-to-fivers were home again, the cars were back at the curbs and in the driveways, it was a beautiful Friday night in mid-May and the air was sweet with the smell of tree blossoms. But the lawns and sidewalks were deserted. Lights were burning in all the houses, but the curtains were drawn and Mo knew the doors were locked. The streetlights had come on and insects spun in the cones of light, the occasional bat zapping through to feed. Something about the mild humidity, the cooling air, reminded Mo of when he was a kid, the evenings after school as summer approached, the excitement of just being loose in the streets, gliding on your bike through the spring air. He wondered how long it would be before the kids here would feel good about being outside again.

For an instant he thought yearningly about going home, back to the house and the unlikely but possible comforts of Carla's arms, maybe even the cleansing heat and abandon of making love to her, they'd slipped a couple of times since agreeing to sleep apart. And then his body remembered the awful embrace of O'Connor's corpse as the last strand was cut and its weight fell onto him as he and Angelo wrestled the rubbery, clutching thing onto the gurney. Maybe he'd need to get a little distance on that before holding Carla, or anybody, again.

He lifted the crime-scene tape, got into his car, started the drive back toward the barracks, thinking, *Maybe this really isn't the job for me.*

When he'd first moved up to investigator at Major Crimes, despite knowing several MCU cops and having seen some bad stuff, he hadn't been ready for what it did to you. The stresses and strains, the opposing forces. The movies had it wrong, it wasn't about car chases and shoot-outs and sexy encounters. Ninety-five percent of the job was sheer tedium—depositions, triplicate paperwork, reviewing regulations, debriefings, reading files, hassling with schedules, go-nowhere interviews, conferences, waiting on bottlenecks at the lab or some other department. The other five percent? Sheer horror. Going into somebody's kitchen and slipping on half-coagulated blood, the smell that doesn't come off your clothes, the contorted face you can't forget. Poking around in some guts or brains or jism or vomit or shit. All the Major Crimes people knew about it: the female victim who looked kind of like your wife, the boy who looked like your own kid, the way you could never look at your own family or friends again the same way.

And the only break from this was the remaining one tenth of one percent of the job, which was the dubious pleasure of chasing down and having it out with a killer.

All this for forty-five K a year.

So why do it?

Mo had pondered that a lot lately. Most of the other Major Crimes types he knew were motivated by a sincere desire to serve, a lot like armed services people, which many of them had been. They wanted to combat evil, maybe they had religious beliefs that kept them going and more or less in one piece. Few of them would admit it outright, because it didn't seem hip or flashy enough. But despite the popular image, these were not hip or flashy people. Most were thoughtful, worried people who had originally, at least, felt the pain of victims and survivors acutely and had sworn something like a private blood oath to avenge their suffering. Even the hotshots who were in it for guns and glamour—they usually adopted the jaded pose because it was easier than admitting that what they saw and did got to them.

Even Valsangiacomo, a real cowboy. Once Mo had run into him down at The Edge. He'd joined him at the bar and watched him toss back shots of Jack Daniel's for a while, then asked him what was with the rapid intake of whiskey. Valsangiacomo, six-one and a body-builder, let his shoulders slump. "This morning, Helena and I, we're about to make love, but the baby comes in the bedroom. So we knock off and take a rain check for tonight, right?" Helena was a gorgeous, dark-haired, full-breasted woman Valsangiacomo had met while visiting relatives back in Napoli, had courted madly and brought back to the U.S. Mo could easily imagine how much you'd look forward to that rain check. "So then today Estey and I get called to a scene up in Bedford. Woman, naked on the bedroom floor, great body, I'm thinking, What a waste. She's been cut all over, bled out, circumstances indicate rape, too, so we have to check for semen. We're exploring her orifices, natural and man-made, with Popsicle sticks and swabs and flashlights. Kneeling in the blood? And now Helena, she's at home, expecting me back, got all kinds of great plans. And I know I'm not gonna be able to do anything tonight, but I don't want to tell her why? Trying not to bring the stuff home, but what're you supposed to say?"

There wasn't really an answer for this problem, so you stopped off at The Edge and poured them down.

Some people were constituted to take it better than others. They shook off the images of the day. They took each case as it came and didn't think in terms of combating all the world's evils. Carla had been on Mo for years to see it like that, but maybe if you had certain kinds of sensitivities, or the habit of looking for the big picture, you couldn't see all the crimes and hurts except in some kind of cumulative way. And the burden had been adding up, Mo felt as if every day on the job eroded his sense of human worth and goodness a little further. How far could you let that go before you bought a big bottle of Thunderbird and lay down in the gutter and gave up on it all?

But what would he do instead? He could get books and read about the color of his parachute or how to define his midlife crisis or whatever it was when you changed careers later in life. He could pay an arm and a leg to some career counselor to give him skills and affinities tests and tell him that he should have been a brain surgeon or a Park Service ranger or something. More likely, take a big pay cut and start a career microwaving frozen beef patties at a burger place.

Mo braked the car in the left lane as he waited for a trio of bicyclists to pedal past the entrance to the barracks parking lot. Thinking about all this had made him irritable and sad, and he waited impatiently for the bikers to slide past, peddling with tiny red lights flickering madly on their bike frames. There were two men and a woman, sleek as plastic greyhounds in skintight spandex in black with rainbow neon stripes, walnut-shaped helmets with tiny spiffy rearview mirrors clipped to their temples, special gloves and shoes. The three of them all seemed to have the same build, slim and long-limbed with standout sinews, as if they were a distinct species, bionic aliens from some streamlined planet. *What's this, the fucking Tour de France?* Mo groused. *Can't even go for a bike ride without three grand worth of clothes and equipment. Something the matter with a T-shirt and shorts?* He couldn't remember the last time he'd seen an adult bicyclist wearing anything but high-tech, Euro-styled outfits, and suddenly the whole trend seemed symbolic of the decline of Western civilization, the universal collapse of values.

Then the last of them cleared the entrance, and he pulled into the lot. He found his space and shut off the car and spent a moment looking up at the bright windows of the barracks building, fifty feet away. People were moving inside, silhouettes in the windows, somebody showing papers to somebody else, talking about it, moving on. Cops came and went under the lighted portico at the entrance, purposeful and competent-looking.

Looking out at it, he suddenly understood Marsden's inexplicable intimacy, what was really troubling him. Marsden was mother-henning, he really loved his squad and was worried about how it would hold up if he wasn't there to oversee it. Marsden didn't always get along with his wife, and he'd never had any children. But everybody had some nesting instinct, and for Marsden the shop had become his home, Mo and Valsangiacomo and the others were his kids. It was kind of touching. Marsden had been there so long he saw this as something precious and worth working for. For a moment Mo glimpsed the place as Marsden must have seen it. Something about the sense of quiet industry here, even this late at night. Confidence and camaraderie. Professionalism, teamwork. A little citadel of comparative order, a bulwark against the world's craziness.

For no reason at all, Mo suddenly felt better, the problem of *why* more distant. *A Howdy Doody copycat,* he thought, *maybe it could be interesting.* He got out of the car and headed toward the brightly lit building, beginning to like the idea of looking into the files and getting a handle on this thing. Anyway, he was in no shape to deal with Carla right now.

6

Monday morning after one of the worst weekends in recent memory. Feeling driven from the house and the problems of domestic life, or rather the lack thereof, Mo sought the refuge of preoccupation and got to the shop bright and early. He put in a call to SAC Biedermann at the Manhattan FBI field office, and as he waited for a call back he reviewed the Howdy Doody files he'd pulled off VICAP on Friday night. He'd been at his desk less than an hour when his phone rang and he took a call from someone who introduced himself as Roland Van Voorden, chief of police of the town of Buchanan. Marsden had patched him through.

"What can I do for you, Chief Van Voorden?" Mo asked.

"We have a body, a homicide. Some kids found the corpse late yesterday afternoon in the old power station here."

"Okay . . ." Mo said, putting a question in his voice and wondering why Marsden had sent this one to him.

Van Voorden answered his thoughts. "Your SI said it might tie in with a case you're working on. That's kind of a pun—whoever did it tied the body up? Like to the wall, with fishline, lots of lines tied to eyelets in the wall?"

Holy shit, Mo thought. *O'Connor was killed just three days ago, if this guy's killed another already, he's on a real tear.*

Mo got the location from Van Voorden, instructed him on securing the crime scene, made calls for technical assistance. Then he signed out and drove to Buchanan, twenty miles northwest of White Plains on the banks of the Hudson River.

He took 287 west, then cut north on Sprain Brook Parkway. The motions of driving were soothing, permitting some good thinking. The proverbial clarity that comes from the open road, he thought. But then, turning onto 9A, he came up behind a big beige Land Rover that he couldn't pass or see around or over, and he lost that fantasy quick. The roads were choked with traffic.

Still. Friday night he'd called Angelo, who had just finished packing O'Connor's twisted corpse away for the weekend. Angelo had anticipated his request for an expedited autopsy but told him there was no way, even bumping back a couple of other customers, that he could get to it before Tuesday. Then Mo had gotten the FBI's Manhattan field office on the phone, where the twenty-four-hour operator told him there was no way to reach Biedermann before Monday. He'd downloaded some files on Howdy Doody from the FBI VICAP site and had a good read for a few hours until his eyes began to water and he went home to the big house and Carla. It was almost midnight.

She was on the couch, reading by the light of the goosenecked lamp, the only light burning in the whole echoing place. She had put on music, a big Mahler symphony that seemed incongruous played that quiet. When he walked in he was glad to see her still up, looking lovely and shadowed in her exotic pajamas.

He said, "Hi," she said, "Hi," and she put down her book. He started toward her to give her a kiss, then thought better of it. His clothes might have a smell on them from bear-hugging O'Connor's corpse, and anyway she didn't look as if she wanted a kiss. Instead he went into the kitchen for something to eat.

"I made some soup, just heat it up," she called in.

That sounded good. Without turning on the kitchen light, he washed his hands, then lit the gas beneath the pot and took a bowl from the cabinet. He got a beer from the refrigerator, popped it, went out to the living room. He stripped off his jacket and shirt, down to the T-shirt, so he could feel better about being near her. "How's it going?" he said. She said, "Fine." The kind of openings people fell back on when they felt the pressure of more important things to say but couldn't get there yet. "Don't ask me about my day," he said, a code they'd worked out for saying it had been gruesome. Of course, what'd it leave to talk about?

The symphony went into a brooding minor-key movement, and Carla looked unbearably lovely as she told him she would be moving out. She'd get a place with her friend Stephanie in Mount Vernon, which might be better anyway because it was closer to her client base. There was no hurry for Mo to find another place, Mom liked him, probably if he did ever get around to the painting and stuff, he could stay on here as long as he liked.

She had obviously planned what she was going to say because it came out smoothly, well-reasoned, logical. In fact, it was surprising how many of the details she had worked out, how far it had gone in her mind while he'd still been thinking the relationship was worth trying to salvage. He said that to her, sitting on the coffee table dangling the beer can between his knees, and she reached over to put a warm hand on his cheek and said, "I think we both would like a relationship that's not about 'salvaging' something." And the way she said it hurt him, as if it were about rescuing junk and recycling it maybe. But she was also right, that was almost as bad, he'd suddenly seen himself as hanging on to *a* relationship rather than *this* relationship. Suddenly he saw that in the three years they'd spent together it had never really felt right, despite some real tenderness and some good sex, there'd always been that disconnect, that sense of coming from behind. Of, yes, salvaging something.

The soup had burned. They'd slept apart, again, and he'd spent the weekend helping her organize her things for the move.

The traffic clotted up again near Briarcliff Manor, and he came out of his thoughts to barely avoid slamming into the rear end of another damned Land Rover. In fact, there was an identical one behind him, a Toyota version, and when he looked down the road, it seemed that every vehicle was some kind of heavy-duty safari truck, with massive, knobby tires and tube-steel grilles and huge luggage racks rearing on the high, square roofs. Big gunboats built for the deep outback, for driving on the thorny, hard soil of African savannas, with plate-steel running boards and spare tires bolted to the back gates. Massive as military vehicles, and getting ten miles per gallon, and all of them driven over the smooth roads of Westchester by anorexic housewives on their way to their manicurists, aerobics classes, orthodontists. *What's happening to us?* he thought with alarm. For a minute he fumed at the vagaries of fashion, mankind's lemming instincts, then decided the hell with it. He put his flasher on the dashboard, lit it up, and carved a path for himself through the intersection.

Van Voorden had given him good directions to the old power station, into Buchanan and then over toward the river and south past the Indian Point nuke plants. He passed the red-and-white tower and rounded domes, continued along the heavily wooded shore, and came up to a white, flashbar-topped Chevy Suburban that was parked across from a dusty little church. The Buchanan cop showed him to a dirt access road, and he rolled slowly down the bluff through a mishmash of trees, vines, broken masonry, abandoned gravel pits, trash. At first he worried about his oil pan, but then the land smoothed out and the trees opened to a big view of the Hudson River.

The old station loomed at the water's edge, a massive brick cube about four stories tall. It had the tall, round-topped windows and decorative masonry of the last century, but now the windows were covered with corrugated sheet steel. Originally it had been sur- rounded by many smaller outbuildings, but in the years since it had been decommissioned these had fallen into heaps of rubble grown over with weeds and vines. The road ended in a dusty parking area near the rearing wall, and Mo pulled up next to a pair of Buchanan cruisers.

The shore of the Hudson here was a kind of no-man's-land, with the power-company property theoretically off-limits to the public but widely used by hikers and teenagers who enjoyed the views and rocky outcroppings. When Mo had been in high school in New Rochelle, he'd sometimes come over this way with friends. They'd bring beer and start campfires and get drunk and make out, looking across miles of slate-blue water, the rolling headlands, tugboats nudging barges upstream, the sparkling lights of the far shore. Twenty years later, the ground was littered with beer cans, Styrofoam cups, fast-food junk, used condoms, blown newspapers and plastic garbage bags caught in bushes, all mixed with industrial rubble left over from the power station's early days: old machine parts, broken concrete walls, railroad ties rotting in haphazard stacks. Hiking paths had been beaten into the grass and sumac brush, meandering along the river. Just to the north, gigantic steel gantries reared on either side of the river, holding sagging power cables from the nuke plant.

Mo followed a path close to the wall of the building, wondering where Van Voorden, or the victim and murderer, had gotten inside. Around on the water side, he found a crumbling flight of broad concrete steps leading to an outlandishly huge, ceremonial doorway. New York, the Empire State. The doors were covered with graffiti-decorated sheet steel, but one corner of the rusted metal had been pried away to make a triangular opening about three feet tall, big enough to crawl through. He was just crouching down to go inside when a man in a brown police uniform came around the far corner.

"Oh," the guy said. "Detective Ford? I was waiting for you, but then I thought I'd look around a bit. I'm Van Voorden."

"Got held up by traffic," Mo told him. The parade of Land Rovers. They shook hands. Van Voorden was tall, bony, with a long neck and a protuberant Adam's apple of such size and angularity that Mo became uncomfortably conscious of his own, bobbing in his throat.

"We don't get much of this here," Van Voorden said. "This is my first, my first, uh—" He petered out, not sure what to call it.

"Let's take a look," Mo suggested.

They crawled through the opening and into an entry foyer that was lit only by thin lines of sunlight squeezing around the edges of the sheet steel over the doors and windows. The room had tiled walls, and the air was humid, earthy, smelling of rot and piss. The mash of litter continued inside, and ferns grew in cracks in the floor.

Van Voorden switched on a big four-battery light and panned it around the vault.

"Basically," he said, "this thing is just one big room, except for in front here there's this entry and a pair of offices or something on each side. We got to go through there"—shining his light on a doorway opposite the front doors—"into the main room, down some stairs, and back under where we are now. I've got some people down there now."

"Is this the only way inside?" Mo asked. He had brought his own flash and lit it up also.

"I think so. The kids that found the body came in and out this way, so that's how we made entry."

Van Voorden led the way into the main chamber. It was, as he said, a single huge room that had once housed the massive boilers and turbines but that was now stripped and mostly empty from floor to ceiling. The room rose straight to the rafters high overhead, cavernous and obscure, lit only by slit gaps in the sheet metal. Swallows swooped to nests in the rafters.

They went down a flight of stairs to a ground floor of buckled concrete and dirt with scraggy bushes growing through, litter everywhere, little circles of wood ash and charcoal where trespassers had made campfires. Mo felt it before he consciously saw it, the subliminally registering ordering of things: a circle of beer cans around a star shape of overlaid boards, zigzags of loose bricks with cigarette butts set into the angles. At the bottom of the stairs, Van Voorden steered him toward the front of the building again, where the lower level was divided into several rooms. Mo heard the mutter of voices and saw other flashlights panning in one of the rooms, and then as they got closer, he smelled the corpse. Despite his reluctance to breathe deeply, he felt a gust of relief blow through him: Not a fresh corpse, the new guy wasn't on a rampage of a kill every other day. This one had to be much older. Maybe even a victim left over from the original Howdy Doody killer, who'd been apprehended, what, four months ago.

The death room was a concrete and brick chamber the size of an average living room, lit by flashlights and by slits of daylight around a tiny, steel-covered window up near the ceiling. Van Voorden introduced him to the Buchanan officers, a woman and two men. They all held handkerchiefs over their faces. A glance showed Mo that they'd done a great job of overlaying the dirt floor with prints of cop-uniform shoes.

Then Van Voorden introduced him to the corpse, and the others obligingly coordinated their flashlights on the wall. Older, yes. In fact, the body had come apart and only portions remained strung to the wall: two forearms and hands with clutching skeletal fingers, an inverted head held in place by poly line around a segment of bare spinal column. The rest had rotted or been eaten by rodents until it couldn't support its own weight, and the torso had fallen away onto the rubbled floor. One desiccated leg was still in place, lines taut from the mummified knee and ankle to the eyelets sunk into the concrete, but the other had fallen. The bulk of the body was a tangled mound on the floor, overlaid by a cloud of delicate white mold. Mo panned his light away from it and around the room, seeing again the telltale organization of objects in the rubble. Holding his breath and leaning close to the inverted head—from the long, golden hair hanging down, he guessed this one had been a woman—he used a tongue depressor to probe in the desiccated jerky just above where the ear would've been. There it was, a little circular pit going down to the bone, another signature wound of the Howdy Doody killer or his copier. No sign of the nylon handcuffs, but he looked closely at the cords, and, yes, it was weed-whacker line, ribbed with sharp edges. Not fishline.

"Like I said, this is the first one of, uh, these I've ever dealt with," Van Voorden said. His voice was muffled by the handkerchief he held over his mouth and nose.

"Who found her?" Mo asked.

"Kids. A couple of boys from town, thirteen- or fourteen-year-olds, I know the one of them's folks. They were out here Sunday, goofing around, dared each other to come back under here. They came in, saw this, then left in a big hurry. I didn't hear about it until this morning. The boys bicycled home and weren't sure whether to tell anyone, they were afraid they'd get in trouble for trespassing in here. But they both ended up telling their parents, and they called me."

The corpse was so decayed that from medical evidence alone it would be hard to tell when the murder had occurred. There'd be rot, mold, animal and insect damage. No finger skin remaining for prints, but Mo saw a half-circle of teeth down in the tangle, and dental records might help them get a name. Once they'd identified the victim, they could talk to friends or family and pin down when she'd last been seen. He hoped it would turn out to be five months ago, and then he could give this one to the Howdy Doody prosecutors.

"How often do you think people come inside here?" Mo asked.

Van Voorden shrugged. "My guess is not that often. Not till school's out, another few weeks. Probably people come inside the building almost every weekend, but I'll bet not many come back under here, too creepy and dark. I know I sure as hell wouldn't."

It sounded like a fair assessment to Mo. His guess was that the corpse was at least a month old, but it could as easily have been here six months or more, especially if the murder had happened during winter. There'd be rat damage but the cold would've kept insects and bacterial rot down until the warmer weather set in.

"Okay," he said, making a decision. "I'm going to ask you all to follow each other single file out of the building the way you came in. Then I'd like you to start taking the metal down off the front doors so the Crime Scene people and the ME can get their equipment through. Avoid handling the area where the gap is, we'll look for hairs and fibers on the surfaces there. Also, if I can ask one of you to wait in the parking area for the others and direct them back here when they come, I'd appreciate it."

They looked at each other, hearing his dismissal, but did as he told them. They knew he was thinking *country cops.* But it was true, he wished they'd had the sense not to mill around in here, obscuring other prints, brushing the rough walls and leaving their own clothing fibers and follicles and danders everywhere. On the other hand, with a month or six months gone by already, a lot of that would be useless anyway. Between cop prints in the dirt on the floor, he could see a solid mesh of rat tracks and a sprinkling of droppings. Out in the big room, there'd no doubt be the footprints of hundreds of visitors, going back decades.

Mo stood back from the body, trying to visualize what had happened here. A woman wouldn't have come into a place like this alone, so either she came with the killer, meaning she knew him, or he caught her elsewhere and made her come here. Or, much less likely, killed her elsewhere and dragged her here.

He startled as a rat appeared in a crack in the foundation, slithered down the wall, and disappeared into another gap. He decided to get out of the room while he waited for the forensic team, and he walked back to the door, carefully stepping in the tracks of the others.

He looked over the big room, the dim light just revealing the rubble on the ground. It was a lousy place to die, lonesome and scary and filthy. What had happened here? What had the killer done to her? How long had it taken? The stacked and arranged geometries in the rubble everywhere nagged at him, signifying a horrible compulsion. Ordering, *controlling,* the environment. It was all about control.

He experienced an unwanted flashback to O'Connor's house, the awful contorted person on the wall. The vision stabbed at him before he shut it down with an effort.

From reading the Howdy Doody files on Friday, he knew that the cause of death was strangulation by the line around the neck. The head wounds had been made by antique ice tongs—when they'd caught Ronald Parker, the Howdy Doody killer, they'd found the tongs in his car, the points of which matched the wounds on his victim's temples. Between the strings and the arrangements of objects, it was clear that the ritual centered on *control,* the killer manipulating his victims absolutely. Nobody had answered the question of whether Parker had done the arranging of objects before, during, or after the killing, or what exactly it signified.

Mo agreed with Marsden, Ronald Parker was the one, no mistake. He had been caught in his car, four months ago, speeding away from his last attempted kill, and the police had found a spool of plastic line, disposable handcuffs, tongs, and other paraphernalia in his trunk. They had established that he'd had prior contact with at least two of the victims. His background matched the profile developed by the FBI's Behavioral Sciences people and the independent shrink they'd consulted, and they had looked forward to running psych tests. Mapping the mind of the monster.

But Parker wasn't answering any questions. On his second night behind bars, he had hung himself in his cell, using the leg of his prison pants. Guards had found him in time to save his life, but not his mind: He sustained severe brain damage from oxygen deprivation. One of the photos in Parker's file showed his cell after they'd removed him, the geometric arrangements of toilet paper, hairbrush, prison slippers. Yes, Parker was the one, but he wasn't in any condition to tell anybody much of anything.

Mo listened to the silence in the cavelike room. It was a scary place, even for a six-foot cop armed with a Glock-17, even during daytime, even with a bunch of other cops just outside. It must have been terrifying for the victim, an agony of fear before the physical agonies began.

He walked farther back into the big, dim room, his flashlight illuminating little more than the ground in front of his feet. Rearing up from the rubbled floor were two large, tapering brick columns, eight feet wide at the base, once maybe ten feet tall but now crumbling and raining loose bricks. At one time they must have been the main support for massive floor timbers, but now they stood solitary, twenty feet apart, casting pools of darkness that the ghost of light from above didn't penetrate. He approached one of them warily, hating the darkness, his right hand traveling to the nylon of his holster and the soothing weight of his gun. It was an irrational fear, the killer was long gone. Given the age of this corpse, it was probably Parker, already behind bars.

The stepped bricks of the tapered columns had been decorated. In the beam of his flashlight, he saw beer cans set neatly on each little shelf and surrounded by chips of broken glass. All this organizing and arranging must have taken hours. Did the killer talk while he worked? Did he make the victim watch? Did he arrange for a while, torture for a while, arrange again?

No, Mo knew suddenly. Abruptly he knew how it worked, saw it clearly in his mind's eye. The image sickened him.

Bam! a metallic blow echoed in the big room. Mo's heart answered with a series of punches inside his chest.

Bam! again, and he realized it was the Buchanan cops starting work on the front door. Sounded as if they were using sledgehammers, for Christ's sake. But maybe it meant that the others had arrived. He got himself under control and began walking toward the entrance, thinking that maybe he'd take a couple minutes of sunshine before coming back down.

7

TUESDAY, THINGS BEGAN TO coalesce. Mo managed to reach Biedermann, who sounded like a chilly son of a bitch, and scheduled a meeting with him down at the FBI Manhattan field office later in the day. Then he got hold of the secretary for Dr. Ingalls, the consulting psychologist who had worked on the Howdy Doody profiling with the FBI's Behavioral Sciences Unit, and was lucky enough to step into the gap left by a canceled lunch meeting.

The White Plains police and St. Pierre had done some good legwork, establishing that while no one in Daniel O'Connor's neighborhood had seen anything particularly suspicious, several neighbors had noticed O'Connor's car in his driveway all day Thursday. A visit to the copy shop he'd managed revealed that he'd been at work on Wednesday but hadn't shown on Thursday. The day staff had wondered where he was and had left messages on his answering machine, but they thought maybe they'd gotten the staffing calendar screwed up and so hadn't gotten alarmed until Friday.

The corpse in the Buchanan power station had been removed, and the Forensic Identification Unit had made casts of her teeth and photos to be distributed to dentists and orthodontists. From a quick inspection of the degree of fusion of the pubic symphysis of her pelvic bones, Angelo had guessed the victim's age to be late twenties, and he declared her blond hair natural. He measured a humerus and provisionally set her height at five-four. So St. Pierre had started a database search for reports of Caucasian, late-twenties blondes over five-two gone missing within the last year.

The psychologist maintained an office on Eighty-fifth Street, an upper-crusty neighborhood not far from Central Park. Mo drove down on the Saw Mill River Parkway, segued onto the Henry Hudson, joined the backed-up cars at the toll station. The big city gathering around him, the view of the cramped New Jersey shore across the water, the odor of some pollutant that smelled like burning chocolate: It made him nostalgic. A spring day, the trees busted out with leaves and blossoms, the sky looking celebratory despite global warming and the New Jersey factory chimneys. He'd lived just north of the great colossus of Manhattan all his life, had come in through its various gateways thousands of times, and yet he never got over the feeling of pleasurable excitement and trepidation it gave him to be wrapped in its dark, dirty, gutsy bear hug. What had he thought he'd do with his life when he was twelve and would come down with his father to go to the Natural History Museum? Dad had done a decent job of encouraging Mo's love of things historical, archaeological, maybe envisioning a scholarly career for him, who knows. If asked where he'd be twenty-seven years later, twelve-year-old Mo would probably have said he'd be doing archaeological expeditions in exotic locations when he wasn't living in his fancy penthouse with a view of the Park. And he'd probably have said he'd be married to Deborah Weinstein, a blond, early-developing girl in seventh grade who for an entire semester had embodied for him the feminine mystique. She used to write him tantalizingly flirtatious but disappointingly vague letters in a round, pneumatic-looking script with smiley faces in the *O*'s.

So how close was he? Now he was thirty-nine and had just broken up with the fourth major love of his life, he was lonely and horny and lived in his ex's mom's house, now even more hollow with the removal of Carla's stuff. He was an underpaid cop feeling alone in the police society that was his only contact with human beings. He spent his time investigating sickos who hurt or killed people, and the closest he got to archaeology was poking around in the desiccated remains of murder victims in abandoned Hudson River power stations.

Mo realized that this level of self-esteem was not going to sustain him through the forthcoming meetings with high-powered shrinks and successful G-men. He made an effort to pump himself back up.

He missed the Ninety-sixth Street exit and had to continue on down to Seventy-ninth, where he got off and headed back up through the little streets, delayed by street repairs. But then the gods of Manhattan bestowed one of their quixotic little miracles, the sudden appearance of a parking place just where he needed it, and he got to the appointment with Dr. Ingalls on time.

Dr. Rebecca Ingalls's office was on the fourth floor of an elegant older building with marble floors and a big elevator of walnut and polished brass. He found the office door open and went in to find the secretary he'd talked to on the phone. A little sign on her desk told him her name was Marie Devereaux. She looked to be in her late sixties, as dour-faced as he'd expected from her telephone voice. She greeted him dubiously and asked him to wait on one of the leather-upholstered chairs, but before he could sit down the inner door opened and a big-boned, blond woman in her mid-thirties came out, laughing as she flipped some papers onto the desk.

She said to Marie Devereaux, "Look at this! Those complete and utter yo-yos! Can you believe it?"

Marie Devereaux looked over the papers and allowed her eyebrows to rise.

"Honest to God!" the blonde said. She turned to Mo and included him in the moment: "Can't tell you the joke, but it involves the bookkeeping practices of one of the institutions I do consulting for. Marie and I had a bet, and she just won. Damn!"

"What'd you win?" Mo asked.

"Tickets to a Mets game," Marie Devereaux said primly. "Detective Ford, this is Dr. Ingalls."

Mo tried not to show his surprise. He had read parts of her profiles of the Howdy Doody killer, insightful but technical, and he'd learned that she was highly regarded in psychological circles, author of several influential books. He'd expected a woman like the secretary: older, serious, stuffy in a Viennese, turn-of-the-century sort of way.

Dr. Ingalls invited him back into her office, and he followed her into a large corner room with tall windows and a collection of potted fig and lemon trees. Desk with laptop computer, a pair of couches facing each other, several comfortable-looking chairs. Ansel Adams photos of Yosemite on the walls along with some wild crayon drawings by kids, all nicely framed. An antique buffet covered with carved wooden birds and rainbow-hued blown-glass vases. A floor-to-ceiling bookshelf covered one wall, but there was no sign of dark leather chaise longues or the other somber furnishings Mo unconsciously expected in a shrink's office.

Dr. Ingalls stood expectantly at her desk. "Hungry? This is lunch, right?"

"Sure, food would be nice."

That seemed to please her. "Can we just order out? There's a fabulous Chinese takeout just two blocks over, they'll bring it up, we can have a picnic here . . . ?" She waited for his nod, then picked up the phone, tapped a number from memory.

He watched her as she ordered, still feeling a little stunned by her informality, her unpretentiousness, her looks. She wore a blue dress, midcalf length, and in her heels she was nearly his height. Big-boned, solidly built, yes, but a good figure. Thick golden hair, a face too wholesome to be pretty exactly, but nice blue eyes, big easy smile. Not at all what he'd expected.

When she got off the phone, she took him back toward the two couches, sat him in one, and settled herself opposite him, a coffee table in between. "I hope you don't mind," she said. "Eating here, I mean. I'm just starved, and we only have this hour. We'll cover more ground if we don't have to go out."

"So how do you like New York?" Mo asked. He was glad to see that surprised her a little, evened them up a bit.

"Is that astute observation, or just an indication you've read my bio?"

"Observation, but it doesn't require any astuteness. Your accent, your informality—Midwest, right?"

She feigned chagrin. "Can't hide it, huh? But you're right. Southern Illinois born and bred, fed on sweet corn and fresh dairy. I did my postgrad work at Columbia, so I lived here then, then returned to Chicago for some years. I moved back here a year ago, and I've loved every minute. How about yourself?"

"New York area, all my life." He shrugged.

"Marie says you want to talk about Ronald Parker and my profiling work for the FBI. What brings it up? I should warn you, I've got to be a little careful here, they're planning to use me as a witness at his trial. Among other testimony, I'll bring in his match to the psych profile I established."

"There's been another murder, up in White Plains. It fits everything I know about Ronald Parker's MO. If there's a copycat out there, I figured the best starting place for his profile is what you guys put together about Parker. I'm meeting this afternoon with the special agent in charge, and my guess is we'll end up reactivating the Howdy Doody task force—you'll no doubt hear from him."

Hearing that there'd been a copycat murder clearly troubled her. Her eyebrows became tildes, two gentle S-curves, and she took a moment before answering carefully, "Ronald Parker is by far the most disturbing case I've been involved with. For a number of reasons."

"Such as? I don't mean to make you go over familiar ground, but this only fell into my lap a couple of days ago. I'm not up on the details." Mo took out his pocket notebook and pen.

Again Dr. Ingalls seemed to need a moment to frame her answer. She got up, tucked her hair into a ponytail, and secured it with a bunchy blue hair band. She went to the window and leaned on the sill, then turned and sat against it, facing him again.

"Erik Biedermann will push you out, Mr. Ford," she said. "He'll structure the task force so that he pilots it and the State Police don't have any say in the direction of the investigation. He'll explain that it's a case of unusual complexity, best left to the 'real pros.' That being the case, do you really need to know the details? I'm just trying to save you time and energy here."

Mo found himself bristling. He'd never met Biedermann, but he'd never heard anything positive said about him. An arrogant Fed, probably a glory hog, with contempt for the various regional police organizations he had to interface with. Mo felt a flash of guilt, thinking of his own reactions to the Buchanan police: *country cops*.

"We'll have to see about that," he told her. "I'm—" He tried to think of a way to say it that wouldn't sound like some kind of macho posturing, then thought of Dr. Ingalls's frankness and spontaneity and decided the hell with it, he'd reciprocate. "I don't usually give a shit what guys like Biedermann want. I'll make my own decisions about my own cases. What I need to know, what I do. We're pros, too. With better solve and conviction rates than the FBI."

She looked at him dubiously, but then grinned. It was nice to see the smile again, Mo decided, you could get hooked on making this woman smile.

"Let me start with Ronald Parker," she began. She crossed her arms and her ankles, a nice shape against the window light. "What I'll do is, I'll conflate what I theorized about him in advance of his capture—much of which proved to be accurate—and what we now know about his background. If we're after a copycat, we'll want to draw any parallels from facts, not guesses."

Mo nodded, clicked his pen.

Okay, she said. What did we know from the victimology? Both

men and women, an unusual pattern for organized serial killers, who usually strike only one gender. At first, she and the Behavioral Sciences profilers had wondered whether the killer might be bisexual. But given that there was no evidence of sexual assault upon the victims, a better guess would be that the choice of victims stemmed from the specifics of the killer's childhood trauma. Serial crimes were often symbolic reenactments of or retributions for psychological injuries sustained in childhood, abuses most often committed by parents, stepparents, or other relatives. The evenhandedness of this killer suggested he had been abused by both genders, maybe both mother and father, or at least *blamed* both parents.

Too, there was a disturbing consistency in the appearance of the victims. All were blond-haired and light complexioned, medium to tall in height. This suggested, again, that the murders were symbolic retributions or reenactments, and Dr. Ingalls suspected the killer would prove to be blond and light-skinned, either because the original abusers were his parents and he'd have inherited their looks or because he was reenacting his own trauma and the victims were surrogate "selves."

"So then we looked at the mode of death itself," she said. "The use of handcuffs, the suspension of the victims using fishline, and the meticulous organization of the objects at the murder scene told us this was all about *control*—exercising absolute control over the victims and their personal spaces was central to the psychological narrative. There are a great number of ways to exercise control, and the specific technique in this case suggested that the murderer had once been similarly controlled, maybe tied up. We even made a note that we might find scarring on the wrists or ankles of the killer, and sure enough, Ronald Parker shows evidence of prior dermal trauma at both sites. I'll show you."

Dr. Ingalls rummaged in a file cabinet and came out with two photographs, which she handed to Mo. There was one close-up of hands and forearms, another of lower legs and feet. She sat next to him on the couch and pointed out the barely visible, irregular lines of paler skin. "These are Ronald Parker's wrists and ankles. We were right that his murders reenacted his own earlier trauma."

Mo was impressed. He tried not to be conscious of her proximity, the smell of her hair, but failed. She got up again and returned to the window, Mo railing at himself for his adolescent vulnerability to the nearness of a beautiful woman. And then that thought hit him on the bounce—was she beautiful? Since when? Looking at her now, he decided, yes, very much so, just not in the typical ways. Jesus, he was in lousy shape, he thought. And Dr. Ingalls was sharp, she'd see it in him.

She went on, looking troubled again: "We thought we were smart, but there were some things we never did pull together. We didn't get to question Parker before he—you know about this?—before he hanged himself, gave himself brain damage. He's not going to be able to tell us certain things."

"Like—?"

"The arranging. What exactly it signified to him, how it pertained to the original abuse he suffered. Also the use of the ice tongs on the head, why he wanted to injure them that particular way. Also whether he did the arranging before, during, after—"

"He didn't do the arranging," Mo said. He remembered the insight that had come to him down in the musty bowels of the power station. "Or rather, he didn't do it directly. Everybody assumed the reason why his fingerprints were never found on the objects, or anywhere, was because he wore gloves—"

"He had a box of latex gloves in the car when they caught him."

"He *did* wear gloves. But he didn't do the arranging. His victims did. While he held their strings. While he turned their heads, moved them from place to place with the ice tongs sunk into their temples."

"Oh, Jesus," Dr. Ingalls said. She went quickly to sit down on the other couch.

"You said yourself it was about control. Parker moved them like

56

puppets. The whole point of the arrangements was just to exercise control—not so much on the environment, on the *victims*. To savor his ability to manipulate a living person absolutely. For hours and hours."

"Oh, God." She looked as if she could visualize it too clearly. "We . . . we assumed the victim's fingerprints were on things because he always killed in their houses, and . . . and you'd expect their prints to be there. But it was also because *they* did the arranging. He *made* them. How horrible!" She blew out a breath, shook her head, troubled. But then she smiled again, *wham,* a solid Plains–states smile, unabashedly appreciative. "You are one smart cop! You've had this case for what, four days? I'm impressed!"

Mo savored that for a second or two. And then Marie Devereaux put her head through the door. "Your lunch is here," she told them disapprovingly.

8

THEY ATE FROM PAPER plates, sitting on opposite sides of the coffee table and leaning forward over white cartons of moo shee pork, kung pao chicken, egg rolls, white rice, wonton soup. Dr. Ingalls hitched her skirt up to facilitate eating, still demure just above the knee, and spread several napkins on her lap. She ate like a stevedore, shoveling the food off her plate directly into her mouth with deft pivots of the chopsticks, smacking her lips. The food was great, Mo hadn't realized how hungry he was.

After a while, Mo said, "You don't seem like a person who would go into forensic psychology."

"I'm not! My main field is child psychology. My whole FBI connection is an accident—they consulted me on some letters from a child being held by kidnappers. Wanted me to get clues about her emotional state, maybe about the identity of her abductors or the location where they were holding her. I got a lot of things right, so they began calling me in on other things, not directly child-related. Given that adult psychoses usually result from childhood trauma, profiling really benefits from a developmental psychology perspective. I'm not proud of the fact, but I apparently have a talent for deducing the mental states of bad guys. So they keep coming to me."

She wiped her mouth with a napkin and licked her lips. "But thank you. If I may say so, you don't strike me as a person who would go into homicide investigation."

"How so?"

"Well, you're too thoughtful, you're too self-critical, you're too uncomfortable with death and pain. I'd have pegged you as, oh, a historian, or a writer of popular books on something like archaeology or current science issues—" She looked at him penetratingly, observing that she'd scored hits.

"What else," he said, feeling a little exposed.

"Divorced recently." And then she looked surprised at herself. "I'm sorry, that's—"

"It's that obvious, huh? How about you?"

She shrugged and went back to her eating, selecting a blackened, curled chili, looking at it closely before cautiously nipping the end of it. "I was . . . engaged . . . in Chicago. He couldn't relocate. It fell apart after a couple of months of living a thousand miles apart." She made a face at the chili's burn or the recollection.

"Which would seem predictable," Mo said. "Prompting questions about why you moved to begin with."

But she pulled away with a frown, leaning against the couch back. "I think we're getting off the topic, Detective Ford. I'd like to get back to Ronald Parker."

So her candor had its limits, Mo thought, and she could be hard, businesslike, if she needed to be. "Yes," he agreed.

She glanced at her watch and offered as an explanation or apology, "Only because I'm conscious of the time—I have another appointment in fifteen minutes—"

"Go ahead."

"Okay. What else did we know about him in advance? Above average height and weight, in good physical condition. That one was simple—four of his victims were men, in generally good shape, and it would take at least parity in strength to overcome them. Also, it would take considerable strength to hoist people up as he tied them to the eyelets."

Mo nodded, remembering O'Connor's weight as he came off the wall.

"High intelligence and good organizational skills, seen in the amount of planning, the assembly in advance of tools and materials, the observation of victims' living habits—he had to ascertain that he could have them in his control for many hours without risk of interruption. We also saw high intelligence, maybe even police experience, in his ability to avoid leaving trace evidence at the scenes. The plastic police handcuffs also suggested a law enforcement background. We were wrong there. But education, we theorized a bachelor's degree at least and Parker had a BS." Dr. Ingalls frowned at herself. "Is any of this helpful at all?"

"Absolutely." Mo looked at his notebook and realized that for all she'd told him, he hadn't made it halfway through his list of questions. He was aware of the time ticking away. "So who *is* Ronald Parker—what's his personal history?"

"As we'd guessed, he was an adopted child. His parents are now dead, and we have no proof of abuse other than the ligature scars on his wrists and ankles. But adoptive, step-, or foster parents account for seventy percent of child abuse. He grew up in New Jersey and New York. Interestingly, he himself went 'missing' about two years before we caught him. I believe at that point his pathology overwhelmed him, and he could no longer maintain the persona of normalcy, so he went undercover when he started killing. We're not sure what pushed him over the brink, made him leave a snug job as a bank teller in Newark. We still don't know where he was or what he did during his two years out of view. But we're afraid there may be other victims we haven't located yet or don't yet recognize as his. He may have spent the two years 'warming up' for the fully developed ritual. If often takes a serial murderer several tries to identify the acts which best satisfy his compulsions."

"Okay," Mo said. "Have we got time for one more? I don't know if you need prep time for your next appointment, or—"

"You're very considerate. Sure, we have time for one more." She said it graciously, but she had begun packing away the food cartons, tidying up.

Mo stood to help her. "Okay. So what connected the victims to him? How did he select them?" This would be critical if they were going to anticipate what the copycat did next.

To his surprise, Dr. Ingalls seemed to become distinctly uncomfortable. She grabbed the cartons and shoved them into the take-out bag, her movements brusque and businesslike. "This was a difficult point for the whole task force, and no one has ever established his connections to all the victims. But we believe he chose them from chance encounters and professional contacts on two criteria. First, that they looked like his archetypal persecutor, the tallish blonde, mid-twenties to mid-forties. Second, that in the course of their contact they somehow 'controlled' him. We know that he made contact with one victim through the bank where he worked and she was a customer. Apparently she accused him of shortchanging her when she cashed a check, and she raised a fuss about it that no doubt gave him a lot of stress. Another was a mechanic who had worked on his car. Parker believed the man had taken too long to replace the clutch and then overcharged him. In both cases, we see people 'controlling' Parker, and Parker exacting retribution by asserting his own control—absolute control unto the death. The others, we're still not sure how they came to his attention, but we're assuming a similar pattern. They had the bad luck to look like some manipulative monster from Parker's past and to interact with him in such a way that he felt controlled by them."

Mo gave that a moment's thought. Serial murder often progressed by a predictable general sequence of events, starting with the procurement phase. This was when the intentional, organized killer selected the victim. Usually the victims were people who somehow fit into the killer's mental world in some specific way—their appearance was right, or their professional roles, or their living habits. Something brought them to his attention and made them seem desirable targets. The killer increasingly incorporated the victims into his delusional scheme as he learned more about their habits and worked out how to gain access to them. The problem was that without some pattern of connection between victims—physical and material, not just some warped psychological link in the killer's mind—it was next to impossible to catch a serial murderer.

"So," Mo said, "given all this, how'd he get caught? I know he botched an attempt and was caught fleeing the scene. How did that go down?"

But Dr. Ingalls was looking unhappy. She didn't answer immediately. Instead she bunched up the trash bag and stuffed it into a wastebasket. Then she sat down in the chair behind the desk, and Mo got the distinct sense she had retreated to the shelter there.

"The FBI took a proactive role," she said. "And it worked. And now, yes, I would like some prep time, thank you. It has been a pleasure, Detective Ford."

He almost called her on her sudden chilly formality, she seemed like the kind of person you could challenge that way. But then the dry voice of Marie came out of the intercom: "Your one o'clock is here."

Dr. Ingalls stood to shake his hand. "Good luck with SAC Biedermann," she said with a touch of sarcasm.

He went to the door, trying to overcome his feeling of being dismissed, angry with himself for expecting anything different. She was watching him as she took the band off her ponytail and shook her hair loose, a disorderly blond fountain that covered her face for a moment before she brushed it quickly back into a more professional-looking coif.

"I may need to consult with you again—" he began.

"Certainly. I'll make every effort to accommodate whenever feasible. Just call Marze, and she'll schedule it."

He felt shitty as he opened the door. But then she surprised him, calling, "I enjoyed our lunch, Mr. Ford." When he glanced back, she was briskly sorting papers at her desk. She didn't look at him, but he was glad to see her smile as she worked. Immediately he felt a lot better.

9

T HE FBI MANHATTAN FIELD office was in the Federal Building, miles south of Dr. Ingalls's office. With a couple of hours
to kill before the three o'clock meeting, Mo opted to drive down,
leave the car in a lot near Chinatown, and walk the rest of the way to
Federal Plaza. It was a good day to walk, not hot enough to work up
a big sweat, and he had always liked this part of Manhattan. If you
managed to step out from under the cloud of cynicism over your
head, you could get off on the sheer diversity of human beings, the
innumerable sizes and shapes and colors of them, the endlessly
surprising things they did. Even the air, the piss smell of the masonry,
the rotting-food aromas of garbage cans, the suffocating diesel
belches of buses, seemed rich with nutrients he was sure fortified
the blood.

He bought a little bag of candied peanuts and munched them as he
strolled. There was a lot he hadn't asked Dr. Ingalls. In fact, there was
no guarantee that the things she or Biedermann could tell him about
Ronald Parker would necessarily apply to a copycat. The copycat
killer operated under yet another layer of psychological complexity,
his close identification with a previous killer making it even harder to
guess his motives and next moves.

One of the things he'd have to get from Biedermann would be the
really deep forensic details. A copycat could reasonably be expected
to deviate from the original, if only because the new killer couldn't
know everything about his role model's work. Mo's idea was to get a

good sense of Ronald Parker, then focus on the new killer's departures from Parker's MO. The lab reports weren't in from the O'Connor murder, but so far he hadn't found any obvious departures. That is, unless the power station murder did prove to be the new killer, not just a previously undiscovered victim of Parker's. But whether by Parker or a copycat, the power station murder would be the first that didn't occur in the victim's own home. That had to be significant. At the very least, fingerprints found on arranged objects could prove or disprove Mo's belief that the victims themselves had been forced to do the organizing.

If they hadn't already caught Parker and Mo had been called in on the new murders, he'd have assumed they were done by the same guy. It all came down to how closely the MOs matched. If they were too much alike, you'd have to consider some troubling alternatives.

Like what? A, the killer of O'Connor *was* the same guy who'd killed all the others, and Parker was the wrong guy. But they had Parker cold, the case against him was rock solid. So that would leave B, and this was kind of scary: Ronald Parker hadn't worked alone, and his accomplice was still out there, just now starting up again.

Of course, there was C, a third alternative that could explain closely matching MOs. This struck Mo as less likely still but in a way more scary. It *was* a copycat situation, but the new killer had access to inside information about the Parker investigation. Or was *involved* in the investigation.

He dodged a speedballing rollerblader, a tall black teenager who wore nothing but a G-string, iridescent green alien-eyeball shades, and Discman headphones. The guy whipped down the sidewalk backward, graceful as Baryshnikov's shadow, weaving in and out between other pedestrians without looking, as if he had eyes in the back of his head.

The interruption was good, Mo decided as he watched the dancing figure recede. With his idea of an insider doing the new killing, he was getting ahead of himself. Best to wait, hear what Biedermann had to tell him.

His thoughts went back to Dr. Ingalls, Rebecca Ingalls, the nice buzz that had grown on him as they'd talked. He was being stupid, he decided, showing his vulnerability. He had long since decided that much of love was about marketability, about station. Everybody had an unconscious or at best barely conscious sense of their own marketability, of how desirable a partner they'd make. Maybe it was an assessment of looks, of sex appeal, of social class, of educational level, of how much money you had—an idea of yourself that you recognized when you glimpsed it in a prospective partner. You might hanker after somebody who was more marketable than you were, the way people got the hots for movie stars, but realistically you seldom went after those people. Relationships did occur between classes of overall desirability, but they seldom lasted. Because the partner who discerned he or she could do better would eventually try to do so.

Is that what had happened with Carla? Mo's sense of their relative marketability was that he held his own with her in terms of looks and smarts, but she came from family money and in the last year with her career taking off she had begun to sense she had opportunities he didn't. Time to move up another notch in the relationship department.

A pretty dismal view of love.

So what did all that have to do with Dr. Ingalls? he chided himself. New York was full of attractive but, to Mo, inaccessible women. It was inappropriate even to put her in the "prospective" category, a sign of his desperation and heart-hunger. She had pulled it all up short when she'd felt their conversation veering too far toward the personal. She was a professional. More importantly, she also knew what her marketability quotient was, and that she could do better than Mo Ford. She saw that, he saw that, end of story.

Feeling lousy again, Mo finished the peanuts, balled up the bag, tossed it at a trash canister, missed, retrieved it, and put it in. He had come up to Federal Plaza. Time to put on the act of being together and functional one more time.

Biedermann's office was on the twenty-fifth floor, a regular palace compared to the institutional, gray-surfaced cubicles his underlings got. Still, the room was done in federal cutback-era utilitarian, with short-pile gray carpeting, a massive enameled metal desk, Steelcase desk chair, a small Formica conference table with six plastic chairs. On a set of shelves, Biedermann had allowed himself the luxury of a few personal decorations: pictures of the SAC with Al Gore, with Colin Powell, with Governor Pataki, with others Mo didn't recognize. A couple of pistol-shooting trophies, a citation or two. A heavy, red-leather, chrome-studded dog collar, and a big bowie knife mounted on an engraved plaque.

"You're wondering about the knife," Biedermann said. He was about two inches taller than Mo, with a military buzz cut gone white-blond, blue eyes in a tanned, strong-jawed face. His charcoal suit was well cut and made Mo envious, given that his only comparably stylish suit had been ruined by Big Willie.

"What's the story?" Mo asked. The knife was obviously a routine icebreaker for Biedermann.

"A joke. Used to work in Internal Affairs, out in the San Diego field office. You're never popular, understatement, when you're IA. So when I moved over to this job, the San Diego staff presented me with the knife. Said I'd stuck it in their backs long enough, I could keep it now."

Mo chuckled dutifully. He thought to ask about the dog collar, but there was a rap on the door frame and three people came into the room. Two were members of Biedermann's staff, a woman and a man who, Biedermann explained, had worked on the Howdy Doody task force, Special Agents Lisa Morris and Esteban Garcia. They both carried manila file folders, edges trimmed with the red and white stripes that meant they were active case files. The third person

Biedermann introduced as Anson Zelek, a tall, thin man in his early sixties with a tight, triangular face, small mouth, up-tilted eyes. He looked vaguely familiar, and then Mo realized he resembled the typical representation of a Roswell alien. He wondered if the look resulted from a face-lift.

Biedermann sat at the head of the table, Zelek off to one side of the room. Mo sat across from Morris and Garcia, savoring the draft of air-conditioning against the back of his neck. He asked them about the structure of the interagency task force on the Howdy Doody case, and SA Lisa Morris listed the members: the FBI, the Manhattan and Bronx PDs, the New York DA's office, the New Jersey State and local cops. The Connecticut State Police and the Westchester DA's office had also been included because they wanted to be up to speed if the killer struck in their jurisdictions.

Then it was Mo's turn. He told them what he knew so far about the O'Connor murder and filled them in on the power station corpse. When he mentioned that he'd just come from a meeting with Dr. Ingalls, Biedermann looked at him penetratingly, more than a little interested. Zelek's tilted almond eyes seemed to perk up, too.

"She's very good, isn't she." Biedermann commented flatly.

"Yes, I thought so," Mo said. "But our appointment today was a short-notice thing, I didn't have the time to ask all the questions I wanted to."

"What else did you want to know?"

"Well, I asked her how Parker got caught, and she said it resulted from a proactive strategy on your part. But she didn't give me any details."

The three agents at the table glanced at each other, and at Morris's questioning look Biedermann gave a little nod. He clearly intended to stay in charge of any information exchange here.

Morris was a smallish woman with red hair in a practical cut, and she spoke with a slight Southern accent. "We had very little to go on, and our killer was hitting about once a month. By the time he'd killed his sixth, we were starting to get a lot of pressure for an arrest. The last several kills were in Manhattan, the mayor put pressure on us, Washington said we had to get proactive. All we knew at the time was that the perpetrator selected tallish, blond victims, and that his murders seemed to be about striking back at people who'd controlled him. Controlling them in return. So we established a likely victim. It was a long shot that he'd notice. We got lucky, and I mean that sincerely." Again she gave Biedermann a look, a checkup: *You sure this is okay?*

Mo felt obliged to break in. "I understood he killed people he'd encountered, but that nobody ever figured out how he acquired them all. How could you place someone in his way?"

Biedermann dipped his chin, and SA Morris went on, "Our profile suggested the perpetrator would follow press reports about his case, that public response to his crimes was one of his motivations. So we engineered a public relations effort. We identified a tallish, blond person we could set up through crafted news reports as a controlling figure, hoping he'd want to retaliate. As I said, we got lucky. We had the intended vic's apartment under surveillance, and when Parker came in, we were there."

It was beginning to come clear for Mo. Jesus. No wonder she hadn't wanted to talk about this part of it. No wonder she'd pulled away so fast.

"You used Dr. Ingalls," he said.

Biedermann took over. "She's a rising star in the field, she'd just published a book that was getting her name in the news anyway. So, with her cooperation, we set her up in a series of articles. 'Supershrink closes in on Howdy Doody killer,' that kind of thing. 'FBI confident profiler will reveal killer's identity.' He had to feel manipulated by her. We scripted her press comments very, very carefully, framing her view of him in terms that would feel condescending, challenging, manipulative. He took the bait. We were lucky."

Mo thought about that for a moment. It had to have been scary as hell for Dr. Ingalls to walk around every day knowing she might be being procured by a very effective, sadistic serial killer. He asked, "So how'd it go down at the end?"

This time Biedermann nodded minutely to Garcia. Like Morris, Garcia was dressed perfectly, crisp white shirt, tie, dark suit. He was a barrel-chested man with a pronounced widow's peak, and as he talked, he gestured with thick, ring-encrusted fingers. "I was in tactical charge of the apprehension unit. By the time we had Dr. Ingalls in position, we knew his rhythm pretty well, knew within several days when he'd try again. We never did spot him as he picked her up, and we never saw him approach the building. Uh, but we had given her a wrist alarm, one of these Lifeline things, that she could press if anything happened, would ring at our end. And one night there he is, a guy walks into her bedroom, he's tall and blond and he's carrying a black duffel. She, uh, she activated her wrist alarm, fought with him, but he saw us starting to move in. We're not sure how he got away from the scene—" Garcia hesitated uncomfortably.

Mo was thinking, *Another FBI bungle.*

"We can talk blame for a few mistakes," Biedermann broke in, "or we can talk *credit,* well-deserved *accolades,* for setting it up, for protecting Dr. Ingalls, and for catching him." He gave Mo a challenging glance, then nodded for Garcia to continue. "Give us the nutshell version, how about, Esteban?"

"He had only been with her for a few minutes, she wasn't badly hurt. When he evaded us at our perimeter, we gave a holler to the NYPD, and a black-and-white spotted him several blocks away."

"Good interagency cooperation," Biedermann put in, still watching Mo. Sitting back from the table, Zelek crossed his legs and looked mildly amused.

Garcia finished, "He resisted arrest before being subdued. In the car we found extra nylon handcuffs, a cordless drill, a pruning shears, the ice tongs, latex gloves, a whole roll of the fishline."

Mo looked at the three of them, and they watched him just as closely. "Fishline," he said finally.

They caught each other's eyes.

"Not exactly fishline," Biedermann said. "A heavy-gauge poly line a lot like fishline."

"To be precise, a lawn-trimmer line," Mo said. "Serrated to cut weeds better."

"Well, yes," Morris admitted.

"But fishline was what you told people. What you told the press."

"Public relations issues are paramount in a case like this," Biedermann said. "Every detail has to be managed, or the whole investigation will get out of control."

"I understand," Mo told him, disliking him. Control was a bugaboo for Biedermann just as much as for Howdy Doody. Him and Flannery both, very different styles of getting things done but both big guys with big ambitions. He wondered briefly how the SAC and the DA had gotten along on the first task force, and how it was going to feel to be an investigator caught between those two jumbo-size egos.

Biedermann continued, "Which brings us to something we'll have to get sorted out right from the start, Detective. We've had experience with this kind of thing, at the national level. If you've got a copycat up in White Plains, a prolific, highly organized, and mobile killer, we're going to have to have a very solid command structure for the investigation. My office will have to have undisputed authority for task force strategy. We'll completely respect your prerogatives, but you'll have to respect ours."

Mo nodded. "I do. Absolutely. I really do. That's why I'm here. So as a first step in our cooperation, I'll need the whole story, copies of all the files, scene photos, pathology reports. *And,*" he said as Biedermann started to speak, "you can expect the same from us. Right now, I'm curious about how closely the copycat parallels the original. If it is a copycat. And I'd like to start with a couple of details that should tell us that right away. What do we know about the handcuffs?"

Morris glanced to Biedermann, and at his nod said, "They were found on most of the bodies. Standard police equipment, Flex-Cuf brand disposable nylon, twenty-two inches long when new but clipped short on Howdy Doody's victims. No way to trace them—they're the brand of choice of about two thousand police departments nationwide, they're cheap, and their use isn't monitored. Plus, anyone can buy them in bulk from Gall's police supply by mail order. As you know, they're easy to slip on quickly, so we theorized he used them right away to get control of his victims. This was verified by Dr. Ingalls's, um, her, uh, experience. Once their hands were useless, he could take the time to do the more elaborate ligature knotting."

Good, Mo thought, *she's brought us to the real issue.* "Yeah, let's talk about that. The knots."

Morris had been holding her files in her lap, and as Mo spoke, she unconsciously pulled the folders against her chest, glancing at Biedermann for a cue.

Mo didn't wait for Biedermann's answer. He reached over, caught Morris by surprise, jerked the files out of her grip. He quickly opened one to find a photomontage of a minor holocaust: bodies hanging on walls, bodies contorted on gurneys, close-ups of temple wounds and skin lacerations, autopsy shots.

Zelek's almond eyes narrowed suddenly. None of the agents moved, but Biedermann lowered his voice half an octave. "I don't think your approach is called for, Detective."

Mo was flipping through the photos and found what he was looking for, a catalog of knots, photographed at close range against the discolored skin of the victims. The photos were arranged in rows in fold-out, clear plastic envelopes, each row neatly labeled and displaying seven sets of knots for easy comparison. Yes, there was the distinctive line, the sharp-seamed weed-whacker poly. It would cut the skin more than a smooth fishline, grip better when wet with sweat or blood. It would hurt more and beget quicker response to the puppeteer's commands.

And, yes, the knots were consistent. The one that had actually tightened around the limb of the victim was an odd type of slipknot, where the line passed twice through a loop of itself and was then secured with three or four wraps—sort of a miniature noose, only doubled. The other was a complicated thing that occurred in the middle of the wrist lines, obviously designed to lengthen or shorten the line as needed. Mo didn't precisely remember the knots he'd seen at O'Connor's house or at the power station, but at a glance he could see these were similar.

If the knots did match, this was going to be a real shithole of a case. Because whatever else might have been made public in the course of the Howdy Doody investigation, the details of ligature knotting weren't. A close match here would signal that they had the wrong guy in Parker, or that Parker had had a partner who was now off on his own.

Or that the new killer had deep access to police or FBI files and was deliberately using Parker's MO to challenge or confound investigators. Thinking about it now, Mo decided the insider theory was looking stronger. The odds of the killer going for the trap they'd set were improbably long. That they had even attempted using Rebecca as a positioned victim suggested that they'd known they were trying to lure an insider.

Mo shut the folder and tossed it back toward Biedermann. Morris and Garcia just waited, not sure how to react. *One of the limitations of a micromanaged shop,* Mo thought. *It destroys initiative.*

"Okay," Biedermann said. "You've established that you're an asshole, and that you think we're assholes, too." His face had a wearily baleful look. "But let's step back a bit and try to regroup here. Let's try to get objective. If there's a close parallel between Howdy Doody and your new guy, yes, one of the obvious suspicions would be that the killer has some kind of inside access to information. In which case, you can understand why we're so leery of letting everybody know every detail. It has nothing to do with what you perceive as our lack of respect for regional police jurisdictions. It's about limiting the circle of people with access to the information. Without that, we'll never be able to figure how anyone got information, if indeed they did. You agree?"

"Yep," Mo said.

"So the way this is gonna work is as follows. First, on the basis of the similarities between the new crimes and the Howdy Doody killings, this office is declaring presumptive jurisdiction. Second, you don't get copies of everything. You want to compare knots, you can bring your photos down here and compare them onsite. Same with pathology reports. Same with scene photos that show the arrangements. Same with *any* detail I choose to restrict access to. You accept that only the lead desk knows the whole story, and that's here, that's us. You play your part, but you *don't* try to do more than your part."

Mo started to object, but Biedermann held up his hand. "I talked to your supervisor after you first called on this. Says Morgan Ford's real good, but he likes to be a lone wolf, he's got reprimands in his file, he causes trouble for his outfit. We don't want that in this investigation, Ford. So you want to play macho here, go fuck yourself. I snap my fingers, someone more amenable takes over and you're out. This office will cooperate fully—*within* an effective command structure for the investigation. So will yours. You don't like that, again, go fuck."

Everyone got tense, except Zelek, who was looking mostly bored. Mo's testosterone kicked in for an instant, but it was followed quickly by the *who gives a shit* hormone. Yeah, he'd like to catch Howdy II, save the world from the latest menace. But it wasn't his sole responsibility. This was a job, not a crusade, and a job he had serious doubts about. Biedermann was an asshole, but only one of many, and you couldn't let them all bend you out of shape.

And anyway, Biedermann was right about this.

Mo shrugged. "Sounds good," he said cheerfully. "So I'll be down here tomorrow with some details on the new White Plains and

Buchanan murders. I'd like access to your files. Two o'clock be okay?"

He was happy to see that his sanguine approach rankled with Biedermann. The SAC's poise slipped just a bit, a pout on his pursed lips, as he saw the goad in Mo's attitude. Zelek was looking at him speculatively. Morris and Garcia just watched their boss, uncertain.

10

I T WAS FOUR-THIRTY by the time Mo left the Federal Building and burst with relief into the air of Manhattan rush hour. The streets had filled with pedestrians and cars and buses, and a mood of eager and irritable desperation had come over the city. *Hard day, get home, run for cover, kick back.* For once Mo wasn't in a comparable hurry.

Before leaving the FBI offices, he'd made a call to Ty Boggs to let him know he was loose and on his way. They had arranged earlier to meet at Ty's favorite Vietnamese restaurant, Pho Bang, over on East Broadway at Mott Street. Ty had to come over from his precinct house in the Bronx, which gave Mo half an hour to cover just a few blocks. So he took his time. He watched with amusement as a riproaring procession of fire trucks tried to get through the traffic, sirens warbling and horns blatting as they stood like everybody else, pinned by gridlock. Everything motionless, and yet the street was a bedlam panic of red lights, massive glistening vehicles with roaring motors and bellowing sirens. Despite the air of urgency, a relentless stream of oblivious pedestrians slipped between the bumpers of the stationary behemoths. New Yorkers.

Paradoxically, the meeting with Biedermann had cheered him up. Dr. Ingalls had been right about how the SAC would want to crowd Mo and the NYSP out. But Biedermann's pushy attitude, the silent spooky presence of Anson Zelek, whoever he was, along with Flannery's machinations: It was all a good reminder to keep his distance from his job. For the moment he was feeling pleasantly disconnected from the whole thing.

The wall of roaring machines finally managed to move, and Mo kept walking. He was looking forward to seeing Ty, maybe he could shed some light on some of the undercurrents here. At the very least, he might help figure out ways around or through Biedermann.

Mo knew Tyndale Boggs from classes they'd both attended at City College eighteen years ago. Ty was older, having served in Vietnam before continuing college. He was a lieutenant in the Bronx PD now, while Mo was still just a State Police investigator, at a sergeant's pay scale. Ty claimed he owed his promotions to being African-American at the right time and place and having a name that more or less combined the names of two great baseball players, but it wasn't true. He got there by being smart and capable and a bulldog on the case. He was in his midfifties, a sturdily built guy with the face of a martyr, all the world's troubles etched into two deep horizontal lines in his forehead. Divorced now, he lived with his sister and her two kids. In Vietnam he'd been shot through the cheek, in one side and out the other, and it had left scars and some ongoing dental problems. He and Mo were pretty close for a while but had drifted apart in the last few years, Mo wasn't sure why.

Mo got to Pho Bang before Ty did, taking a table near the front and ordering an iced lychee-nut tea to tide him over. It was just five, a little early for the dinner rush, and the place was mostly empty. When Ty came through the door, he moved into the room like the shadow of a rain cloud, dark and a little menacing. Mo thought he'd aged a lot since he'd last seen him, six months ago.

Ty pulled back a chair and put himself in it, already slouching before his pants hit the seat. "Hey," he said.

"Looking good," Mo told him.

Ty grunted and grabbed a menu. Mo took it as a cue to look at his own.

"I just spent an hour and a half with your buddy Biedermann,"

Mo said after a few minutes. He had explained the Howdy Doody copycat when he'd first called.

"Lucky guy," Ty said. He grabbed a handful of chow mein noodles from the bowl in front of him, tipped his head back, poured them into his mouth. A waiter came to put ice water and a teapot on the table.

"Fun to work with?" Mo asked. At Ty's flat-eyed look, he asked, "You think it's just his style, or has he got a particular bug up his butt about Howdy Doody?"

"Both."

Ty was often surly and closemouthed, but this was extreme even for him, Mo decided. "Hey, Ty," he said, "if this is a bad day for you to talk about this stuff, we could—"

"Nah." Ty brushed the idea away with the back of his hand. "It's just Howdy Doody wasn't a lot of fun, I'd just as soon not deal with it any more than I have to. I'll do what I have to to see it to trial and then be glad to see its backside."

"What was so bad? Biedermann?"

"Biedermann's a dickhead, yeah, but there's other stuff, complex, made it hard to work the case. I like my serial killers neat."

"You want to tell me?"

But the waiter had come back. They both ordered. Mo chose a bowl of noodle soup, Ty several dishes he ordered in Vietnamese. Two smartly dressed young couples came in and took one of the circular tables.

Ty waited until the waiter was back in the kitchen. "Yeah, I'll tell you, but it's all pretty vague. I'm not sure what the shit is." His face took on a perplexed look, forehead lines turning into crevasses. "There's something working behind the scenes. Everybody knows it, nobody knows what it is. I mean, besides the thing with Biedermann and the shrink, that profiler they brought in."

Mo felt a stab of some strong emotion. "What was that?" he croaked.

"It was understood, you didn't mention it, but sometimes it complicated things to pretend it didn't interfere. Not technically professional misconduct, I don't think, she's a civilian. Good-looking, can't blame Biedermann. Not sure if they're still an item, but him pressuring her to be used for bait, that had to put some kind of strain on 'em." Ty poured himself a cup of steaming tea and gulped down the tiny cupful in one scalding swallow. He set the cup down and frowned at the pot.

That explained a lot about Biedermann's and Dr. Ingalls's attitudes toward each other, Mo thought. He agreed with Ty: If they were still an item, it was strained. Serial killers did that to you. But whatever their current relationship, he couldn't deny that, yeah, they'd make a good match: two big, handsome, confident, Anglo-looking, up-wardly mobile professionals. Real equality in the marketability factor there. He felt an irrational disappointment and hated himself for it.

"What else?" he prodded.

"There's something with the investigation, like another layer that we're not supposed to know about. You'd see it all the time, the way information would be shared or mostly not shared. The way Biedermann would put a lid on this line of inquiry or that and meanwhile be whipping your ass for progress in another area. I tried to figure it out, then just said what the fuck, what do I care, I'll just do my bit, close the case and get out. Another thing, one day I'm chatting up this girl down in Human Resources, and she mentions Biedermann requested my personnel file. Not just me, turns out, he looked at job files of everybody in the NYPD who worked on the case. So I talk to Tommy MacArthur, he's my counterpart on the Newark side, and Biedermann did the same with them. We're wondering why he's so interested in our backgrounds. I ask, 'Can this guy just do that?' and the answer apparently is, yes, he's got some special clearance."

"The possibility of the inside link," Mo said. Yet another indica-tion that's what they were thinking. It was one possible explanation for Biedermann's attitude, especially given his background in Internal Affairs.

"Maybe, but dig this," Ty said, shaking his head and picking up some heat on the subject. "About nine months ago I had to go back for some oral surgery, about the tenth time over the years? So I'm back and forth with the Vets Administration for my records, you know, they're supposed to cover this shit, I got these bone chips in the gums and over in my mastoid. They sit there fine for a few years, then they decide to move around, give me pain." Ty grimaced and rubbed his jaw. "So I call up Records, I know some of the people there pretty well by now, and this VA guy says, 'Hey, Boggs, yeah, I just got a request for your records the other day.' I'm thinking who the fuck, he tells me it's FBI, as a federal agency they have access. And I'm wondering why the hell Biedermann's going to go back twenty-seven *years* before he's gonna trust me to do my job, not have a sideline as a serial killer. And this from a guy knows damn well niggers don't do serial."

It was a fact that almost all serial killers were white, Mo reflected, almost none African-American. He could understand Ty's resentment. Biedermann's caution did seem excessive.

"Any ideas why he's thinking that way? What he's looking for?"

Ty shrugged. He took another cup of tea, this time swishing it through his teeth like a mouthwash.

They sat like that for a while, Ty sprawled in his chair, both of them watching as the restaurant began to pick up a few customers. One of the newcomers was a young Vietnamese woman who loitered near the register, obviously waiting for someone. She was wearing high heels and a short black dress that showed off her legs, the most exquisitely shapely legs Mo could ever recall seeing in his life. With her dark hair and slim figure, she reminded him just a little of Carla, and looking at her, he felt the bottom fall out, all the hopeless tender yearnings of a lifetime suddenly catching up. Like he had a hole where his heart was supposed to be. To make it worse, after a few minutes a comparably handsome young man came in, and the way the woman's eyes lit up broke Mo's heart. The guy wore pleated black pants and a white shirt with blousy sleeves, a Vietnamese Valentino. They kissed hungrily before going to a table, and their pleasure in seeing each other was too much to take, Mo had to look away.

But then, welcome distraction, the waiter brought their food. Mo's was a bowl the size of his bathroom sink, a nest of noodles in steaming broth mixed with slices of beef and whole shrimp and topped with a pile of cilantro and mint and basil leaves. Ty lined up his several dishes in front of him and went at it with his chopsticks, a man who knew how to eat.

"So how's Carla?" Ty asked between bites.

"I'm single," Mo said.

Ty's face twitched, but he didn't stop eating. "You knew it was coming. For like the whole last year."

"Yeah. But if it's not your idea, you're never quite ready for it."

"Got any other irons in the fire?"

Mo shook his head.

"Me, I don't even try when I'm in an oral surgery phase," Ty confided. "I'm enough of a son of a bitch even without it, nobody should have to put up with me."

Mo couldn't argue with that. Instead he concentrated on eating. The soup was delicious, the vegetables crisp and the mix of flavors always surprising.

After another long silence Ty said, "A couple times, at the task force meetings, there'd be some guys Biedermann didn't introduce. Usually it was this gray-faced guy, quiet—"

"The alien? I just met him. Name's Anson Zelek."

"The alien, yeah. When I saw that guy, my first thought was *Washington*. Then I thought, hey, Biedermann's office is on the twenty-fifth floor? That's the National Security floor. So I figure, the way Biedermann runs us like puppets, I think he's a puppet, too. Like somebody further up is pulling *his* strings, that's why he's such a hard-ass method man." Ty crammed a bite of rolled and stuffed beef into his mouth and chewed carefully.

An interesting irony, Mo thought: Takes a puppeteer to catch a puppeteer. Ty's take on Zelek sounded about right: some Washington-level spook type. In Mo's experience with the FBI, it wasn't that unusual to have some outside agent sitting in, usually when a case involved supervisory issues or possible links to other investigations, often RICO cases. Another thought occurred to him: "Was the Westchester DA at any of the task force meetings?"

"Yeah, Flannery, him or one of his assistants. Another asshole. If the new guy's killing in Westchester, Flannery will be all over it, won't he? Oh, you lucky boy."

Mo thought of another question: "So who's pulling Biedermann's strings? Zelek?"

Ty shrugged again. Halfway through his meal now, and sometimes he winced as he chewed. "Who knows? And, hey, Mo, who really cares? You want my advice, if this copycat turns into another big one, just fall in line, do your part. Why worry about what Biedermann's got cooking?"

Ty was getting cranky again, and Mo decided not to press for details just now. "Do me a favor, though," Mo said. "Let me look at your files? Talk to me about the case as we go?"

Ty gave him the flat-eyed look. "Sometimes I think you look for trouble, so help me. I never did figure out why. Speaking as a looey myself, I don't envy Marsden. You're a real asshole sometimes."

"Thanks, Ty," Mo said. "I knew I could count on you."

11

VENGEANCE MUST BE APPROPRIATE *in degree and in kind.*
That was certainly a guiding principle. How would you say it
in Latin? the puppeteer wondered. Carve it onto a plaque, put it over
the door of the house, like the grandiose mottoes universities posted
over the administration building's main entrance. Lofty significations
in a dead language, was that a nice irony or what?

But of course it was not only about vengeance. For all that
Machiavelli and others had philosophically elevated the principle, this
was much more than a petty, personal desire for retribution. This was
an act of rebellion, a vehement defense of personhood in an era when
the state and the stampeding, faceless masses would crush the individual. Maybe the old banner from the American revolution would be
more appropriate: *Don't Tread on Me,* illustrated with a crude, coiled
snake embroidered beneath the words. The implication being *I bite.*

Don't control me.

Mr. Smith was out shopping. The mall in Danbury was a huge,
gaudy affair, big enough to disappear into, with the added advantage
of being across the state line. It was one of nine malls he rotated
through for supplies. Not that these purchases should ring any alarm
bells, but there was a certain pleasure in taking such precautions. It
reminded him that he was a guerrilla, a secret army of one.

He parked in the middle of the lot, locked the car, sniffed the May
air. Sun still up, sky clear: a pretty nice evening. He decided he
needed to get out more often.

Most of the supplies could be bought at the home-building supply store, a sprawling hangarlike building across the parking lot from the main shopping complex. The battery of his cordless drill seemed to be discharging too fast, and Mr. Smith had decided that a replacement was in order. Got to keep your infrastructure in top shape. Another bunch of eyelets, a dozen or so, stay ahead of the game there. He still had two spools of the line, so that could wait, but it might be nice to get another box of gloves. Also some more of that deodorizing cleaner, the kind designed for pet smells, with enzymes that literally digested urine and other odorous fluids.

The store contained a dazzling selection of sizes and brands of everything. And all of it so clean and well displayed. Do-it-yourselfers cruised the aisles with pushcarts groaning with two-by-fours, gasoline-powered leaf-blowers, circular saws, sections of PVC, gallons of housepaint. *Enjoy it, you sonsabitches,* the puppeteer thought. *God knows you've sacrificed everything for it.*

He brought his selections to the cashier. She was a pretty young woman who wore a plastic name badge that told impatient customers that she was in training, a way of explaining her slow and inept processing of their purchases, her hesitations and apologies. The puppeteer felt sorry for her as the line grew. When it was his turn, he paid in cash with exact change, for which she gave him a grateful smile. A pretty, dark-haired girl.

Next, some more specialized purchases in the palatial main building of the mall. Sharper Image and Brookstone, delicious high-tech shops full of cunning electronic devices easily adaptable for other purposes. Then some basic components at RadioShack, where the cashier asked for his phone number and he declined to give it, telling the guy he was on enough mailing lists already. Then Lechter's, which sold excellent cooking utensils, including a brand of knives of such good steel that they could be reground and honed to surgical sharpness. So few people nowadays knew the power of a good blade, how amazing a truly sharp tool could be. Of course, you had to know how to grind them properly, a once common skill now mostly lost among the general population. Americans, among so much else that they'd let slip, had forgotten the blades that the Vietcong used with such effectiveness, the fast work a smaller man with a razor-edged long knife could make of a big, heavily armed, and encumbered GI.

He left the temple of commerce happily burdened himself, carrying several shopping bags full of things bought with honest greenbacks. At first he congratulated himself that it had all gone well. But then he ran into a hitch as he was trying to get out of the parking lot and had to wait in traffic snarled at the mall exit. A light was malfunctioning and there were some repairs in progress on the entrance ramp to Route 7, so a cop was directing cars, wearing a clownish orange reflective vest and an orange plastic shower cap over his police hat. All the drivers were a little confused, their reflexes dulled by the anesthetic of shopping, slowed by this deviation from routine. The cop was having a hard time alone, really it was a job for two men. When the Mr. Smith started to cross into the intersection, the harried cop stuck out a white glove and shot him a wide-eyed glower. He waved his other hand like a scolding schoolmarm, side to side with one finger raised, and stepped into the path of Mr. Smith's car before turning to direct the cross-traffic. Sitting there, locked into the intersection like a beef steer crowded into a cattle chute, Mr. Smith felt the artery in his neck bulge, twist like a snake. Heat poured into his face. Blood pressure spiking, he could practically feel the hippocampus bloating at the base of his brain, convulsing like an exposed grub. The contempt and the arrogance of the cop's gestures. For a moment it occurred to him to teach a lesson to this cop, to watch from a distance and trail him home. Then he thought of accelerating the next phase with Number Four, things were almost ready anyway.

But that was stupid. He deliberately shed a degree of heat, reminded himself of the need for caution. It was more than a personal safety issue, it was virtually national security. You didn't lose control, you *took* control. That's how you struck back. That's how you made the *statement*. That's how you made them pay, and that's how you gained ascendancy. Over yourself, over others, over life. This was to a large degree a metaphysical quest.

Still, it was good that it didn't take too long for the cop to turn and beckon him to advance. The orange-capped blond head nodded reassuringly and almost apologetically, and the pressure backed off a few foot-pounds. Time to go home.

The puppeteer used his remote to open the gate and then cruised up the long driveway. Mid-May, the place was beautiful in the sunset light, a little mysterious. The Smith house. Big oaks sheltered the grounds, last year's leaves thick on the forest floor among a low growth of myrtle. After the turn, the lawn and the rise to the house.

The house was not large, but it was fine as a second residence for a single man, and with its double garage and the little wing he'd added in back, it had all the room he needed. A classic Westchester woods house that looked as if it had grown up out of the soil: steep, moss-stained roof, ivy-grown stone walls, massive chimney, little windows. Around here they called the style Rustic Tudor, but he always saw something Bavarian in it. A Black Forest fairy-tale house. It had been built long before the area became the upscale enclave it was now, and in fact the land behind the house, down toward the stream, had been a garbage dump forty years earlier. That was in the era before environmental constraints and zoning and permitting. Now the old dump was long overgrown, a scrubby forest choked by kudzu and marked by the occasional rusted-out hulks of round-backed Studebakers and DeSotos. It made a handy place to bury the dogs and was crucial to the later phases of the conditioning process, a proving ground of sorts.

He regretted that he had only three acres, but the size of the estates on either side, the old dump, and the highway dead zone not so far away gave him abundant privacy. You couldn't see any other houses from anywhere on his property, and from the front windows of the house you could see cars passing only during winter.

He drove up to the garage and parked in front of the right-hand door. He took his purchases into the workshop and, after switching on the lights, began putting them away into cabinets and drawers. The electronics shop occupied its own corner of the big room, opposite the heavier machining equipment, and for now he set the scale he'd bought at Brookstone on the workbench there. The scale was a clever device that not only weighed you but measured your body-fat content by passing a weak electrical current into your flesh through the chrome plates you stood on, which were really elec-trodes. Having read the machine's technical specs, he'd been delighted to find that the current it used was exactly what he'd calculated for the next direct neural-stimulus experiments and would save him time customizing components. He gave the scale an affectionate pat and looked forward to dismantling it later.

When he was done, he went to the surgical room to check on the dogs. The two of them waited whimpering in their separate cages. A golden retriever and a German shepherd, both about two years old, adopted through ads in the Hartford advertising weekly. They were good dogs, still handsome despite the incongruous bald domes that capped their heads above their worried eyebrows. He'd shaved them yesterday and had rewarded them with treats for their good behavior. Now he spoke to them soothingly as he inserted the hose through the mesh and refilled their water bowls.

Back in the main room, he cocked an ear toward the house and heard nothing, which suggested that things were still in order there. Then he took a seat at the workbench and opened the *Times* he'd picked up from a coin box at the mall, scanning it carefully and then refolding it. He looked over the *Daily News* and the *Journal News* just as carefully. Monday's article on the O'Connor murder had been disappointingly vague, and there was no follow-up today.

When he was done with the news scan, he unfolded the cash-register receipts from the day's shopping and spread them out on the table, going over the figures. The one from Lechter's got his attention fast. He took out a calculator and tapped in the numbers to double-check. He'd been right the first time—they'd overcharged him. *Son. Of. A. Bitch.* That big, oafish guy at the register, smiling insincerely while he rang up the charges and either fucked up or deliberately jacked the price five dollars.

The artery writhed in his neck again. The top of his head felt too small to contain the pressure inside. The five dollars wasn't so important, it was the *principle* of the thing, the system grinding along and *controlling* him, maneuvering him to its advantage, bilking him. And, worst of all, he couldn't go back to the mall and make a scene, couldn't risk standing out or making a profile in any way. He had to be patient about these things, he reminded himself. But his impotence was enormously frustrating. He was caught, controlled, just one little puppet in a great big puppet show, and there was not a goddamned thing he could do about it.

Except, he reminded himself. Except what he was already doing. Except the job at hand. When the tabloids had finally gotten wind of the links between the killings in New Jersey and then Manhattan, they'd called them the work of a "monster." Mr. Smith didn't really mind that, though he'd have preferred more acknowledgment of the insight and skill they'd required. On one level, yes, anyone who could do that kind of thing *was* a monster. But he was just doing as he'd been taught. He was doing what he'd been trained to do, made to do, the thing he was good at, the thing he'd been assured it was essential for him to do. If he was a monster, they had made him one, and it was only fair that they faced the consequences now.

The thoughts ate at him, piranha in a feeding frenzy, a thousand small, savage bites, and his hands shook as he filed away the receipts. Despite his self-control he knew from experience the thoughts and the pressure wouldn't quit without the relief of some catharsis.

Fortunately, he wasn't without recourse on that score.

He turned off the garage lights, quietly unlocked the door to the kitchen, then slipped inside the dark house and shut the door soundlessly behind him. The shock value of a sudden appearance. Once he was inside, he crossed the kitchen and stood near the door to the living room. There was a little odor of mildew and urine, and the only light came from the digital clock in the microwave. He waited, then deliberately stomped his feet and banged a pot on the counter.

In the following silence he was gratified to hear a quick shift and scrape from the dark room beyond, as if a small animal had withdrawn into a corner and now stood waiting. A palpable sense of fear and expectation.

"I'm home," he announced. A stern, paternalistic voice. "I'm coming in." All he got for reply was another light shifting sound and some more cowering silence. It was very gratifying.

12

WEDNESDAY CAME UP WET, a light rain misting down from a low, pewter-colored sky. Mo didn't mind, it meant that he could work inside without looking through the windows at another beautiful spring day that he couldn't take the time to get out into. He settled into his chair, ignoring the banter of Estey and Paderewski across the room. A bunch of materials from the O'Connor murder had come through, including a summary of the legwork the White Plains PD and St. Pierre had done. St. Pierre was inexperienced, but the guy was a bundle of energy. Already he had interviewed the victim's sister in Poughkeepsie, the people at O'Connor's copy shop, and a woman he had recently started dating. His notes said O'Connor had been thirty-two, no kids, divorced two years ago with the ex now living in California. An avid bicycler and kayaker, amateur nature photographer. The girlfriend said they'd been dating for about six months, and both she and the sister had gone to pieces when St. Pierre had interviewed them. At Mo's suggestion, the White Plains people and St. Pierre were keeping a close eye out for disagreements or altercations O'Connor might have had with people, anything that might have made him seem "controlling" and established him as a target for the killer. White Plains was still trying to reach the former wife in Sacramento, but everybody knew this one was not about a vengeful ex.

Reading a life story summed up like this gave Mo a pang. Reduce any life to its outwardly visible facts, a pile of paper, and it'd seem generic, arbitrary data without a soul. Mo's own postmortem life summary would be pretty bleak. Between the paper and the meat thing left at a murder scene, it made you have to ask just what a life was. The answers suggested were not uplifting.

Mo looked to get something more useful from the lab materials that had also come through. Angelo had performed the autopsy Tuesday afternoon, and his report was there. Time of death was very early Friday morning, meaning that O'Connor had been caught at home before work Thursday and the killer had used him for maybe eighteen hours. Angelo's notes said that after O'Connor had been suspended from the wall, he had been able to support his weight on his leg and arm cords, and he'd only strangled to death when his limbs could no longer keep tension off the neck cord. The close-up photos of wrist and knee ligature sites showed abrasion and directional bleeding that was consistent with him being alive for a time on the wall.

The thought of a man straining to hold himself until his strength failed and he slowly choked, that was hard to take. Mo took a moment to shut his eyes and rub the bridge of his nose.

The extensive bruising around ligature sites suggested that O'Connor had been forcibly manipulated for a long time. No sign of sexual assault, unusual for a ritualistic killer of this sort. Organ condition and muscle tone good, meaning that O'Connor had been fit and in good health, lending credence to Dr. Ingalls's claim that the killer would also be quite strong. Angelo had made incisions through the temple wounds and had provided both photos and cross-sectional drawings of them. Mo was no expert on old tools, but the size and shape of the wounds looked about right for a pair of antique ice tongs with sharpened points. Just like the tongs long since recovered from Ronald Parker.

Angelo had provided a group of close-up photos of the ligature knots, which would provide the most telling comparisons to the original Howdy Doody killings. By this afternoon, when he went back to the FBI Manhattan field office with these materials, Mo would have some idea just how deep this shithole was. He couldn't tell without comparing them side by side, but looking at the knots now he had a sinking feeling. They jibed closely with what he remembered of the knots he'd glimpsed in Biedermann's files.

And, yes, the handcuffs on O'Connor's wrists were the Flex-Cuf brand Special Agent Morris had identified on Parker's victims. Angelo had simply read the brand name and logo off the straps.

Finally, there was a sampling of photos of the arranged objects found at O'Connor's house, clearly showing that several kinds of designs and patterns were repeated. The zigzag lines with objects in the angles, a starburst of smaller objects around a larger, and so on. Some kind of arranging of victim and objects was not uncommon with serial murderers, and the exact nature of the arrangements could reveal a lot about the psychology of the perpetrator. A focus on the genitals of the victim would suggest a sex-derived psychopathology. Swastikas, crosses, or other symbols could provide clues to the perpetrator's cultural background. Use of flowers, facial covering, or concealment of wounds might represent symbolic burial and suggested that the perpetrator felt remorse or shame. In fact, the FBI's Behavioral Sciences Unit had put together an encyclopedic catalog of such arrangements, with exhaustive analysis of the psychological implications of each.

These photos would also be interesting to compare with Biedermann's photos of Ronald Parker's arrangements. And, Mo reminded himself, with the arrangements and other details of the power station scene.

By the time he'd finished reviewing the new materials, it was eleven-thirty. Estey had left the office. Paderewski had her feet up on her desk and was leafing through a magazine and listening to music on earphones as she took a coffee break. Mo had just decided it was time to do likewise when the door swung open and St. Pierre came in. He came over to Mo's desk and moved papers aside to make room to sit on it.

"You got time for an update on the power station corpse?" St. Pierre gestured with the file folder he was carrying.

"Show me," Mo said.

"Forensic ID is working on two main avenues. On the odontology side, we got X-rays and photos of the teeth, and I've personally taken copies to every dentist in the county. Our tooth people say she had a grinding problem, excessive wear, and if she sought treatment, like one of those mouth guards you wear when you're sleeping, that might help speed up the dentists' matching her teeth with a patient." He tossed several photos on the desk, shots of upper and lower jaws from different perspectives. "On the jewelry, the earrings were nothing much, but the ring seemed unusual enough that it might have a history. So I've been taking photos of it to jewelers all over the county, see if they've ever seen it, maybe sold it or done work on the setting." St. Pierre slipped two more photos out, gave them to Mo.

Angelo had found the jewelry among the ruins of the corpse. The ring did look distinctive, a small opal in an ornate antique setting, the kind of thing that might be an heirloom.

"Good work," Mo said sincerely. St. Pierre the eager beaver.

Mike took the compliment like a puppy getting praised, practically wagging his behind. "Finally, we're in line for facial reconstruction, but that'll take some weeks. I also gave tissue samples to the DNA lab in Albany for a definitive ID when we get something to compare it to."

"Any fingerprints on the arranged objects?"

"Good prints on everything. And we're on for a match search. But that could take a while, too—"

"How about the ligature cord? I'm especially interested in the knots."

For the first time, St. Pierre looked troubled, his eyebrows moving independently as if they couldn't decide where to end up. "The line is a .95 serrated poly weed-whacker line made by Unibrand and sold at hardware stores, Home Depots, Wal-Marts, impossible to trace.

About the knots, um, I asked Lazarre for 'em, she stalled me. I didn't get what it was about. Maybe you should talk to her."

Mo could see where this was leading. Liz Lazarre was chief evidence technician at the county lab up at Grasslands. Her domain was a suite of sealed, positive-pressure, HEPA-filtered rooms that contained little more than bright lights, drying racks, huge, white enamel tables, and photographic equipment. The tables were kept sanitary and were big enough to accommodate anything deemed likely to reveal evidence, from a thumbnail to a car bumper to a couch. She would have put the power-station weed-whacker cords on one of her tables, gone over them with tweezers and microscopes, and photographed them under various types of light. Liz was nicknamed Eva Braun, an attempt to signify her dictatorial style, although Mo didn't really know whether the original Eva had been as hard-nosed as her buddy Adolf. Mo had a sinking feeling about why she had stalled St. Pierre.

"In other news," St. Pierre said proudly, "I just got a call that my wife has gone into labor, and I'm going home right now to attend the delivery. I'll probably need tomorrow off."

Mo just looked at him, the big sunny face, the boyish smile. He seemed unaware of the ironies here, his talking in the same breath about desiccated corpses and babies being born, or his taking only one lousy day off to acknowledge the new life that was coming while giving the rest of his days to death.

"That's great, Mike," Mo said. "Good luck. I know it'll go great." He shook St. Pierre's hand, gave it a real squeeze. He knew he would be scared shitless in St. Pierre's shoes.

Across the room, Paderewski was looking at St. Pierre, smiling and clapping her hands. How she heard anything through her earphones, Mo couldn't understand. "You going to give out cigars?" she asked.

A telephone call to Liz verified Mo's suspicions. Liz was a smoker who lived in torment from her inability to light up on the job, crabby from constant nicotine deprivation. It wasn't easy to tell just how you got on Liz's good side, or if she actually had one, but you certainly didn't want to get on her bad side. So when she told him she'd already sent the ligatures and knots to the FBI Manhattan field office, expedited at Biedermann's "request," Mo didn't complain. Instead he thanked her and drove to the county's Grasslands Campus in Valhalla, ten minutes north. The ME's office.

Angelo spent his days down in the basement, working with dead bodies and coworkers and assistants who often struck Mo as not much more lively than the customers. The amazing thing was that they all took their lunch down there, munching away in a staff lounge right across the hall from the big cold-storage locker containing stainless-steel bunks designed for very deep sleepers.

Angelo was punctual about his mealtimes, and Mo found him as expected, feet up on the table, avidly reading some technical journal while eating a big submarine sandwich. His assistant was there, too, hunched over the table and eating potato salad out of a plastic container. Angelo shot his forefinger at Mo and stood up to greet him.

"I thought I might see you today," Angelo said.

"Oh?"

"Well. It's not often I've got three of yours in here at once. Who do you want to see first? Willard and O'Connor I'm done with. The power station lady is going to take a little longer, just because of her condition. We're doing some microscopic tissue analysis and some insect work on her—there're some egg casings and larvae that will help us draw a bead on how long she was there. You want to see?"

"Not today. Actually, I came to see you."

"I'm flattered. Let's go back inside, we'll talk." Angelo had heard the gloom in his voice, got the message. He balled up his sandwich wrapper, tossed it, and led Mo down the corridor toward the autopsy suite. They went through a pair of swinging doors and into the main room, a big, windowless chamber with tile floors and bright lights.

Six white-enameled surgical tables took up most of the area, and the far wall held two dozen stainless-steel-faced drawers intended for current customers.

Once he'd shut the door behind him, Angelo said, "Rumor has it Carla's gone. How're you doing with that?" He looked at Mo and stroked a nonexistent beard, looking more like a psychotherapist than a cadaver-cutter.

"Ah, not so good. You know."

Angelo turned away and crossed over to the wall of chrome, where he pondered for a moment before yanking one of the handles. The long drawer slid out and there was Big Willie, skin bluish, huge chest split with the crude stitching of the Y-incision, head and neck braced in a green plastic block. Angelo looked at Willie critically for a moment before saying, "I know. You're in mourning. But for what? RIP for Carla and Mo, or for love itself?"

It was an insightful question, and Mo spread his hands, turning so he didn't have to face Big Willie. "When you start pushing forty—" he began. Meaning that, yes, after a while you did begin to fear it could die out of your life, maybe the one just past was the last ever. "Listen, help me with your buddy here," Angelo broke in, patting Willie's arm. "I need this drawer, but we'll want him around while your review is pending, and anyway we haven't located any next of kin yet, don't know how to dispose. I've got to move him over to storage. Wheel that gurney over here, would you?"

Mo obediently rolled the gurney over next to the drawer. Angelo adjusted the height and locked the wheels.

"We'll just flip him. It's okay if he's on his face, he'll end up on his back in the fridge." Angelo positioned himself at Big Willie's legs and stood looking at Mo expectantly. Mo put his hands under the massive shoulders and lifted when he got Angelo's nod. "There you go. Good. Good," Angelo said encouragingly. It took all of Mo's strength to turn the body onto its side, and then it suddenly followed through on its own and rolled joltingly onto the gurney.

They wheeled Big Willie into a side hall and to the locker. Angelo opened the insulated door, and the light inside came on automatically, like a refrigerator. It was a small, cold room with two rows of five-stacked steel bunks on either side, set up on vertical chain conveyors that raised or lowered them. A couple of bodies lay on the right-side bunks, giving Mo the uncomfortable feeling of having intruded into some stranger's bedroom. They locked the gurney's wheels, and Angelo pumped a pedal that raised it to the level of one of the left-side shelves.

When he'd gotten the height right, Angelo turned back to Mo. "I don't even want to hear the over-the-hill crap," he said. He positioned himself to roll Big Willie, and when they both heaved, the body flipped over and landed on its back on the shelf. Angelo adjusted one of Big Willie's arms and then released the gurney's lifters and brakes, saying, "It's bullshit, Mo. One, you're too young to be thinking that way. Two, you were lonely in that relationship. If you want my opinion, it's good luck for you that Carla had the gumption to break it off." He raised his eyebrows, *Right?*—driving the point home with his dark eyes.

Mo shrugged. Break it off, try a little harder, how could you tell when it was time for one or the other? Where was the line? Mo had always landed on the try-harder side. "Maybe we could talk about business," he said after a moment. "Your postmortem on the power station corpse, not your post on my relationship. Can we get out of here?"

"Sure." Angelo still held his eyes, letting Mo know he didn't entirely accept the dodge.

They left the locker, Angelo pushing the empty gurney as they headed back toward the autopsy room.

Mo breathed the warmer air of the corridor with relief. "I'm interested in the ligatures—"

"Found four in the remains. Sent them up to Liz."

"Who looked them over and sent them on to Federal Plaza."

Angelo nodded thoughtfully as he wheeled the gurney back into the bright main room. "Mm. You'd like to see them, huh?"

"Well—"

"Fortunately for you," Angelo said, "I kept some close-up photos of my own. Always keep shots of such items in situ." He winked, turned to a stainless sink, and began washing his hands. "Never hurts to have a little backup documentation."

"I take it you've worked with Biedermann before," Mo said.

Twenty minutes later, Mo was back at his desk, looking over photos of the knots, copies printed off Angelo's scanner and color laser printer. On the left, a knot in place around the wrist bones and blackened tendons of the power-station corpse. On the right, a knot from O'Connor's fully fleshed wrist. Same cord, the serrated poly line. Same knots, the little double noose with three or four turns of line, the complex midline tensioning knot. Details so specific that it would ordinarily lead one to suspect that the two were killed by the same guy. Nice to know before meeting with Biedermann and his lackeys again.

Mo checked his watch. So far so good. One more errand to run, and then he'd better get over to Federal Plaza.

13

M O WALKED THROUGH A broad expanse of chest-high, gray cubicles filled with FBI personnel at their computer screens. The plastic access authorization tag flopped on his lapel, marking him as an outsider. He followed the room's central corridor to a row of offices and conference rooms against the outside wall, where the first person he saw was Dr. Rebecca Ingalls. She was standing just inside the door of a conference room, wearing a green dress and matching jacket, talking to someone just out of Mo's view. Silhouetted against the window, her figure hit Mo hard: strong thighs and sweet belly curve, surprisingly narrow waist. The sight of her gave him a good feeling, until the broad-shouldered form of SAC Biedermann stepped past her and came out to greet him.

"Aha. Detective Ford, come on in, welcome," Biedermann said. The words were warm but the voice was not—Biedermann was apparently working on his social skills but had an absence of native talent. "Dr. Ingalls was good enough to make time in her schedule. I thought she should join our little powwow, look over your materials, and get up to speed on this new situation. Rebecca, I believe you've met Morgan Ford of the State Police?"

She nodded and shook his hand. "Nice to see you again," she said. *Bang,* an Annie Oakley smile, Great Plains bright and dead on target.

"Good to see you," Mo agreed.

They took seats at a big table, just the three of them today, Biedermann at the head with Mo and Dr. Ingalls opposite each other.

Mo opened his briefcase and set out some of the materials he'd brought; Dr. Ingalls put out a file and a notebook. Biedermann's end of the table was conspicuously empty.

"So let's see what you got." Beidermann rubbed his big hands together expectantly.

"Well," Mo said, "you've already gotten the materials from our labs, the pathology reports, and my personnel file. That doesn't leave me much to bring but my opinion, which I'll be glad to share with you if you'd like. Then I'd like to see your files."

A look of dislike crossed Biedermann's face. "Now hold on here—"

"My opinion is that if Ronald Parker's attorney finds out how completely this new murder parallels the ones attributed to Parker, he'll go to press before he goes to court, claiming you nailed the wrong guy. That whereas I can't show these knots and cuffs and ligature abrasions to the newspapers—" he tossed copies of Angelo's photos toward Biedermann—"I can, in fact I am obligated to, disclose exculpatory evidence to his attorney. Who doesn't have to play by the same rules I have to, and who will happily blow the lid off your secrecy game. However, I'm willing to forget that obligation for the time being if I see some files appear on this table in the next sixty seconds. The deal for today was not a powwow but for me to look at *your* materials."

Biedermann's jaw inched forward, a G.I. Joe look that he probably practiced in front of a mirror. Dr. Ingalls looked a little taken aback by the immediate antagonism between the two men, but she was also curious, observing closely.

"I told you yesterday," Biedermann said curtly, "that I don't take any bullshit from you." He reached behind him for a phone, tapped a number, waited, said into the receiver, "Get me Frank Marsden, White Plains barracks State Police." As he waited, he said to Mo, "You're out, Ford. It's that simple. Marsden will can your ass so fast—"

"Actually," Mo cut in, "I just talked to him before I came down here. Put him in touch with a lady by the name of Francine Jacobs, in our personnel office? He was upset that you had requested my file, and *his,* without the courtesy of consulting him. He's pissing mad already and disinclined to be told what to do. Do yourself a favor and try a more cooperative management style." Mo kept his voice even and just watched Biedermann's reaction.

Biedermann hesitated, one hand holding the phone out from his face and the other flat on the table, staring at Mo.

"One other thing you should know," Mo added, "is that Richard Flannery is taking a personal interest in this case. You've met the Westchester DA, right? He has asked me, personally, to keep him, personally, informed, and to let him know if I need his help with anything." Mo had decided that one way to survive working with both Flannery and Biedermann was to play them against each other. It was one thing for Biedermann to push around a lowly detective, another to get macho with the elected top legal authority of New York's richest county. "In fact, I talked to him just before I came down here. He asked me to give him a full update tomorrow. Maybe you should call him instead of Marsden."

Biedermann still held the phone, and it could have gone either way, but then Dr. Ingalls laughed, shook her head, tapped the back of Biedermann's hand with her pen. "God, I love my job!" she said sincerely. "You guys are giving me a *text*book demonstration of hierarchical competition behaviors! Erik, you've heard similar criticisms before, maybe it's time to acknowledge there's some truth there? Also, Detective Ford has already had some great insights, and I don't think you can afford to do without his obvious talents. Let's get to work."

Biedermann, to his credit, hooked a wry grin on one cheek. He tossed the receiver back onto the cradle, got up and went to the door, cuffing Mo hard on the shoulder on the way. "Esteban," he called to the outer office, "you want to bring us the Howdy Doody files?

Thank you very much." Then he waited at the door, looking back at the two of them. "Looks like we got the makings of a great team here," he said without enthusiasm.

The original Howdy Doody's cord was Unibrand .95 serrated line, just like the line taken from O'Connor's body, available in bulk spools at over three thousand outlets throughout the country. Likewise the eyelets, three-eighths-inch galvanized-steel question marks manufactured by Save-Rite Hardware and available for fifty cents apiece nationwide. Likewise the disposable handcuffs, Flex-Cuf brand, a three-eighths-by-one-sixteenth-inch band of nylon. The most telling parallels were the knots, which matched, and the bruises and abrasions on the ligature sites, which told the tale of identical abuse and manipulation of the victims. Finally, there were innumerable parallels among the types of designs prevalent in the arranged objects. None of these were details that had made it to the press.

The three of them looked over the materials, compared photos side by side. For a while Biedermann stood behind Mo, leaning over him as he reviewed the materials, the proximity of his big body making Mo feel claustrophobic. When he went back to his chair, he just sat, fiddling with a pen, looking thoughtful and almost sad. Dr. Ingalls took the materials as Mo finished with them, and when she was done, she blew out a breath. She clasped her hands behind her head and sat leaning back in her chair, staring at the ceiling.

Mo was the first one to talk. "Ronald Parker is the wrong guy."

"No," Biedermann insisted. "Not a chance."

"How can we be so sure? Okay, you caught him in his car with all the paraphernalia, his profile fits, but maybe he was, I don't know . . . set up? Maybe—"

"Morgan," Dr. Ingalls said quietly, "there was an eyewitness. Given all this, I'd doubt the eyewitness myself—except it was *me*. We arranged a trap. Ronald Parker came into my apartment. He . . . hurt me. He had the equipment with him. My testimony against him isn't just going to be about the profile match." She looked at Mo as if wary of his reaction.

"So what does that leave? Parker had a, an accomplice, someone who knew the signature inside out, and now that Parker is in jail he's going it alone?"

"Maybe," Dr. Ingalls said. "Except for two points. First, Ronald Parker was alone when he came to my apartment. Second, even if two people got together to commit murders, no two people could share the identical psychopathology. Their different psychological needs would sooner or later have to be expressed in the crime. Especially if they were no longer working together."

"An identical twin brother?" Mo hazarded, knowing he was reaching. "Parker was adopted—could he have reconnected with his twin somewhere along the line? I mean, you're always reading about the separated-at-birth thing—"

Dr. Ingalls shook her head. "We went back, found his birth records. A single birth."

"Leaving the inside-job scenario," Mo said. "The new killer is someone close to the original investigation and is masquerading as a copycat to confuse the issue. So who knew this much about the investigation?"

He looked at Biedermann to see his reaction. Having observed how the SAC ran things, how close to his chest he played his cards, the answer couldn't be flattering. Mo was willing to bet that very few players had all the information needed to duplicate the crime so closely. Someone in Biedermann's office. Maybe somebody in the New York DA's office. Maybe somebody in the New Jersey or New York PDs, but judging from Ty's resentment over the way the investigation was controlled, probably not even there. Who else? Zelek, the alien, or someone else at his level? Then there was the issue of using Rebecca as bait, suggesting they had reason to suspect the insider possibility early on. Mo thought to confront Biedermann with that, then decided he'd pushed his luck enough for one day.

"Even that scenario has its problems," Dr. Ingalls said.

"Such as—?"

"Motive. Why would a law enforcement employee kill these people, who are apparently randomly selected? And even if it's driven entirely by a psychopathology, if you've got the forensic knowledge to avoid leaving evidence, why bother to imitate someone else's modus operandi when inventing your own would be so much more . . . satisfying? When imitating would *suggest* to police that the perpetrator has inside information?"

"And I have to say," Biedermann put in, "I resent the implication that anyone in this office is in any way involved." Mo realized it was the first time he'd spoken in a long time.

"So what's the alternative?" Mo asked.

Nobody answered. After another minute, the phone behind Biedermann buzzed and he picked it up. "Biedermann. Yeah. Yeah. Okay. Two minutes," he said. When he had hung up, he stood and went to the door, shrugging his big shoulders, getting his air of authority cranked up again. "I've got other things to attend to. Detective Ford, I propose we table this discussion until we have more data on the power-station murder. We'll convene a full task force meeting when we have that material." He gave them each a nod, his eyes lingering on Dr. Ingalls, before leaving the room.

Dr. Ingalls busied herself with putting her materials into her briefcase, and Mo did likewise. Being alone in the room with her felt suddenly awkward. Throughout their meeting, Mo realized, he'd been acutely conscious of her interaction with Biedermann, seeking clues to the current state of their relationship. They called each other by their first names, but that didn't mean anything, given that they'd worked together for the better part of a year. Then there was that moment when she defused the confrontation, laughing and demonstrating some kind of emotional authority over Biedermann—

He was startled when something hit him in the chest. A little wad of tinfoil skittered across the table, and he looked up, astonished to see Dr. Ingalls watching him, just putting a piece of gum into her mouth.

She chewed a couple of times, then grinned at his surprise. "You're thinking Erik's a pain, huh? Hey, it's three-thirty—you want to get a cup of coffee?" The words were potentially flirtatious, but her smile was heavily wry, almost regretful. Still, his heart did a sudden flip and deftly landed on its feet.

"Sure," he said.

14

B UT SHE CHANGED HER mind as soon as they got outside.
"Would you be up for a walk instead? If what everybody tells
me is true, days like this are rare in Manhattan. Carpe diem, and all
that."

Mo agreed readily. The rain had blown over, and an expanse of
blue was pushing the wet weather away, a ridge of clouds sliding
away above the city like an opening eyelid. After half a day of rain,
the streets were wet and everything had a fresh, scrubbed look, and
yet a nice breeze took the humidity away. She was right, it was not
something to be squandered. They turned south on Broadway and
headed toward Battery Park.

Rebecca walked with big, easy strides, swinging her briefcase in a
wide arc. She looked like an outlander, big and blond and gazing
around with the enthusiasm of a tourist. "You have to understand,"
she said, "my one regret about my profession is that it involves sitting
inside a lot, talking a lot. I love it here, but I still get a little
claustrophobic."

"I can imagine. I'm kind of a city boy, but I still like to walk every
chance I get."

She gave him a quick, approving glance. "I liked the way you
handled Erik when he wanted to yank your chain. You had done
some preparation for that eventuality?"

"Some amount of that is typical in interjurisdictional projects."

"Well, that's what I thought we could talk about." The regretful look was back. "I think you need to be aware that Erik is tough, but he's sincerely trying to make a good job of a complex situation."

"You don't think you're letting your personal relationship with him bias your judgment?"

She glanced over at him to see if he'd meant it the way it sounded, a little taken aback. "You do do your homework, don't you?"

"I'm just trying to keep my own professional objectivity. Critical thinking, question the biases of your sources. A good habit, don't you think?"

"Very wise. You sure it's purely a professional interest? No biases on your part?"

She was getting back at him, turning it back around. But in a nice way, probing but not judging. She must be a knockout shrink, he decided, a hard person to hide anything from.

"Let's speak in declarative sentences," he proposed. "We're both accustomed to interrogating people—admittedly different schools and styles, but I'll bet between us we could answer each other with questions forever."

"Declarative statements only." She nodded with a wide smile, liking the challenge. "Okay. So let's get something out of the way. I think you like me. I think I like you. That's okay with me. Yes, the relationship between Erik and me probably did get in the way somewhat during our Howdy Doody work, but not to any crucial extent. No, I don't think it's biasing me now."

Mo walked along beside her. Jesus, she could spike it right back over the net at you. Jesus, it felt good. Looking at her now, he saw something besides a handsome female: rather, a self-inspected person, unafraid of her own nature, accepting of her own style. Committed to dealing with life on the terms she'd set for it. He wanted to ask, to verify, whether her relationship with Biedermann was a thing of the past, but that was an interrogatory and the declaratory, stripped of camouflage, would be something like *I want you to be available for a relationship*. Which was way too fast, under the circumstances.

They had come up behind a family of Japanese tourists, a mother and father and four kids who walked in a line across the whole sidewalk, arranged by size like six organ pipes, largest to smallest. They wore shorts and white socks and gaudy running shoes and bright sweatshirts with brand logos on them. The littlest girl jumped over cracks in the pavement while the father wrestled with a large foldout map of Manhattan, turning it upside down and back again. Probably looking for the Trade Center towers, two blocks over. Rebecca slowed, watching them with pleasure, and Mo held back with her. The kids were cute. It was good to let the previous statements settle in. They didn't say anything for a full two minutes.

"I am usually called Mo," he stated finally. "I would like to call you Rebecca."

She looked at him, pleased. "This is fun!" she said. "Who'd a thunk? Oops! Does that count as a question? Oops!" And she laughed at herself.

Four o'clock and Battery Park was nicely spacious, lawns and trees and iron fences ending at stone breakwaters, the water of the Upper Bay beyond. The very toe of the stockinged foot of Manhattan Island, the bow of the big ship. Pigeons patrolling the sidewalks, pecking at cigarette butts and flipping them away peevishly. The usual scattering of lovers, thoughtful solitaries, joggers. A few tourists gazing over the gunmetal blue water at Ellis Island and Miss Liberty, the dirty-orange Staten Island ferry forging along. A park crew was emptying trash containers, two guys working the metal baskets and a woman driving a golf cart heaped with garbage bags. A breeze puffed in from the southeast, bringing in a sea smell.

They stood for a moment at the water, leaning against the railing. Rebecca had gotten serious again. "My point about SAC Biedermann was going to culminate in a warning."

"Warning?"

She nodded. "You have to understand, I'm relatively new at

working with the FBI. The closest I've ever come to the level of intrigue there was consulting on a federal program dealing with early childhood education, that had a lot of political complexity and pressure. But I know that there are dimensions here that simply can't be . . . shared . . . with every police agency that might be interested. I'm not party to them all myself, and I don't want to be. I don't know you that well, but I can guess you're the kind of person, the kind of investigator, who wants to know everything. And who doesn't quit and doesn't . . . take orders well." She gave him a tiny smile to show that she didn't mean it as criticism.

"What was the warning?"

"Just that maybe the compartmentalization Erik wants is the best thing. That you probably don't really want to know everything or get involved as deeply as you'd usually insist on."

Mo thought about that for a moment, trying to figure out where this was going. "Does that guy Zelek have anything to do with these 'other dimensions'?"

"I assume so."

"Can you give me any idea of what these other dimensions are?"

She tossed her head, *yes and no*. "I have my own speculations, but they're just that—speculative. But I think Erik was transferred here from San Diego specifically to handle the Howdy Doody case."

"Do you know why?"

"Not entirely. But just from comments he's dropped, I believe he had been dealing with a similar case out there."

"What!"

The regretful look. "Not a big string of murders. Maybe two."

"Do you know if they caught the guy?"

"I'm assuming not. Hopefully, they'll establish that it was Ronald Parker. We still don't know where he was during the twenty-month period when he vanished, and maybe he was out in California, beginning to develop his ritual."

"Yeah. Except that now this copycat, or whatever, has come along."

"So you can understand Erik's concern. I think he's deeply upset by the copycat."

"You want to tell me your speculations?"

She pondered that, frowned, shook her head. "I'm thinking I'd like to play the declarative game again. You've asked me about five questions in a row." She was trying to be light about it, but he could see that something was disturbing her.

"I would like to keep walking," he said.

She moved away from the fence and chose to head back toward the park entrance and the looming cliffs of Manhattan buildings. "I consent with the understanding that I'm getting hungry and would like to eat soon."

"I would like to have dinner with you," he said.

She stopped walking and turned toward him. "Mo, there are scary aspects to the study of human psychology and neurology. My work sometimes involves pain and lives that can't seem to get straightened out, but in general it's not so bad, it's about healing. But not everybody comes into psychology with altruistic motives. People also come into it with the intention to use the science as a tool, a weapon, to create suffering and pain."

"Like Ronald Parker, his obsession with control? Manipulating people. Hurting them."

A beat, a hesitation, as if she were about to say something important. Then she appeared to think better of it. "Yes," she said. "Like that."

They turned and walked on, scattering a clutch of pigeons that had crowded around a hot dog someone had dropped. One of the pigeons had to run away, dragging an injured or deformed wing. For a moment Mo felt an intense kinship with the bird. The fellow loser.

When they got to the street, Rebecca put her hand on Mo's

shoulder. "I heard your suggestion about dinner. But not now. Maybe another time. I want to get a cab and go home now." No smile at all.

"I'm disappointed. But I'll hail a cab," he said. The declarative sentences were making them sound like automatons now. Using statements of fact to obscure, not reveal, their feelings. He realized there were a lot more questions he would have liked to have asked and a lot more declarations he'd have liked to have made.

A yellow Honda taxi pulled over and Rebecca got in, folding her legs elegantly before swiveling inside. The instant the door shut, he badly missed her presence at his side, the movement and light that went with her. A little wave, a weak smile, and gone.

15

THURSDAY MORNING.

Mo had spent the night twisting in tangled sheets, hating Carla's mother's empty house, thinking about Rebecca Ingalls and trying to figure whether the way he'd felt around her was just the product of his vulnerable, reboundy state of mind or was something better. Later, exhausted, he'd had a hard time disentangling the spooky complexities of the case from his attraction to her, and finally he'd slipped into shallow nightmares about sexual rejection and manipulation by sinister forces. And then when he'd gotten up and staggered as far as the bathroom mirror, the sight of his face was a shock that reinforced all the negative conclusions he'd come to. On his forehead and left cheek, the bruises from his fight with Big Willie had turned into irregular rings of green, yellow, purple, and he had insomnia bags under his bloodshot eyes. So he retreated from the bathroom to the kitchen, where he washed down a handful of vitamins and Saint-John's-wort capsules with two cups of black coffee, instant because Carla had taken the coffeemaker when she left. A hot shower and squirts of eyedrops helped only a little. The house was a mess and so was he, might as well go to work.

But first he had a different kind of errand. If there was one perk he enjoyed about being an investigator, it was the relative degree of autonomy. You weren't at the desk all the time, you were on your own, you could set your own priorities. St. Pierre had called to let everybody know Lilly had delivered her baby after an easy labor, the baby was great, and they were back home now. Mike was taking his one day off for the big event. Mo decided to take an hour off himself, bring some flowers over to Lilly.

The flower shop he remembered six blocks from the St. Pierres' had gone out of business, so he had to stop at the A & P, picking the least-dried-up-looking bouquet of carnations and whatnot. Looking at the thing on the car seat, it struck him as inadequate: bunch of clear plastic, universal-product-code sticker, little pouch of freshness chemicals stuck in. He wasn't in shape on these gestures. His social reflexes were rusty.

But it had been this way the other two times he'd dropped by the St. Pierres' house. After one of his visits, he'd decided that this self-savaging came from being around a real family, which made him conscious of his own lack of one. Mike and Lilly had two kids before this new one, one in first grade and the other still toddling around in falling-down Pampers, both with red-blond hair and ruddy cheeks like their father. Lilly had stayed pleasantly chubby between pregnancies and was now a full-time mom. The house was a chaos of plastic toys and half-finished projects, and it always smelled like baking, diapers, coffee, and a clean-clothes smell emanating from a dryer that seemed to run continuously. Whenever Mo came by, the kids would be hanging on their parents, taking all kinds of physical liberties with their clothes and anatomies. Bunch of happy mammals in their den.

Mo pulled up at the house, feeling like shit. You couldn't help think of the contrast with your own situation, living in your ex's mom's mostly empty house. Your life without any kids or sibs, just a mother and father who had moved from Scarsdale to Kissimmee, Florida, an elderly Jewish lady with a million interests from animal rights to Zen, an elderly Catholic guy with none.

It wasn't envy, who could envy the noise and mess? It was just— what? Finally he decided screw it, stick to the agenda. Give Lilly the bouquet, kiss the baby, shake Mike's hand, get back to work.

He got out and went up the walk, beating the plastic bouquet against his leg.

It was a stolid, middle-class neighborhood, and the house looked a lot like Daniel O'Connor's. That same hue of aluminum siding, the same little trees. Which might explain what Mike had been feeling that day at the death house, only a week ago, poor son of a bitch.

Mike let him in, smiling shyly and giving him an awkward hug with his big, lanky frame. Apparently you got emotional at times like this. They went back through the kid mess into the bedroom, where Lilly was up and folding some clothes at the bureau as the two older kids sat on the bed, looking at the new arrival.

The baby was asleep but looked uncomfortable, her red face wrinkled around some internal discomfort.

"She's beautiful," Mo said. He handed the bouquet to Lilly. "You're looking great, too, Lil. Congratulations."

Lilly was wearing baggy sweatpants and a huge shirt, and she looked tired. But she was also flush with some kind of energy, some kind of authority and self-acceptance. The proverbial glow. She accepted the bouquet and kissed Mo on the cheek. "You're so sweet. Thank you."

"Her name is Andrea," St. Pierre's older kid, the girl, told him. "She weighs seven pounds ten ounces."

Mo looked down at the little head lost in swaddling. Babies had a smell around them, he realized, a mix of laundry whites and milk, talcum powder and piss. The toddler, a boy named Peter, looked suspiciously up at him and then started playing with a knitted baby bootee.

Brittany expounded further: "She cries at night. I helped change her diapers. Mom was in labor for only two hours. Do you have a gun like my dad?"

"I guess I'm getting better with practice," Lilly said. "Move over, Brit, let me sit for a minute." Brittany scooted over, and Lilly took the baby on her lap. She leaned back against the head of the bed and just looked over her brood for a moment. The sun was hitting the half-open venetian blinds behind her, putting a barred halo around her, and Mo thought, *Madonna and child, White Plains, USA.*

"How're you doing, Mike?" Mo asked. "Did you get Paderewski's cigars?"

St. Pierre chuckled wearily. "I got pretty wired up yesterday. Didn't sleep at all last night. It's a good thing I took the day off."

"My handsome stranger," Lilly said fondly, taking his hand. "It's so nice to see my husband during daylight hours. I'm going to have to have babies more often."

Mike rolled his eyes. Mo smiled, joked around, tried to figure out what to say to the kids. Mike sat down on the bed, too, eyes drooping with fatigue, and took the little boy on his lap. After a little while Mo said he'd let himself out, and he left them there, the five of them. Big mammal pile. Happy for now, tired, coping. A family.

Not for everybody, but Mo could see how for a guy like St. Pierre it was really not too bad.

Next order of business: Flannery had commanded an appearance, the first jerk of the chain. So Mo drove across town to the county offices building, a massive glass and steel edifice that Mo thought made a nice palace for somebody like Flannery, full of enterprise and just as big, shiny, and bogus as he was. He took the elevator up and waited ten minutes in the outer office before a secretary showed him into the DA's inner sanctum.

Flannery was on his treadmill, dressed in gray sweats. On the console of the machine were a radio phone, a legal pad, a water bottle. His legs scissored steadily, long, firm strides, as the belt scrolled beneath him.

Flannery didn't slow down when he saw Mo. "Detective Ford! Good to see you. I know it's early in the investigation, but what with this thing up in Buchanan, and you going to see the FBI people yesterday, I figured it was time for an update."

Nice to know Flannery was keeping a close watch on everything, Mo thought. He told the DA about the power-station corpse and brought him up to speed on the precious little they'd learned from the O'Connor scene. Flannery asked a couple of good questions about Angelo's pathology findings, showing off a little and reminding Mo that he had gone to medical school before switching to law. Mo told him about the line, the knots, the other similarities.

"So," Flannery summarized, "even if the power-station corpse turns out to be left over from Ronald Parker, we've got strong parallels in the O'Connor murder. Too strong to ignore. What's your take on the possibilities?"

"A partner of Ronald Parker's that we didn't know about. Or somebody with deep access to information about his crimes."

Flannery bobbed his head thoughtfully, staring out his window at the White Plains skyline as he upped his tempo. The big arms swung vigorously, but he wasn't breathing hard, not much sweat on the tanned bald dome. The guy really was in great shape.

"How's Biedermann like that one?" Flannery asked at last. "The insider scenario? Because this case has been his baby, that's how he wanted it. The connection would almost have to be to his office, right?"

"I suggested that. He was offended. At this point, even with his trying to limit access to information, there are quite a few possible connections—the NYPD, the New Jersey people. It would take an extensive internal review to see just who knew what. I understand your people sat in sometimes, too."

Flannery frowned. "Damned right we did! We knew the guy could move into our jurisdiction. And we knew the Feds would bungle it. As they obviously have done. I'm not going to let this new guy kill seven, eight people in my town, thanks."

The phone wheedled, and Flannery slapped the radio handset in front of him, cutting off the ring. For another moment he kept on striding, but their exchange seemed to have spoiled the pleasure of his workout. He punched a button, let the belt carry him to the end of the machine, stepped off. He grabbed a towel, and the first thing he dried was his head, polishing it with a few hard swipes.

When he was done, he fixed Mo with bright blue eyes that were completely without the bearish good humor people associated with Flannery. "You're an observant guy—what do you make of Biedermann?"

"He runs a tight ship. Seems to have taken catching this guy as a personal commitment." Mo thought to mention the presence of Zelek, the silent alien, but decided it wasn't worth bringing up.

Flannery nodded. "Uh-huh." Mo could see the wheels turning, the politician figuring his angles. Then the DA seemed to make a decision. "Okay. This is good, Detective. This is very helpful. Let's you and me make this a regular thing, you talk to my secretary and set up a catch-up session for once a week. Unless there's a big development and we'll do it often as needed. Given the need to keep information flow contained, I want your contact with this office to be through me, personally. *Not,*" he added quickly, "that I don't trust my staff. Just so we play along with the SAC's plan. Just so nobody starts thinking of my people the wrong way, if this turns into something like that. Which we do hope it won't, don't we?"

The phone was ringing again, and Flannery tossed his towel back onto the treadmill rail.

Mo had been thinking to ask about the DA's plans for the Big Willie investigation, how long his indentured servitude to Flannery might last. But this wasn't the moment.

Flannery picked up the nagging phone. Instantly his face lit up, a big *just you and me* grin. "*May*-or *Rus*-so! Just the person I wanted to talk to." He smiled as he said it, but when he looked up to toss Mo a wave of good-bye and dismissal, his face went totally serious again.

A disquieting transformation, Mo thought, not so much the sober look as the ease he moved between moods. He was glad to get out of there and back to work.

16

PROBABLY HE WOULDN'T HAVE called Gus Grisbach if he hadn't been in such a bad mood. It wasn't that he was refusing Rebecca's advice—don't get involved any more than you have to—so much as trying to find out just what he was supposed to avoid getting involved in.

When Mo had first moved up to investigator, he'd been lucky to be paired for a time with Larry Mackenzie, a good mentor who had initiated Mo not only to investigative technique but to some of the nonstandard procedures that were standard. Before he'd died of prostate cancer, Mac had bequeathed to Mo a monster of a nonstandard resource, Gus Grisbach's phone number. Gus had been an NYPD investigator for many years before taking a bullet in his brain and opting for early retirement. Gus's logical faculties were as sharp as ever, but the bullet had burrowed a messy hole through his socializing instincts, which had never been great to begin with. But retirement hadn't stopped his fanatical fight against crime. If anything, the injury had inflamed Gus's hatred of criminals to a white heat. Given that he was confined to a wheelchair and couldn't beat the streets anymore, he'd set himself up in his apartment with, supposedly, a couple hundred thousand dollars' worth of computer equipment. Gus got information for cops. Since what he did wasn't legal, no one formally acknowledged his existence. His number and a word of introduction were guardedly handed down from generation to generation of investigators like priceless heirlooms.

Mo called from a pay phone, got a curt answering-machine message, and left his home phone number for a call back. He was thinking it would be nice to know more about Biedermann, about his career history, his move from San Diego, the murders there. Maybe a clue to Zelek and the "other dimensions" Rebecca had mentioned.

Back at Major Crimes, he worked the phones and fax machines, combed the databases. St. Pierre had done great work on Tuesday and Wednesday, and at one o'clock Mo fielded a call that had promise. An unidentified corpse could take weeks or months to put a name to, or it might never be ID'd, but here was a jeweler who thought the ring looked familiar. Mo sent him back to his billing records, and after another half hour he called back with the name of the person who had commissioned him to clean and reset the stone, one Irene Drysdale. The name wasn't on the list of possibles they'd put together from missing persons lists, but there was an Irene Bushnell, a resident of Ossining who had disappeared about six weeks ago. Mo spent another hour calling back dentists and asking them to look in their client lists for either name. By two o'clock, he had a positive match on the teeth. For once everything had fallen together like clockwork.

"Her name was Irene Bushnell," Mo explained to Marsden a little later. "Born Drysdale, married last year. Her mother reported her missing April third, we're presuming that's the date of death." He had gone to Marsden's office with the news, and now he sat in front of his desk, both of them pissed off at what it meant.

"Mother? What about the husband?" Marsden didn't look good, the gray-green skin of his cheeks contrasting sharply with the rash next to his nose.

"A truck driver, long-distance hauler. He was verifiably in Nebraska at the time."

Marsden didn't say anything for a moment, just flipped through the faxed X-rays of teeth, frowning. "Yeah. And Ronald Parker was in jail and brain-damaged at the time."

Meaning that there was a serial killer on the loose in southern Westchester County, and a particularly screwball fuck at that, someone driven to imitate Howdy Doody's elaborate kills. And somehow possessing the knowledge needed to imitate them to perfection.

"Well," Mo said, "at least this explains some details of the O'Connor murder."

"Like what?" Marsden snapped.

"The air-conditioning. Whoever killed Irene Bushnell was disappointed that she wasn't discovered for six weeks. He wanted to make sure if O'Connor sat for a while he'd be in good shape. Also the positioning, right in front of the big windows. Suggests it was important to the killer to have the murder noticed, and he wasn't going to take any chances."

Marsden glared at him, slit eyes. "One visit to that profiler, and you're talking psychobabble already. Okay, so what did you establish with Biedermann yesterday? Did he specify which part of his anatomy we're supposed to suck?"

Mo wasn't sure how much he should tell Marsden. "The parallels between Ronald Parker and this new guy are very close," he said. "Given how close, we'll need to reestablish the Howdy Doody task force, only now we're in on it, and so is White Plains. Biedermann will take complete control, and we're supposed to bring him coffee and stuff."

Marsden bobbed his head as if he'd expected it. "So what's next?"

"St. Pierre's off today, but tomorrow we'll go talk to the mother and the husband. We'll want Irene Bushnell's work history, her social habits, see who she might have gotten mad at her. It's about control, so we'll keep an eye out for who might have felt controlled by her."

"Okay. You guys be sure to look for sources for fingerprints for her—civil service work, other employers, maybe arrests."

On one level, you'd think, *Why bother, we know who she is, and we can't match 'em to the corpse anyway*. But Marsden had already taken a step ahead. Mo looked at him for a moment with admiration. "You're pretty good," Mo said.

Marsden thought so, too. A little self-satisfied grin. "The power-station scene is an oddball. If this guy's trying to be an exact copy, he's already blown it, he didn't kill her in her own home. Which means we might learn something new from the scene. Starting with, whose prints are on the arranged objects?"

Mo nodded: Marsden, too, had suspected that the puppeteer made the victims do the arrangements. Irene Bushnell had spent her last hours in that cavelike hellhole, obeying every command of a controlling monster.

"You want to talk about Biedermann?" Marsden asked. The way he said the name suggested he didn't have a lot nice to say, especially after learning that the SAC had looked into his personnel files.

"You said you knew him. What's going on? I heard that he was transferred to the New York field office just to handle the Howdy Doody case."

Marsden shrugged. "I don't 'know' him. Talked to him on the phone, heard things. I know he was a war hero in Vietnam, he's thought of as having a political future—directorships, Justice Department, stuff like that. Takes his job very seriously."

Mo grinned at the understatement. "Some of this is over my head. I mean, what happens if there *is* an inside element here? Somebody with access to information about Howdy Doody, doing the new murders? Who's responsible for internal review when there are so many agencies and jurisdictions involved?"

"What happens is nobody knows how to handle it and there's a lot of distrust and internal bloodshed. A circle fuck ensues. If Biedermann was transferred here specifically to handle the Howdy Doody case, I'd guess it's because the insider possibility was something they were already considering. That's why they chose somebody with an

Internal Affairs background. It would also explain why he doesn't tell anybody anything."

Mo thought about that. If that was true, it suggested that Rebecca was right, there had been prior murders back in California, with MO's similar enough to the Howdy Doody MO to trigger the insider concern. In which case—

"So there's two ways you can play this, Ford," Marsden said. He had been watching Mo shrewdly and obviously didn't like what he saw. "One, you can pull your usual bullshit, try to go around Biedermann, run with your hunches, play Mo Ford messiah cop cowboy, and get us all in trouble. Two, you can play this extraright, SOP all the way, every piece of paper in place so that we can account for our every move and it was all by the book and nobody in our department takes the heat when something fucks up. Do I have to spell out which option I'd prefer?"

When Marsden spoke like that, the exaggerated precision, the chill coming into his gravelly voice, it was time to make serious agreeing noises and get out of his office. "No. I hear you," Mo said.

"I'll tell you something else," Marsden went on. "Look at me. I'm feeling like shit. We're moving my goddamned angiogram up, my cardiologist has already scheduled bypass surgery for right after because he's pretty sure what the angio is going to show. My point is, I don't need any more stress."

Mo felt a pang of dismay at that. Marsden was more than smart, he was tough and fair and straight up, and he took care of his own people. If he left, the complexion of this job would change, and it could only change for the worse.

"I hear you," Mo said again. "By the book. Don't worry," he added, meaning *about me fucking up* and *about the surgery*. Marsden squinted at him skeptically and shifted his gaze to some papers. Mo left the office sincerely hoping he wouldn't have to renege on his promise.

17

MO HAD DINNER AT A restaurant, burger and fries and house salad, and got back to the house well after dark. He pulled up in front and sat looking at the tree-shadowed façade for a moment, summoning the energy to go inside. What the hell was he doing here? It was the kind of older burb he'd envied as a kid but now mostly resented for its complacent affluence and aloofness. The street was dark with heavy foliage that cut the streetlight glow into puzzle patterns, the houses were separated by wide lawns and thick hedges. The windows in all the others were warm and yellow, while Carla's mom's house had the black, curtainless windows of abandonment. The air was humid and too hot for May, the oven breath of global warming coming over the Northeast and making it feel like the Deep South. That Gothic, muggy, overgrown feel. Kudzu was already well established here, he thought, how long before the Spanish moss came along?

Bitch, bitch, he chided himself. He took his briefcase off the seat and left the car.

Inside, he went through the empty living room and into the back of the house, where he put on some lights that revealed the holes where Carla's stuff had been. The gap once occupied by her nice antique rocking chair. The place where the stereo cabinet had stood, where a fifty-buck boom box now lay on the floor amid dust bunnies and pen tops and lost coins revealed when they'd taken the sound system to her car. The bookshelf was still there, but now his own

122

books lay jumbled on half-empty shelves, and the pretty things were gone from its top, leaving only faint impressions in the dust. All that remained were a couple of his shooting trophies, chrome and blue plastic, which without Carla's curios had lost the look of ironic kitsch and now appeared just garish and distinctly déclassé. Especially in the unflattering light of the ceiling lights—she had taken all the floor lamps.

He hit the fridge for some beer but there wasn't any left. Instead he found a carton of lemonade and sat for a moment, swigging it from the box. Tonight he'd intended to spend some time looking over the rental classifieds, but he'd forgotten to bring home a newspaper, and now he was too tired to go out to buy one.

For a while he thought about Dr. Rebecca Ingalls, the way she looked and talked as they strolled toward Battery Park. But immediately he railed at himself. *She's way beyond your reach, get real, take a look around—what're you going to do, invite her over?*

The other pisser was that while he was mad at Carla for taking it so lightly, for moving out so easily, and while he agreed it was probably necessary, he still missed her. A night like tonight, back when, he'd court her. He'd put his hands on her waist, holding her hip bones, and kiss her forehead, her nose, her lips. She'd smell like a night-blossoming flower, stoning him instantly. Still standing, he'd bring one leg just a little between her legs, and he'd feel her begin to respond, and after a while they'd be making love and all this deep Dixie heat would become intriguingly sensual, a complement to the primal sweat and scent of lovemaking—

He caught himself slipping and pulled away from the thoughts, emptying his head again with an effort.

In the bedroom, he took off his shoes and then his gun and holster, which he hung on the chair next to the bed. Then he unbuttoned his shirt and threw it onto the floor with the other dirty laundry. Probably he should put on some music, chase the emptiness away, but he just needed a minute to charge up his energy. He felt the dark, empty house around him, cottony silent back here except for the faint drone of the refrigerator through the kitchen wall.

It was the shits.

A hard week. He wasn't really constitutionally well configured for homicide work. What had Rebecca said? *Too uncomfortable with death and pain.* That was part of it. Tonight he knew the week's images would come back, the bad pictures, the bad thoughts. O'Connor strung up in his agonies. Big Willie's broad, convulsing back and later his cold flesh and dead weight as the body tipped onto the gurney. Irene Bushnell's head and spinal cord hanging upside down against the bricks as the rat came down the wall—

He startled when he heard a noise from the front of the house. A thump and a series of clicks and then nothing. His ears strained against the silence. Then he slid the Glock out of its holster. Barefoot, he crept out of the bedroom, through the kitchen, and into the dining-cum-living-room. Beyond was the dark, streetlight-mottled front room, and the hall where the stairs came down. Another clunk, a shifting sound, and his pulse began to shake him.

"Mo?" Carla's voice.

He blew out a breath of relief and quickly stuck the gun into the waistband of his pants. "Yeah."

She came into the dark room tentatively. "You still awake?"

"Yeah," he said again.

They went back into the lighted rooms. Carla wore a short, summery dress of some filmy fabric, and she looked shapely and very female. Yes, she still got to him. She came into the living room and looked around at the unresolved mess with an expression of concern. Mo sat on the couch, leaving her the option of standing or sitting next to him.

She sat, eyeing the Glock when he pulled it out of his belt and set it on the floor. "Jesus. Who were you expecting?"

"I don't know."

"How are you? Your bruises are getting better, that's nice."

124

Mo made an indeterminate gesture.

"I remembered some other things I needed to get. And I wanted to talk to you. Wanted to check in." She looked at him warily. Part of the rhetoric of parting had been that they'd stay close, they'd keep in touch, maybe do things together now and then.

"How're things in Mount Vernon?" he mustered. "Heavenly?"

"Come on, Mo. Please?"

He made another ambiguous gesture, *okay* or maybe *whatever*. Actually, she didn't look that good. She held herself tensely. Her eyes were a bit too bright, and she looked slimmer, almost too thin. "So what've you been up to?" he asked, trying a different tack.

"I've been doing some great work on the book. It really is very handy to be a little closer to the city, I can go back and forth if I need to. I finally got an in to that voodoo group in Brooklyn, got to observe some prediction rituals with this old Jamaican woman. Pretty amazing. Oh, and I also scheduled an interview with Hope Christianson, she's very big right now. The Christian prophet?"

"Great." He got the sense that she was beating around the bush, avoiding something.

She chuckled insincerely. "All these people I interview? They take it so *seriously*. I mean, they read the future, they talk to the dead, some of them channel guiding spirits. They make me feel like I've been, almost like, I don't know . . . a hypocrite. I've always been so . . . *rational* about it."

"You came here to talk about that? At ten o'clock at night you drove up here from Mount Vernon?" He felt like hurting her, just a little.

Carla put her hand on Mo's thigh. Deliberate or just habitual he couldn't tell, but instantly his body ached for more. He didn't move.

"This is stupid," she went on, "but I had a scary premonition. It seemed very real. About you. I thought I should tell you."

"Hey, terrific," he said blackly.

"Mo, please? Do you want me to tell you or not?"

125

"Sounds like these people you're researching are getting to you. I didn't take you for the gullible type. I thought your book was going to be an objective look at—"

"That's completely not true! I've always taken my intuition seriously, I've just never claimed it was infallible. If you think it's stupid, fine, but let me tell you and you can decide yourself. And then I've got to get a few things together and go."

"Okay. Go ahead. Shoot." She really did seem to need to tell him. He slouched down against the couch back, looking disinterested.

"You're taking an attitude, *sure, I'll humor you,* to get back at me. I can understand that. Look, I'm sorry we didn't work out, okay? But we *didn't*! We had to face it, didn't we?" Her bright eyes rimmed with tears that she quickly wiped away, and suddenly her sincerity got to him. So he sat there on the couch with her and listened, facing the doorway to the shadow-mottled living room, the bare front windows overhung with heavy oak branches.

It was after the visit to the mudda-woman in Brooklyn. Carla had tried a visioning technique the voodoo priestess had recommended, she said, and unexpectedly she had seemed to break through into some other place. Telling him now, Carla leaned forward intently, staring with her dark eyes into the middle of the room as if still seeing it, as if watching some invisible movie. Mo felt a little chill.

In this other place were moving shapes. There was a big, dark place, but with apertures of light, not really windows, that gave it just enough light to see by. The moving forms were hurting each other, and there had been hurting in that place before.

Carla's voice had gotten a little shaky. "It was like the time, remember, when we went up to Adirondack State Park?"

She didn't go into details, knowing he'd remember it all too well. Summer before last, they'd driven upstate to get away, out where things were clean and pretty. They'd planned on staying at a motel, but on the first day they'd taken picnic stuff out to the woods, just driving until a spot took their fancy and they pulled over and walked away from the road. Bright sunny day, wading through some tall-grass fields and then into the forest with the idea of eating and lazing around on the blanket and then making love outdoors. They went in a couple hundred yards, sat down in a nice grove of trees. Carla leaned back and then sat forward suddenly, looking at the palm of her hand. *Ow,* she said. Something had poked her. Mo looked and there was a piece of an animal jawbone half-buried in the soil, and she'd put her hand on a tooth. Okay, bad coincidence, but they just moved down the little ridge a bit, set up again. This time Mo saw bones in the soil, not just one but several, ribs and long bones, and then a cloven black hoof sticking up. A dead deer. That was okay, the woods were full of deer, they had to die somewhere, coons and dogs had probably spread the body around. So they moved the blanket and the tote bags over the ridge another thirty yards and spread out again on the edge of a little clearing. But then the breeze shifted and brought a smell that was too familiar to Mo, and he scanned the woods with sudden unease. Suddenly the landscape became *full* of bones, as if they were springing out of the soil, and not clean ones either, many with rotting flesh and hair. Skulls, legs and hooves, rows of ribs with tattered hide attached, knuckled sections of backbone. Whole sheets of empty, maggoty hide emerging from the dirt, or half-submerged in puddles of green-scummed water. It was a charnel place, the earth full of dead things. It was all wrong, it was hideous, why would so many animals die in one place? They practically ran back to the car, and after they'd driven fifteen miles and found a park office, the ranger had laughed and told them they'd had the bad luck to picnic in a regional roadkill disposal site. The state highway crews and park personnel picked up dead deer and other animals and threw them into scrapes they'd bulldoze each spring and cover over in the fall.

So Carla's vision or premonition or whatever had happened in a place like that. Mo got the picture.

"You were one of the people there, Mo," she whispered quaveringly. "When I saw it was you, I tried to see the details, I thought I should know so I could tell you?" She looked to him for understanding.

"What details?" he asked. He realized he was whispering, too.

"I could sort of see auras around the people, the moving shapes. And there were lines of, like, energy or . . . power . . . between people."

"Lines."

Carla nodded. "I tried to see the details. Lines from your hands, lines from your feet, from your head? They moved with you, or maybe they . . . they moved you? I know it doesn't make sense." She looked disappointed with herself.

Mo was thinking that this cut a little too close to home. To Howdy Doody and the copycat. He'd never told Carla one word about the new cases.

"I tried to see the other forms, people, in there with you. They had the lines on them, too. The people were, this is hard to explain, they were *telescoped,* or superimposed . . . or one behind the other behind the other, farther and farther away. I wanted to see them more clearly, and all I could get was the image of like, a *doctor.* Not in a white suit and stethoscope, not a physical resemblance, but someone who knew things about the human body? A bad doctor. The closest association I got was like a Nazi medical experimenter, I don't know, like Dr. Mengele or somebody."

Carla had gotten shakier and less sure of herself as she went on, groping for the right words, trying to crystallize her impressions, and Mo looked at her with alarm. She'd seemed so confident and in charge of herself when she'd moved out, only five days ago. He almost wanted to ask about the voodoo mudda-woman she'd visited, whether drugs had played a role in whatever ceremony they'd done. Then he thought better of mentioning it. It would make her furious.

"Maybe this isn't good for you," he said. "The book, the people you're seeing—" He almost said, *Moving out of here. Ending it with me.*

128

"I don't like it when you tell me how to live," she said.

"I'm not, I'm just—"

"I thought I should tell you this! Okay? Have I ever done this before? Have I ever made exaggerated claims about any of this? You *know* I'm a skeptical person, you *know* I wouldn't tell you this if I didn't think it was important. God, I knew you'd laugh at me and feel superior—"

"Carla, Jesus, I'm not *laughing*—"

"How many times have you told me about one of your cases and how your 'gut' or your 'instinct' or your fucking 'radar' steered you in the right direction? That every investigator does it that way, that it's vital to police work. Right? So, what, I'm not supposed to use those same things when I'm figuring out somebody's personal problems? Or when I get clear signals from my own goddamned 'radar'? Maybe you should face up to your own hypocrisy!"

She was right, he'd never quite thought of it that way. But reflexively he tossed it back at her: "Another way I single-handedly fucked up our relationship."

She stood up quickly. He tied to hold her arm, but she shook his hand loose. "I've got to go. It's very late. I left some of my CDs here."

"Look, I'm sorry. You're right." He let her see his desperation. And she paused, looking down at him, those fine cheekbones and dark eyes. He could feel the nearness of her body, her smooth olive skin and supple waist and her sweet summer-night smell. After another moment he said quietly, "Stay here with me tonight, Carla."

For an instant she almost seemed to consider it. Then she turned away, went to the shoebox of CDs on the floor, began sorting through it. He watched as she found several and then went to the closet, where she dug around inside and pulled out a pair of her sandals.

He walked her to the front door, stood in the dark hall with her.

"I don't know what it means," she said. "I guess, just take care of yourself."

"I will. Thanks. You, too, okay?"

Then she was out the door and stepping lightly down the front porch steps, a fey shadow in the hot night air. He watched until she'd gotten into her car and pulled out, thinking, *Believe me, Carla, I'm not laughing*.

Later, he was still awake, lying naked on the bed in the dark, too hot to cover himself even with a sheet. The empty house bothered him. Carla's description of the "place" being dark with apertures of light, with the ambience of that patch of woods full of death, stayed with him. You could picture it all kinds of ways. It could be the power station, for example, a big dark place where bad things had happened. Or it could even be this house, the empty, dark rooms with tree shadows cutting the streetlight into sharp blue shards, and the hurting that had happened was what they'd done to each other as the relationship began to fall apart. Or someplace else. Or nowhere but Carla's imagination, something going wrong with her.

This was nuts, he'd have to get another place. This house was perfectly nice and he really *hated* it. He felt the empty rooms upstairs, the basement down below, sandwiching him between layers of darkness. After another hour, he sat up, took the Glock out of its holster. Glocks were weird guns, he hadn't initially endorsed the State Police shift to the Glock over the old Smith & Wesson Model 65 because he didn't like the feel of the Glock—the overlarge, too square handgrip, the blocky barrel. But they fired nicely, had a reliable magazine and a manageable recoil. And once you learned it, the trigger was sweet. In the State Police you were trained to walk toward your target, emptying your whole magazine, and some Glock advocate had once said, if your adversary could still get off a shot at you after you'd fired eighteen shots from one of these babies, you *deserved* to die.

Mo got up, holding the gun, and prowled through the house. He hated the pressure of the empty rooms and the acid light in them, and he wanted to strike back at them, push back the perimeter. *What is this, Ford,* he asked himself, *angry at what you're scared of, or scared of what you're angry at?* He walked stealthily through the living room with its glistening floors, then the hall, holding the gun as if he expected to use it. *Come on,* he thought, *come and get it.* He went up the stairs just as quietly. Long hallway to either side, six dark doorways. Stopping to listen, hearing only his own heart and the occasional slight tick and rustle of the house, two A.M. and only now beginning to cool down. He leapt through into each room, one after the other, landing with legs wide in shooting stance and pivoting quickly left and right. Dark, empty rooms, stuffy air, shiny floors, bare windows with a few dead flies vaguely visible on the sills.

Come on, he thought furiously. *Come at me.*

But there was nothing there, as he knew there wouldn't be. He was prowling naked and mad and scared around his ex's mom's house, hunting nothing but Mo Ford's loneliness, and he knew it, and no goddamned Glock was going to be any help at all.

18

ONE DAY FOR THE NEW baby, for the tired wife, for the
nesting instinct, and then St. Pierre was back at work bright
and early Friday. Mo almost said something, but then thought Mike
might take it the wrong way. They got back into the routine with
only a few words about Mike's domestic life.

They decided to divvy up Irene Bushnell's mother and husband,
then rendezvous back at the power station to assess the scene again,
try to figure what it might reveal that the O'Connor home did not.
St. Pierre took the mother, who lived in Tarrytown, leaving Mo to
drive to the victim's home outside of Ossining, ten minutes farther
north.

He drove with one hand on the wheel, the other rubbing his eyes.
He'd slept for maybe two hours. After his existential hunt through
the house, he'd gone to bed and dropped off to sleep. But after only a
few minutes, the phone had rung. The bedroom was still pitch-dark,
and the clock told him it was almost four A.M. He groped for the
phone, knocked it off the table, found it in the tangle of clothes on
the floor. When he finally he got the receiver right and put it to his
head, his voice was a croak. "Mo Ford," he said.

"Detective Ford," the voice said. "You wanted my assistance."

"Gus," he said. "Thanks for returning my call—"

"What do you need?" Grisbach's voice seemed barely capable of
the expressiveness needed to make a question. Although he'd never
met Grisbach, Mo had a clear image of him: somewhere in Man-

hattan in a darkened apartment filled with arcane high tech, pale-skinned and hugely fat in his wheelchair, a spider at the center of his web.

"I was hoping you could get me information on—this is a little touchy—on an FBI guy. I'm involved in a task force, I just figured I should know more about who this guy is so that—"

"Name?"

Mo felt a moment of relief. He'd been afraid that looking into a federal agent might be beyond Grisbach's reach, or something he wouldn't want do for any number of reasons. Fortunately, it looked as if his first hunch was right: Gus's past career had left him with a city cop's typical distrust and dislike of the FBI. "Erik Biedermann," he said. "Currently SAC in the Manhattan field office, formerly out in San Diego. Supposedly fought in Vietnam, I don't know which service. I'm particularly interested in his work on maybe two murders in the San Diego area, maybe two, three years ago. Anything you can find out about his transfer here. Any connections to, uh, other agencies." When Mo stopped, he could hear the tapping of keys at the other end.

"Anything else?"

Mo thought about it. "A guy named Zelek. Anson Zelek, also FBI." Just out of curiosity.

Keys tapping, then: "I'll call you."

"Look, I'm really grateful—" Mo began. Then he'd realized that the line was already dead. No, Grisbach wasn't much for social niceties.

He'd rolled over and tried to go back to sleep, and then the alarm was ringing and it was time to get up. Daylight had been like sand in his eyeballs.

The address St. Pierre had given him for Byron Bushnell was a ranch house with dirty white-aluminum siding in a poorer, semirural neighborhood of similar homes. It was easy to find because it was the only lot on the road that contained a fifty-five-foot semi with a Kenmore tractor, a vehicle bigger than the house itself. Mo parked on the worn grass next to a white Toyota pickup and got out. A movement in the window caught his eye, and then Byron Bushnell opened the front door.

Bushnell looked like shit. He was a smallish man with sloping shoulders and long hair, T-shirt, jeans worn low on his hips, cigarette in his lips. His red, swollen eyes suggested he'd been crying or drinking or both, and the smell of stale cigarette smoke hit Mo like a wall as he came up the steps. When Mo introduced himself and offered condolences, Bushnell just turned around and made an ambiguous gesture with the back of his hand. He went back into the house, threw himself on a recliner, fumbled on a side table for a can of Bud. He put aside his cigarette to suck at the can, looking at Mo with crazed, hostile eyes.

"I'm hoping you can tell me more about your wife, something that will help us identify her killer—her contacts in the community, her friends, her job, what she did in her spare time, that kind of thing." *Also about her husband,* Mo thought. Copycat MO or not, you always started with the husband.

"You don't catch the fucker, I will," Bushnell said. "I'll fucking feed him his own nuts."

"We'll catch him. With your help." Bushnell was pretty unsteady, would require a lot of steering. Mo made a show of getting out his notebook and pen and looking officious. "Why don't we start with her employment? Did she work?"

"Why don't we start with you can go fuck yourself. Cops don't give a fuck about us, gonna hassle us every time, and now Irene's dead you're gonna do *what* for her?" Bushnell finished off his beer and flung the can across the room. It hit the wall and fell to the floor with several others. He stared at Mo with *I don't give a shit* in his eyes.

Mo paused, undecided on how to proceed. Bushnell was going to be a tough one.

After a moment Mo put down his notebook, went over to the beer cans on the floor, picked them up one by one, put them on the dining table. The last one he held up as he looked back at Bushnell. "You got any more of these?"

The gesture took Bushnell by surprise. "Icebox," he said.

Mo went into a kitchen that made his own look like something out of *Good Housekeeping* and opened the refrigerator. It contained mostly beer of different brands. He broke a couple of cans out of their yoke, went back into the living room, and handed one to Bushnell. Mo popped the top on his, not really wanting to drink this early. But what the hell, he decided. He loosened his tie and took a seat at the dining table as he sipped.

It took a while, but he managed to wring some details out of Bushnell. Apparently Irene had worked five days a week at different houses for a cottage industry run by another local woman, a company called The Gleam Team. On the lifestyle side, she had church and her mother and some girlfriends down the road. Byron and Irene liked to catch stock car races when they could, and on weekends the two of them hung out at a couple of local bars. They played pool with an informal circle of regulars, Irene was pretty good. They had both grown up in the area, so ten years after graduation they still knew a lot of people from high school. Mo got the impression of a lifestyle stuck overlong in the fast-and-loose stage, a passionate but often rocky marriage, occasional run-ins with the local police for fighting or driving while intoxicated. No, Bushnell couldn't think of any altercations between Irene and anyone, nothing where anyone would have thought of her as controlling.

After an hour, Bushnell was running out of useful detail even as his nostalgia was gaining momentum, and Mo decided it was time to throw him a curve, see how he reacted. "She sounds like a really great person," he said sympathetically. "You're hurting pretty badly, huh?"

Bushnell's face registered anger for an instant, the resistance of a man to emotional probing. And then the face crumpled and tears gushed from his eyes. "Six weeks she was gone, but I was still hoping, I kept hoping maybe . . ." His body folded forward as he wrapped around his pain and cried wrenchingly, the convulsive heaving of someone giving up to loss.

Scratch Bushnell as any kind of suspect, Mo thought. He folded away his notebook, stood up, clapped Bushnell's quaking shoulder as he went out.

The power-station scene had changed completely. Mo bumped down the access road to find the parking area filled with cars, trucks, vans. Lots of federal license plates. He spotted St. Pierre's car among the others.

The whole building was ringed with yellow tape, and sections of the ground outside had been cordoned off. One of the FBI vehicles was a big Evidence Response Team technical van with satellite dishes on its roof, its back doors open and people working on equipment on the platform. Another was a truck-mounted generator running at a high idle and trailing heavy cables into the building. The sheer amount of resources in play meant that Biedermann was taking this very seriously.

Mo followed a pair of FBI techs around to the main door and was surprised to come face-to-face with Dr. Rebecca Ingalls. Her eyebrows jumped as she recognized him, and then she smiled.

He was conscious of not looking his best, but he returned the smile. "What are you doing here?" he asked.

She shrugged self-deprecatingly. "I'm doing—what do they call the TV sportscasters, the ex-pros who don't call the plays but sit there and—"

" 'Color.' You're doing color?"

"Yeah." She frowned. "I'm trying to do psychological background, the implications of choosing this place to kill her. What it means that it's not her home, what that tells us about this killer. I was downstairs, but I, um, I needed a break." She tilted her head back, shut her eyes, gave her face to the muted sun for a moment.

"I know what you mean. Any conclusions?"

She brought her chin back down. "No. Other than it's a terrible place to be tortured to death." Obviously, she wasn't enjoying this visit to the Westchester countryside.

Mo nodded. The sheet metal over the main doors had been removed and the front of the big brick building gaped into the open air. Faint voices echoed inside, and a fetid, humid smell wafted up out the dark opening.

"Erik's inside," she said.

"Too bad." Mo scuffed at the fractured concrete of the walk.

That gave her a little amusement.

He hesitated, then started inside. But she called to him, "I was talking to your colleague—Mike, right? He's such a sweet young man. He thinks you're the greatest, you know." That was flattering, Mo thought, surprised. Rebecca went on, "He has complete faith you'll solve this, that nobody could stop you, you're another Sherlock Holmes. Also that Erik is the Antichrist."

Better and better, Mo thought. "St. Pierre's a good guy," he acknowledged, "but he only moved up to Major Crimes a couple of months ago."

She caught his eyes quickly before turning back to the sun. "I'll be down again in a few minutes," she said.

The lower level of the power station was bathed in lights. Biedermann's people had set pole lights at all four corners of the big room, three brilliant panels on each, and two more light installations shone down from the stair railing. In the light, the place looked worse, filthy and moldy, full of dead vegetation, used condoms, other trash. There were probably twenty ERT people in the rubble now, crouching or standing with heads down, scanning the ground. Mike St. Pierre sat on the bottom step, looking a little overwhelmed.

"Hey," Mo said, coming down behind him.

"Hey."

"Where's Biedermann?"

"Back in the murder room. He's just now letting people get to work, they had photographers in here for a couple of hours, don't trust ours to do a good job."

"Is he telling you anything?"

St. Pierre shrugged, scuffed at the layer of dust and soil on the broken concrete floor. "The dirt's a good thing, something not at any of the residences. Footprints, signs of struggle might tell us more about how it went down. They did these overhead photos, scene mapping. Biedermann acts like he'd like to take the place down and reassemble it somewhere, like an airplane crash. But I was gonna tell you—"

But he stopped as Rebecca came down the stairs to stand beside them with a determined expression. The three of them looked over the scene for a moment, not speaking. Seeing this much focused human industry in one place was impressive.

"So what do you think happened here?" Mo asked her at last.

"Something went wrong," she said immediately. "This wasn't part of the plan."

"'Plan'?" St. Pierre asked.

"Not 'plan' exactly. But this was a mistake, a slip of control."

"And it's about control," Mo mused.

She nodded. "Erik had his crew do some video with overhead boom cameras. He's looked at sections of it, thinks there are indications of a struggle, maybe even of sexual assault. From marks in the dirt and other trash—you can't really see it from ground level."

That was smart, Mo admitted grudgingly. Biedermann was exploiting the particulars of this anomalous scene to maximum advantage. And if Irene Bushnell had been raped before she was killed, it did signal a radical departure from the Howdy Doody MO. Still, all the evidence in the world, short of finding fingerprints they could match with prints on record somewhere, wouldn't help them locate the killer. Mo's instincts told him the answer lay with tracing Irene Bushnell's contacts with other people. Somewhere, her world had intersected the killer's world, she had caught his attention. Somehow, he had gotten her to this place. He thought of Byron Bushnell, the possibilities that their social life suggested, The Gleam Team, her church. And he'd bet good money he and St. Pierre and the local contacts of the NYSP could do a better job than the federals at following up on those things.

"So what's he looking for here?" Mo asked. "What's he expect to find?"

Rebecca answered immediately, "Sometimes it's almost as if he already knows who it is and hopes to find verification of that from trace evidence." Then she looked surprised at herself, as if she hadn't intended to say so much. She frowned, then pointed with her chin back toward the death-room door. "But why don't you ask Erik?"

Biedermann was coming out of the room with a cell phone to his ear. He looked serious and a little haggard, rubbing his hand across his brush cut with exasperated strokes. When he glanced up and saw Mo, he scowled. Mo gave him a laconic salute.

When Biedermann came up to him, he slapped the phone shut. "Detective Ford," he said.

"Very impressive," Mo said, gesturing at the booms and lights and the army of investigative talent. "Coming up with anything interesting?"

"We'll talk about it at the next task force meeting. Right now I've got to get back to Manhattan."

"Dr. Ingalls says you're considering the possibility of sexual assault."

Biedermann moved past him on the stairs, scowling at Rebecca. "The possibility, yes. I will definitely keep you informed." He trotted on up the stairs with the stolid agility of a big, fit man, never looking back. At the top he gave curt orders to one of his people, pointing around the room. Then he was gone, out the front door.

Mo watched his broad back disappear from view, disliking him again. The lack of courtesy, that proprietary frown at Rebecca.

"Good of him to keep us informed," St. Pierre suggested. "Hey, Mo, I was going to tell you—"

Mo said, "Rebecca, one more question about Erik, and then I promise I'll shut up about him. You know in his office he's got that knife on a plaque, right, a gift from the people he supervised at Internal Affairs?"

"The backstabber joke. Erik says every IA supervisor gets one when he moves on."

"Right. And he's also got that dog collar, the fancy red one with the studs and stuff on it? He was going to tell me about that, but we didn't get to it. What's with that?"

She grinned. "Another joke, a gift from his team when he left San Diego. Same general idea. It's got an inscription on the dog tag that says something like, 'You can have this back, we've worn it long enough.' Suggesting Erik is a tough boss."

Mo chewed his lips, nodding, still gazing up the stairs. "Right. I'll bet he is."

She looked at him, and after a second her eyes widened. "Wait a minute. Where are you going with this?"

He gave it a second's thought. "Nowhere. Don't worry." And that was the truth, he'd been letting himself think out loud, bad idea, and it really was presumptuous of him anyway, way too premature.

19

DRIVING THE ROADS OF Westchester again, heading back toward White Plains. This time the parade of SUVs was diluted with leftovers from the previous automotive phenom, deluxe minivans.

What St. Pierre had been trying to tell him was some information he'd gotten from Irene Bushnell's mother. In his usual self-effacing way, he said, "I don't know if this is worth anything or not, I mean maybe I'm reading more into it than—" Mo had tried to instruct him in the art of appearing confident, with the goal of inspiring a similar emotion in others, but he wasn't there yet. But what St. Pierre had correctly identified as important from his interview with the mother was that, one, she thought Irene might have been having an affair recently. It was an opening, a window into circumstances of Irene's life that her husband wouldn't know or wouldn't want to admit to anyone.

The second detail was that Mrs. Drysdale said her daughter had been very interested in the Howdy Doody killings, had followed news of the investigation in the papers, talked about it now and again. It was the kind of detail that cried out for attention, either an irony or a coincidence or—Mo hoped—a clue to her connection with whoever killed her.

It was two o'clock and Mo wanted to go interview Mrs. Drysdale immediately. Rebecca volunteered to come along with him to Tarrytown, provided Mo gave her a ride back to New York afterward. From a strictly professional standpoint, he told himself, it made sense to have a female, especially someone well-trained in psychology, present at a second interview with an older, grieving woman.

So now they drove along, not saying anything. Rebecca's face was serious, verging on angry.

"I'm just keeping my mind open," he said at last. "I'm, what do they call it, 'thinking out of the box.'"

"You're thinking that Erik is the person inside. The person who knows the Howdy Doody MO well enough to imitate it so closely. And that really disappoints me, because I thought you were a more self-inspected person. He's not a serial killer, and you are obviously letting"— she stumbled over the next part—"letting other emotions bias your judgment. At the very least, I thought you were a better investigator."

He drove along, feeling cheerful. "My other emotions like what?"

"I'm not going to be baited into juvenile banter. I didn't come along to play footsie with you. I thought I should take the opportunity to head off a really, *really* unprofitable and destructive line of thought on your part."

His cheerfulness faded fast. "Why are you so certain nobody should look at Erik? Because you know him so well? Because you couldn't possibly sleep with a killer?"

Her eyes blazed and she craned around to look behind them as if she were debating stepping out of the moving car. "This was a mistake. Take me back to the power station. You are overstepping professional bounds, Detective Ford."

"I'm not saying anything about your professional judgment that you didn't just say about mine."

She started to snap back but then accepted it. "I'm not sleeping with a killer," she said under her breath.

Which could be interpreted two ways, Mo thought. *Not sleeping with. Or just not with a killer.*

"He's been involved from the beginning," Mo said. "He's very,

142

very jealous of who gets information about the killings. He's showing very intense interest in the case, giving it more personal attention than I've ever seen any SAC do, ever."

"He was *assigned* the case, he's keeping information tight because there's the insider possibility, and he's a very *good* agent in charge who gives *every* case his close personal attention."

"And he's a very controlling personality—"

"How many of those are there in the State Police, the FBI, the various district attorney's offices, do you think?"

Mo tossed his head and admitted, "Just about all of em." Yes, he had been premature in voicing suspicions of Biedermann, probably it was the guy's attitude on the stairs that had made him say it out loud. She was right to tell him so. And maybe she was right, maybe bringing her along now had not been such a good idea, given the degree of his own fucked-upedness.

In Tarrytown, he turned off Route 9 and headed east. St. Pierre had told him that Mrs. Drysdale worked a two-to-ten evening shift at Quality Plastics, a big warehouse and plant on the outskirts of the city, and he was trying to remember just where it was. With any luck, they'd get a few details from Mrs. Drysdale, he'd drop Rebecca at her place by five o'clock with curt good-byes, he'd get back to Carla's mother's lovely house by seven.

"Can I make a personal observation?" she asked. She had been leaning against the passenger door, arms folded, watching him drive.

"Yeah. Sure. I guess." He hoped it wasn't too unflattering.

"I'm not very good at beating around the bush, playing word games. You'd think I would be, because I use words to finesse people into constructive perspectives on themselves all day . . . But I hate fencing with people about important things. It goes against my philosophical commitments, it doesn't come naturally for me, and it never leads anywhere good. I don't know you very well, but I think you're the same way. The no-bullshit type."

"True. Thanks."

143

"I'm saying this because, if you don't get yourself taken off this case by being stupid and impulsive, you and I will probably be working together. So I want to tell you that I am not currently involved in a personal relationship with Erik Biedermann. I don't say it as some kind of an invitation, I say it as something I don't want to have to dance around every time you and I consult. Not one more time."

"Okay. I'm sorry, honestly—"

She held up her hands, stopping him. "I don't do invitations that way. Here's how I do them: Mo, so far I think you're pretty great. I think I know where you're at right now, emotionally. Let's get together off duty, maybe for dinner. And then let's be sure our personal interests, if it ends up we have any, stay out of our professional collaboration."

And instantly he felt terrific again. He pulled up at a stoplight and looked over at her. She was watching him, dead-eye serious, straight on. Turned toward him, one thigh curved beautifully on the seat, she looked stunning and formidable. The traffic moved and he accelerated again before he could answer her.

"You are something else," he told her finally. "You know that?"

The Quality Plastics plant consisted of a pair of gigantic rectangular steel buildings with a low brick office wing stuck on the front of one, next to the company sign and three dead saplings in circles of redwood bark. *Industrial "park,"* Mo thought, disgusted. *Another Orwellian Newspeak oxymoron.* At the front office, he showed his ID and the guy in charge said yes, he already knew about Irene Bushnell's death. He led them back to an office substation in the warehouse section of the plant, paged Mrs. Drysdale, left them there.

The warehouse interior was cavernous. Quality Plastics made all kinds of things, stored here under bright fluorescents in stacks and on girdered shelves that reached to the ceiling, forty feet above. Just down the aisle, a worker was using a forklift with a spindle attachment to load a roll of bubble wrap the size of a minivan onto a high shelf. Farther down, another lift was moving around huge slabs of pale green foam. The air was sharp with the smell of plastic and the propane exhaust from the forklifts.

Mrs. Drysdale emerged from the distance, a little figure lost in a canyon of plastic products. When she got closer, Mo could see that she was a short, dumpy, sad-faced woman wearing jeans and a red sweatshirt emblazoned with the Quality Plastics logo. She was probably only around fifty, but her hair was gray and hung limply halfway to her slumped shoulders. When she walked up to the substation railing, she told them if they wanted to talk to her, they had to come back to where she was working. "I was gonna call in sick today," she said, "but then I didn't want to be alone at the apartment. I gotta kept my mind off it."

They followed her back through the warehouse between towering stacks of foams and wraps. Other employees looked at them curiously, this guy in a dark suit with *cop* stamped into his forehead, and this big, gorgeous blonde, following the short, sad figure of Mrs. Drysdale. Back in the middle of the building, she stopped at the first of a row of huge foam blocks, each the size of a city bus. The row stretched for half a block.

"These're the buns," she explained. She been carrying a hand-held computer inventory device and now switched it on. "They're going to the band saw later, I gotta keep track of the cutting lots." They did look like gigantic loaves of bread, except that they were made of flesh-toned plastic, Caucasian with an uneven tan. Mo prodded the nearest bun and yanked his hand back when he found that the surface was a tough hide that felt just about like human skin. Mrs. Drysdale found a tag stapled to the bun and pecked listlessly at her computer.

"Mrs. Drysdale," Mo began, "Detective St. Pierre mentioned several points that came up when he spoke to you earlier, and I felt we should follow up on them immediately. I'm sorry to have to discuss details that may be difficult for you, but the odd fact you tell us may be the one that allows us to catch Irene's killer. And we very much want to catch him."

Mrs. Drysdale walked on toward the next bun, her frumpy back to Mo and Rebecca as they followed her. She looked alone and lost between the fleshy loaves.

When she stopped again and began pecking at her computer, Mo continued, "You suggested that Irene may have had a, uh, a relationship with someone."

"Her and Byron," Mrs. Drysdale said quietly. "They would never settle down. I told Irene, you get married it's supposed to mean something. Just out of high school, it's okay you shop around, you flirt, you get your guy jealous, maybe guys fight over you, that feels good. But you're twenty-seven, you can't live in a soap opera." She slapped the computer with the flat of her hand. "This darned thing. I hate these things. Never comes out right." She scrabbled her fingers over the keyboard and slapped it again, her face puckering.

"Why did you think Irene was having an affair recently?" Rebecca asked softly. "What did she say that made you think that?"

Mrs. Drysdale began the walk to the next bun, and they followed. On the way, a pair of teenaged employees came buzzing around a corner in a golf cart, hot-rodding at all of eight miles an hour. They saw Mrs. Drysdale and slowed, sobered up, drove away. Word of her grief had traveled fast among the Quality Plastics staff.

Mrs. Drysdale would probably have walked the whole length of the warehouse without saying anything, but Rebecca caught up with her. She took her arm gently, steered her toward a thigh-high slab of foam, sat her on it. "This is a very difficult time for you. It's a time when you need to take care of yourself. Why don't you rest here, talk to us if you can? Sometimes it helps to talk about a loved one you've lost." Mrs. Drysdale was quietly crying, and Rebecca began stroking her forehead. Mo was impressed at how easily it came to her: reaching out, comforting, taking care. Rebecca crouched in front of her, one hand on Mrs. Drysdale's thigh. Good body language for a nonadversarial interrogation, Mo realized, getting below the subject's height so as not to be imposing, giving her complete attention, a posture that was consoling but that also compelled a response.

Mrs. Drysdale slumped, completely out of gas. "She asked me questions. 'Mom, what if I had an affair with a guy?' It was something she wanted to talk about. First time I told her, 'I don't want to hear about this, you know how I feel.' Then a week later she's asking, 'When Dad was alive, did you ever fool around with another guy?' 'You think if By does something with somebody else, it's okay if I do?' Things like that."

"Did she ever say anything that would suggest who the man was? How she met him, or where?"

"'Mom, did you ever think what it would be like to have a guy with some money?'" Mrs. Drysdale remembered. "'Do you think I should have my hair redone?' She was thinking maybe a Princess Di cut, make her look kind of upper class. So I don't think it's one of their regular friends."

"That's excellent. That's just what we're looking for," Rebecca prompted. "You're doing fine."

So whoever Irene Bushnell's secret flame had been, Mo was thinking, she'd been conscious of the marketability factor. Knew she was reaching up.

Mrs. Drysdale was responding well to Rebecca's encouragement. "That made me think maybe it was somebody she worked for. And I thought that would be a bad idea."

"Tell us about that."

"I don't know anything. She cleans . . . *cleaned* houses, you got to have some money to have someone in to clean, maybe it was one of the people she worked for. I don't know."

"Would Byron know? Would they have talked about it if she were in love with someone else?"

Mrs. Drysdale scowled. "Never." Then her eyebrows tilted up in the middle again, hopelessness. "Maybe the lady who runs The

Gleam Team, but Irene wouldn't've said anything to her, she'd be afraid of losing the job."

They gave her some time, but she didn't say any more. She fidgeted listlessly with her inventory computer. With the foam on all sides, they sat in a quiet that felt like clogged ears.

Mo broke the silence. "You told Detective St. Pierre that Irene had an interest in the Howdy Doody murders. How did you know she did?"

"She saw that TV thing, *Unsolved Mysteries,* before they caught him, we watched it together. She thought it was horrible, him tying people up with fishline. Couple of times, we'd talk and she'd mention it. She knew everything the papers wrote about it, how many people died, that stuff."

"Did she ever suggest why the case particularly interested her? Was she interested in other sensational murders or other news events?"

Mrs. Drysdale just shook her head. "Sometimes. Mainly just Princess Di—the car crash. She bought a commemorative plate."

Rebecca took a turn, probing gently, trying to find the trigger for Mrs. Drysdale's memory. But nothing came. She sat collapsed in on herself on the sagging foam slab. After a while a buzzer went off somewhere and she got up, dusting foam crumbs off her jeans.

"I shoulda been done here, they got to get these to the band saw." She began her lonely walk down the aisle of buns, paused at the next, pecked at her computer, slapped it in frustration, wiped her eyes. Rebecca looked after her with sympathy, caught Mo's eye. He nodded. This interview was over.

As soon as they were back in the car, she asked, "So?"

"So let's have that dinner," Mo said.

"Can't tonight. I've got a conference call scheduled with two psychologists from Stanford, the kind of thing that could go on and on. I meant, so what did you get from Mrs. Drysdale?"

He gave up, got to business. "I'd say, two things. One, the lover.

Maybe Irene was having a fling with the copycat, he decided to kill her, he set it up on some pretext so they went to the power station for a tryst. Two, the possibility of the connection to her job. She knew a little about Howdy Doody—maybe she was cleaning, found some paraphernalia she thought was suspicious, he found out and had to kill her."

"Neither of which scenario fits the Howdy Doody motivational profile at all."

"Yeah, but neither does the power station. You said yourself something went very wrong."

"True." Rebecca thought about that, looking troubled, staring through the windshield at nothing in particular.

Mo caught the same mood. There could also be no connection at all between Irene Bushnell's murder and her job or her hypothetical affair. And too much was unexplained, the whole copycat problem was far too complex. Why imitate Howdy Doody? With Irene, maybe to throw the police off. But then, what, the guy learns he likes killing that exact way and randomly selects and kills Daniel O'Connor? Besides, how does he know the Howdy Doody weed-whacker line, the knots, the other details?

They drove for a time without talking. After a while, he said, "You were very good with her. I admired your technique. I also appreciated your sympathy for her."

"I was just going to say the same thing to you." Rebecca smiled. "You're a paradoxical person, aren't you?"

Mo shrugged. He could feel himself falling toward her. It had an oddly inevitable feel. The comfortable feel of their silences. The pleasure he took in the sight of her when he glanced over. The sense of her being always right *there,* smart, observant. And yet completely unpretentious. When he'd first felt the tug, he'd questioned whether it was just his being lonely and horny and on the rebound, one of those. More and more this was feeling like something bigger. You had an instinct about that, you had to trust it. It would always surprise you, guaranteed it would catch you off-balance. He'd never quite felt this way with Carla, with her it had always been *trying,* three years of fishing for the feeling but never really getting it. Eventually coming to care about her deeply, and, yes, that was one kind of love, and he'd been willing to try to make that enough. Maybe he was nuts, needy, whatever, but this felt completely different. This felt like the needle on the compass swinging around to lock on magnetic north. No, it was like two gears meshing and beginning to turn together. No, it was . . .

He shook his head, surprised at how far gone he felt.

20

MR. SMITH WAS WORKING on the dogs. He had been looking forward to this all week, but now he felt a little tired, one of the drawbacks of living in two places and having, really, two jobs. The day job was necessary in more ways than one, but this was his real work, his real avocation. He took a deep breath, enjoying the familiar alcohol scent, and rallied.

He had never ceased to be amazed by the fact that the brain didn't have any sensory nerves in it. To avoid surface pain, he'd injected the German shepherd with a local anesthetic, a shallow subdermal shot just above and behind each eye. Now the dog was strapped flat to the stainless surgery table, looking up at him with soulful brown eyes as he drilled, wide awake but probably feeling almost nothing. There was a little blood, but he'd calculated bone depth very carefully before setting the stop on the bit, and he was confident the brain itself was untouched. He was good at this.

"Atta boy," he said encouragingly as he removed the bit from the second hole. "Good dog." The dog looked at his face for cues. Mr. Smith was sure he'd have wagged his tail if he'd been able to move it. Friendly bugger.

The next step was much trickier: inserting the blades at the right angle and to just the depth needed. He didn't have cranial imaging capacity on the premises, and the canine cranial anatomy was very different from the human head's. But he'd taken the shepherd to a country veterinarian in Massachusetts, telling the doc that his dog had been hit by a car, just his head, seemed all right but could we get a couple of X-rays? The vet had been glad to comply, and Mr. Smith had asked if he could take the films home, just in case something came up later he could give them to his regular vet. He repeated the same transaction with the golden retriever at a veterinarian in Pennsylvania: "I'm visiting from out of state, and my dog just got hit—" He'd paid in cash, of course.

The end result was good films of both dogs' heads, lateral and dorsal views, and as he worked on the shepherd, he referred frequently to the X-rays, displayed in an illuminated viewer. Not as good as CT scans but not bad under the circumstances. In Vietnam, he had often worked with less.

Mr. Smith had made the blades himself, regrinding some fine paring knives he'd bought, leaving a thin shaft five inches long and only an eighth of an inch wide, quite rigid, surgically sharp at the end. He set his angle with an old medical protractor, felt the first contact with the surface of the brain, and tapped the back of the handle until the blade had sunk to a depth mark he'd made in advance. No real resistance, just soft stuff. Mr. Smith thought, *And that's all that doggy friendliness is, all that mammalian bonding, all that trust, all the things that restrain the killing urges—just a quarter inch of soft, wet, pink stuff.* Sad, really. One might have wished those things were made of a more durable substance.

A tremor shook the immobilized body, but still the shepherd stared up at him with those watery, soulful eyes. Mr. Smith withdrew the blade, set a slightly different angle, repeated the procedure. This time the eyes seemed to go blank for a few seconds, almost as if when the neural circuits were severed some part of the animal's consciousness disappeared. Blood welled out of the wound, which Mr. Smith dabbed away before he did the other side.

"Good boy," he said a minute later. "Good boy. All done."

The dog watched him, the eyes different now, as if it were thinking about something else, something remote and vaguely troubling. Sometimes this gave Mr. Smith a pang, seeing that mysterious thing go away from the eyes, human or canine. *The most elegant and important aspect of a being, dog or man,* he thought, *and yet we don't even have a name for it.*

He closed the wounds with a few swift sutures and wiped away the blood. Then it was time to put the dog back into his cage. A couple of days for recovery, then on with the conditioning phase. This time it would be a differential experiment, with the German shepherd serving as the control and the golden retriever receiving the implanted electrodes. He'd compare their progress, the speed at which they became conditioned, the durability of conditioning afterward, the ease of manipulation. Very exciting.

He released the straps, leaving the head restraints until last. The little buggers could be tricky at this stage. When the last belt was removed, the dog drew his legs close to his body but still lay there, looking disoriented. Mr. Smith put his arms around the barrel chest and lifted the shepherd to its feet on the table, a little worried that he'd miscalculated, cut a motor circuit. But the dog stood on its own, shaky at first and then gaining strength. Mr. Smith watched its brown eyes, the preoccupied distance punctuated by erratic darker glints and shadows, primal urges and emotions flitting and fading. Like sharks just below the surface of the night sea, he thought, there, gone, dark on dark.

"Okay, champ," he said. "Time for bed." He lifted the dog, feeling the tremors in its big body, and carried it to the open door of its cage. It stepped into the wire mesh box and turned around and looked at him vaguely and then suddenly lunged at his face with a throaty snarl. Mr. Smith reared away just too late, the long canines ripped into his neck just above the shoulder before he reflexively clubbed the muzzle with the side of his arm. The dog's bald head smashed against the metal door frame, and before it could recover, Mr. Smith slammed the door shut. The shepherd made one more lunge against the mesh with that same gargling primal growl. Mr.

Smith put his hand to his torn shirt and looked at the blood on his fingers. His heart was pounding, his whole body ringing with adrenaline. Jesus, that was *fast*. Ouch. It was amazing how their reflexes actually improved when the neural inhibitory mechanisms were removed.

The thought pleased him, and he smiled at the dog, who was still shivering but calmer now, looking rather baffled. "Good *boy*! That's my *good boy*," Mr. Smith said approvingly. "What a good dog!"

Several hours later, the wound disinfected and bandaged, he felt a flash of gratitude to the shepherd. The bandage was irritating right there, just below his collar on the right side, but it was only a shallow surface slash about an inch long. And that adrenaline rush had awakened him completely, swept away the cobwebs. Here it was the middle of the night and he was still going strong.

He reeled a length of cord off the spool and clipped it with a wire cutter, moving with deliberation so that the subject could observe the details. The subject, Number Four, was already bound by six lengths of trimmer line and knew the feeling of restraint, the not-so-subtle bite of the cord's serrations as they sank into the skin. He had told Number Four to be quiet, not to utter a single sound until told to do so. Once all the cords were tied, he would do some lecturing, it was time for some context. The biggest advantage in conditioning humans as opposed to dogs: They could receive verbal communication.

They also had good imaginations. They could imagine future or threatened discomforts.

Mr. Smith held the end of the line close to the subject's face and demonstrated the knot again. "The basic Pavlovian model of conditioning is very simple," Mr. Smith explained. "The organism, in this case you, has several basic biological programs, and behavioral conditioning exploits those to reinforce or discourage specific behaviors. Avoiding pain is a biggie, isn't it?" He snugged the loops of the knot and looked at the subject. "You can answer. Avoiding pain is an important motivation, isn't it?"

"Yes." A shaky voice.

"Really, really important?"

"Yes—"

"Very good. You do what's expected, you don't get pain. You *don't* do what you're supposed to, and you get hurt. Very simple. What's another motivation?"

"Getting reward," the subject mumbled.

Mr. Smith nodded approvingly. He gestured for Number Four to raise the left arm and was pleased to have immediate compliance. Then he slipped the looped end of the cord over the wrist, drawing it tight and tighter and watching the face until he saw the first twitches of pain there. The wrist was badly abraded from earlier, and the line cut into bloody tatters of skin.

"Good. And reward can be as simple as the cessation of punishment or the providing of pleasure or wants or needs. For us humans, punishment or reward can be simply physical, but it can also be emotional—psychological. For example, would my approval of you constitute a reward? Make you feel good? Encourage a specific behavior?"

Number Four hesitated, which suddenly infuriated Mr. Smith. He thought for an instant of doing something drastic, but he got himself under control quickly and decided to show his disapproval with just his body language, yanking lengths of cord off the spool with vehement gestures. Test subjects should be responsive to such nuances.

He was glad to see that the subject noticed, looked more frightened. "Yes!"

" 'Yes' *who*?" Mr. Smith said nastily. He would push his control here, make it suffocating, not leave any room at all.

"Yes, Daddy."

Better. "Say it three times."

"Yes, Daddy. Yes, Daddy. Yes, Daddy." Saying it, Four's eyes watered from fear. It was always odd to see an adult in this situation, to hear the words, but you had to do it, had to hearken all the way back to a subject's emotional foundations. And fathers were so often oppressors, weren't they.

"Good," he said, curt and authoritarian now as he looped the elbow knot and gave it a jerk that had to hurt. Skipping the neck cord for now, he gathered the last two lines and secured them. Once they were knotted, he tested each line in turn and found them satisfactory. Just enough slack for some movement.

"But of course, we humans are not animals, are we? We talk, we establish complex relationships, we have long memories of our lives, don't we? You can answer."

"Yes, Daddy." The subject looked sick now, weak, hunching naked and pale-skinned against the wall.

"Which means that simple behavioral conditioning is not enough, not for an animal as complicated as we are, is it? We need a subtler approach, too—a psychological approach. So to supplement the Pavlovian conditioning, we move on to the psychoanalytic model, which calls for us to establish *narratives* that describe our lives, especially our early lives. Because our experiences when we were children, even infants, shape the way we think and feel and behave now, as adults. Right? You can answer. And lift your right leg, too."

Number Four lifted the leg and stood, balancing with difficulty, crying, knowing the hurting parts were coming. "Yes. I mean, yes, Daddy."

"Put down the leg. Now raise the left. Good. Down. Good. Now your left arm—lift it and salute me. Good. Down. Good. Now your right arm, the same. Good. Now smile." They did this for a time, Mr. Smith picking up the tempo of his commands. "Good," Mr. Smith said, and threw the knuckleball: "Now tell me—do you hate me?"

Number Four had behaved well, had learned all this so quickly, but now hesitated. This part was tricky, they were never sure about the emotional terrain.

"Answer me." Mr. Smith picked up the tongs and was gratified to see the subject's eyes widen. The nostrils flared, a sure sign of a hormonal state of alarm. The temple wounds were still oozing, the memory of that pain would be fresh. "Don't you hate Daddy now? Don't you wish I would go away? Don't you wish you could move without me telling you? You can answer. Don't you want to hurt me? You *better* answer." Letting the anger come into his voice.

Tremblingly, quietly: "Yes. Yes, Daddy."

Too scared, not enough anger there yet. "What don't you like? What's the thing about Daddy you hate the most?"

"Control," the subject croaked. "Daddy's control."

"Control. Very good. It's imperative that you understand, deeply understand, how important this is, why the issue of *control* is so important. What is control, really? The fact is, the desire for control underlies our every move, from our basest self-interested activities to our highest aspirations. I'll bet you don't think so, but it's true. What's 'democracy'? It's about *control*, isn't it—people rejecting the control of the few and demanding control of their own lives. What's 'religion,' what's 'prayer'? A passive-aggressive attempt to control what God does—'Be nice to me because I'm being subservient and grateful and properly observant,' or 'Please let me live or be healthy or get rich'!" What's 'art'? An attempt to impose order on chaos, to control physical media, and to manipulate the emotional responses of other people! Right? You see how important this is?"

Four nodded, nervous about where this was going. Mr. Smith thought about it himself, hoping that the subject was ready for this. "So our lives, human history, it's all about people vying for *control*. And control can be a cruel weapon, can't it. To get what you want from others. A way to victimize others."

Against his will, he felt himself succumbing to his own rhetoric. It was all true. Abruptly he felt himself on the verge of tears. A knot in his throat choked him as he tried to talk. "Look at me, my life. I was controlled from the time I was a young man. I was bright and promising, *because* I was so bright and promising and idealistic, *that's* why they had to control me. To use me. They used my best attributes to control me—my desire to serve my country, my desire to help heal my fellow man, my intelligence and skill. They took all those good things and turned me into a monster—because *they* needed a monster! So look what I've become! A whole life spent in secrecy and intrigue, a whole *life* undercover, *quarantined* from the rest of the human race as if I had some kind of *disease*! Could I get married? Could I have kids? No—nothing! I've got *no* one, no relatives or loved ones. My memories? An archive of horrors! And on top of that, on top of *all that,* they want to catch me and kill me. There are *teams* of people with no other goal than to destroy me! And that's why we have to make a statement, don't we. Pitiful as it is, hopeless as it is, we have to make our solitary statement of defiance, don't we? Just you and me."

Suddenly the injustice of it enraged him, the artery in his neck twisted painfully, the pressure seemed to lift his scalp. He knew he was losing his medical objectivity here, wanting to inflict some pain in return. But fortunately the two goals overlapped.

"Jump," he commanded suddenly.

Number Four, caught by surprise, obeyed with a jerk after a momentary hesitation.

"Good. Now three times, fast. Good. Stick out your tongue. Good. Now three times, fast. Now jump again. Faster. Again. Again."

Four jumped, the hard plastic of the cords swinging and rustling.

"So what do we have to do when people control us? Keep jumping. You can answer."

"I, uh—"

"You said you hate Daddy. You said the thing you hate most about Daddy was—"

"Control," Four rasped.

"And what do you have to do—*have* to do!—when people control you?"

"Hurt them. Hurt them back."

"Keep jumping. Faster! Yes, hurt, but more important, *control* them back. So why don't you hurt Daddy now? Make him stop?"

"Scared."

The subject was breathless now, red in the face. But it was going well: answering faster now, the tempo picking up. "Why don't you try? You should *try* to make Daddy stop, shouldn't you?"

"It hurts too much when I—"

"It's gonna hurt a whole lot fucking worse if you don't try!" *Come on,* Mr. Smith was thinking, *do it. Give in to it. It's paradoxical, developing resistance within a framework of submission, but you can do it. It's the next important step, and you're very close.* "Come and hurt Daddy. Come now, or *I'll* come and hurt *you.* I'm gonna come hurt you. Here I come, Daddy's gonna come—" He clicked the points of the tongs together, *clack clack.*

The subject was crying, gasping, but the badgering was beginning to work. Number Four lunged toward him, arms outstretched, hands clawed, mouth a rictus of hatred. A raging early primate, a fearful primitive reptile striking at its enemy. Mr. Smith stayed just out of reach as the cords drew up short, bit the wrists and ankles hard, brought the leaping naked body to a stop with a wrenching jerk. Four sagged against the tangled lines, the knots drawing blood.

"Again. Hate Daddy. Come hurt Daddy." Mr. Smith leaned temptingly closer.

Wide eyes, a flash of resistance, then the desperate lunge again, the cutting cords, the collapse.

"Again," Mr. Smith ordered. A tempting step closer, maybe just maybe within reach.

And again and again.

Finally a scream of rage, veins and tendons standing clear in the neck, blue eyes bloodshot, muscles cording with the lunge. The wrenching yank of the cords snapping taut, the sound of elbows and knees hitting the floor, the tangling and writhing.

Jeez, that was a doozy, Mr. Smith thought. Maybe it was time to back off. You had to pace this stuff, or you could damage the subject. He didn't want to end things prematurely tonight.

He put down the tongs and came forward warily, watching the arching, gasping body. "There," he said. "That's all for now. That wasn't so bad, was it?" He came closer, bent, reached out one hand, touched a shoulder. Four ignored the contact. He leaned closer, stroked the forehead, wiped away blood and tears. Four calmed a little, already partly conditioned to the routine. Amazing.

Mr. Smith sat cross-legged on the floor, arranged the lines, and drew the panting body to him. He loosened the wrist lines a little, held the weeping face against his shoulder. "There," he said again, comfortingly. "There, there. All better now. Everything's going to be fine. Daddy won't hurt you now. That's all for now." He stroked the blond hair, rocking gently, waiting to feel the quaking sobs subside. He massaged the neck, kneading, soothing. "There. See, Daddy *loves* you, doesn't he? And you love Daddy, too, don't you? Do you love Daddy? You can answer."

The subject stopped breathing for a moment, held perfectly still with face still buried in Mr. Smith's shirt. A heartbeat, two, three. Then, "Yes, Daddy." A muffled voice.

"Say it." Putting just the tiniest edge of threat in his voice.

"I love you, Daddy."

Mr. Smith nodded approvingly. But it wouldn't do to make it too easy. He let his hand tighten hard on the back of the neck and bent to put his lips right against Number Four's ear. "Say it three times," he whispered, letting the edge show clearly now.

21

M O HAD DECIDED TO work Saturday, and to his surprise St. Pierre insisted on coming along. Maybe it was the overtime pay, a new baby cost money. Biedermann and any new forensics from the power station would have to wait until Monday, but the interviews with Mrs. Drysdale had opened several doors, and it was important to move fast on these things. You waited too long and memories faded, witnesses or suspects heard you coming and ran for cover. Best to steamroll it right along.

Friday night he had dropped Rebecca at her apartment, a nice building not too far from her office on the Upper West Side. Her good-bye at the curb in front had been shy and maybe a little reluctant. A handshake, but a nice one. On one level, he felt as if they were racing toward something. And yet despite her direct, candid way of talking about their feelings, she was being discreet, pretty balanced—taking things out into the open, but also setting limits, keeping a reasonable degree of professionalism. An admirable combination.

Rebecca was right, he had no real cause to consider Biedermann any kind of suspect. But at the same time, his instincts told him something was wrong with the guy, and it shouldn't be too hard to shoot down or support his suspicions. First, he'd look at whatever information Gus might come up with and maybe talk to Ty again. If either produced anything at all shady, there was an easy second step: determine where Biedermann had been on the day Irene Bushnell had disappeared and that Thursday Daniel O'Connor had not shown up at work. Simple. So he put it out of his mind and concentrated instead on what he could do, which was look into Irene Bushnell's employment contacts. Even with all the high tech in the world, you still couldn't beat traditional investigative techniques like legwork, interviews, and deductive processes.

Saturday morning he and St. Pierre arrived in separate cars at the home of Mrs. Ferrara, the lady who owned The Gleam Team. She ran the cleaning business out of her home in Ossining, a well-cared-for white cape built in the sixties. She had a husband who was mowing the lawn when they arrived and two kids who watched suspiciously as their mother took her police visitors to an office at the front of the house. Mo and St. Pierre and Mrs. Ferrara sat there as Joe Ferrara, who looked as if he could use the exercise of a walk-behind, went back and forth past the big window on his riding mower. The drone of the machine coming and going made conversation difficult about once a minute.

But Mrs. Ferrara was helpful. She was a tall, slim woman in her late forties, dark hair pulled up into a single, thick braid. An intelligent face. She was wearing shorts and grass-stained running shoes and a man's work shirt: Saturday was obviously a day for yard work at the Ferraras'. Mo let St. Pierre take the notes.

She told them she had started the business about eight years before and now supervised twelve cleaning people full-time. Her job was to do the advertising, scheduling, payroll, client relations. Right now, The Gleam Team cleaned for fifty-two clients, most of them residential. At the time of her death, Irene Bushnell had been cleaning for seven clients, two of them twice a week, the rest once. However, in her three years with The Gleam Team she had cleaned for others and had occasionally substituted for other employees, so the total number of clients she'd contacted was twenty-one.

"Irene was a good girl," Mrs. Ferrara said. "She was more regular than the average, and she didn't break things often, or steal things. Those're the two most common problems."

"Did she ever talk about personality conflicts with any of the clients?" St. Pierre asked. "Disagreements, uh, somebody being bossy? Somebody making passes at her?"

Mrs. Ferrara had a couple of file folders, one with Irene's name on it, and now she looked inside them. "I keep a note of any problems in my client and my personnel files, usually you hear about it from both sides. But Irene—well, here's a complaint she was late . . . here's a complaint she broke a mirror . . . Here's a complaint *she* made about a watchdog that tried to bite her. Um, but that's it. A better than average record."

Mo took the papers, scanned them. "Do you often encounter problems with sexual contacts between clients and employees?"

The question seemed to embarrass Mrs. Ferrara. "I used to do cleaning myself. You get a certain amount of . . . well, of interest from male clients. You're cleaning their bedrooms, sometimes you're in their house alone with them, so . . . But our contracts expressly forbid it. If you're thinking Irene had a, um, contact, all I know is, not that she told me. No."

Joe Ferrara droned past the window while St. Pierre dutifully jotted in his notebook. Mo could imagine his notes: *Interviewee says victim did not rpt. any sexual contacts, which are contractually forbidden.* Mike seemed to enjoy the stilted language of police reports. Mo wondered if he ever jotted implied subtext like *Not that she told me, no, but I wouldn't be totally surprised.*

They ended up with Mrs. Ferrara giving them a printout of the names and numbers of all the people Irene had ever cleaned for, with checks next to the seven clients she'd served at the time of her death. A lot of phone calls and interviews, Mo thought, automatically doing an investigative triage assessment. And it would probably lead nowhere.

He and St. Pierre were out at their cars, discussing their game plan, leaning on the open doors and sweltering in the noonday heat when Mo's pager vibrated. He looked at the number, recognized Marsden's office phone, and with a flash of prescience thought, *Oh, shit, and it's only been a week since O'Connor.*

St. Pierre had to stop for gas, so Mo got there ahead of him. When he pulled off the road and parked among a row of police cars, his first thought was, *Oh, yeah, one of these places. The secret landscape.* They were on a country road eight miles north of White Plains, with heavy woods on both sides except here, where the road bridged a little stream. Less than a mile down the road it was a nice residential, semirural burb of upscale estates. Same distance the other way was 684, the six-lane interstate that fed cars to Manhattan, forty miles south. The stream broadened as it headed away from the road, turning to a marshy flat of mud, grass, and scrubby trees among which State Police and North Castle township uniforms now walked cautiously. In the distance, the banks steepened and trees closed around the waterway again. This was neither country nor city, but had the worst attributes of both: Like the city, it had traffic noise and exhaust fumes from the interstate, close overflights from Westchester Airport, a heavy scattering of trash, sometimes bad people on the loose. Like the country, it had a lonesome feel, it was full of bugs and mud, it had lots of cover and no streetlights. It was the kind of no-man's-land where no one really went, too urban and dirty to picnic or fish or make out, too rural and lonesome to seek any other entertainment in. Parents didn't let kids play in places like this: the edge of highways or railroad tracks, those areas out behind the mall or just the other side of the new development or around the back of the landfill. Dead land, soiled land, unpeopled land. No one seemed to notice, but look around and it was always right there. This kind of place was great for killing or dumping, and Mo had seen a lot of bodies turn up in garbage bags in similar spots. Probably five thousand people drove by every day, probably thirty thousand an hour on the interstate. And not one of them had any idea of the kind of things

164

that sometimes happened just the other side of that highway berm. Didn't really want to know.

St. Pierre arrived, and they stepped over the guardrail and headed down the embankment onto the banks of the stream. A North Castle cop pointed them further into the marsh, back among crippled-looking, stunted sumac trees. There was a mud and sulfur stink here, a rotten smell that seemed made up equally of decaying vegetation and human pollution. Mo's feet squelched in mud and instantly cold water soaked his socks.

As they picked their way upstream, Mo could see a man-made shape materializing among the scrub, and soon he saw it was a concrete culvert, an old one, something that had either washed out in some past flood and stranded itself here, or that had been replaced twenty years ago and just left to decompose. The near end was a round cement tunnel six feet high and maybe ten long. The far end, where most of the other cops clustered, was bigger, a square, shallow box of cement about eight feet on a side.

Mo nodded as he saw a few faces he recognized. Then he and St. Pierre squelched around the corner and saw the corpse, hung inside the square end of the crumbling culvert.

The victim was a young woman this time. Naked, as they always were, a blonde with a fine figure now discolored by blood and bruising. The cords holding her had been poorly measured, allowing her body to bend backward with her belly out and her head back against the wall. The knee lines had snapped and hung down. From the scrapes on her skin, it was clear she had fought back.

She had been a real beauty, Mo thought. Immediately he felt a rush of anger at himself for the inappropriate thought, but then forgave it: You had to acknowledge what a waste it was, you had to appreciate and mourn what she'd been. The day you stopped doing that, you were in real trouble.

"Who's in charge of the scene?" he asked.

"That'd be me." A portly, uniformed cop pushing retirement age lifted a hand, and Mo read his nameplate: Officer Bradley.

"So who found her?"

Bradley made a gesture as if apologizing for something and consulted a little pocket notebook. "A resident up the road, a Mrs., uh, Mrs. Pilz. She goes jogging with her dog nearby, the dog slips the leash and runs down here, won't come back. So Mrs. Pilz comes to get the dog. Dog must have smelled the body."

Mo bent to inspect the cords and remembered suddenly that contrary to popular misconception, corpses *do* breathe. Not so they'd fog a mirror, but when you leaned this close, you smelled the gases gusting out of their skin, corruption venting through the pores. Still, he caught a whiff of perfume in the rot smell, a lot like that one Carla used, what was it, Sunflower.

After a moment he leaned back, feeling like shit, having seen what he expected. The handcuffs were nylon Flex-Cufs, logo right there. The line was serrated trimmer line, the knots were thrice-wrapped double nooses. The extensive abrasion at ligature sites and on elbows and knees told him she'd been used hard before she died. Yes, and the temple wounds.

He felt a little weak as he stepped back, the proximity of violent death undoing him once more. There was something else that made him shaky, too, a feeling only certain people, certain cops, knew. It was a hatred of whoever did this, a rage that had no outlet and so went around and around in you and made you crazy and sick. It was more than the ugliness of murder, more than the waste of life and youth and beauty, it was the *unfairness* of one person being singled out to receive so much of someone else's pain. And this puppet thing was the worst, the control and persecution that went on and on and outraged every sensibility about self and self-determination.

St. Pierre was just standing there ankle deep in muddy water, trying to look professionally detached and not succeeding.

Mo asked Bradley, "Did Mrs. Pilz recognize her? A neighbor maybe?"

"Says she didn't get close enough. Didn't want to look."

Mo knelt to inspect the lower body. Given the cement wall, the puppeteer hadn't put in eyelets but had tied the cords to stubs of rebar emerging from the crumbling top of the box. The knee cords had tightened hard before they'd broken, probably before death, and were still sunk deep in creased flesh. It wasn't supposed to be part of the MO, but the power-station scene and the smeary stains on the concrete floor here were suggestive, so he looked closely between her legs and at her inner thighs.

Yes, Rebecca, he thought wearily, *you're right. Something's gone wrong with the "plan."* Because it looked as if she'd been raped along with everything else.

He stood up again. Bradley was yammering at St. Pierre, but Mo ignored him as he took a turn around the culvert. He wanted to toss his shield down and walk out of here, this was really getting to him. People dying, love dying, Sunflower perfume, traffic noise, mud. Maybe you couldn't be an effective cop if you had too many of your own existential concerns. Or maybe it was good you were hit like this every time.

"Mo." A familiar rough voice made him turn back toward the road.

Marsden was squelching toward him, his suit pants rolled a couple of turns to stay out of the muck, exposing pale ankles. He puffed and wheezed as he came up and surveyed the body and the scene. "Aw, fuck," he gasped. "Aw, fuck." He nodded hello to St. Pierre and Bradley, then stepped up onto the culvert box to peer closely at the corpse.

"Guy's beginning to fuck up, isn't he?" he asked over his shoulder. "MO is drifting. Hitting once a week, weird environments, ligatures getting sloppy. We got the arrangements of objects?"

"Not that I've seen yet."

Marsden nodded. "He can't be procuring with the care Howdy Doody used, either, doesn't take the time."

"I think she was raped, Frank," Mo told him quietly. "Biedermann is looking at rape in the power-station case, too."

Marsden looked. He was still huffing when he turned back to Mo with eyes that were just black slits, as if he had no eyeballs at all and the cracks beneath his hooded lids revealed just an empty, dead black inside his head. He said, "You know, I'm really beginning to dislike this bastard. You?"

22

THEY CAME UP WITH an ID on the first house-to-house, when one of the uniforms had the bad luck to canvass her parents and inadvertently break the news, ass-backward, the worst way. She was Carolyn Rappaport, a student at SUNY-Purchase who had come home yesterday for the second-to-last weekend of school. Her parents had been worried when they hadn't seen her in the evening, but the campus was only a short drive away, she was twenty now and sometimes went out with friends until all hours or even stayed the night at girlfriends' houses, they'd tried to get her to call in but since she'd gone off to school she didn't always. Now they theorized she'd gone jogging late Friday afternoon, and the killer had somehow acquired her on her run.

Mo stayed at the scene until after dark, when the North Castle PD left a car to guard the area but the investigation knocked off for the night. No point in pushing it, nobody had found anything even in daylight. A search of the streambed a quarter of a mile on either side of the culvert turned up no clothes or puppeteer paraphernalia. A variety of footprints at some distance, on the drier banks, but for thirty feet around the culvert there was at least two inches of water, and the mud beneath retained no useful impressions. They'd bagged some beer cans, cigarette butts, a broken pair of sunglasses, even an old toaster, but everybody knew they'd gotten nothing from the scene.

Mo sat wearily in his dark car, the lone North Castle cop a

hundred feet behind him, invisible in his own car. The smell of Sunflower perfume was still in Mo's nostrils, connected to some ache inside him. He wondered how Carla was doing. He rolled the window down and looked out over the barely visible landscape. With the darkness had come a cool humidity, rising with the mud stink, and peepers were calling here and there from the marsh. The bushes and sumac trees down in the streambed were nothing but blots of darkness, separate near the road but blending into one continuous curtain of shadow further out. Three quarters of a mile to the southeast, over the dark trees, the interstate droned continuously and gave off an unnatural glow.

Just a nice May night here in the gap, the in-between space, the dying land.

He'd still have been killing her at this hour yesterday, he thought. The two of them would have been together in that lonely dark, playing out that awful, unequal drama on the box end of the stranded culvert. Who could do such a thing? Skip the psychology, that was too awful and anyway too speculative to think about. No—who could, physically, have accomplished it? The killer had to have felt safe here. Had to have known about the culvert somehow, you couldn't see it from the road. Probably had to have known about the rhythms of life around here to avoid being seen, to know screams wouldn't be heard. Had to know how to get in and out of the tricky terrain in darkness.

Abruptly Mo's ears registered the crunch of gravel nearby, footsteps in the dark, and in an instant he was breathless and his Glock had materialized in his hands. And then a flashlight's beam came and went, the North Castle man being considerate and shining it on the ground so as not to blind Mo.

"How's it going, Detective?" the guy asked. "Nice night." He bent to the window, big, square gray uniform, face almost invisible. He noticed the gun in Mo's lap.

"Hey," Mo said. "How about you? You got the all-nighter."

The cop jutted his chin at the Glock. "I just did the same thing a few minutes ago. A raccoon or something, I about pissed myself."

They both chuckled, then sobered and stared off at the dark marsh together for a moment. And then they said good-night and the guy crunched back to his car.

Mo sat for another minute, bringing his pulse back down. Jesus, he was getting jumpy. It took him a while to find the line of thought he'd been pursuing. Okay, who could have done such a thing? Unless he was just really desperate and really lucky, it had to be somebody who knew the area, who had been here before.

Did he walk, or drive? Did he wait, or arrive and strike suddenly? Given the short time since O'Connor, had he been watching Carolyn for a while, or was this some impulse thing that he happened to be ready for?

But all the questions seemed to circle around to the other who, the other how—the mental state it took to accomplish this, the mind of the killer. And Mo really needed to skip that tonight. The air was beginning to feel cold. He rolled up the window, started the car, and drove off wondering if maybe this was the dead place Carla had seen in her vision or prophecy or whatever the hell that had been.

The ringing phone jerked him out of sleep. Mo rolled and grabbed the receiver, hands shaking with the sudden acceleration of his heartbeat. One-thirty-eight in the morning.

"This is Gus," the flat voice said.

"Gus," Mo said, sitting up, struggling to get brain cells online. "Thanks for calling. Yeah, thanks, I—"

"Got some stuff on your guy Biedermann. You're probably onto something. Guy's got a buttoned-down life. His trail's been swept."

" 'Swept' meaning—"

"Meaning someone has erased chunks of his past. Not everything, but systematic enough to have to've been deliberate. Starts thirty years ago, Biedermann's in the army. Got a Silver Star for some operation in Cambodia, another couple of medals for outstanding service. Records are fine for a while. Then he practically disappears for ten years. But I placed him at a couple nonservice scientific conferences over the years, like this American Psychiatric Council conference on violent psychology, 1970. Another one on neuroleptic pharmacology. In 1972, I got him speaking to a congressional panel on Vietnam, basically part of a scripted Nixon choir on drastic tactical options for what everybody knew was a losing situation in Nam. Subject and contents secret, probably because nuclear options were discussed."

"So he's been affiliated with, what, secret technologies, or—"

"Shows up here and there for the next five years in congressional hearings, intelligence conferences, and some medical conferences for the next five years. Subject not always clear, but I say birds of a feather, so I look at the other personnel at these things and he's usually on the same bill as some CIA counterintelligence people, some FBI, some Delta people—"

"Delta as in Delta Force?"

"Yeah. Secret army branch, the army's version of a SWAT team. High-tech, radical tactics, cutting-edge science, high-level command structure. Need it lethal, quick, surgical, secret, Delta's supposed to be the tactical tool of choice. Can be used for foreign or domestic, with presidential clearance. But they're fuckups like everything else federal right now. They were there at the Branch Davidian fuckup in Waco."

Gus was quiet briefly, giving Mo a moment to think about it. So Biedermann had had a broader career in law enforcement and intelligence, and it had been kept semisecret—so what? Mo had been approached by the FBI himself, turned them down for various reasons.

"His name shows up in another interesting place," Gus went on. "You remember last year, there was this stuff in *Time* magazine about this special army unit that supposedly went and killed AWOL

American GIs in Vietnamese and Cambodian villages? The black-ops guys from back then, the guys who'd done the killing, were talking about it for the first time."

"Yeah, I remember—"

"Then a week later, whole thing blows up, *Time* and CNN back away from the report, all the witnesses go back on their testimony, various army bigwigs come out and say it was bullshit, right? Guess whose name comes up?"

"No kidding."

"Oh, yeah. Biedermann's name had been dropped by a couple of the black-ops vets as being up in the chain of command back then. So then last year when it's sweep-it-under-the-rug time, they call out our boy, decorated veteran and now a successful FBI guy, all aboveboard and trustworthy. Says, yeah, he was in charge of some secret missions, but it wasn't killing our own guys, God no. It was Russians, some Russian spies they were after, that's who the Caucasians were they were shooting and gassing in those villages. It's all right there in *Time* magazine."

"Yeah, I read that." Which would be plausible, Mo thought, except that the whole show of refutation, after the *Time* and CNN pieces came out, was so obviously a cover-up attempt.

Gus apparently had the same thought. He was laughing, or at least that's what Mo thought it was, a series of sharp hisses. "I fought in Nam myself, just a grunt, no heroics, never got even a scratch on me," Gus said acidly. "Personally, I hated the fucking Cong, wanted to kick their asses good, couldn't stomach the whole apology thing after. But you don't gotta be a genius to smell the bullshit on the cover-up. We used to talk about it back then, we all knew what would happen if we fell for some slant girl or lost faith in the war and ran off and went native. Everybody knew there was a unit that'd come after you and make you dead."

Mo knew from legend that getting that much personal communication from Gus was rare, significant of deep feelings on the subject, at least to the extent that Gus was capable of anything like feelings.

"What about his FBI career?" Mo asked. "Anything on his time in San Diego?"

"Oh, yeah. And here's where it gets funny. In 1983, Biedermann pops out of the service, joins the FBI. Got decorations and prior intelligence work, so he moves up fast, he's going along in Internal Affairs, a nice niche for a former spook, right? Except that in 1995 somebody waves a magic wand over him and he's suddenly turned into SAC in San Diego. Spends a year like that, goes back into IA, then two years ago, bang, he's SAC again, this time in New York. Like he's yanked out for something specific."

"Like what?"

"Hard to tell. He handled a number of cases out there, probably has quite a handful here. What's relevant, who knows? You were interested in maybe a serial string in San Diego, but there were probably half a dozen he was involved with down there. Take me a little longer to get details on 'em all."

Going down his list, Gus gave Mo the basics on Beidermann: address in Manhattan, not far from Rebecca's office on the Upper West Side. DOB, car model and registration, Internet service provider. Mo dutifully jotted it all down, wondering how the hell Gus could dig up all this. He had already gotten a lot to think about, but another question occurred to him: "Gus, do you know when he started in New York?"

The machine-gun chatter of a keyboard, and then Gus said, "Okay, yeah—transferred New York field office October '98."

Mo wrote the date in his notebook. "Thanks. Thanks a lot, Gus. So, what about the other guy? Zelek?"

"I was just getting there. There's no Anson Zelek. Doesn't exist. Not in the FBI. Nothing in the FBI's public personnel records or in payroll. And not in CIA either. DIA's harder for me."

Shit, Mo thought. "Any suggestions?"

"Yeah, I got a suggestion. You're over your head. Rethink your priorities. Get a life." Gus cleared his throat into the phone, an angry, phlegmy gargle. And then the phone went dead.

Mo rolled onto his back and stared at the dimly lit ceiling. The room was pitch-black except for the dull red glow of the numerals on the digital clock radio. The big empty house creaked and shifted stealthily all around him. After a while he groped on the floor until he found his Jockey shorts and draped them over the clock's display. Better.

Jesus, he was thinking, *how fucked-up is this going to get?* Who the hell was Zelek? Of course, maybe Zelek was peripheral, not important. But who the hell was *Biedermann*? Because there was a big problem with the idea that Mr. Expertise was brought East specifically to go after Howdy Doody. Biedermann came to New York in October '98. And Howdy Doody's first known kill wasn't until January '99.

23

SUNDAY, AFTER THE NIGHT'S developments, it seemed kind of natural to go do some shooting practice. Just to keep in shape, Mo told himself, always a good idea, nothing at all to do with Biedermann, no.

The Dale Shooting Center was a private range in New Rochelle, halfway to Manhattan. Mo liked Dale because the equipment was top-notch and the place was open at the odd hours he sometimes felt the need to practice. So he packed up his two guns, the Glock and the little Ruger .22 that he occasionally wore on his ankle, and went down there.

When he walked into the lobby, he got a surprise that made him think *synchronicity*. Or maybe it was more like *serendipity*. Because at the counter, getting her headphones, was Dr. Rebecca Ingalls.

When she turned to see him, her face lit up. "Mo! What are you doing here?"

"I was going to ask you that."

She showed him a compact Smith & Wesson .38 automatic. "After my, um, unexpected visitor? After my near-death experience with Ronald Parker, I thought I should learn to use one of these. I bought it four months ago and come to shoot about once every two weeks. I'm not very good. Maybe it's a philosophical resistance on my part, I've never been a gun fan. But, gee, I did try to *talk* to the bastard, and I didn't seem to get anywhere, you know?"

He admired her ability to maintain a sense of humor about it. "So why drive up here from New York?"

"Mainly because everybody I asked said this was the best range around—I suppose that's why you're here. But I also thought it would be good to get out of the city. I'd just as soon not risk running into any of my clients or patients and have to explain why I'm here."

They signed in, got headphones and booth assignments, and headed down the corridor to the range area. Rebecca was wearing jeans and running shoes and a short brown leather jacket over a white shirt. He'd never seen her so informally dressed or so pretty, and the way she looked was a blunt hit to the chest. The sum of all longings.

"Is this fate, or what?" she asked. "Running into you. I was thinking of you."

"Oh?"

"Well, I was thinking you and I made a very effective interview team."

"I thought so, too."

"And," she went on, rocking her head side to side as they walked, an effort at nonchalance that wasn't convincing, "I was thinking we should, yeah, face it, have a date. A date that we admit is a date." She had obviously made a commitment to directness in emotional matters, but it wasn't always easy for her. He liked that a lot.

"That'd be good," he told her.

They both clammed up as they came into the range. Not too many shooters today, just two booths in use, the room thumping erratically with their shots. They took stations eleven and twelve, setting out their boxes of ammunition, checking their weapons, loading. She stepped back from her booth and seemed to be having difficulty with her magazine, but he didn't offer to help, figuring it might seem condescending. Instead he put up the Glock and emptied the gun at the man-shaped target, eighteen quick shots. He hit the target return button, and when he looked away, he found her staring at him, round-eyed. He pulled down his headphones and so did she.

"What in the world were you doing?" she asked.

"What do you mean?"

177

"Shooting so fast. Aren't you supposed to aim?"

But the target gusted up to his station and they both turned to look at it. It was a pretty good cluster, Mo thought, one messy hole obliterating the little X at dead center where maybe eight shots had gone through, and then a scattering within two inches. But two holes were out almost the width of his hand, clear evidence he was not in top shape.

"Jesus," she said, looking over the target. "I didn't know people could actually *do* . . . that. So this is something you do a lot?"

Mo shrugged, not knowing whether she'd consider shooting skill a character asset. "Not really. Just a natural thing. Good distance vision or something."

"Uh-huh," she said skeptically. She looked at the unloaded bullets in her hand, dismayed. "Now I'm embarrassed to shoot."

But she got over it. She finished loading, got ready to fire. He stood back to watch her, realizing it wasn't her shooting stance that he was looking at but the in-curve at her waist, the length of her fine legs as she braced herself and took her two-handed grip. He could tell she was a lousy shot from the way her gun moved around. *Here's where you're supposed to come up behind her and help her stabilize her arms and talk into her ear about her form and grip and all that cliché stuff,* he thought, and the idea of being that close to her made his belly warm, his limbs loose. He felt dazzled, irradiated by her, so after emptying another magazine he moved down a booth just to get away from her. She stepped back to look at him quizzically, and he made a gesture at the target track, implying something wrong with the equipment. She nodded and went back to popping away.

Mo shot with the Glock for a while longer, raising the challenge by taking out the numbers on the target rings. Then he shot with the little Ruger, which was not at all as accurate, barrel too short, not really designed for this distance. But still he could feel the rust falling away as his body merged with the weapons and intuited the geometries and velocities and recoil factors. He had been truthful with her, it really was an instinctive thing. But, no, he was not a bad shot.

They had a late lunch together, leaving her car at the range and driving in Mo's to a roadside dairy freeze on the north end of town, with picnic tables along the back end of the parking lot. At the counter they ordered deep-fried everything, burgers and corn dogs and fries and rings, and took the food to a tree-shaded table on the bank of a narrow river. They were on a busy commercial strip, fifty feet away half a dozen kids were bouncing around on the restaurant's faded-plastic playground equipment, it was nothing like the no-man's-land of last night, but still the river scene brought Mo back there.

Rebecca must have seen something in his face. "We could go somewhere else. I just always liked these places when I was a kid—"

"No. This is fine. I was thinking of something, yesterday—"

"Crime scene?"

"This is so nice, I don't think this is the time to—"

"I'm a psychologist. Spill it, Mo." She nipped an onion ring, holding his eyes.

"You'll hear about it tomorrow. It's the Howdy Doody copycat," he admitted gloomily. "Or whatever he is."

She pried it out of him. Grudgingly he told her about Carolyn Rappaport, the obvious deterioration of the copycat's MO, the probability of rape. Neither of them touched the food. Rebecca was a good listener, drawing out his emotional responses to the scene as well as the forensic details. When he was done, he felt cleansed of the shocked confusion that had gripped him since last night. But he'd acquired the heat of it again, the anger and fear that were growing in him.

"Look," he said, "I need to talk to you about something. Can we talk confidentially?"

"Of course!"

179

He glanced quickly around at the other customers: a family of four, two tables away, jabbering and munching, oblivious, and some other people over near the playground, too far away to overhear. "I need you to hear this right, not assume I've got weird motives. It's about Erik Biedermann."

For once she didn't object. "Okay."

"I have some information about his past, about his appointment to the New York field office, that bothers me." Mo felt a moment's trepidation, wondering if it was wise to trust her so much so soon, but he plunged on anyway. He told her about Biedermann's role in the black-ops hit squad, his interest in the psychology of violence, his "swept" intelligence background. Rebecca's eyes widened as he talked, and it made him feel better: *She didn't know this. She didn't knowingly sleep with an assassin. Biedermann the hit-man.*

"He's got a very strange history with the FBI," he concluded. "He gets yanked out of IA and put in charge of murder investigations. Only problem is, at least with Howdy Doody, the murders start *after* he arrives on the scene."

"What are you *saying*!"

Mo dropped his voice further. "Biedermann moved to New York in October of '98. The first Howdy Doody murder was committed in January of '99. And that guy Zelek? He's not FBI. He doesn't *exist*."

That got to her, and she had to think about it. Finally she said, "Can I ask how you know all this?"

"No."

She took another minute, watching the kids in the playground enclosure. By degrees her sunny face became shadowed by something she saw there. At last she lifted her chin toward the kids. "See how sweet they are? Little wild creatures, innocent, just wanting to play. I prefer to work with children, because I fall for them and they inspire me to do my best work. Also because the basic elements of human psychology are right there, not yet overlaid with the complexity we adults acquire. Little sweet people, unspoiled human nature, right? But watch them for a moment, Mo."

He wondered where she was going with this, but he did as she instructed. There were six kids of different sizes, four girls and two boys, clambering on a boxy jungle gym, scooting down a tube slide, swinging from rings. The youngest was a boy of two or three with a tilting walk, the biggest was a chunky girl of maybe seven. The kids would back up at the ladder to the slide, jostling for position, impatient with each other. The little one struggled on the ladder rungs, nervous about the height, going slow. As Mo watched, the big girl looked quickly over at the chatting parents, then yanked the little kid off the ladder and onto his ass on the ground. She stepped on his hand as she went over him and up the ladder. He screamed and began crying and then threw gravel at her.

"Mom!" she yelled.

"Jimmy!" one of the women called. "No throwing! Jimmy, come here please. Right now. Jimmy, I mean it!"

"Predictable," Rebecca said, turning back to Mo. "Because the fact is we're not nice creatures. Even when we're kids. At our most innocent, we have all kinds of nasty feelings—anger, hate, competitiveness, jealousy, sadistic impulses, vengefulness, you name it. We are full of guile. We hurt others. Look at how a girl that young is already manipulating the situation. And Jimmy—if Jimmy were an adult experiencing an intensity of emotion comparable to what he's feeling now, he'd probably try to kill her."

Yes, Jimmy was really going to pieces now, a full-tilt tantrum, clawing at the chunky girl as his mother tried to drag him away.

"My point," Rebecca finished sadly, "is that psychology has its scary dimensions."

"You said that before. I still don't know what you mean."

She toyed with a loose strand of hair as if debating something inside. "Can we drive? Just drive around for a while, then you can take me back to my car?" For the first time since he'd met her, Mo saw a deep uncertainty in her face, something like fear.

"What I mean," she said, "is that the study of psychology has gone two ways. I shouldn't be surprised— I mean, what human endeavor hasn't? We invent things that serve to help and heal, and we use those same things to hurt and kill. Metallurgy gives us both guns and surgical tools, chemistry's used for both poisons and medicines. Nuclear science has given us invaluable medical imaging devices and the atomic bomb." She was leaning against the passenger-side door, both to face Mo and, it struck him, to keep some distance between them.

Without thinking about it, he took them onto the Hutchinson River Parkway, north. "So you're saying the science of psychology can be used as a weapon, too."

She nodded. "Some of it is common knowledge, of course. There's the cliché of 'brainwashing,' where prisoners of war are isolated and exhausted and their egos systematically broken down, and they're made to tell secrets by various means. Recently you hear a lot about the science of 'creating untenable psychological discomfort'—remember when Noriega was in his compound in Panama, and the U.S. forces broadcast loud rock and roll at him twenty-four hours a day? Or at the Branch Davidian compound, the ATF continuously broadcast the screams of rabbits being slaughtered? To wear them down, confuse and demoralize them. And it works."

"Screaming *rabbits*?" The thought gave Mo the creeps.

"From my doctoral work, I know a little more on the subject than most people. But especially since I've been working on forensic profiling, I've done some . . . odd . . . research and have been called in on some unusual cases. So I've glimpsed . . . the tip of some iceberg. I've encountered at least two of what I'd call *manufactured personalities*. Where the healing science I study has been used to make lethal weapons."

"What the *fuck* is a 'manufactured personality'?"

She wasn't looking at him anymore, and she wasn't seeing the countryside they drove through, either. "I was called in by state prosecutors on the case of a serial killer out in Oregon. They had caught the murderer, and they wanted my input on his early years to help the prosecution psychologists. There were three of us, two psychologists and a neurologist, and we were all, well, we all became certain this man had been . . . deliberately tampered with."

"Oh, man—"

"I'm sorry. But on every psych test and personality inventory, he showed emotional and cognitive responses like a lab-conditioned *animal*. What was worse, his brain scans showed two symmetrical lesions in his temporal lobes. He'd had *brain surgery*, Mo, but he had no recollection of it and there were no records of it! We knew he'd been in the army in Vietnam, so we asked for his service records, but we kept not getting them. When we told the prosecutor we couldn't do without his service medical records, *poof,* we got canned. We were taken off the case. I guess they found somebody else, some whore psychologist who'd ignore the obvious. By then, the three of us, the psych team, had dug up bits and pieces, enough to suspect this man had been part of an experimental weapons program. A program that manufactured assassins—remote-control killers. We were sure he had been made into a specialized killing machine. A programmable sociopath. He'd had brain surgery to help suspend normal inhibitions against killing, and he had been conditioned or trained to accept 'programming' from his controllers. They'd *target* him, see, send him after Ho Chi Minh or local Cong sympathizers or Russian spies or whatever! We believe that he came back to the U.S. and was never able to reintegrate into normal society. He was driven to keep on killing. And he wasn't the only one. I was peripherally involved in a similar case, with another Vietnam vet perpetrator, in Indiana."

Mo drove for a while in silence, now fully aware of where he was going and why, angry at Rebecca for withholding this information from him earlier. Wanting to confront her with the reality, the urgency, of what they were up against.

"In other words," he said, "he was a *puppet,* basically operated by his superiors. And when his strings were finally cut, he just kept on doing what he'd been programmed to do."

She seemed to notice where they were for the first time. "Where are we going? I thought you'd just drive around—"

"I mean, really, who the hell would even *think* of broadcasting rabbits screaming? Where would you even get a tape of rabbits being slaughtered? You'd have to be a sicko to even think that one up."

"Why are you angry at *me,* Mo? I can't see how I have in any way—"

"Answer me, Dr. Ingalls." Mo drove them down the exit ramp and onto the side road. They were very close now. His anger rose, pressure he couldn't hold. "I don't know shrink vernacular, but let me be more scientific. Wouldn't you have to have a rather morbid imagination to think that one up—screaming rabbits? And what happened to all those experimental assassins? Isn't it possible some of them went into other areas of government work? Why not? Keep them on your side, keep them for possible future use, keep them quiet? Keep them off the streets? Suppose they were really *very* well organized, *very* smart, capable guys, very useful guys. Isn't it possible, Dr. Ingalls, that your Erik Biedermann's service in Vietnam was as one of these programmed assassins? Given that we *know* he was associated with, *commanded,* a black-ops hit unit! It was in *Time* magazine, okay? Isn't it possible that maybe in his own special way he's, what'd you say, 'failed to reintegrate' into normal society?"

She was getting angry now, too. "I want you to turn around now, or tell me where we're going. Every time I get in a car with you, I'm practically abducted, Mo, and I'm not—"

"I'm taking you to where you'll probably go tomorrow anyway, to do your 'color' thing."

"I don't *wish* to go today, thank you—"

"And isn't it possible that the reason *you* get called in on these cases is that your knowledge of these 'unintegrated' killer guinea pigs is an asset in the profiling you do? Your demonstrated willingness to keep quiet about it?" Mo yanked the car around a curve, jostling her against the door.

"My 'demonstrated' . . . Mo, I can't *prove*—what am I supposed to—"

"That in a way, you're whoring, too, you're given a nice incentive to keep quiet, with your nice fat consulting fee—"

"That's it! That's unforgivable. You let me out of this car, or I'll press charges."

But they were there. Mo pulled off and braked hard, the car skating to a stop on the gravel shoulder. A technical van, a couple of State Police cruisers, and St. Pierre's car were there. Mo shoved open his door and got out and went to sit on the guardrail with his back to Rebecca. He couldn't see anyone upstream, they were all out of view among the tortured sumacs. A hazy, milky sky hung over the flats, depressing as hell.

After a while he heard her door open and close. He glanced to the side and saw her standing on the bridge, looking out over the marsh, a little wind tugging wisps of hair around her cheeks. He felt about as shitty as he could remember ever feeling.

He gave it another minute, all he could take, and then went to lean against the railing near her. "I'm sorry," he said.

She didn't acknowledge him.

"I really want you to forgive me for losing it back there. For acting like you're to blame. It's just that a beautiful girl died out there, and I'm feeling bad about it. This stuff you're telling me scares the shit out of me. I want to do something about it, but I don't have any idea what to do. Will you look at me, please?"

He was grateful that she did, eyes blue-gray and still very guarded.

"I don't want to have a fight with you. I'm, I'm kind of . . . attracted to you. Not just 'attracted,' wrong word. Better than that."

His vocabulary had completely stalled out on him. What was it about shrinks, he wondered, that they make you yammer this way? "I think you're really great, and I want you to . . . feel the same way about me."

This was not how or where he'd have preferred to say it. But her eyes warmed a little. Then she gazed back out over the scene.

Something clicked for him then. "You're not disagreeing very hard. About Biedermann. There's something else, isn't there?"

St. Pierre came into view, deep in the marsh, saw Mo, waved. Mo tipped his chin in acknowledgment. Rebecca turned away, arms still crossed. She walked across the bridge, staring at her feet, then came back to Mo.

When she looked up at him, her eyes were wet, from the gritty breeze or what, he didn't know. "Thanks for saying all that," she said quietly. "For a cop, you handle your own emotions very well, did you know that? I think you're like me, you don't like beating around the bush when it's something that matters."

"True. Thanks."

"So I'm going to tell you something I shouldn't, and hope that you'll understand it. And hope that you'll work with me on what it means. Um, personally as well as professionally."

"Anything."

"We'll see about that." She grinned miserably. "So, Mo, what kind of sex do you like?"

The question startled him. When he looked at her, she just seemed scared, not flirtatious or ironic. "Question like that, I have to wonder what you want, a straight answer or some—"

"A straight answer."

"I guess I like mutually satisfying, loving sex. Technique-wise, I guess I'm, uh, pretty conventional. Open-minded but probably pretty traditional."

"Yeah, well, me, too. Well, you were right that Erik and I were an item," she said bitterly. "I was very lonely when I first came to New

York, I don't want to go into the *why* of it. It ended for a variety of reasons. One of them was that we didn't . . . mesh . . . sexually."

"Why are you telling me this?" He didn't want to hear it, didn't want to risk ruining things for them later.

"Because one of the things he did that I didn't go for was, he wanted to tie me up."

All Mo could do was stare at her.

"I'm open-minded, too. I tried it the once. He used scarves. Didn't like it, just was not my personal . . . preference. Told him. He wasn't violent at all, just basic bondage, no pain or derogation or anything, just *control*. And he never suggested it again. But, you know, I thought, I couldn't help but think, afterwards . . . that given what we were working on, it was kind of . . . inappropriate? The resonances should have been a turnoff? They sure were for me."

"You were working on Howdy Doody."

She tossed her head, the *I'm a fuckup* gesture. "Yeah. A guy who tied people up."

Rebecca took a few steps away, turned back looking sick in the muted sunlight. She blew out her cheeks. "I feel like I'm going to throw up. Didn't want to tell you this. I mean, it's such a lousy way to . . . But I felt I had to tell you. Didn't I? Under the circumstances?"

He couldn't think of what to say. So he just took her arm, steered her back toward his car. Opened the door for her, let her settle numbly into her seat, closed the door. What he felt was a volatile mix of emotions: protectiveness of her, hatred of Biedermann, fear of what this could all turn into. A wild yearning barely reined in by caution and decorum and messy circumstances.

When he'd gotten in, he turned to her. "So where do we go from here?" His voice was hoarse.

"Good question," she said grimly.

24

THEY DROVE BACK TO Dale Shooting Center, caravanned into the city, left her car at her building's garage, went out to dinner. They weren't dressed for anything fancy, so they headed down Broadway and grabbed an Indian meal at a midtown cafeteria-style restaurant they both knew.

They made a pact to not talk about Biedermann or the murders for the duration of dinner. And they didn't. She was good at keeping pacts, Mo decided, something else to admire about her. So at first they didn't say much, just watched the other patrons eating, the sullen-looking busboy clearing tables. Mo was thinking about what he'd said to her on the bridge, how he didn't know how to talk about feelings with words that were his own, not some cliché lifted from a movie or a novel. *Attracted* seemed shallow, cheap. Maybe he was uptight about trying to talk intelligibly to a Ph.D. Maybe, more likely, he just wasn't used to trying to find the right words for this, and maybe it was time to get some practice. You could get rusty in this. Looking back, he couldn't tell where the getting together with Carla had turned into the falling apart from Carla, the two were seamlessly merged or were the same thing. It had been a long time since he'd explored the vocabulary of love.

But the storm in the car had broken through some restraint they'd both maintained. Some dam breaking. For a while there, they'd both been stripped pretty raw, but Mo liked what he'd seen of her. And he liked that he could be real with her and she still seemed to be moving toward him.

"When we first met, you indirectly asked me a question," she said, interrupting his thoughts, "and I didn't fully answer you. I'd like to now, though."

"I don't remember."

She picked at her food. "Why I came to New York when I did, basically ending my relationship in Chicago. I was impressed that you picked right up on that."

"You don't have to—"

"No, this is fine." She shook her head, smiling again, some of the sunny warmth returning. "This is something I want you to know, something very important to me. Down in Decatur, I really was a hell-raisin' farmer's daughter of the old school. Got married when I was barely nineteen, had a daughter six months later. Marriage lasted about that long after, neither of us was ready at all. Just because of where I was at back then, Rachel went with her father. Later, he remarried and had a couple more kids, which meant that with him Rachel had siblings and a better nuclear family than I could offer. So we just kept to that arrangement, her living with him. But all these years, she's been with me every weekend. Then last year, my ex and his family and Rachel moved to New York—he'd gotten a big job at NBC. So there I was, with my practice and my boyfriend in Chicago, my beautiful daughter in New York. So I had to choose. Easiest choice I ever made—I couldn't live without her. And that's the answer to your question."

He smiled with her. "Funny how the one thing we think of as a mistake at the time can later turn into the one thing we know *isn't* a mistake." Meaning, *getting knocked up at eighteen.*

"I like that. A very nice insight, Mo."

"So they live in Manhattan?"

"New Jersey—just over the bridge. The only reason I was up at Dale shooting today was that Steve, that's my ex, and family are at his family reunion, back in Illinois, so I don't have Rache this weekend. And I miss her like crazy!"

Mo chewed, thought about that. "Do I get to meet her?"

"Maybe."

That was okay, Mo decided, it was early and she didn't want to make mistakes where her daughter was concerned. He respected that.

They talked about families and earlier years, and somehow Mo got into telling her about the graduate courses he'd taken over the years. Evening classes, an odd mix of subjects, no real intent to get a degree. Some English lit, his biggest pleasure had been reading *The Canterbury Tales* in Middle English: plain and simple, one of the world's great yarns. Then for a while he'd thought to get out of the investigative side of the job, maybe move over to more technical forensic work, so he'd taken a year of organic chemistry. That was a killer and he decided he'd get too impatient with lab procedure, at least out on the street you got to improvise now and again. Then a couple of Islamic Studies courses, mainly because he'd been hit hard by a book of Rumi's poems given to him by the first woman he'd lived with. Then career stuff again, a software aps course that was fun.

After a while, Mo realized they'd been at the restaurant for a long time. Their talking was completely genuine, but part of him recognized it for what it was—stalling. They both knew that when they walked out of the restaurant, it would be night in Manhattan and they'd have to decide what they did next. And there was only one thing he wanted to do: to be closer to her, to rub up against her, to move on to a new level that he could tell was coming, inevitably, thrilling and scary in a good way. He was feeling irradiated by her again, only this time he couldn't fight it.

Talk about *chemistry,* he thought dazedly.

As usual, Rebecca faced it straight on. "It's getting late," she said reluctantly. "It's that point of the evening when people who like each other have to figure out what to do next, isn't it."

"Yes," Mo said. He felt a little breathless.

"Also the point at which big mistakes are often made," she went on, being very deliberate. "Mo, this has been great, but I raised enough impulsive hell in my first twenty years to last a lifetime. You and I have a lot more to talk about, and I'd love to bring you to my apartment where we can do it in privacy. But I need to be clear on issues of, what would you call it? Timing. Pacing."

"You mean sex."

She liked that he'd cut to the chase, it wasn't always her job. "I have a daughter to think about, I need to do things responsibly? Look like I've got some semblance of stability?"

"Sure. Yeah, no, I understand completely."

"Just for now—"

"Right. Of course."

"Which isn't to say—"

"No, it's fine. Honestly."

That was such a blatant lie that they both had to laugh out loud. It felt good, real belly laughs. People's heads turned. When they were done and she had wiped the tears out of her eyes, they went out into the noise and light of Broadway at night.

The tang of exhaust-scented May night air sobered her. She stopped and turned Mo toward her. "Mo, I'm serious about keeping an even keel. I've subjected Rachel to enough of Mom's emotional upheavals. We can go back to my place if you think we can both respect that." She searched his eyes, and, yes, he could see she was serious.

"So stipulated," he said.

For a moment, when her apartment door closed and they came out of the entry-hall light into the darker living room, all resolutions wavered. The dark was full of a magnetic pull, and Mo took an involuntary step toward her. But then Rebecca hit the lights, tossed her purse, went into the kitchen to switch on the overheads.

"Want something to drink?" she called.

"Like alcohol?"

She leaned back into the doorway to grin at him. "Like, yeah."

So she opened a bottle of wine and brought it back into the living room with a couple of glasses. Her apartment was pretty and upbeat and comfortable and in good taste yet unpretentious. Eclectic furniture and colorful paintings, obviously the home of a person who bought things because she really liked them and not because they matched each other or proved anything. The big rug on the bright oak floor was an antique, blue-gray, braided oval, Midwestern chic that somehow worked nicely in this Big Apple apartment. On the bookshelf mantel were photos of Rebecca with a blond-haired child at different ages. One was a studio photo of a pale fifteen-year-old whose lips parted just enough to see the glint of braces.

Rebecca sat at the far end of the couch, poured them each a glass of wine, and then followed his gaze. "That's Rachel. I have to tell you, she was prettier before she got her nose pierced. Honestly, maybe I'm old-fashioned, but I don't understand it, this ritual self-mutilation—"

"She looks like a good kid. Very pretty, like you," Mo told her. Then he lied, "Really, you hardly notice the nose thing."

But the words *ritual* and *mutilation* hung unhappily in the room. Rebecca frowned, acknowledging it. "So maybe it's time we talked about the . . . the problem. If there's any truth in what you're saying about Erik—"

She stopped. But he knew she meant, *Then we have to do something.* Or maybe she was already a jump ahead and meant, *Then we're both in danger if he thinks we suspect him.*

Mo tasted the wine, a crisp white that seemed to clear his head. Despite his body's longing for her, there was serious business at hand that couldn't wait.

"I don't know what's going on here," he told her. "But I have to tell you, from day one, the whole thing of you being bait for a trap, that didn't hang together for me. It was too long a shot that the killer would take notice. That they put any credence in its working says to me they knew beforehand they were playing the scam to somebody who was inside the loop, who would for sure react."

"But how does Erik fit into that at all? It was his idea!"

"I don't know. But there's another thing that ties him in," he said. "Again, I'm not sure exactly how. But from everything I've heard about the night Ronald Parker came here, it sounds like big-time bungle, even for the FBI."

"You could say that, yeah."

"I mean, how did Parker get to this building without being noticed? How'd he get through the FBI's perimeter?"

She nodded, sipped her wine, staring blindly into the whorl of the rug. "You mean, someone was helping him. Telling him what to look out for, how to get in and out. Or maybe screwing up my surveillance and protection just enough to let him through."

"Where was Biedermann that night?"

She looked really miserable. She swallowed, but didn't answer.

"So he was on the detail here. Our hands-on, runs-a-tight-ship SAC."

She nodded.

Mo stood up, took a turn through the room. Bad enough to think that a highly placed federal agent could be a killer. Worse by far to think he would happily kill a woman he had been in a relationship with.

Rebecca said, "Mo, I don't know anything about this end of criminal investigation. I'm a *psychologist*! I wouldn't have any idea how to prove or disprove something like this, or—"

She looked so at a loss he knelt in front of her and held her shoulders, trying to think of something reassuring to say. "Look. I can't figure Biedermann's involvement, I mean, what, he's the killer, or he's one of several killers, or what, I don't know. But I don't believe this case is hopeless. We've got some very good leads in the power-station murder, it looks like Irene Bushnell was having an affair, we think it may be someone she was working for. This new guy, Biedermann or whoever, is deteriorating, he's making mistakes, we can come up on him with a traditional forensic approach. St.

Pierre and I have drummed up a lot of leads, and I'm sure we're going to get DNA evidence from the Carolyn Rappaport murder. We're gaining on the son of a bitch, okay?" He spoke with more confidence than he felt.

She just looked downcast, hopeless. "That was her name? Carolyn Rappaport."

"And I've got some ideas how to help us figure out Biedermann. At the very least, it should be simple to implicate or clear him in direct participation in the murders."

She raised her head. "How?"

Mo hesitated, sensing this was not quite right but plunging on anyway. "Well. It involves *you*. There's something you can do better than I can."

Now she sat straight and hugged her arms around herself, her eyes sparking, confusion and outrage mixed. "Gee, where have I heard this before? About how *I* am perfectly positioned to catch the killer—if I'm willing to take certain little risks?"

Mo realized what he'd done, that in his own way he'd recapitulated Biedermann's exploitation of her. The thought made him sick. "You're right," he said immediately. "I hadn't thought of it that way. Jesus. No, you're right, forget it, absolutely—"

"Let's hear it, Mo." They locked eyes. "Go on and tell me your plan, I'll listen. That much I can promise, at least." She really was furious and said that last as if any other implied promises were now being reassessed, put on hold.

25

B UT IT REALLY WAS pretty simple. The best time, Mo had decided, would be Thursday, when they'd scheduled another "Pinocchio killer" task force meeting at the FBI offices—information sharing on the Carolyn Rappaport murder. There'd be a good crowd, and all Rebecca had to do was excuse herself from the conference room for five minutes and take a glance at Biedermann's personal calendar. She had only to ascertain where he'd been on the dates that Daniel O'Connor and Carolyn Rappaport were killed. Simple.

Still, he'd left her apartment with the sense that he'd blown it. She'd cooled, she'd gotten stiff and formal. Keeping her distance from men who asked her to do dangerous things. He couldn't blame her. He'd been an idiot to suggest it. On the other hand, once he had, he couldn't dissuade her from going through with it. She had a lot of . . . what would they call it in the Midwest? Pluck.

In any case, the plan left the first part of the week to make progress with the legwork. Monday began with a meeting with Mike St. Pierre, mainly to discuss Irene Bushnell, the power-station victim. Regardless of the other complications of the puppet murders, Mo felt, they had to build the case on the reliable bedrock of traditional criminology, forensic science, and logical deduction. Because, human cruise missile or not, Pinocchio was a flesh-and-blood man who had somehow come into Irene's physical proximity and gained control of her. And given that she had died at the power station, a place she was unlikely to spontaneously visit, at a time when her husband was driving his truck in Nebraska, Mo was willing to bet she'd had repeated contacts with the killer—enough for him to know something about her. Eventually, if you looked closely enough, if you played through the film of her last days, you'd see Pinocchio enter the frame, make contact.

And St. Pierre was doing a tremendous job of connecting dots. By eleven o'clock, he had called all the people Irene Bushnell had worked for and had made up charts depicting every household's members, her work schedule, and her other contacts within the community. He began setting up the interviews and other background work that might help them identify Irene's supposed lover or murderer or both. Mo was grateful to have a methodical, focused young investigator doing this kind of homework, and he told St. Pierre so. Mike tried to conceal how much the praise meant to him.

St. Pierre had gone to seed since the baby came. When Mo commented on it, he explained, "No sleep. Lilly and I got to get up five times a night." His eyes were tired, but there was a glow in them, too, which Mo assumed had to do with his new fatherhood. Mo had been given to understand that a nesting instinct took over when you had a kid, you felt very close to your wife, priorities shifted, and so on. The tired but happy mammals. When Mike had come in this morning, Paderewski had commented on the puke stains on his shirt, and St. Pierre had looked proud rather than embarrassed. And yet he was still cranking out this great work.

They split up and spent the afternoon talking to the clients Irene had been working for. By the end of the day, Mo had slogged through three go-nowhere, uncomfortable interviews: People got scared and tightened up when murder struck so close. The first client was a frazzled, red-haired mom of three carrot-topped kids in a massively ostentatious house in Briarcliff Manor, for whom Irene had cleaned Tuesday and Friday mornings. Among other details, she told him that she and the kids had always been there when Irene was, the husband always at work in the city. Scratch the possibility that hubby had been Irene's secret flame.

The second client was a middle-aged couple, the Tomlinsons, who lived in an older house in downtown Ossining. They both worked in banking, the husband usually telecommuting because he was mobility-impaired, a member of the polio generation of the fifties and mostly wheelchair-bound. Without kids or pets, they didn't need cleaning often, so Irene worked there for just four hours every Monday, leaving around one o'clock for another of her jobs. They knew nothing about Irene's life. Mo found them dour and suspicious, and their house struck him as oppressively, overly tidy. They'd gone with a new cleaning company since Irene's disappearance.

The last client was a single woman in her early forties, a lady exec at a hardware distributorship, and her aged mother. Neither knew anything about Irene's personal life, and they seemed to resent Mo's assumption that they might.

A dead-end day. Mo thought of driving into the city to see Rebecca but then doubted that he'd be a welcome visitor. Back to Carla's mom's house. He decided he'd call Rebecca later, see how she was doing with some of the research she was planning to do on U.S. military psychological experiments.

The thought occurred to him: It would be nice, someday, to have a more cheerful subject to discuss with her, a better excuse to call her.

Tuesday morning, he got a call from Flannery's secretary: The DA expected him at one o'clock for an update on the Pinocchio killer. Another command appearance, back by popular demand. Mo almost told the secretary that Flannery could go fuck himself, Big Willie or no, but then remembered his need to keep Flannery allied as a counterbalance to Biedermann. He spent the morning at his desk, running through some paperwork while St. Pierre sat with the phone pressed against his head. The tedium side of the job.

When Mo arrived at the DA's office, Flannery was at his desk, dressed in a sharp pinstripe suit that emphasized his massive shoulders. The teddy-bear charm was a bit thin today, Mo decided. Flannery looked preoccupied as he waved Mo to a chair and sat tapping the desk with his pen.

"How're you doing, Detective?" he asked.

"More or less adequate. You?"

"Task force meeting day after tomorrow. I'll be there myself. I want to make sure I'm up to speed on the case. Thought you and I should touch base."

This was predictable, Mo thought. The DA would be making his first appearance on the new task force, with an audience of other self-important guys to impress. He'd want to bring up some nuanced points to show how on top of things he was, project the proper air of authority. Mo summarized events since he'd seen him last: the complete lack of progress on Daniel O'Connor's murder, the precious few leads on Irene Bushnell's murder, nothing solid on the Carolyn Rappaport case other than the indications of the killer's increasing psychological imbalance.

Flannery's frown deepened by degrees, and at last he held up a hand. "You think I'm a pretty complete bimbo, don't you? Another asshole politico with no brains, no integrity, no commitments other than making himself look good. A guy whose best talent is spotting necks to step on on his climb to success. Have I got that about right?"

Mo did a double take, getting a sour grin from Flannery.

"Hey, I'm telepathic!" Flannery said acidly. He stood, went to his window, looked out over the forest of construction cranes across the plaza. The daylight reflected off his bald dome. "Look, Mo—I can call you Mo, right?—you can think whatever you like about me personally, I'm an asshole, whatever. Fine. But I want to tell you something. Authority isn't just *handed* to anybody. Being the big guy, able to get the big jobs done, requires that people around you *believe* you're the big guy. Yeah, my job is part theater. So, yeah, in the interests of earning some clout, I like to look good. I like to have some extra strings to pull to get things done. And, yeah, in the interests of the public's sense of security and well-being, I like to *look* like I know what I'm doing, like I'm confident about positive outcomes. No question." Flannery turned back from the window, came to stand in front of his desk. His blue eyes bored into Mo's, and he was actually breathing hard with the intensity of feeling. "But just remember, whatever your opinion, it is *not* about *me*. *It is about getting the job done!*"

Flannery hurled the last words at Mo and then, *wham!*, brought a meaty fist down on the desk. The desktop was a solid slab of mahogany, but the pen set and phone jumped half an inch.

The blow startled Mo, but he managed not to move, not even to blink. "So it's lonely at the top?"

Flannery just stared at him, shaking his head sadly. "Cool customer, huh? Well, that's good, because this is a shit heap, isn't it, and the pressure's about to go up. Carolyn Rappaport was the daughter of the school superintendent. I know the Rappaports socially, they've communicated with me directly about their daughter's murder. People feel very *threatened* when this kind of thing happens to the daughters of prominent citizens, 'Mo.'"

"We're doing everything—"

"'Everything'? My understanding is, Carolyn Rappaport was killed Friday night. You got out there Saturday. When did I hear about it? Monday. When were you thinking you might get around to telling me about it? How *ready* do you think I sounded when Bill Rappaport called me yesterday? How *in charge* did I sound?" Flannery had gotten cranked up again, but then caught himself and brought it under control. He leaned back against his desk and folded his arms. "Any other little details you haven't gotten around to telling me?"

There was a lot to tell somebody, an ocean of complications, but Mo needed time to think about how to go about it. Whether telling Flannery was the right place to start. "I don't think so," he said.

Flannery's face brightened. "Oh. I see. Like you didn't get anything worthwhile from consulting with the psychologist, what's her name, on a profile for this creep? Not a *crumb* of insight you could share with the district attorney? And you didn't learn anything from Erik Biedermann about where the FBI is going with this? After he put on his three-ring circus at the power station last Friday?"

Flannery was showing him that he was keeping tabs on the investigation, on Mo personally, and Mo almost asked who was reporting to him. But he was sick of the game. He stood up and went to lean against the desk himself. He was still a little shorter, but at least they were side by side, it wasn't so uneven. Flannery's leathery neck wrinkled as he turned his head. Up this close, Mo saw other things in his face beside the bearish charm. The wrinkles on his forehead and around his eyes told of cunning and striving, but beneath that was anxiety, even sadness. Maybe the DA did have an agenda beyond self-aggrandizement, maybe even something like the personal crusade to combat evil that motivated many cops. Including Mo Ford. In which case, not unlike Mo, he daily faced an endless, losing battle.

Against his better judgment, Mo felt for the guy, and he decided against making a smart-ass comeback. Instead he said, "Look, I'll send you copies of my notes. But I don't have time for this bullshit. There are a lot of possible leads, most of them will prove to be dead ends, I can't tell you anything substantive other than what I already told you. Biedermann doesn't tell me anything, you'll have to talk to him directly if you want more. If there are nuances you're missing, that's what these task-force meetings are about. We'll all know more on Thursday."

Flannery nodded at that. "Okay." He checked his watch with a weary gesture, then got off the desk and went around to sit in his chair again. He jotted a number on a scrap of paper and shoved it across to Mo. "Okay, Detective. This is my personal cell phone number, it's always with me. What you're gonna do is, right here while I'm watching, take out your cell phone and peck that sucker into your phone's memory. So you've got *one button* to push to *call me the fuck up* when there are developments! So you have no goddamned excuses."

Flannery watched expectantly, his eyes hard. Playing the big boss. Mo looked at him for a moment, then decided what the hell. He took out his Nokia and programmed in Flannery's cell number.

A glint of satisfaction flitted over Flannery's face, the guy getting his jollies from pushing Mo around. "Very good. Then I'll see you Thursday. And thank you for your time."

Mo was at the door when the DA called to him again. "Oh. Just so you know. A heads-up about, what'd you guys call him, Big Willie."

Mo turned to see Flannery with a big grin on his face. It gave him shock.

"I got a call from the attorney for Willard's family. Turns out he's got a rich uncle in Philadelphia. They're considering a wrongful-death civil suit against you personally. And they're urging me to press criminal charges as well."

Terrific, Mo was thinking. On top of everything else, a tangle of legal hassles and expenses. Court appearances, the other side's calculated vilification of him. Win or lose, the harrying of months of litigation. As if his life weren't enough of a mess. As if Rebecca wouldn't have enough doubts about getting together with a guy like him.

"So what'd you tell them?" he croaked.

Flannery was really enjoying this. "I told them I was reviewing the incident and considering the possibility of criminal charges. But just between you and me and the wall, I'm not inclined in that direction. At this juncture, anyway."

Flannery's mouth grinned. Mo nodded to show he'd heard what he intended—another reminder about Mo's obligation to do his bidding, about who was in charge.

★   ★   ★

All in all, a crappy day, ending in a stuffy, humid night. The Southern Gothic feel had returned. Mo got to the house after dark and immediately took a walk through the place, just something it felt good to do. He turned on lights as he went, revealing empty rooms, glaring oak floors, dark, bare windows. When he'd toured all three floors, he shut off the unnecessary lights and went to make a sandwich from some pastrami and rye bread he'd picked up. The food helped, gave his stomach something to do besides clench. He wanted a beer but didn't want to impair his reflexes with alcohol. And he had a lot to think about, needed a clear head.

The phone at his elbow went off and made him jump. He grabbed the receiver.

"Morgan, hi—it's Detta. How are you, honey?"

Detta was Carla's mother. She was a small, dark-haired, energetic woman who looked a lot like her daughter. With all the rental real estate she owned, she had made some money, and she'd used a good share of it for face-lifts, fitness training, cosmetics, a youthful wardrobe. Seeing her and Carla together, most people took her for an older sister.

"Not so good. You've talked to Carla? You know we're, uh, we're having some trouble—"

"She told me she moved out, honey. I'm so sorry. You know how much I've always liked you. I've told Carla that many times."

"Thanks." Mo was thinking feverishly. Detta was okay, but when someone prefaced what they were going to say with how much they liked you, you were usually in trouble. "Detta, I know I've got to move, I've already checked out a couple of places, and—"

"Morgan. Is *that* why you think I called? To give you your eviction notice? Honey, you know I think of you as *family*."

"Well, thanks—"

"Really, I was calling about Carla." Detta's chipper suburban real estate agent's voice picked up a note of concern. "I'm worried about her, Morgan. She doesn't look well. I'm concerned about that book she's writing, those *people* she's seeing. How did she seem when you saw her?"

Mo dodged the question. "Haven't seen her in a few days. Was there something in particular?"

"She was here yesterday, and, honestly, I don't think I've ever seen her so . . . troubled, um, distant. *Different.* At first I thought it was you two, I know how hard that can be. But she was talking this *spooky* talk. She's seeing *voodoo* people, she's seeing every kind of crazy psychic, I don't know all the details. The scariest part is, she sounds as if she *believes* all this supernatural business! She told me she's been seeing an old woman in Brooklyn, what did she call her—a *mudda-woman*. That's some kind of a Jamaican witch, I think. I've called her at Stephanie's, late in the evening, and Stephie just tosses off, 'Oh, she's down in Brooklyn,' as if she's, she's taking a night secretarial class instead of . . . slaughtering goats and drinking blood, or whatever they do."

Detta's voice had risen until it had a nearly hysterical ring to it. Now she lapsed into silence, and Mo heard her draw desperately on a cigarette.

"And every time I talk to her," Detta went on, "she makes these mysterious comments, she's had these bad, what, *visions* or prophecies, I don't know what you call them. Morgan, isn't that one of the symptoms of schizophrenia? That scares me to death! It runs in our family, I never told you this, but my sister—"

"What do you want me to do?"

"The last time I saw her, we were drinking cranberry juice at my kitchen table, and Carla was telling me all this hocus-pocus. And she was squeezing her glass so tightly it *broke* in her hand! And there was red juice all over, and she cut her fingers. And I thought, oh, my God—"

"Detta, I'm convinced. But what do you want me to do?"

"Morgan, honey, I know you're not, you know, *responsible* for her anymore. But I don't know who else to ask. I was just thinking, I know you still care about her, maybe you could talk to her. You're a *policeman*, maybe you could go to Brooklyn? But in such a way that, whatever Carla's involvement is, it doesn't get her . . . you know. In trouble. With the law." She smoked for a moment, then finished craftily, "I just think so highly of you, honey, and I'm sure we can work something out with the house."

So she was bribing him: Make sure Carla's all right and you can stay on. Mo felt like telling her how much he liked the goddamned place. And yet the thought of Carla having a hard time—that was painful. A lot of tenderness still there, a well of it inside him.

"Detta, I'll talk to Stephie tomorrow, I'll try to see Carla, I'll do what I can about the Brooklyn thing. I'll call you soon, okay?" *Like I need this right now,* he was thinking.

She was grateful. She'd always thought of him as family. She was just a little desperate, that's all.

As Mo hung up, the last thing he heard was Detta sucking on her cigarette.

26

WEDNESDAY AFTERNOON. Mo had always liked Brooklyn, but he had only been to this section of Bed-Stuy maybe twice in his life. It was generally avoided if you weren't local, weren't black. He was glad Ty had agreed to come with him, and he wondered briefly how Carla had managed to connect with the Jamaican voodoo circle here. How she ever got in and out: white girl in a cute red Honda Civic. For once he almost didn't mind wearing the cop look, the indelible brand. Between him and Ty, a white guy and a black guy cruising the streets in a Crown Vic, they'd look like some kind of heat from a mile away and people would keep a respectful distance.

He'd met Ty at his Bronx PD precinct station, and they'd driven in Ty's car down the Bruckner, across Hell Gate, and through Queens. Brooklyn always seemed to Mo a nation unto itself, four times the size of Manhattan, with plush residential neighborhoods, small-town shopping districts, devastated warrens of crumbling masonry, chic big-city downtowns, you name it, and every color and nationality and persuasion of human being.

Ty drove in stony silence. Man of few words most of the time, but Mo had once observed him addressing his troops, an hour-long harangue that demonstrated Ty had hidden talents as an orator. Ordinarily Mo would have tried to pry a word out of him, but for once he didn't mind his silence. It gave him a chance to just look at the sights of Brooklyn sliding by. Brooklyn had this unique ambience, this *moxie,* that he never got tired of looking at.

Another dead-end day. It was a phase of investigations that Mo dreaded—the sense of stalling, of time passing and the trail cooling. He and St. Pierre had compared notes on their interviews with Irene Bushnell's clients and agreed that nothing looked promising. There were a few more interviews to run down, but he didn't have a lot of hope for any of them.

Ty broke into his thoughts: "That looks like it." He jutted his chin at a three-story brick building with a cement stoop covered by graffiti. It was one of a row of similar buildings, not too run-down, but it stood out because the metal front door was painted yellow and green. Plywood had been nailed up behind the bars on the first-floor windows. A tall young man lounged on the stoop, wearing a Rasta tam and a T-shirt that revealed weight-trained muscles. His sunglasses made him look like a praying mantis and did nothing to conceal his alertness: a sentinel. Mo spotted Carla's red Civic at the curb just down the street.

The guard's head swiveled to watch them as they parked and approached the stoop. Mo was conscious of the neighborhood's attention, people pausing to watch these two intruders.

"What up?" the guard asked. He still half-leaned against the doorway, arms crossed on his chest, giving them his eyeless gaze.

"We're looking for Carla Salerno," Ty said. "She here?"

"Wrong place," the guard said. He didn't move a muscle. A group of teenagers at the next stoop had turned and were watching them with a lot of interest.

Mo felt Ty's body go tense. Ty had limited patience for attitude, especially when his teeth were hurting. Mo knew that though he was four inches shorter and thirty years older than the guard, Ty could and would have the guy in the gutter on his face if his next word was less than cooperative.

Mo moved so that he was in front of Ty. "Not a police thing," he said. "She's a friend of mine. Do me a favor, just tell her it's Mo."

The sunglasses glistened at him for a moment. Without turning away, the guard gave a short rap on the door. It opened a little, and the guard conferred briefly with someone through the crack. Then the door closed and he turned back and leaned against it again. "Chill an' we see," he said.

When the door finally opened again, Ty opted to stay outside. "I don't need to get involved in relationship stuff. I'll just stay out here and keep an eye on Junior." He sat on the railing of the stoop and gave the guard the evil eye. "But call me if you need me, huh?"

Mo was ushered inside by a slim black woman who locked the heavy door behind them.

The building had obviously been built as a six-flat, but the interior walls of the entry area had been removed so that they stood in a much larger room, lit only by electric light. It was empty except for about a dozen folding chairs scattered along two walls, occupied by three middle-aged women and a gray-haired old man. From their look of patient expectation, Mo understood this was a waiting room, something like a country rail station or a doctor's lobby.

The young woman led Mo up the stairs, toward the echoing sound of television theme music. "Mudda Raymon, she very old," she explained. "We take care of her. But I tell her what you want, she say she waiting for you. She say she happy to see you." A musical Caribbean accent.

"I don't need to take her time," Mo said. "I'm just here to see Carla."

She led him into another room that had been made bigger by knocking out walls, this one set up as a combination living room and bedroom. The air was hot, thick with the smells of cooking and body odor, and the only light came from a big-screen television at one end of the room and a number of candles around an altarlike assemblage of portraits and curios. An old person's room, Mo decided: An aluminum walker stood near the bed, and one table held a blood-pressure cuff, a bunch of prescription bottles, a hairbrush thick with white strands. Around the room stood pots of flowers, some fresh and some dead and hanging from dry stems.

Mudda Raymon sat in a Barcalounger in front of the television. She was a tiny old lady, skeletally thin, with a fog of white hair around her narrow, mottled skull. She wore a flowery quilted robe from which her corded neck and wrists emerged like dried twigs, and she didn't look up as they came in, just watched the credits passing on the big screen. An oxygen tank on a wheeled cart stood next to her chair along with a hospital tray table that held a glass of water, the television remote, eyeglasses, a box of Kleenex, an ashtray full of cigarette butts.

"Mudda, this the policeman of Carla," the young woman said. Mudda Raymon didn't move or say anything, just watched the credits flowing up the screen, her lips drawn back in a toothless smile.

They waited like this for a full minute. As his eyes adapted to the dim light, Mo saw that there were other people in the room: an old gentleman in a three-piece suit, apparently asleep in another chair, and a tall teenage boy and another older woman who were sorting seeds or beads at a little table. Another bodyguard type, big and alert, in a chair near the back wall. A half-closed side door led to a well-lit kitchen, from which Mo could hear the sounds of dishes, murmured voices, a baby crying.

The film ended and the screen went into a haze of static and then flipped bright flat blue, the blank screen of the video. Still the old woman stared at it.

"Okay," Mo said finally, his voice loud in the muffled air. "This is great. Now where's Carla Salerno?" He had given up on the old woman and directed his scowl at the others.

But there was Carla, coming out of the kitchen, carrying a tray. She looked at Mo with disapproval as she passed him to set the tray on the table next to Mudda Raymon. A smell of jerk spice wafted in with her.

"Hey, Carla," Mo said. She was wearing a kitchen apron over

jeans and a halter top, and suddenly he felt stupid with his mission to rescue her from the voodoo infidels on the basis of Detta's neurotic, racist worry. For all that it was dark and stuffy in here, it was a pretty ordinary room, no sign of dead goats or bowls of blood, a lot cleaner and more together than his own rooms. Then he saw the way Carla's hand shook as she set a spoon in the bowl. And he thought, yeah, maybe this was bad for her, maybe she was tangled in something here, maybe she wasn't quite all right. She seemed to have taken a role as some kind of nurse or servant for the old woman.

"Mudda, do you want to eat now?" Carla asked.

For the first time, Mudda Raymon moved. Her little head shook decisively twice. "No. Talk to policeman now." Her voice was surprisingly deep, almost a man's voice. She turned to face Mo more directly, beckoned him with a flip of her mummy's hand. "Come 'ere, boy. Come on, don' be 'fraid ol' mudda-woman." When Mo didn't move immediately, she went on, "You be 'fraid of me? Huh?" The thought made her laugh. "Shit," she said. "Big man 'fraid of everyt'ing. Shit." She snorted derisively and turned back to stare at the blue screen. Her eyes were lightly cataracted with blue-white veils that reflected the cathode light.

Across the room, Mo noticed, the nattily dressed old man had opened his eyes and was watching them intently. He hadn't stirred, his chin was still on his chest, but his eyes were sparking in the blue glow. Since the old woman had begun speaking, everybody seemed very alert, very focused.

"Mudda Raymon," Mo began, "I don't want to bother you. I just—"

"Dis differn't kind o' church, huh," Mudda said disinterestedly. "Dis not Jew synagogue, not Mother Mary church, you half-half bastard. You don't know dis church. Big man, 'fraid everyt'ing, shit. Oh, you 'fraid inside your head, you 'fraid of black-old Mudda, you 'fraid yourself. You 'fraid to be 'lone, 'fraid bad man eat the world up, what else." She shook her head and clacked her tongue in disdain.

"Mo," Carla said quietly, "I've told Mudda Raymon about you, and she would like to give you a session. You should know, it's quite an honor, Mo, she's a very . . . special person. I think you should listen."

"I appreciate the offer," Mo said, "but I didn't come here for that. Your mother called me, she was worried about you, I promised her I'd check up on you. Tell me you're all right and I'll go."

Even in the dim light, Mo could see Carla's anger flare. "God *damn* Detta! So you come down here like a good little Boy Scout, embarrassing me, insulting these people, barging in—what, is this something you cooked up to—"

Mo knew she was going to say something like *to try to get me back*. But she was interrupted by a sudden roar of static from the television. Mudda Raymon had found the remote on the tray table and thumbed it, and the screen flashed from blue to a field of fine rainbow-gray static. Mudda Raymon adjusted the noise level, watching the volume tracker on the screen. When the sound had subsided, she put down the remote and half-turned to Mo.

"I like de TV," Mudda Raymon said conversationally. "You like to watch de TV? Got good shows?"

Mo hesitated, then answered, "Once in a while."

"See, dis show." Mudda Raymon leaned forward, reached a gnarled finger toward the screen. She traced a shape in the snowstorm of static. " 'Bout a man, he got trouble. You see him dere?"

She was crazy, Mo was thinking. Somehow all these gullible, desperate, superstitious people had granted her some kind of mystical authority, and here she was just a shrunken, senile, old mummy. But despite himself he followed her finger, and, yes, there were larger moving shapes in the static, as if the TV were one channel off the station and picking up just a ghost of some show. Maybe people moving in a room or trees tossing in a storm. Or no, maybe boxing or pro wrestling.

"See, he got all kinds trouble." Mudda Raymon's blue-white eyes were locked wide on the screen. "Look, he fight, now he fight himself, now he fight 'nother man. Now he fight big giant man, he kill big giant man. Now he fight himself again, always fighting. You see him now? You know him?"

So we're getting a session whether we like it or not, Mo realized. He wondered why Carla had told the old woman so much about him, even to the Big Willie thing. On the screen, phantom shapes swam in the static, vehement ghosts, whirlwinds in a sandstorm.

"All de deads," she droned on. "He have so many deads. See dere? An' de deads hurt his heart, make his heart sick. Make him always 'fraid, make him sad like he gon' die. Poor man, first he t'ink he can fix de bad men. But bad men like a river, no end, bad men like de ocean. So he t'ink, *all* men bad men, *nobody* no good, he heartsick. Oh! An' now he got new trouble."

Mudda Raymon shook her head and laughed, her eyebrows going up on her forehead in delighted surprise, as if she really were watching a TV sitcom or family drama. Mo started to say something to cut this off but then stopped. She was quite a show, no doubt about it, might as well see it through to its end.

Mudda Raymon's brows came down, and she leaned toward the screen with a little more urgency. Her milky eyes never wavered from the static snowstorm, but she looked dismayed now, her head shaking on its stalk of neck. "Now, dis part bad. Oh, yah, de puppets! De dancing puppets. Everybody damn' puppet. Poor bastard."

Mo felt the skin contract on the back of his neck. Carla had come up with something like puppets in her vision, too, and he could swear he'd never told her a word about those cases. The heat of the room was insufferable, how did these people stand it?

The deep voice rasped on in its monotone: "And dere de dump-yard, dat bad. De old dump-yard. Oh, and dis—dis so bad. See! De *puppet*-puppet! See de *puppet*-puppet, de bones puppet-puppet." She leaned back now, pulling away from whatever she saw in the haze of static. "You got to watch him. He watch you. He come get you! De puppet-puppet gon' come get you! Dis so bad! Okay, no more dis, no more." Suddenly Mudda Raymon was groping on the tray table for the remote, and she knocked the water glass onto the floor. The crash of breaking glass startled everyone in the room. Even the old man snapped his head off his chest. Then Mudda Raymon found the box and the screen went black.

The old woman was shaking all over and panting with emotion or exertion. She looked as frail and weightless as an old puppet herself, Mo was afraid she was going to have a heart attack. He looked to Carla with concern, but still no one moved.

"Poor bastard," Mudda Raymon told Mo, puffing. "You give me some dat air now." She flipped her hand at the oxygen tank.

Mo obeyed, opening the valve and letting oxygen hiss into the tube. Mudda Raymon took the mask from him and held it to her face with one clawed hand, breathing greedily and watching him over the edge of the clear plastic. Bent close to her, he could see her eyes clearly, the faint blue film of cataracts in the yellow globes. When he saw the expression there, he almost jumped back. Not fear or cunning or confusion. She was looking at him with utmost compassion. Pity.

He stood back, wanting badly to leave this dark, suffocating place. Part of him wanted to tell her, *Save it, lady*. But another part wanted to plead, *What was it you saw?* Or maybe it was more like, *Help me, Mudda, I'm all fucked up.*

He took a step back from her. "Okay," he said. Mudda Raymon was looking away again, so he turned to the other old woman, who had stopped working, was just watching him. "Thanks. That was good, yeah. I appreciate it." He took out his wallet, feeling as if he were on a stage but had no idea of his lines. "You want me to pay something or what? I mean, I don't know how this works." The woman just watched him with round eyes.

Mudda Raymon made a sound like an old hinge creaking, and she shook her head. "Dis one on de house. Poor bastard."

Mo thanked her again and turned around to leave. Carla walked him down the stairs. They didn't say anything until they got to the bottom and stood in front of the triple-locked door.

"You sure you're okay?" he asked her.

"I was going to ask *you* that," she said, half just tossing it back at him, *Don't patronize me,* and half meaning it.

Out on the stoop, Ty was sitting across from Junior, giving him the dead-eyed look. The guard returned it with his impassive insect sunglasses, but he seemed to have lost conviction. *You only need sunglasses if you ain't got the look, Junior,* Mo thought. He was glad to be in the open air again.

"How're you two getting along?" Mo asked.

Ty got up and brushed off the seat of his pants. "Swimmingly," he said. Then he added, "Fuck happened to you? You look like hell."

27

W ITHOUT ANY MAJOR NEW leads and a lot of new players signing on, the task force meeting didn't accomplish much beyond establishing a basic command structure. It was all Mo could do to pay attention. Instead he found himself staring at Biedermann, as if he could see through the skin of his forehead and into the convolutions of his brain. A "manufactured personality"? A human cruise missile? Impossible to say for sure. There were dark sides to the SAC's personality, true, but there were dark sides to everybody's personality.

The other aspect of the meeting that interested him was the interplay between Flannery and Biedermann: How would these two alphas get along in the same room? But Flannery took the strong, silent approach, not saying much, just asking for clarifications every now and again, taking notes, looking in charge and competent.

The alien, Anson Zelek, wasn't there, but it was a good-size crowd anyway, enough bodies and bustle to camouflage the scheme to look at Biedermann's calendar: Mo and Marsden from the State Police Major Crimes, a guy from the Manhattan DA's office, some New York City and White Plains cops, a couple of Flannery's people, Biedermann and two of his team.

And Rebecca, of course. Rebecca, who excused herself from the conference room for five minutes and came back looking different. She tried to hide it but couldn't resist shooting Mo a look, *Trouble.*

★   ★   ★

They made a point of not leaving together, but rendezvoused at her apartment an hour later. Even though he'd been cleared through the lobby super, when he tapped at her door, he still heard the approach of her footsteps and recognized the pause before the door opened as her looking through the peep to be sure it was him. A woman who wasn't taking chances.

They went to sit in the living room again, which was bathed in a murky daylight from the overcast sky outside. Mo sat at one end of the long couch and Rebecca took the other.

"Okay," she began. "This is pretty bad, Mo."

"First, come over here," he said, making a decision.

"We've got a lot to discuss."

"Come over here." He patted the cushion next to him. Their connection had felt strained ever since he'd proposed she look into Biedermann's whereabouts. Not that he was any expert, but what they were about to discuss was not likely to create what anyone would call a romantic ambience tonight. It was best to try to connect, reaffirm there was something special between them, before they got to it. When she still didn't move, he added sincerely, "If I don't get next to you soon, I'm going to go nuts."

That got to her, a little anyway. She moved within arm's length, but he didn't reach out for her yet. "Okay—" she began.

"Closer," he insisted. "Please." She looked at him dubiously, but sidled nearer. "Whatever else," he told her quietly, "we need to be a team here. We can't trust anybody, we're not sure who to say what to. But we have to start somewhere. So let's make a team, you and me."

She laughed a little, shaking her head. "I like the way you establish priorities. You're completely right. I guess I'm not as accustomed to dangerous situations as you are, I'm not handling this well. But you're right about a team. I like that idea."

She was so close, speaking so softly, that he could hear her heartbeat in her voice. And then she climbed onto his lap, put her arms around his shoulders, put her head next to his so that her hair made a secret golden tent around his face. It was the first time he'd been this close to her and it intoxicated him. The warm scent of her, the weight of her body on his thighs, the suppleness of her waist beneath his palms as he held her lightly. When he shut his eyes, he felt himself tumbling. From here, he'd want to stroke her and explore her and take away their clothes. But she had asked him to be patient. Best to let her lead. And, yeah, they had a lot to talk about.

They did a couple of minutes of team-building and then she got off his lap, told him how it had gone. The plan had been simple, just a starting place. Biedermann's daily activities would have been recorded in a calendar at the unit secretary's desk. And Mo had been right, Rebecca was a familiar figure in the offices, enough that the secretary would trust her, know her, not think anything of her request. As a paid profiling consultant, practically FBI herself, Rebecca's line was simple: "Henrietta, I need to catch up with my billing, but I just realized I haven't kept up with my records since this new puppet guy has come up, I wasn't sure at first if I'd be needed on the new task force. Can I just check Erik's calendar so I can get my own dates and times straight? Just for the last couple of weeks." Henrietta said, "Sure," slid the book over for Rebecca to look at, went back to some paperwork. Sure enough, there were the daily entries showing Erik's appointments and conferences, his visits to crime scenes and other out-of-office times. This calendar was for May only, didn't go as far back as the day Irene Bushnell had disappeared. But it did go back far enough to see where Biedermann had been on the day Daniel O'Connor had been tortured to death, and the day Carolyn Rappaport had died, only six days ago.

"Mo—he took a personal leave day on May thirteenth. His whereabouts are off the book, he could have spent the whole day killing O'Connor." They were side by side now, close enough that he could feel her body shivering.

"What about Friday? We know he was on duty then, we saw him at the power station."

"Yes. But remember, he left not long after you got there? He was talking on his cell phone, said he had to get back to Manhattan?"

Mo remembered well, the big, agile man trotting contemptuously past them up the power-station stairs. "So what was his appointment back in the city?"

"That's just it. He didn't have one. There's nothing in the book. No other appointments that day. From the calendar, you'd think he spent the whole day at the power station."

Shit, Mo thought.

For a split second, the desire to quit swamped him. Walk away from the job, just walk, forget about Biedermann and all the sad, dead puppets. Take out a loan and go back to school or something. Biedermann's schedule didn't constitute anything like proof, but it sure didn't offer the exculpatory evidence he'd been hoping for. It meant the G-man had the opportunity to have done the killings.

But a question nagged at him: If Biedermann was the killer, who the hell was Ronald Parker?

It was as if Rebecca had read his mind: "I keep thinking I should take another look at Ronald Parker. Because whatever else we *don't* know, we *do* know he was involved. But we didn't think we needed to look that closely at him, psychologically—we *had* the killer, we saw all the standard indications of serial-murder psychopathology, case closed. All anybody wanted was evidence to convict him, him alone. Not to figure out who he was, how he got that way, or what his connection to something . . . larger . . . might have been. And then he gave himself brain damage right away, there wasn't much point—"

"Okay. So we should visit Ronald Parker. Is he . . . can he talk?"

"Some verbal ability, but very dissociated. We might get something if we ask the right questions. But we can also take a closer medical look. They took brain scans after his attempted suicide, trying to determine the extent of the damage. But nobody looked at the scans for . . . anything else."

Mo didn't ask what else they might look for, that would have to be her department. He was thinking ahead to what he knew how to do, the forensic side of it. Somewhere there was a link between Ronald Parker and the Pinocchio killer and Biedermann, a pattern that connected them. They just hadn't quite seen the whole picture yet.

Rebecca fixed some coffee and they talked for another hour. Mo told her about progress on Irene Bushnell, that maybe her lover had been a cleaning client. The idea that the murderer had a personal involvement with his victim constituted a deviation from the original MO, but as a psychologist Rebecca found it credible, especially given the rape and other features of the Carolyn Rappaport murder. They guy was starting to fall apart.

Rebecca had seemed strengthened by their team-building, but as they talked a crease began to form between her eyebrows. When Mo finished with the details on Irene Bushnell, she had her own news to report. "I did some research myself," she said. "I cruised around on the Web and made calls to a couple of colleagues. It's a little hard to separate sensationalist paranoid material from fact or from reasonable extrapolation. But I know a little more about those government programs I told you about."

Mo had felt better getting back to police work, the solid ground of forensic procedure. Every time they went into the military psychology stuff, he felt the tension come up in him.

"Okay—"

"Everybody knows about MKULTRA, the army's LSD experiments on servicemen during the 1960s. But not many know the goals of the experiments, or that there were other exotic psych programs. In Lexus I found some articles from the early 1980s, about a handful of lawsuits against the government by former MKULTRA guinea pigs who claimed they'd gotten lasting brain damage from the experiments. They had been subjected to chemical and conditioning experiments which altered their behavior, in the hopes they'd become fiercer soldiers, better fighters. They all acquired what we now call post-traumatic stress syndrome. Its main neurological manifestation is the hyperactivation of the hippocampus, the fear reflex, which can stay with a person for life."

"So what happened to the lawsuits?"

"They just faded away. I imagine some deal was cut. To show you how bogus the court proceedings were, the government denied anything like that happened—*and* cited national security privilege in denying the plaintiffs access to information. A perfect catch-twenty-two."

Mo nodded. Here he was, thirty-nine years old, and only now getting a sense of how deep things were, how much happened behind the scenes and below the surface. Even at the level of city politics, it happened all the time, as Flannery and his maneuverings demonstrated. Imagine what took place at the national and international level. He had no doubt Biedermann's occasional alien visitor, Zelek, was part of some big machinations. But what? The parts didn't fit, the picture just wouldn't come together.

"What else?" he asked.

Rebecca rummaged in her briefcase, took out a handful of printouts, scanned them briefly. "There was another project, called . . . oh, yes, SCOPE. The acronym means Socially Conditioned Operational Performance Enhancement. That's the one I told you about the other day, where they tried to create programmable assassins. One of my colleagues on the West Coast sent away for Freedom of Information Act documents a few years ago. He faxed me what he got—you're welcome to take a look."

She handed Mo a sheaf of papers. Twenty pages had been blacked out in their entirety, even the letterhead was a big blotch of ink at the top of each page. Another thirty pages, apparently censored by someone else, consisted of lines of heavy black marker broken only by the occasional *but* or *and* or *the*.

"That's informative," Mo said, handing them back. "Makes you almost think these guys have a sense of humor."

"The admission-denial thing again."

"So how does anybody know anything about these programs?"

"That's where reasonable extrapolation comes in. Every information system leaks. There had to be people who knew about these programs, but who opposed them on ethical grounds. Or who thought to make hay out of whistle-blowing. What happens is their leaks get branded 'paranoid fringe' and discredited. Their info shows up in little publications on obscure presses, homemade newsletters, low-budget Web sites. What gives leaked SCOPE information credibility is that it's all based on real science, real people, real historical events."

"So what was the science?"

"Basically, the experimental subjects were given classical conditioning to enhance certain social responses, augmented by extensive psychiatric work that tailored the pain or reward to the individual subject's past—family relationships, traumas, and so on. Then hypnotic techniques embedded specific programs, like the targeting." Rebecca paused, shuddered, went on, "There are also credible claims of neurosurgical intervention. As we saw in that case in Oregon."

"Brain operations."

"Yes."

Mo thought about it. "Would the resulting . . . psychological profile . . . be consistent with what we're seeing here?"

She looked troubled. "In some ways. It's hard to say. We need more information."

Outside the weather lowered further, and the belly of the sky seemed to swell and then open. Rain began to fall, silver and thick as a school of fish, and some leaky drainpipe near the windows spewed a fountain that splashed heavily on the window ledge. The room got dim, and it seemed forlorn in there, Rebecca's cheerful interior washed in such a sullen light. Mo got up, turned on some lights, began pacing around the room. Rebecca looked lost in her own thoughts, too. With the lights on, the window light grew much dimmer, and the rain on the glass blurred the world into an indistinct abstract, full of vague and dark shapes.

Mo looked back at Rebecca, sitting with her elbows on her knees, chin on two fists, staring at nothing. Very beautiful, very troubled.

It was good that they had a team, he thought, but even so it seemed a little lonesome, just the two of them against who knew what.

28

M R. SMITH WAS WORKING the golden retriever. He'd named the dog Johnny, counterpoint to the German shepherd's Frankie. This stage was often therapeutic, he'd found, a chance to get outside, get some exercise. Just a man and his dog in the great outdoors. Even if what they were doing wasn't exactly *Dog World* material, was it.

The old dump was a good place to work dogs in this phase. The whole area was well out of view of roads or houses, although at the southeast end, where the land tilted toward a little stream, one of Westchester County's innumerable upper-middle-income developments had sprung up in the last ten years. The terrain was a wide, gently sloped basin of several hundred acres, covered by forest and littered with relics from its landfill days: here an ancient Studebaker, there a badly rusted piece of farm machinery or an icebox or fifty-gallon barrel of who-knew-what, humping out of the leaf-covered soil or draped in vines.

The junk was an asset in several ways. It kept people away, especially these upper-income neighbors: parents who wouldn't stoop to strolling in a landfill, spoiled kids who didn't wander around after school but were hustled off to dance lessons and soccer practice. Almost as important, the rusting relics aided the conditioning process by creating all kinds of nooks and crannies, good denning for rabbits, raccoons, mice, grouse. Something to arouse the dogs' killing urges.

The dogs you could take out here fairly early on, because in the unlikely event someone saw you, you and your mutt looked from a distance like a Hallmark card or something out of *Field & Stream*.

Thursday evening of a pleasant if too hot late-May day. The puppeteer held Johnny's leash in one hand. Over one shoulder he carried a small backpack full of supplies: an army-surplus folding spade, a child's garden rake with a sawed-off handle, meat tidbits for rewards, a heavy steel-cable tether designed for large livestock. And the radio sending unit. He had rigged the retriever with two sets of implants that delivered an electrical current to parts of the dog's brain. One set simply caused pain; the other hyperstimulated the hippo-campus, site of the rage and fear reflexes so essential to conditioning. One of Mr. Smith's concerns had been that the wires and receiving unit on Johnny's bald skull would be rather visible, and they could get snagged on branches. So he'd bought a sweater that matched the dog's fur color and had cut off and customized one of its sleeves. It ended up as a pullover cap that covered Johnny's neck and head, with holes for eyes and ears, camouflaging the shaved dome and snugging the electronic components against the skull. In the dimming light, from any kind of distance, no one would see anything but a man and man's best friend, out for a woodland romp. The dog was on a leash now, but for the workout he planned, the direct neural stimulus would be his means of control. If it worked as expected, the technology would constitute an exciting advancement in animal conditioning. The control unit was a little box adapted from a radio-controlled toy car. Thank you, Radio Shack.

Right now, he was putting off the exercises and just savoring the evening. A moment of comparative serenity, time to ponder. Later tonight, with his human subject, he planned a lecture on control, on resistance, on protest, on the necessity and urgency of what they were doing together. It was important to tailor the speech to each individual, according to what he knew of the subject's past, beliefs, values, habits, et cetera. That made it much more effective. So the variant of the lecture he was developing now made use of the current subject's liberal political values. The subject was a defender of free speech and agreed with the Supreme Court that burning the American flag was a legitimate, protected form of expression—protest speech. Mr. Smith didn't agree, but he was certainly willing to use the analogy if it allied the subject's values with the project at hand. And, in fact, it was a very close analogy.

"You and I are conducting an act of protest," he rehearsed out loud. Johnny's eyes rolled up to look at him nervously. "We are protesting the actions of our government, the most nightmarish, despotic acts ever committed by any government or society. Yes, it seems ironic—some would even say hypocritical—that to protest killing and degradation and oppression, our protest takes the form of killing and degrading and controlling innocent people. Yes, these are heinous acts that should be reviled. But you must think of it as you do desecrating the American flag. It's an extreme form of protest, an outrage against common sensibilities, that is *justified by the extremity of the wrongs it protests. That* is what we are engaged in. *That* is the mission you are helping to carry out. Yes, you are being asked to make a great sacrifice—*as am I!* But it is a sacrifice we *must* make if we are going to change the course of events—which it is our lot, our *duty,* our *destiny* to do!"

His voice rose as he continued, and Johnny looked up at him with eyes bright yet somehow flat, something a little dead about them. The tremor in the dog's right rear leg picked up. Smart dog, knew his master's moods already. Mr. Smith found himself breathing hard, not from the walk but from the anger that flared as he thought about the topic. The vein in his neck bulged against his shirt collar, the skin between his shoulder blades began to perspire. There was so much to tell, so much to protest. If he didn't watch himself, he could go on and on. Not good. You had to boil it down to something short and simple that the subject would easily remember. A neurolinguistic program easily activated by the appropriate stimuli.

So he brought his breathing under control and tried again: "We *must* make this ultimate sacrifice because nothing less will capture the attention of our violence-saturated, apathetic nation."

Better, but it still sounded a little overblown, eighteenth-century. *Fuck it,* he thought. *There's time, focus on the task at hand.* But just thinking about it had spoiled his mood.

They were deep in the center of the old junkyard now, where some of the older trees still stood, swarmed with kudzu that made leafy tents around their bases. A row of rusted-out fifty-gallon drums formed a low wall, their contents long leached into the soil but still giving the area a stale stink, caustic soda maybe. Johnny shied at the dark leaf shadows or maybe the chemical smell. That was good: Put him on edge, get those old fight-or-flight chemicals perking.

Mr. Smith paused to scan the evening woods. Stop, look, and listen. In Vietnam, you learned to scout the landscape, and you did it right or you died. But nothing moved nearby except the gently swaying treetops. A couple of lawn mowers droned somewhere in the downhill development, and a distant car horn honked amid the universal faint hiss and roar of the highway, but that was it. Time to get to work.

"Okay, fella," he told the dog. "Okay, Johnny boy. Come on." Obviously the retriever had learned the nuance of this tone of voice, the bogus friendliness that signaled the beginning of a session, because his hindquarters began to quiver. Sometimes test subjects would snap at this stage, you had to be especially careful during the first session outdoors. So Mr. Smith kept a wary eye on Johnny as he put down the pack and took out the cable tether. He clipped one end to the dog's harness and looped the other through a flange of iron on a half-buried hay rake. Only when Johnny was secure did he unclip the leather leash.

He stood back and rummaged in the pack until he found the plastic bag of steak chunks. He took out one, offered it. Led by his nose, Johnny came forward, and Mr. Smith backed away until the cable drew up taut. Johnny tugged hard at the line but couldn't go any farther. You didn't want to make mistakes about the range; no, sir, you did not. Mr. Smith tossed Johnny the meat and the dog snapped it out of the air.

Standing just beyond the arc of the cable, Mr. Smith took out the radio control unit and thumbed the switch. A bead of red light came on. Mr. Smith showed Johnny the fierce little crimson eye, and sure enough the dog began to growl and shake all over. Less than a week of lab work with the setup and this boy had the routine down pat! Johnny was obviously rarin' to go.

"Good boy," Mr. Smith said sourly.

The left-right toggle was rigged to activate one set of implanted wires that would give the dog an adjustable dose of pain. The forward-back toggle fed a variable current into the hippocampus, directly activating the fight-flight reflex. Used independently, the two could act as a kind of experimental control, allowing you to differentially test the conditioning value of each. Or you could use them together and really drive the poor sumbitch wild.

Mr. Smith had looked forward to a little more serenity this evening, at least a longer pretense of the man-and-his-dog thing, but working on his lecture and recalling all the outrages and indignities and horrors had put him out of sorts. Johnny was, after all, a pain in the ass, rambunctious and disobedient, especially compared to the German shepherd. Maybe he'd start with the pain.

He thumbed the left-right toggle, just a little off dead center, and Johnny's eyes seemed to bulge. The dog made a noise like a hinge that needed oiling and rotated his head robotically, as if working a kink out of his neck.

"You look stupid in that getup, Johnny," Mr. Smith said. "What're you gonna do about it, you little fuck?" And he thumbed the toggle over another few degrees.

Half an hour later it was getting too dark to see well. Time to head back to the house. The dirt around the rusted hay rake was clawed up in a semicircle, dug deep from Johnny's lunges, his straining at the tether. Johnny had shit himself a couple of times during the double-stimulus periods and would need to get hosed down, but otherwise this had gone great. During the short-range tests, the dog had practically broken his neck a dozen times, trying to get at Mr. Smith when the direct hippocampal stimulus had been activated, and he'd lapsed easily into quiescence when the stimulus was removed. He had shown an amazing ability to learn commands in minimal time when subjected to electronically reinforced pain-reward conditioning. Then, when Mr. Smith had let him off the tether to sniff around and roam, the controls had worked just fine at a distance. He could drop Johnny into the dirt or turn him into a man-eater from a hundred yards away. Mr. Smith would have been delighted if he wasn't so preoccupied with emerging complications.

Before leaving the circle of vine-tented trees, he took out the spade and the rake. He shoveled and raked the soil and leaves until there was no trace of Johnny's exertions. When he was done, he scanned the landscape carefully. Only one far-off lawn mower running now. A faint whiff of barbecue, family life going on all around, unknowing.

That thought made Mr. Smith angry again. All the things he was excluded from. The easy companionship of loved ones, the pleasant routines of normal life. Dinner on the deck, TV, carousing with the kids, bedtime stories, making love, the sweet sleep of the innocent. Forbidden. Denied. Forget about it.

"Let's go, Johnny," he said. The whites of Johnny's eyes flashed briefly as he heard the tone of voice. Mr. Smith gave the leash a yank and they started home. Back to reality.

Calm down, Mr. Smith commanded himself. *The direct-neural-stimulus experiment is going flamingly well, couldn't be better.* The thought gave him a moment's pleasure, but then it occurred to him that, yes, indeed, it was good work, the kind of thing that if you didn't have to live in the twilight world, if you'd had a real laboratory, if you'd been able to publish and speak at conferences, you'd have made terrific progress in all these years and you would have gotten all kinds of recognition, research contracts, honors, university chairs, a fucking Nobel Prize.

All denied him. All impossible.

Besides which, there were the other problems. Number Three was turning out to be a huge problem. Three was like a snowball rolling out of control, gathering size and speed, bearing down on Mr. Smith's operations. He should have *known* Three would be a fuckup. A mistake in so many ways. Because of Three, he'd have to attend to some serious damage control, some countermeasures, and that always meant increased risks. Dr. Rebecca Ingalls was at the center of it again. And her hotshot cowboy-cop new boyfriend, Detective Morgan Ford.

For a moment his mood brightened. Thank God he'd had the foresight to put the listening devices in her apartment and could more or less keep up with where they were going, what they were thinking. And what an incredible stroke of luck that she had dared to pair up, even after her first relationship disaster, with another principal investigator on the case! What were the odds? It was a sign, a gesture of favor from fate, that his work would and should continue.

But they were both too smart. They were getting too close, prematurely. Each in his or her own inimitable little way, they had managed to grab threads that could unravel the whole show. And there was still a lot to be done, the protest hadn't attained the magnitude that it needed. It was time to give serious thought to doing something about Number Three and about putting major obstacles in the way of the two lovebirds. Dampen their enthusiasm in a big way.

The problem with damage control was that it was risky. It meant conducting missions away from your preferred turf. It meant showing too much of your hand, too much about your level of knowledge or organization. It meant *losing* control, surrendering control to others or risking it to the whims of fate. The first such mission had almost upset his apple cart big time. *Son. Of. A. Bitch.*

Mr. Smith was getting worked up again. He wasn't paying attention, and when Johnny suddenly bolted, the leash ripped out of his hands. The dog tore through the woods with a growl, after something—another dog, Mr. Smith saw, a little black mutt. Some damned pet on the loose. Johnny would rip it to pieces, and people would come looking for it, and—

There was no point in calling Johnny back. The black dog was high-tailing it in a wide circle through the trees, with Johnny gaining fast. Mr. Smith opened the backpack and quickly found the radio-control unit. He thumbed the switch, saw the light flash on, and pushed the pain toggle over all the way.

Johnny's body stiffened in midleap and he careened headfirst into the trunk of a tree. He tumbled stiffly to the ground and screamed, not a doggy yelp but a mechanical sound like a car screeching to a stop. The little dog disappeared into the darkening woods as Johnny flopped and humped.

Mr. Smith let go of the toggle and the big yellow body stopped convulsing. After a moment Johnny staggered upright and stood drunkenly, head bobbing like a dashboard folly. He got his bearings and then unexpectedly tore off in the direction the little dog had gone. Mr. Smith, running toward him, hit the pain toggle again. Johnny arched and went over, flailing against the pain, making that screech like air brakes.

Mr. Smith released the toggle when he was twenty feet away, and Johnny just lay for a moment on the forest floor, his chest heaving. When he got up, every muscle was quivering. He lurched several times and cowered at Mr. Smith's approach. And then he lunged.

Mr. Smith had just time to shove the daypack into the snarling mouth. As Johnny wrenched it out of his grip, he managed to snag the trenching spade and wrestle it free of the bag. He whanged Johnny on the head with the folded implement and sent him sprawling, then opened the blade and followed up with a hack to the neck. The blade bounced harmlessly off the radio receiving unit. Mr. Smith's face felt like it was going to explode as he swung and missed, swung and missed, and then connected as Johnny lunged back at his throat. The dog went down and he hacked him again and again on the top of the spine with the edge of the spade. Mr. Smith's heart was hammering, his neck was a snarl of pulsing veins, a nest of snakes.

When he was very sure the dog was dead, he caught his breath and carefully scanned the landscape for observers. *Mo-ther fuck-er.* That had been too close for comfort. But the darkening woods were still, tranquil, the distant noises unchanged.

The soil was soft and moist here, and it turned easily. He dug a shallow trench, cut the electronics off Johnny's head, and put the bloody tangle into the bag that had held the meat treats. He rolled the dog into the grave, and when he'd covered the body, he dragged over an ancient car door and arranged the soil-sodden metal over the spot. Then he raked leaves and dirt around the area until it was indistinguishable from the rest of the forest floor.

When he was done, he felt better. Somehow the act of smoothing the ground had smoothed his mood. The dog's death represented the loss of a considerable amount of research effort, but it wasn't the first time, and he had learned a great deal. The neural implants were enormously promising, he still had the German shepherd. Anyway, given the situation with Number Three and Rebecca Ingalls and Morgan Ford, he had other concerns besides canine conditioning experiments. The pure science was a luxury he couldn't afford for a while, he was in a fight for his life now. And that was something he knew well, even looked forward to. It did focus the mind and galvanize the spirit, did it not, to have your back to the wall.

He headed back toward the house, already planning it out. He felt refreshed and more lucid than he had in weeks. A little shot of adrenaline could do wonders for your state of mind. Time for some serious damage control.

29

THE THING OF NOT having a decent suit bothered Mo. He hadn't gotten around to replacing the one ruined by Big Willie and was half considering buying another on his way into the city. Not to try to impress Rachel, there was no way he could guess what would make an impression on a fifteen-year-old kid, he needed a good suit anyway, why wait on buying a new one? So for a while he debated stopping at Harry's, on Forty-second, on the way in. Finally he decided that there wasn't time, he'd have to make do with what he had.

"We're going to grab dinner at around five thirty," Rebecca had said when she'd called, "and it occurred to me you two should maybe get a glimpse of each other. Nothing fancy, just this midtown pizza place Rache likes. Before I drop her off at her dad's, over in Englewood." She made the invitation sound offhand, but her voice gave her away: trying too hard to be casual.

"You sure Rachel wants an unexpected visitor?"

"You're very considerate to ask. Don't worry, I talked to her. She said it was fine."

"You and I, we're dealing with some pretty hairy stuff. You sure this is the time?"

She answered immediately, as if she'd given it thought, "We've got to keep our priorities. I long ago resolved that I wasn't going to let bad things I encountered in my professional life keep me from attending to what matters in my personal life. Right?"

It was Sunday, midafternoon, and he'd spent the first part of the day looking at three dismal apartments and trying to figure how he could decide on one when he was uncertain of so many things. Was he still going to be a homicide cop, and if not, how much would he make in whatever new career he started, how much rent could he afford? Where should the place *be,* given he didn't know where he might end up working? He'd gone around and around on it all long enough. It would be good to see Rebecca. Dinner in Manhattan might be nice, even if the prospect of meeting Rachel was kind of intimidating.

Ricci's was not as casual as he'd thought. The restaurant had a front door framed by two trees in big pots, Italianate motifs sandblasted into the frosted glass of the windows, real tablecloths. About half the tables were full. Mo scanned the room and didn't see Rebecca anywhere, but about halfway back he spotted a teenager sitting by herself, face hidden by a sheaf of blond hair striped with hennaed purple. He waved off the hostess and made his way back.

She was busy torturing one of her fingernails, scowling and picking at it, and didn't look up as he came to the table.

"Are you Rachel?" he asked. Knowing it was her from the photos.

She lifted her head, eyes widening in surprise and then quickly narrowing with suspicion. Rachel had her mother's good nose and cheekbones, but she had plucked her eyebrows into thin lines and wore unflattering mascara the same color as the hair stripes. The little ring in her nostril looked uncomfortable. "You're the detective?"

"I'm Mo Ford." *The detective* sounded pejorative, but he smiled anyway. "I'm glad to meet you. Your mother has told me a lot about you."

"She's in the bathroom." Rachel tossed her chin toward the back of the room and looked back at him as if surprised to find him still there. "You can sit down."

"Thanks," Mo pulled out a chair, put his jacket over the back, and sat. He tried to think of something to say, came up short, decided to take a drink of water. "Am I late? You guys been here long?"

She flicked her gaze at him, still fussing with her fingernail. "We were early. My mother is a stickler for punctuality."

"Well, I have to say, she wears it very gracefully." He couldn't tell if she'd said it with disapproval. She was still watching him, but not steadily. Instead she looked his way in intense bursts, her gray-blue eyes meeting his briefly and then glancing around the room and at her fingers again and back at him. He asked, "So I hear you're fairly new to New York yourself. How are you liking it so far?"

"It's okay. I'm pretty used to it by now."

"You're doing well, then. I've lived around here all my life, and I still can't say I'm used to it. Sometimes this town seems like a big loony bin to me."

Her eyes checked in quickly, gauging his intent, then flicked around the room again, lingering on the back of the dining room. Looking for her mom.

"Are you finding it a lot different from Chicago? I've never been there."

"Pretty different." Again she looked toward the back of the room, and Mo automatically did, too, wishing Rebecca would return soon. He wasn't making much headway. This was the closest he'd ever gotten to a fifteen-year-old. Probably with a high-powered professional father and mother and an upper-income lifestyle and so on, she wasn't much impressed by what she was seeing in those quick appraising glances. Suddenly he wished he'd stopped for the new suit.

"Got a question for you," he said impulsively. "Your mother, she always says what she's thinking, even if it's blunt or a little shocking sometimes. At least around me. Is she that way with everybody?"

"Tell me about it," Rachel said. She rolled her eyes.

Mo forged on, "Because if I were frank like that? Right now I'd say, oh, something like, 'Hey, Rachel, we can both sit here and wait for your mom to rescue us from each other. Or we can yak a little and impress her. Make her feel good.'"

This time her gaze lingered a bit longer, skeptical.

Mo rolled his shoulders uncomfortably, but opted to keep the pressure up: "Or maybe I'd put it, 'Give me a break, make it look like we're getting along here. So *I* can impress her.'"

On some level she seemed to kind of like that. She stared at him, bolder now. "I mean, what kind of person would want to spend all his time with, like, looking at dead bodies and chasing down crazy psycho murderers?" she asked. "Doesn't it gross you out?"

When Rebecca came back, she smiled hello to Mo and kissed her daughter on the top of her head before she sat down. Her hair was loose on her shoulders, and she wore black jeans with a snug black, sleeveless top. The sight of her almost knocked Mo off his chair.

"I'm sorry I took so long. Both stalls were occupied—you might say it was a standing-room-only crowd back there. I hope you two are getting along. Rache was a little peeved with me because we were supposed to go bowling tonight—"

"It's a Midwestern thing," Rachel said. "He wouldn't understand."

Mo asked, "*Bowling?* There's a bowling alley in Manhattan?"

"We go to some lanes over in Fort Lee, just across the river. I know it's silly, but—"

Without thinking about it, Mo stood up, put his jacket back on. "Let's go," he said. "Let's head over there." He'd never bowled in his life, but anything would be better than sitting here with this kid resenting him, trying to figure out what to say while dodging discussion of how gross what he did for a living was. "There's time before you have to go back to your dad's, right? They got a grill there, we can get hamburgers or something?"

It hadn't been his intention to try to win points with her, but Rachel gave him a look of surprise and reappraisal.

Actually, the drive was kind of fun, Mo acting as tour guide for the West Side and the George Washington Bridge, Rebecca laughing softly at his jokes, Rachel lounging in the backseat and catching his eyes occasionally in the rearview mirror. The Star Bowl was an older place in an older shopping center, a pollution-grimed façade with neon in the neo-deco style that had long since come and gone. The shopping center was in a pocket of Fort Lee that had been cut off twenty years ago by the new bridge access interchanges, which made it hard to get to and must have knocked the whole section into a downward spiral.

"How'd you find this place?" Mo couldn't help asking. He was thinking, *Star Bowl? More like Dust Bowl.*

"Convenience. Rachel's dad lives only about ten minutes away, in Englewood. Usually we bowl and then I drop her off."

Inside, the women showed him the ropes: how you rented the wizened-up leather shoes, smooth-soled and stinking of foot powder, and found a ball with finger holes the right size and spread. There were twelve lanes, only about half in use. Mostly the other bowlers were solidly built, middle-aged guys and their equally bottom-heavy wives. At first Mo had to consciously quell his startle reflex at the explosions of pins that echoed like gunfire through the place.

"I don't know about this," he told them. "I'm going to look pretty stupid."

Rachel was looking around the place and frowning appreciatively as she laced her shoes. "Yeah, but we do this ironically. Half the fun is that this isn't our kind of thing, it's totally weird anyway, it's okay to look dorky. Look at these other people—even when you get good at it, you don't exactly come across as fashion plate."

Rebecca showed him how to place his fingers on the ball, then demonstrated the steps and slide, the arc of the ball arm. He liked having her next to him, showing him how to do this stuff, watching her body move. At first having Rachel observing put him on edge, but after a while he realized he couldn't hide anything, his response to Rebecca would show no matter what he did. So instead he concentrated on having a good time. And it turned out to be kind of a riot, not so different from shooting a gun at the range, really, aiming at the target and letting go with a slow-moving bullet. On his first toss, the ball bounced hard and careened into the gutter. The second wasn't much better, and for a moment he wished he had his gun with him, could pull it out and take the heads off the pins with ten quick shots. Show off. But he got his third ball down the alley and knocked down a few pins. Maybe he could get the knack for this after all.

He turned back to the bench to find the women grinning and clapping lightly. Sitting side by side, they looked disconcertingly alike despite the difference in age and hair and clothes.

"What," he said.

"We were just enjoying your form," Rebecca said.

"Mom!" Rachel scolded, scandalized. To Mo she said, "You looked like a clown. You just about fell over. Probably everybody in the place was looking at you."

Mo threw himself down on the bench. Lesson one was surely that you couldn't let these kids get under your skin. "So go ahead. Show me how it's done. Show me how the pros do it."

Rachel jumped up to pull her ball out of the rack. "At least I don't like fall down all over myself." She wasn't smiling, but Mo realized this was something like trash talk, almost affectionate. Jesus, this was educational, he thought. And then—*kablam!*—the guy two lanes over knocked down all his pins with a crash that made Mo jump practically out of his skin.

"Rache," Rebecca said mildly, "show Mo some mercy. Try to be kind to us thirtysomethings, huh?"

"We're being *ironic,* Mom, remember?" Rachel rolled her ball hard and brought down most of the pins.

30

B ACK AT CARLA'S MOTHER'S house, Mo did a few chores, sweeping away the dust bunnies, cleaning the dishes. It had been hard to drop Rebecca off. Now his thoughts flipped back and forth between two very different worlds. The dark, dire shit, this luminous, soaring feeling. He felt as if he were dividing into two separate halves, light and dark, hopeful and hopeless. But whatever else, he sensed that Rebecca was right about keeping priorities: You couldn't let the bad things screw up what mattered in your life. Especially in the current situation, when he felt increasingly manipulated by circumstances: Flannery, the Big Willie thing, the puppeteer, Biedermann, the job in general. If you weren't careful, they could take over your thoughts, your life, your future. So you had to cut their strings, consciously rebel against their control, by sticking to your priorities. By staying human.

When he took the trash out to the cans behind the house, he stopped at the back fence to breathe the air, look over the dark neighborhood. The yards back here were broad and sheltered by heavy oaks and felt a little wild—he startled a raccoon, which went scuttling under the gate and into the pitch-black of the alley. Mo leaned on the pickets, inhaling the humid air. Muggy, but cooler than in the house. Mostly the neighborhood was quiet aside from the thumping bass of a car stereo on the next street over. That and a dog barking a couple of blocks away, mindless and regular as a machine. It was only May 30, and the weather forecasters were already talking about a dry summer, global warming, El Ninõ disrupting climate patterns. If Detta was going to sell this place or even rent it out long term, she'd better invest in air-conditioning.

Bowling: hard to say how it had gone. You could see where Rachel would be a tough nut to crack. Maybe he should read a book on adolescent psychology, pick up a few tips. A smart kid, like her mother in some ways, obviously determined to raise some hell of her own. But she had softened up a bit toward the end, goofing with him as they ate burgers in the Star Bowl's grill. He could see where it might be fun to have a kid around. And then there was the moment when Rachel had gone off to the bathroom, and he and Rebecca had slipped into discussing the Pinocchio case, the Biedermann problem.

Rachel had come back and probably overheard a little of it and had asked, "What are you guys talking about?"

"Ah, we were talking about Erik, actually," Mo had said. "Erik Biedermann."

"Who's 'Erik'?" Rachel had asked peevishly.

And Mo suddenly had felt the importance of this evening to Rebecca: Whatever she had felt about Biedermann, she had never introduced him to her daughter. Oh, man. That felt very good.

Yeah, it had been good to see Rebecca with her daughter. Thinking back now, he realized that the mom thing, the nurturer role, was a big part of what made her so attractive. Sexy, yes, funny, smart, but definitely somebody with her feet on the ground. Somebody connected to something more important than just herself and her career and so on. Unlike too many of the people Mo knew.

He didn't know how he'd done with Rachel, but the outing had distracted him nicely for the better part of four hours. A little relief. But now, with the night deepening around him, it all began to return. Programmed killers. Sick rituals of torment. Mudda Raymon's rasping voice: *All de puppets.* Secret government weapons projects. Worst of all, the indecision about whom to trust, where to go from here. In a way, seeing Rachel and Rebecca together had upped the stakes, because it pointed out what was really at risk: She had a family, it wasn't just about one person. So whatever he did, he couldn't put Rebecca in danger. Had to shield her from some of this. But how? Probably the best bet would be for him to quit the State Police, have her stop her consulting work with the FBI. Of course, somebody, Biedermann, might correctly see their quitting as an indication they were onto the big picture, and feel compelled to do something about them anyway.

His thoughts went around and around until they exhausted him and it was time to knock off for the day. He went back inside, slung the Glock in its holster over the chair next to the bed, went in to take a shower. He started warm and soapy just to get the day's sweat off and then gradually cranked the cold and lingered until his blood-stream cooled. He toweled himself off, feeling better, not so oppressed.

He had cut the lights and put a T-shirt over the clock radio and was lying in the pitch-dark bedroom when a small noise registered in his mind. The big house always made ticks and thumps as it cooled down at night, and sometimes there were mice in the walls, little scurryings that came and went. But this was a creak, the whispered complaint of wood as weight came to bear on it. He tilted his head to hear it better and heard nothing for a long moment. He had just convinced himself that he was just jittery when he heard it again, the squeak of boards moving against each other. A floorboard. Immediately the air in the house seemed different: inhabited, watchful.

His eyes still hadn't adapted to the dark. All he could see was the black of the room, obscured by the misty phosphene fizz in his eyeballs. Moving very slowly so as not to make any noise in the bedding, he groped for the chair. The Glock hanging there. His fingers found the nylon webbing of the strap, followed it down to the holster. Which was empty.

"Don't get excited," a voice said.

It was Biedermann. In a flash Mo felt a wave of heat move over him as he realized how stupid he'd been, how he'd let his guard down. How hugely he'd underestimated Biedermann. How stupid to have lingered in the shower for so long, deaf and blind. Someone could have come through the front door with a battering ram, and he'd never have known it.

Biedermann snapped on the ceiling light. The big man stood in the doorway, with Mo's Glock in his two hands. When Mo's eyes adapted, he could see that Biedermann was wearing a dark gray turtleneck, black jeans, black gloves, and an expression of high focus. The guy had steady nerves and knew his way around guns: The steel circle of the barrel wavered none at all from its aim at Mo's left eyeball.

"Sit up," Biedermann ordered.

Mo pulled himself up, trying not to be obvious about his drift to the left side of the bed, where he kept the little Ruger .22 under the edge of the mattress. "How're you going to do it, Biedermann? Try to make it look like suicide? Or are we going to do the puppet thing?"

"We'll see how it goes. Right now we're going to talk." Biedermann took a step closer, into the center of the room, wary as a wildcat.

"Why're you here?"

"You really think I don't monitor my staff better than that? Rebecca going over my calendar on Thursday was pretty obvious. She came back into the conference room looking like she'd seen a ghost, and I know we ain't got 'em in the twenty-fifth-floor restrooms. I also know her well enough to know she didn't think that up herself. Some people are naturally devious. Rebecca isn't one of them."

Mo made a *what're you gonna do?* gesture and dropped his hands helplessly onto the bed. The left hand he let fall right at the edge of the mattress. Six inches from the other gun. He'd flip off the bed, away from Biedermann. Grab the Ruger as he fell, come around the end shooting.

Biedermann said, "Tell me what you put together. What you think you know."

That was good, Mo was thinking, Biedermann's urge to yammer, to explain. Distract him even an iota, gain just enough time to roll, drop, lunge, fire.

"That you headed a black-ops hit team in Vietnam. That you're a trained, conditioned killer, you were a guinea pig in a secret medical project. That you're doing something here, you're pulling strings to keep doing it, you've positioned yourself perfectly to cover your tracks."

Biedermann's eyes were unreadable. "Jeez, pretty good. At some point I'd like to hear how you came to know all this. But keep going."

Now Mo's hand trailed just over the edge of the mattress, four inches from the gun. Had to roll and make the grab in one movement. "That you're a fucking mutant. Kind of an android, built to kill. That you like to tie people up."

"I do believe you're trying to provoke me!" Biedermann said, astonished and a little amused. "But before we go any further, don't bother with the little Ruger. Because I collected that, too, while you were in the shower. I figured you'd be the kind of guy would keep an extra nearby."

Mo felt the breath go out of him. Suddenly he didn't have a plan. Biedermann was ten feet away, had the guns, was bigger and probably had a lot more hand-to-hand training. *Life's a bitch and then you die*, Mo thought, part of him just feeling *who gives a fuck?* The urge to walk, get out, was deeper than just the job, he realized. Just shuffle off the mortal coil, cut every last string, enough bullshit is enough.

"What else, Detective?" Biedermann prodded.

"Why're we bothering with this? Go ahead, do your thing. Or is making me talk part of the thrill, the control thing? Is that it?"

"On the off chance that it's part of the thrill, why don't you go ahead. Tell me *why* I do all this nasty stuff."

"Because your brain has been altered, and now you're a machine that's just a little broken. You're a good actor, but you're one of the guinea pigs who didn't 'successfully reintegrate' into normal society."

Biedermann shook his head, looking a little insulted. "Rebecca. Tsk. Jeez, Bec, thanks for your high opinion of me. So you two are getting something going. Good for you both—you slipped that one past me. Jeez, I'm a little jealous. She's quite a gal."

"Let's get this over with. I'm going to get up now, and if you don't shoot me, you'll just have to fight me." Mo moved to the side of the bed, swung his feet over, waiting for Biedermann's shot.

But Biedermann surprised him again. He flipped the Glock around in his hand, tossed it onto the bed. Mo looked at it there, its weight denting the bedding, easily within reach.

"Go ahead," Biedermann said. "You can have it. But we've still got a lot to talk about."

Mo snatched up the gun. Biedermann watched him, then looked behind him and drew Mo's desk chair closer. He sat in it, leaning forward with forearms on his knees.

"I don't usually make late-night visits like this," Biedermann said. "Kind of dangerous with a guy like you. But you've been finding things out and it's time we talked. My office is not the right place to tell all, under the circumstances. You want to hear what's going on? You can point the gun at me for a while, even things up, if it'll make you feel better."

Mo thought about it and decided he didn't need to. He set it down on the bedside table, began to put on some clothes. "Okay. So tell me what's going on."

"What I'm going to tell you has gotta stay secret. I've got two, no, three, choices here, and I'm trying to do the right thing. One choice is to tell you, bring you in, use your smarts. Another is to bust your ass in some way, maybe crank up interest in the Big Willie thing, get you

242

thrown out so your credibility goes to shit and you're out of my hair."

"What's the third choice?"

"Kill you," Biedermann told him. He said it without any anger or pretense, and Mo had to believe it really was an option he'd considered. "Secrecy is kind of important here."

Mo pulled on his pants and a T-shirt and sat on the bed as Biedermann explained. The big house was dark around the one room, the ceiling light oppressive, the air stuffy and congested.

"You're right, I ran some teams in Vietnam and Cambodia. Not much of a secret with all that press last year, is it? You're right— Rebecca's right—it's about an experimental army psych program. The program was intended to make specialized fighting men for particular missions through alterations in their neuropsychological makeup. But I wasn't one of them."

"Who were these guys?"

"Some were convicts who cut a deal to get out in exchange for their participation, most were just draftees. But you don't just take ordinary guys and turn them into human cruise missiles. These were guys whose background suggested they would make good material. The medical boys looked for histories of childhood abuse, violent tendencies, juvenile arrest records for crimes like arson or cruelty to animals. Sometimes guys with preexisting neurological conditions that made them, that, uh, disinhibited certain social functions."

Mo felt his anger flare, the monstrosity of the whole thing. "And if they didn't happen to have the right neurological conditions, you *created* those conditions, you surgically—"

Biedermann held up his hand. "I did nothing of the sort, you dumb shit! Don't you get it? I was the fucking *janitor*!" He had some heat of his own here, Mo saw. "Who do you think my unit went after in Cambodia? Yeah, we killed Americans. It wasn't any fun, believe me. But the program, the experiment, went blooey. Their neuropsych alterations induced psychoses nobody anticipated. These were guys whose *signal* was breaking up, you know what I'm saying? Guys who knew how to kill just about anybody anywhere, who weren't afraid to get killed themselves while doing their job, but who were not responding to their controllers anymore. Who were dangerous as hell and could easily turn on their handlers, and also, *also,* could not be risked in the wild. And, yeah, I admit it, guys who could expose a very unpalatable government secret, one that could affect public opinion about the war. Yeah, it was a big mess, *and I was in charge of the goddamned cleanup crew. I still am.*"

Biedermann's eyes blazed, the most intense and genuine emotion Mo had seen in him. Against his will, Mo felt a pang of sympathy. Biedermann had had a long, lonely, thankless career cleaning up one of his country's nastiest messes. A man who lived in the social equivalent of the in-between land where Carolyn Rappaport had died—a scary, soiled world where a whole society's hideous secrets played out. A world that was all around, always near, but that nobody wanted to admit was there. You couldn't envy the guy.

If what he said was true.

Mo didn't completely trust him, but he couldn't deny that the story did put a lot of the pieces in order: the sudden changes in his appointments, the congressional hearings he spoke at, Zelek the spook sitting in on meetings.

"Zelek—he's part of your . . . cleanup unit?"

Biedermann nodded. "Technically, my boss. Although such distinctions get blurry. Come to think of it, I'd like to get the three of us together sometime, sort this out. Sometime soon."

"So, what, this copycat killer is a, a guinea pig, a cruise missile, who came back, and now his training or conditioning or whatever is catching up with him?"

"Basically, yes. More than half the original subjects were brought back home. They were reconditioned in extensive therapy, they were given every chance to live a normal life—"

"But some of them didn't 'take.' How many?"

244

"That's classified information."

"How many have you had to . . . 'clean up'?"

"Classified."

"And you knew somehow that Howdy Doody was going to start killing in the New York area. That's why you were transferred out here. How did you know?"

"You're about right, but that's classified, too. I'm bringing you on board, Detective, but you're not security cleared and you're not coming on board all the way. Don't take it personally—even my staff at the Bureau isn't on board all the way. Believe me, you don't want to be. But you can forget about grilling me." Biedermann stood up, flexed his big shoulders. A very fit man for his mid or late fifties, Mo decided, one of those rare specimens. But he looked tired, the dragged-out look around the eyes, a guy with too much on his mind. "And now I gotta go. Big day tomorrow and I'm beat to shit. This is past my bedtime."

Mo stood with him, some nagging thoughts just below the surface, feeling wary again. "So what am I supposed to do? Now that you've told me this?"

Biedermann made a weary face. "You're supposed to help me out and not start fucking with my operation. You're supposed to let me make use of your talents but not ask for more information or more of a role than I can allow. I had only those three choices tonight, Detective. I couldn't let you start rocking the boat and maybe expose a bunch of stuff that can't, *can not,* be exposed. So I could kill you or try to fuck you over so you're too busy to hassle me—and believe me, I'd feel completely justified in doing either. Or I could ask for your cooperation. I took the last choice because I'm trying my damnedest not to compound the mistakes that've been made in the past. So help me out here, huh?"

Biedermann turned his back, and Mo followed him into the darkened kitchen. The streetlight glow in the front rooms bled through, giving everything a metallic blue shimmer.

"How the hell do you live like this?" Biedermann said over his shoulder.

"It's a temporary situation."

"I'd fuckin' hope so. A relationship thing, is it?" Biedermann headed out into the empty living room, looked around. "Could be a nice place, though, if you had any furniture." In the hallway, he said, "What's Rebecca say about you living in this mausoleum? You have her over here yet? Elegant, candlelight dinners, all that romantic stuff?"

"That's classified information."

"Funny guy." Biedermann opened the front door.

"You going to give me the Ruger back?"

Biedermann turned to him in the half-lit hallway, a big, dark silhouette with a buzz-cut halo against the doorway. "Ah," he said dismissively, "it's back in there. I just shoved it into the middle of your mattress where you couldn't get it in a hurry."

By the time Biedermann had gone, it was after one o'clock. Mo checked, and he did find the Ruger. His mind was buzzing. Biedermann's explanation had the ring of truth, but there was a big problem, and thinking back he decided the G-man had deliberately shut their discussion down, decided it was time to go, when they'd come too close to it. Okay, so maybe Pinocchio was a former guinea-pig cruise missile that Biedermann's unit knew about and was detailed to catch. But who the hell was Ronald Parker? How did he tie in? And why was the new killer using an identical MO?

Who was Ronald Parker? Rebecca was right, it was time to go take a look at him. Because, one thing for certain, Ronald Parker was no Vietnam vet. If Mo remembered right, the guy was only thirty-one years old. He'd been only five when the Vietnam War ended.

31

M O SAT IN TY'S OFFICE in the Bronx precinct building,
feeling frustrated, slowly soaking his clothes with sweat—the
building was too old to have central air, and Ty's window condi-
tioner was defunct. He was reviewing Ty's papers on Ronald Parker's
Bronx victim, boning up and looking for ideas. It was all routine, files
relevant to Parker's forthcoming prosecution, Mo got nothing new
out of them. There were more bales of papers in a storage room in
the basement, Ty told him, but those were just the usual detritus of
any investigation, useless but held pending the trial under Rosario
guidelines.

Ty was working at his desk, a dark, angry face bent between
toppling stacks of papers. He must have deduced Mo's frustration
from his body language. "Not to sound condescending, but
maybe it would help if you knew what the hell you were looking
for." It was the first time either of them had spoken in over an
hour.

"Ahh. I'm fishing." Mo kicked a file drawer shut and sat looking at
it resentfully as he tried to roll the kinks out of his shoulders. "Come
on, Ty. Tell me you've got something for me. One juicy tidbit."

Ty just looked at him. *What the fuck are you talking about?*

Mo clarified, "Something that bugs you about this case. An
irrelevant detail that won't stop whispering in your ear. Something
that doesn't fit."

"I already told you everything about that," Ty said. But then he seemed to think about it, and to Mo's surprise he nodded. "But, okay, yeah, got one more for you. Maybe. On the knots."

Mo perked up at that.

"Back when this first fell in our laps, I looked at the knots pretty closely. I thought they were familiar but unusual enough they might tell us something? One of my guys is good with that shit, had him look 'em up. Turns out they're military knots. Not anything super-unusual, but he found them both in an old army technical manual—should be in the files somewhere. The one's called a cat's-paw, that's the slipknot on the vic's limbs. The other's a running-end bight, lets you tighten up a line from the middle. Could mean nothing, but could maybe tell us something useful."

"Right," Mo said. It was true: Ligature knots were a whole forensic science in their own right, could reveal a lot about a killer—background, professional training, state of mind, even left- or right-handedness. He'd glanced at the battered manual in Ty's files, *Army Publication TM5-725,* published in 1968.

"So one time, I mention it to Biedermann, you know, maybe the military connection is suggestive. He tells me he's got it under control, thanks very much and fuck off. End of discussion."

"So what's the problem?"

"Only that I've never seen any detailed reference to the knots, names or origins, in any of the task force materials. Another thing Biedermann is keeping very to himself, you gotta ask why."

Mo nodded. Again, Ty was right, details of the knots' provenance should have been more prominent in the investigation, Mo hadn't seen written reference to them even in the file he'd snatched from Special Agent Morris that day. He wished he could tell Ty what he knew: The military link made sense in the light of last night's revelations, the army behavioral-mod programs, human cruise mis-siles. And it made sense that Biedermann would sit hard on the facts here, keep discussion of the knots to a minimum.

The best he could do was nod again, give a shrug, *What's a guy gonna do?* Ty shrugged, too, *The world's full of assholes,* and bent back to his work. Mo pulled open the next file drawer.

But after three more hours, he decided he'd had it. He hadn't gotten to the Rosario materials in the basement, but those would have to wait for another day. It was quitting time anyway.

He said good-bye to Ty and walked out blinking into the late-afternoon sunshine and bustle of the Bronx. He had cut across the street and was walking toward his car when a shiny black Chrysler product with federal plates and heavily tinted windows pulled across his path. In the rear side window, emerging out of the dim interior like a fortune in one of those Magic 8 Ball toys, a pale, triangular face right out of Roswell swam into view.

Anson Zelek.

The window slid down, and the alien's tiny mouth smiled. "Good evening, Detective Ford," he said. "How fortunate to run into you. Do you have a few minutes?"

Somehow Mo wasn't surprised. He didn't bother to ask how they'd known where he was, just took the door as it opened, got in. Zelek offered his hand and Mo shook it reluctantly. A narrow, soft hand without much grip. The car was just slightly stretched, enough to allow a small fold-down desk and a thick Lexan bulkhead between passenger compartment and the driver's seat. Mo glanced at the driver, a big, expressionless guy who didn't turn his head. Zelek didn't say anything to the driver, who must have already gotten his instructions. The electric door locks snicked closed as they pulled out.

"I won't take much of your time," Zelek said. His voice was smooth, a doctor's bedside voice. "Erik Biedermann tells me that you and he had a chat last night. I thought I should follow up."

"Yeah. A 'chat.'"

"He says that you and Dr. Ingalls have shown a lot of curiosity and insight about the puppet murders. That he has given you an overview of the real scope of the problem and explained why your cooperation is so very important."

"That's about it, yeah."

Zelek nodded, and the big, almond eyes blinked slowly in acknowledgment. Up close, he looked a little more human, his eyes not really black but dark blue, his skin etched with fine wrinkles, white hair thinning so the gray scalp showed through. Early sixties, Mo guessed. The hands folded calmly on his thigh were wrinkled, too, but clean and deft and perfectly manicured, a surgeon's hands.

"What I'd like to do this evening is get to know you a bit myself, and also to deepen your context on the situation—"

"You know," Mo broke in, "it's interesting to meet a guy who doesn't exist. Who doesn't have a past. It's my first time."

Zelek heard the implication, that Mo had looked for his name, and the eyes narrowed slightly. He opened the briefcase on the seat between them and took out a couple of folders, then leaned back against the door and scanned several pages quickly.

"Speaking of pasts," Zelek said, "you have an interesting one. Liberal arts education, interest in history, philosophy, the humanities. A seemingly paradoxical decision to join the State Police. But then, look at this: citations for merit while in uniform, awards for marksmanship— fabulous shooting, I'm very impressed—and as an investigator, several commendations for what looks like great work. *But,* but: disciplinary problems, difficulty with supervisors, mm, a charge of misfeasance, a couple of suspects killed in the course of investigation resulting in internal reviews and charges currently pending against you. On the personal side, let's see: unmarried, a series of relationships that—"

"I got the point. You did your homework. My life's an open book. What about it?"

Zelek put away the files and paused to look out the window at the tinted landscape of the Bronx. The car had turned north on Third Avenue, traffic moving well for a rush hour, and Mo wondered where they were going. Wherever, it was clearly prearranged.

Zelek turned back, held up a placating hand. "My point is not to criticize you. Erik, now—yes, frankly, Erik looks at this record and sees an unpredictable investigator, a man with a chip on his shoulder and a dubious respect for authority. Perhaps an exposure risk for our mission. But I see something else—I see an intelligent, talented man with too much integrity to put up with niggling bureaucratic impediments, or the . . . ethical compromises . . . the job sometimes requires. One of those rare individuals truly committed to justice and fairness. In other words, the kind of person who can see our current problem in the right light. Who can be counted on to do the right thing."

Mo had to smile at the obviousness of the sales pitch. He leaned back against the comfortable leather seats and crossed his arms behind his head. "I'm finessed as all hell. I take it you're going to tell me what the right thing is?"

The big, serenely remote eyes lingered on Mo's face. "Let me see if I can summarize what you and Dr. Ingalls are feeling. What to do? You've stumbled into something big and complicated and unsavory, you're honest citizens, and your every instinct cries out for some action on your part. But what? No layperson is ever prepared for the levels of intrigue associated with national security issues. You feel at risk yourselves, not knowing whom to trust—as your more-than-casual interest in Erik demonstrates—or whom to tell. How to proceed with your investigation. What channels or mechanisms a citizen can use to do something about a problem like this. Go to the press? Mm, no—not yet, anyway. Go to the authorities? Maybe, but which ones? Civilian, military? Anyway, who'll believe you? And will talking about it put you at risk? If so, of what—just ridicule and lost credibility? Or outright, mm, physical danger?"

"Obviously, you've got all that right. From that, I'd figure, A, you have a background in psychology. Or, B, you've had this conversation before. Or both, right?"

Again Zelek ignored him. "And maybe, just maybe, you've

thought, 'Maybe it really is best just to be quiet about this. Maybe my roiling the waters will imperil an important government mission that, ultimately, I agree must proceed.' I sincerely hope that has at least occurred to you."

Mo nodded. It had. Yet another factor contributing to his indecision.

Third met Boston Road, and they continued north through a dense, colorful, funky shopping district. Mo had expected the car to turn back, to circle while they talked.

"Mind if I ask where we're going?" he asked. "I have some plans for later."

Zelek's mouth made a little perfect cherub smile at the bottom of the triangular face. "I appreciate that. I'm pressed for time myself, which is why I thought we could chat as I run one of my weekly errands. Detective Ford, the thing I want to stress is that *this is the last one*. We've kept a strict . . . accounting . . . I assure you. It has been a long, *long* haul. But now it's coming to an end— if and when we catch one, final, demented killer. Wouldn't it be nice to close out this rather dark chapter of American history? Mistakes were made, but lessons were learned, and now *it's finally coming to an end*. What would be the point of making a public issue out of it?"

"So you want me to stay shut up about it. And what else?"

The car continued onto Southern Boulevard, and Mo realized they were passing the lower end of the Bronx Zoo and botanical garden. To Mo's surprise, they turned into a service-access entrance to the zoo complex. The driver rolled down his window and said something to a guard, who opened a gate to let them through. Then they were inside, following a curving lane through the big trees and brick buildings of the zoo. It was after hours, and the grounds were empty except for the occasional zoo staff, walking or driving little green, three-wheeled trucks. The car wound between two buildings, and at the back pulled over among several other cars, huge green

Dumpsters, metal utility sheds, and watering troughs and other junk associated with large-animal maintenance.

The driver got out, put on sunglasses, went around to the trunk, opened it. Seeing him now, Mo knew he was not just a chauffeur. Zelek got out his side and bent to insert his face back into the doorway. "This is my Monday-evening ritual. My time is very limited, but I very much wanted to talk with you, and I thought we could converse as we did this. Sort of kill two birds with one stone."

Mo got out. The zoo was an island of comparative stillness encompassed by the vast sound of the metropolis on all sides, a silence broken only by the occasional shriek of some jungle bird. The driver came around the car carrying a big cardboard box, and Zelek led them between a cluster of sheds toward the rear entrance of one of the main buildings. Mo hadn't been to the zoo in a long time, and he'd never been around back, but it clicked for him as they got closer and he caught the smell: the Reptile House. Never his favorite. He'd tended to prefer things with fur and some body heat.

Zelek rang a bell at the side of the door and waited, the smile resting at the bottom of his face. The driver stood with the big box held against his chest. Something rustled inside, fur against cardboard, then the scrape of a claw.

When the door opened, Zelek shook hands with a zoo staffer, a pretty young woman wearing a stained apron over a light blue uniform. They talked briefly, nodding, smiling. The driver gazed at Mo with his sunglasses and hooked his chin at Zelek. "Mr. Belmont is an avid member of the New York Lepidosaurian Society."

"Mr. Belmont," Mo said.

"That's snakes and lizards," the driver explained. A small grin.

But the zoo staffer had moved back inside, and now they all filed into the building. The smell was more powerful back here, a mix of moist concrete, cedar-chip bedding, feces, and the sharp musk of scaly bodies. As the smell hit, whatever was inside the box began scrabbling in earnest.

"Let's have Annette do the honors today, shall we?" Zelek-Belmont called back to the driver. "Detective Ford and I have more to discuss, and I'd like him to have the good view."

They were in a dimly lit hallway that ran the length of the building, with many doorways leading off to either side. Mo realized they were backstage, in the service area behind the cages of the Reptile House. The left-side doors must give access to the cages. On the right were other rooms: storage closets, veterinary surgeries, additional containment rooms with wire cages. The reptile smell was overpowering, and Mo wanted to say to Annette, *What's a nice girl doing in a place like this?* But she just gossiped happily with Zelek. A fellow reptile enthusiast.

At the end of the hall, they went through another door and into the public section of the building. It was a carpeted lobby with branching hallways, dimly lit but with tasteful décor and good ventilation. In the huge solarium cage to their right, two massive, torpid crocodiles lay like fallen tree trunks in a shallow pool. Then they turned down a narrower corridor and the driver handed the box over to Annette, who disappeared into another service door. Zelek led them down a row of glass cubicles and finally paused in front of one large cage. The driver took up a position thirty feet farther down, looking suddenly very alert. On duty.

It took Mo a moment to see the snake. Brown and black, irregular diamonds mottled the big body and camouflaged it well against the artificial rocks and dead tree limbs. Then he spotted a second snake in the shadows under an overhang. This one was even larger, thicker in the body than Mo's thigh.

Zelek pointed them out. "*Python reticulatus*. The largest of the Serpentes. The big one is Samantha, perhaps the largest snake in captivity, twenty-seven feet long and two hundred sixty pounds. I have an affection for the family Boidae, the constrictors. They're expensive to keep up, and the Zoo receives a lot of financial support from our little society. Plus, Annette, bless her soul, is as enamored of the Boidae as I am. Which is why I'm allowed to help out with their feedings."

The snakes weren't moving. They could have been fake, made out of the same plaster as the rocks. *A quality of stillness only a cold-blooded animal can manage,* Mo thought.

"But I didn't answer your question," Zelek went on. He continued staring into the cage as if he couldn't take his eyes off the snakes. "What do we want you to do? Well, just what Erik told you. Help us with the forensic end of it, by all means continue your excellent work, but don't go chasing after big game. The proper authorities—that is myself, Erik, and our team—are fully informed. You and Dr. Ingalls can rest your consciences on that score."

From behind the cage came an echoing metallic *clank.* The big pythons didn't budge, but in the next cage to the right a smaller snake began to ooze slowly along a dead tree limb.

Zelek noticed, too, and said, "That's our friend *Python boeleni.* Also a fine specimen. He's smart—he knows it's his feeding time, too."

Another series of metallic sounds from backstage, and now there was activity in many of the cages, silent glidings and shiftings. Zelek acknowledged the huge mud-brown snake to their left: "But it's not anaconda's turn. That's next week."

"What about," Mo said, "when we come up with things that don't make sense? Or that we don't know whether you're onto them or not?"

"They don't feed very often," Zelek explained. He raised his chin to point out the hatch that had opened at the top of the python cage. A metal basket appeared in the opening, with a pair of plump white rabbits moving fitfully inside. "Only about once every two weeks. *Reticulata* have slow metabolisms, and though they do crush the skeletons fairly well before ingesting, they eat their prey whole. So they take a long time to digest their dinner." Zelek had been watching the rabbits descend with keen appreciation in his alien eyes. "To answer your question, all you have to do is come to Erik

255

with any inquiries or concerns. Not to anyone else, please, you'll only jeopardize our mission. But, again, that said, I hope you and Dr. Ingalls will leave the big picture to us. We're *very* familiar with it. We're almost done. *The last one, Detective!* Let it be."

Mo thought about it. "And if we don't?"

"They're always fed after hours," Zelek continued, "because the general public . . . well, it offends some people. Children in particular tend to get upset. Not good for the zoo's public relations or fund-raising for the Lepidosaura." Zelek laughed at his own understatement, a small, warm chuckle. "But it's just nature. It's the larger design of things, ancient, beautiful in its symmetry. It's just the food chain."

The rabbits got dumped as the cage neared the fake-rock floor of the cage, and they stood uncertainly near each other, sniffing and staring with round, pink eyes. Just pet store bunnies probably left over from the Easter sales season. They looked afraid to budge. Mo was thinking, *Their genes know the scent of the ancient enemy.*

And then first one and then the other python began to move, just a lateral tick of the big heads at first, and then the slowest of slow adjustments of head and body. And then the hypnotizingly slow pour of the checkered bodies along the contours of the rocks. Straightening out of her coils, the big one was unbelievably long. The rabbits began leaping against the side of the cage, against the glass, up the rocks, in and out of the pool, up the glass again. Scrabbling, falling, leaping again.

"My point," Zelek said, "is just that you have done fine work, the proper authorities are in charge. I know this whole affair is probably upsetting to you and Dr. Ingalls. But I hope that after our talk today, you can put your minds at ease." He watched the cage with satisfaction for another moment, then said, "Their slow movements are actually quite deceptive. When they need to be, they're lightning quick. Once they scent their prey, it's all over quite fast."

32

ON TUESDAY MORNING, Rebecca called to thank Mo for the evening of bowling and to say she'd been able to arrange access to Ronald Parker on Thursday at the psychiatric facility at Rikers Island. That was good, because the rest of the case appeared to be flatlining. He and St. Pierre hadn't come up with any useful leads on Irene Bushnell's possible lover and had started to look to the other murders for progress. But there wasn't any. Carolyn Rappaport had been killed by somebody who left no trace of himself other than his genetic material, useful for convicting but not for locating him. The O'Connor case had even less going for it.

After work, Mo thought about maybe going in to see Rebecca but then felt too out of control, too fucked-up. He was still processing the events of the last few days. Biedermann's revelation that he was the cleanup man, not the killer, had at first calmed his immediate fears. But then the session with Zelek, that was a real picnic. The alien hadn't uttered a single threatening word. But the image of the rabbits being crushed in the relentless coils, and then the endlessly stretching snake mouths—that was going to stay with him for a while. Mo didn't know which chilled him more, the idea that Zelek had deliberately scripted the scene or that the guy was truly oblivious to how grotesque it had been.

The visit to Mudda Raymon had stayed with him, too, disturbing him to the extent that he almost wanted to go back there and grill Carla about what she had told the old woman. Maybe even have another session with the mudda. But that was getting superstitious, losing his objectivity.

Bottom line, he didn't want Rebecca to see him like this, shaky and off-balance. Not until they knew each other better, not until whatever they were doing was stronger.

On the way home he stopped at a Burger King on the strip and sat in his hot car, stuffing down a Whopper as he watched the seagulls wheeling over the parking lots, flashing brilliant pink-orange in the light of the lowering sun. He stared suspiciously at the drivers of every car that came through the lot. Any one of them could be the killer, Mo might have seen him every day for years. That was the thing about serial killers, their ongoing secret presence among ordinary people. The masquerade. Ponder that one too much, it could bring you down.

Without thinking about what he was going to do, he got out and walked across the parking lot through the stink of the drive-in's Dumpsters. At a discount shoe store, he bought a pair of calf-length rubber boots, then got back to the car and drove seven miles to the swamp where Carolyn Rappaport had died.

It was just sunset by the time he'd parked and pulled on the boots, but he knew the sky would stay bright for a while. Enough light to navigate by. He headed down into the marshy streambed.

The extensive dimpling of the mud under the water told him that Biedermann had had crews out here since last week. He wondered if the SAC had done something high-tech, like flying over the scene with a helicopter and computer-controlled scanning cameras and who knew what else.

He knew there was nothing physical for him to find here now. He was really after the atmosphere, the sorrowful ghost of the place. The reverberations of the awful things that had happened here. When you had a lot perking just below your conscious thoughts, the ambience of the crime scene could guide the flow of your intuition. Hidden details and half-formed ideas sometimes came forward. He squelched upstream, into the thin forest of stunted sumacs, trying to visualize the place as it had been eleven nights ago.

The culvert loomed, a brighter mass that cast a solid shadow on the standing water. Black in the tunnel. Mo stared at it, trying to shed the echoes of Mudda Raymon's "vision" and focus instead on the hard realities. It wasn't easy. Between his father's lapsed Catholicism and his mother's equally lapsed Judaism, he'd been born into a family environment that was pretty neutral, metaphysically speaking. But like most kids, he'd experienced an almost religious fascination with the supernatural and paranormal. As an adult, he'd worked hard to banish his native superstitiousness but hadn't totally succeeded. Yes, he was susceptible to Mudda Raymon's bullshit. Yeah, the old woman had named a few existential bogeymen: *Now he fight himself, always fighting.* Maybe it was just that Carla had talked about his inner conflict, his self-negation and self-criticism, his ambivalence about his job, about the twentieth and twenty-first centuries, about life. But what about the *puppet* thing? How could old Grannie have picked such a relevant-seeming scary? Maybe Carla had told Mudda Raymon of her own vision of the puppetlike beings with lines of energy from their hands and feet. On the other hand, that left you to wonder how *Carla* had picked up on it.

Puppet-puppet watching you. Puppet-puppet gon' come after you. It gave him a chill. Jesus, he hated being scared of things. Every cell in his body rebelled against feeling fear. Fear mastered your mind, your blood, your heart, fear *controlled* you. He hated feeling controlled. Right now he felt controlled by Pinocchio. Strung on lines, manipulated. Another reason he was here: some ritual confrontation with that. A symbolic breaking loose. It was hard to always be struggling against an invisible, unknown enemy. Sometimes you needed the catharsis of physically fighting back. It occurred to him that cutting the strings was not only necessary to staying human, it was necessary to being an effective investigator. Being able to cut through red tape, shake loose of procedural constraints, come at your opponent from the unlikely angle. Something to remember.

Mo checked his Glock, took out his flashlight, and slogged deeper into the marsh. Up ahead, the setting sun cut the trees into two distinct parts, orange-bright on top and green-black below the shadow of the ridge. Dark foliage converged on the stream a half mile up, and he instinctively headed toward the embrace of shadow, willing all the bogeymen to come fight him.

Farther in, the water deepened as the marsh narrowed between wooded hills on either side. The roar of the interstate was more distant here, absorbed by the trees. *This is good*, Mo thought, *I needed this*. His head was emptied by sheer nervous alertness, any thoughts coming forward hung clear for him to inspect.

Carolyn's killer: He'd have to have parked his car along the road. But none of the nearby residents had reported seeing a car near the bridge. Didn't mean anything, maybe nobody happened to notice, maybe he'd pulled it into the bushes. Or maybe he'd walked or ridden a bike from someplace miles away. Or maybe he'd walked from nearby, maybe the police had unknowingly already interviewed the killer—one of the neighbors.

The sun now lit only the tops of the tallest trees. Here and there, far up the right slope, windows of houses came alight and pierced the darkness, but the marsh was a gloomy flat narrowing between masses of shadow. Still, he resisted turning on the flashlight. Best to save it for the real dark. Best to merge with the darkness, let it enter him, tell him its secrets. Let the animal panic of solitude and dark come up in him, give him some juice.

Mo trudged on, sometimes in the water and sometimes on the brushy banks. None of the State Police teams had come up this far, although Biedermann's people might have. It was almost night now, but he found he could make out the contours of the land. At one point a pale shape seemed to come forward out of the gloom and momentarily goosed his adrenaline, but when he got closer he could see it was just a washing machine, the old barrel-shaped kind with the ringer on top, rusted and half-buried in streambed silt.

By the house lights, he guessed he was approaching a residential area, and sure enough, he soon found himself only a hundred yards behind a large house, brightly lit with many windows. An outside spotlight was on at the other side, and he could hear the drub of a basketball. Farther on, the lights of another house were just visible through the trees.

Suddenly he felt like an outcast, a voyeur among these well-maintained residences, peering at these orderly lives from the disorder of his own. Probably time to turn back. No monsters had come out of the swamp to confront him except the usual inner demons of loneliness, self-criticism, sagging morale. Anyway, somebody might see him, get scared, call the police. Or shoot him: After Carolyn Rappaport's murder, people's nerves were probably on edge around here.

He turned and began to slog back. As his fear-fired nervous energy ebbed, he felt disappointment come on. Aside from the initial high drama of confronting his scaries, this had been useless. No great inspirations had come to him, just two nagging questions, both familiar. One was *Who was Ronald Parker?* Clearly that was a big one, and he'd barely avoided throwing it in Zelek's face during his pep talk. But maybe they could narrow it down when they saw him on Thursday. The other was *Who the hell would think of recording and broadcasting the screams of rabbits being slaughtered?* No doubt the session at the Reptile House had brought that to the fore again. There seemed to be a connection between those two questions.

Ten minutes later he emerged from the tree shadows and into the more open marsh, where the culvert materialized out of the darkness again. He stopped to look at it, remembering Carolyn Rappaport's body hanging from its wires. She'd spent her last hours as the puppet of a very sick being. *De puppet-puppet,* Mudda Raymon had said. Why'd she start saying it twice? Maybe some peculiarity of the Jamaican patois. *De puppet-puppet gon' come get you.*

And just like that the sense of it came to him, an answer to the questions. Holy Jesus. It would put a lot of things together seamlessly: Ronald Parker, screaming rabbits, Zelek and Biedermann, human cruise missiles. Suddenly a rage-filled optimism washed through him, the sense that he had put something important together. *Yes,* he thought, running the scenario through the details of the cases. *Yes, yeah. What a fucking nightmare. Oh, holy shit.* He had no idea what to do about it, but he exulted bitterly at seeing the pattern. Who should he talk to about it? Not Biedermann, definitely not yet, maybe not ever. Marsden? Maybe, have to give that some thought. St. Pierre, no, let him do the great work he was doing without biasing his judgment, keep him out of the line of fire. Rebecca, no—at least not until they'd had a chance to look at Ronald Parker.

He had just vaulted the railing at the end of the bridge when another insight hit him: Irene Bushnell had cleaned for the middle-aged banker couple on Monday mornings, leaving—they said—for another job at one o'clock. But the schedule Mrs Ferrara had provided showed Irene working only a half day on Mondays. Where had she been going for the rest of the day? How could he and St. Pierre have missed something so obvious? His instincts told him it was just the very end of a loose thread. Grab it and pull carefully, the whole thing could unravel.

33

THE INSIGHT ABOUT Irene Bushnell's schedule was the most tangible idea to follow up on, especially after Mo called Byron Bushnell and learned that, yes, Irene worked Monday afternoons, Byron didn't know where, and came home at around five-thirty. So on Wednesday Mo dispatched Mike St. Pierre to Ossining again to meet with Mrs. Ferrara and the Tomlinsons, try to pin down where Irene had been going after she left the Tomlinsons' house at one o'clock Mondays.

Mo felt a little better. When an investigation got down to questions this specific, even with a detail this small, it usually meant you were getting somewhere. And by Wednesday night, after hearing what Mike had discovered and having had another tough interview with Byron Bushnell, he was sure they were onto something useful.

He'd have liked to follow up on it first thing Thursday, but the day would be occupied with something else that couldn't wait: Ronald Parker and the larger issues he'd been advised to avoid, the hidden pattern he had glimpsed during his sunset pilgrimage to the marsh.

The chief of staff at the psychiatric detention facility at the County of New York prison complex at Rikers Island had agreed to give them access to Ronald Parker at one o'clock. Rebecca proposed that they drive over together, but Mo had to attend a BCI staff meeting on unrelated issues at eleven. They decided to rendezvous at the prison at twelve-thirty.

Mo caught sight of her from a distance as he came into the prison's main administrative lobby: a tall woman with a Hollywood figure that looked out of place in this institutional setting. She took a few steps, paused impatiently, turned, strode again, not seeing him yet. For the interview with Parker, she had dressed in a pinstripe business suit and high heels and had coiled her hair at the back of her head. But the severe outfit only seemed to enhance her femininity, Mo thought. *Can't hide the real thing.*

She didn't smile when she saw him, just searched his face with her eyes, and he realized how nervous he was about seeing her again. They'd talked on the phone twice since Sunday, and each time it had seemed a little stiff or awkward. Maybe it was some kind of fallout from his meeting Rachel, maybe he'd flunked some kind of test. Maybe seeing him with her daughter had shown Rebecca what lousy stepfather material he was. Strange, how four days apart could change things.

"So how you been?" he asked. They shook hands. Professional colleagues.

"Busy. Too much so. Yourself?"

"Same."

"How's Rachel?"

"Oh, fine, fine."

Awkward, uncomfortable, stilted, Mo thought.

They turned toward the admitting desk, signed in, received visitor's badges, and were escorted through a metal detector to a smaller entry room where guards patted them down. Then they waited as one of the guards paged Dr. Iberson, head of the psychiatric unit. The guards stood with hands folded, and nobody said anything. Rebecca opened her briefcase to review a file and check her microcassette recorder.

Mo sat uncomfortably, feeling the crushing claustrophobia of the prison complex around him. Not a happy place. People arrested in the County of New York were ostensibly held here pending trial, but everybody in law enforcement knew it was where you could send someone for a prison term without them ever getting a trial. Prosecutors convinced of someone's guilt but without enough evidence to convict just stalled, postponed trial dates, and finessed paperwork until the suspect had served a few years anyway. Then they'd release him due to lack of evidence. Due process in the new millennium.

Dr. Iberson turned out to be a very tall, thin man, the played-basketball-in-college type, with a pink scalp under thinning hair. He shook Mo's hand perfunctorily, but gushed over Rebecca, telling her he had followed her career with interest. Then he led them to an elevator.

The three of them stepped inside, Rebecca between the two men, and stood facing the doors as the car rose. As Dr. Iberson babbled psychology shoptalk, Mo felt his frustration rise. If he were alone in the elevator with Rebecca, he'd grab her and hold her against him and kiss her deeply, maybe she'd like that and maybe she wouldn't, but for better or worse they could sort it out from there. He knew where his own awkwardness was coming from. Some of it was the horror of the revelations he'd had in the swamp, the danger it posed. But more it was four days of thinking about her: She had percolated into him, everything felt very *important*. It was hard to know where to begin. He had no idea what she was feeling, but he knew four days could also let uncertainties and second thoughts creep up on you.

He startled as something touched his back. Rebecca was nodding interestedly at whatever Iberson was saying, but her hand had come up beneath Mo's jacket and shyly tugged at his shirt. She burrowed two fingers down just below his belt at the small of his back and just held the contact. *Hello, it's me.* A secret affirmation. Mo smiled as he felt heat spread from her touch.

"Ronald is in our equivalent of intensive care," Iberson told them as he led them through another sliding steel door. "You'll understand when you see him. His injuries are over four months old, but we're still observing his behavior to monitor his rehabilitation. Also to assess the degree of risk he poses to himself and others. The way the unit is configured, he's under observation by medical staff twenty-four hours a day."

"Are you seeing any adaptation?" Rebecca asked. For Mo's benefit, she explained, "The loss of brain function due to injury is often reversible. Sometimes the damaged area recovers partial function, and sometimes the brain appears to compensate by re-assigning damaged functions to other neural circuits."

Iberson nodded. "His motor skills are mostly back. Verbal skills, he carries on a private monologue all the time, but his responsiveness to others is intermittent—possibly because he gets temporal-lobe seizures. It's hard to assess, because when he does talk, he's usually pretty dissociative. One problem is that we don't know how much is the result of the brain damage he inflicted on himself and how much was preexisting." Iberson was having the time of his life, Mo thought: medical shoptalk with a gorgeous woman, the best of all possible worlds.

They came to another steel door operated by a guard in a glass cubicle. He frowned as he double-checked Mo's identification. Then the door slid open to reveal a big, brightly lit room where a nurse sat at a central desk, doing paperwork. Two walls of the room were made of clear Lexan and heavy wire mesh, beyond which were the individual cells, apparently furnished in standard hospital-room décor.

"Well!" Iberson said brightly, rubbing his hands briskly together. "Here we go."

But Rebecca put her hand on his arm. "Dr. Iberson, we may need to request specific medical examinations or tests of Mr. Parker after our interview. Would that be possible?"

Iberson beamed. "We've done a pretty thorough workover, and you're welcome to see his files, but sure. What're you looking for?"

"We would also like to interview him in his own quarters. We believe he'll be more at ease, more communicative, and we may be able to learn things from his environment—"

"Like the arranging? I assumed you would. Ronald is the only resident of the unit just now, so you won't be disturbing other patients—"

"And we'd like to interview him alone. Just Detective Ford and myself, no staff present."

Iberson's smile faded.

Rebecca patted his arm. "It's just that the smallest number of interviewers offers the least disturbance to the subject." She dropped her voice confidingly. "And there are also issues of confidentiality regarding an ongoing investigation that's very sensitive. I'm sure you can appreciate that."

Iberson frowned in confusion, liking her touch but resenting being excluded. He nodded, led them into the room, pointed out Ronald Parker's cell, showed them how to use the intercom if they needed assistance.

When he and the nurse were gone, Mo said, "I think you may have just lost a fan."

Rebecca just squared her shoulders and gave him a look. Then they carried folding chairs to the door of Parker's cell.

Mo's first impression of a typical hospital room proved to be wrong. Yes, there was the standard adjustable bed, a bank of monitoring equipment, oxygen fixtures, a television mounted on a bracket high on the wall. But the equipment was built in and covered with Lexan, the TV protected by a Lexan box. The bedding was paper of a texture like quilted paper towels, suicide-proof. No windows. There were no drawers for personal effects beneath the enameled counter.

Ronald Parker sat on the edge of the bed, dressed in loose paper pants and shirt with paper slippers on his feet. Mo guessed he was a little over six feet, broad-shouldered, his dark blond hair short on the sides but long enough in front to fall almost to his eyes. He was leafing through a magazine, his lips mouthing words, head bobbing, body swaying as if he were singing and moving to music.

When they came close to his cage, he looked up and went still. Round gray eyes. He had a pleasant, almost boyish face, full lips and cheeks. At first glance Mo couldn't imagine him as a guy who had tortured and killed seven people. But looking closer, you could see something haywire. A look of confusion and desperation on his creased, lopsided brow.

"Hello, Ronald," Rebecca said. "I'm Rebecca, and this is my friend Morgan. Do you mind if we talk to you?"

For a moment Parker just looked at them. Then his head bobbed, left and right, up and down, could mean anything, but Rebecca took it as an assent. She moved her chair close to the wire mesh and sat down. Mo sat off to the side.

"Thanks." Rebecca looked around approvingly. "This is a nice room, isn't it? They're very nice here, aren't they?"

Parker bobbed and nodded, yes or no or maybe.

"Do you remember seeing me before?" Rebecca asked pleasantly. For the hundredth time, Mo was impressed by her: Her voice was warm with real compassion, but everything about her approach was strategic. She had put her recorder in her jacket's side pocket and started it before they'd come to Parker's cage. He could see where her background in child psychology would come in handy in a case like this.

Parker's shoulders shrugged, but then they started moving up and down and around, again as if he were moving to music or working out a muscle kink. He did look intrigued by Rebecca, though, his eyes riveted to her.

"Morgan and I drove up to see if you're happy here. Dr. Iberson says you hurt yourself, and we wanted to make sure you're all right."

"Hurt everything," Parker said. His voice startled Mo, a smooth, bank teller's conversational voice at odds with his crazed-looking, uneven brow. "You got that right. *Everything.*"

"I do know what you mean," Rebecca said wryly. *Ain't that the truth!* Mo knew she was pleased to get a response out of him. They'd gotten lucky, caught him in a receptive moment. Or maybe it was just Rebecca's presence, her skill. Parker's willy-nilly forehead creased in appreciation of her understanding.

They went on like that for fifteen minutes: the weird, weighted pleasantries, Rebecca's oblique probes, Parker's cryptic responses. Sometimes the murderer would clam up, frown, pull away. Sometimes he'd ramble incoherently. Throughout, Rebecca stayed warm, focused, easy, compassionate. She never pushed too hard, just stuck to the friendly, unassuming tone. Never probed too persistently, never oversteered. Never tried to *control* Parker. Mo just observed, did his best to disappear.

The only movable objects in Parker's room were a collection of magazines, some toilet articles, and the TV remote, which were arranged along the edge of the stainless steel countertop: magazine, hairbrush, magazine, hand lotion, magazine, toothpaste, magazine, tissue box, magazine, remote. At one point, Rebecca pointed to the pattern and said, "That's pretty. That makes it better, doesn't it?"

"Then it doesn't hurt," Parker said. "You have to get it right. It's important."

Rebecca nodded. "When I was a kid, my mother used to make me straighten up the top of my dresser? I had all these plastic horses and I'd dump them there when I was done playing with them, in a great big tangle. I was supposed to have them in a row. She'd get so mad at me! I wouldn't get dessert if I didn't do it, and one time she called my father and he had to swat my bottom!" She chuckled ruefully at the memory. "What did they do to you if you didn't?"

Parker had listened with growing intensity, and now his whole body was dancing to the nonexistent music again. He frowned and looked away. After a moment he stood up and began working at the counter, rearranging things.

"I bet you had to get the strings on your wrists," Rebecca said quietly.

Parker moved his hands hurriedly among the objects. Strong hands, Mo saw. He could see the faint discoloration of scarring on the wrists just below the cuffs.

"I would hate that," Rebecca prompted. "That would make me very angry."

Parker was rocking his whole body as he moved the objects into configuration after configuration. "Anger is an appropriate and necessary response," he said unexpectedly. "Provided you focus it. Your anger is a great source of energy. It's a source of power."

Rebecca took the change of tone in stride. "Did you get angry when they did it to you?"

"You answer their control first by asserting self-control and second by controlling them in return. You demonstrate your resistance in such a way so that no one will mistake the message."

Parker's language had changed, Mo realized. His tone was firm, his grammar precise. It seemed not so much a spontaneous response as a lecture he had memorized.

Rebecca had heard it, too, of course she had. She put one hand up onto the mesh that separated them, a reassuring gesture. "I'll bet it was your dad told you that! You know how I know? Because that's just how my dad talked."

You didn't have to be a Ph.D. in psychology to see she had socked an arrow close to the bull's-eye. Parker gave her a different sort of look, a dangerous look. Yes, Mo thought, there was definitely a killer in there. For a moment the fluorescents buzzed in the silence of the room as Parker bobbed and shifted and glowered uncertainly at her.

At last he lectured her sternly, "And you never, never talk about your daddy."

Rebecca was right there with a reply: "Your daddy's name was Albert Parker, right?"

Suddenly Parker was at the cell door, his big fingers clenched through the mesh and gripping Rebecca's hand. Mo moved to free her, but Rebecca shook her head, *no*.

Parker's forehead pushed against the wire. He held Rebecca's fingers pinned, her skin turning white with the pressure as he continued to bore his gaze down at her. "Exactly right. Very good. My daddy was named Albert Parker," Parker echoed in his lecturing tone. His jaw muscles clenched.

The pressure on her hand had to hurt, but Rebecca didn't show any response. "Did you love him?"

"He did cruel things to me when I was a child, and he died of cancer in 1988 when I was twenty."

"Cruel things like the strings on your wrists?"

Parker yanked at the mesh so hard the whole door flexed and rattled in its frame, and his fingers dragged red lines across the back of Rebecca's hand. "I *said,* you never, *never,* talk about your *daddy!*" His eyes bulged out, as much with fear as with anger.

Rebecca took back her injured hand and said soothingly, "Okay—"

But Parker shouted her down. He was shaking the mesh in explosive convulsions, staring at her with red-rimmed eyes. "You're not getting this, are you! You don't know what the fuck you're dealing with, do you? You don't know how bad this is! I mean, we are talking about some very, very scary *shit* here, and you're sitting there like it's all *normal,* like you have the *faintest idea* of what the *fuck* you are talking about—!"

Mo stood up and moved protectively toward Rebecca, but without looking toward him she gave him a tiny hand signal, *wait*.

"Ronald, I'd like to understand, honestly I would. Can you tell me?"

But Parker was just shaking the door, teeth bared, eyes bulging as he pressed his face into the wire, really gone now. His fingers looked as if they'd tear off, bloodying the wire around the bent knuckles. Even Rebecca stood up and stepped away.

And then with one last titanic convulsion it was over. Parker returned to the bed and sat, partially turned away, arms crossed over his heaving chest. Tears streaked his cheeks as he swayed and mouthed words and his feet made papery noises in their hospital slippers. For a few more minutes, Rebecca tried valiantly to soothe him, resume their friendly chat. But she was like a fisherman who'd had a big fish strike and slip the hook, casting and casting and pulling in nothing. She had lost him.

When Dr. Iberson came in, they stood at the unit's exit door for a moment, looking across the room at Parker bobbing and swaying in his cell.

"Ronald does this," Iberson said, "just shuts down if he feels we're too intrusive." He had been hurt by his exclusion from the interview, and now he glanced at Rebecca's scratched hand with what looked like satisfaction. "He's resistant to lines of discussion that strike him as manipulative or controlling."

"Understandably," Rebecca said. She winced as she used a tissue to blot blood from the scrapes on her hand.

The guard opened the door. Out in the hall, Iberson asked, "Do you still want to run any new diagnostics? We've done everything. You're probably interested in his CT scans, and you're welcome to look them over. But they won't tell you much except that he's got some damage in a dozen loci in each hemisphere. He's lucky he retained as much function as he did."

"Thanks—it would be terrific to have copies." Rebecca gave Iberson a weary smile and put her hand on his arm. He brightened. But when they turned to walk down the hall, her mouth became a thin line. Blaming herself, Mo realized. Another way she was like him: a person who raked herself over the coals for her failures.

Iberson was feeling better, eager to help her again. "And I suppose you'll want the tapes, too?"

"Tapes?"

"Observation tapes. He's fully monitored, audio and video. Suicide watch. It's set up like a bank security system, the tapes run for forty-eight hours and then record over themselves. Sometimes you can learn a lot from these stream-of-consciousness ramblings. I have to say, so far there's nothing informative, it's mostly dissociated gibberish. But you're welcome to copies of the current tapes. Or you could get copies of earlier tape cycles from the FBI. The SAC, Biedermann, he asks for copies pretty often."

Rebecca seemed to find some energy. "Yes," she said, "thank you. Copies of the current tapes would be very helpful." And she gave Mo a glance that said maybe this hadn't been a total loss after all.

34

M O GOT TO REBECCA'S apartment at eight o'clock, wired with a nervous buzz. He had to tell her what he'd figured out, and it wouldn't be fun for either of them.

They had arranged the rendezvous in the stupefying heat of the Rikers prison parking lot before getting into their separate cars. Mo had driven back to the White Plains barracks for a quick conference with St. Pierre. When he was done there, he headed back down to Manhattan. A lot of driving.

Rebecca let him in and double-locked the door. She had changed into tan slacks and shirt, white socks, and had let her hair down. She led him into the living room and sat down on the couch. She didn't offer him a drink, and he didn't want one. There was work to be done.

"Mo, this is getting scary for me. I think I know who Ronald Parker is."

"Did you review the tapes Iberson gave you?"

"Some of them. It's time-consuming, you have to do a lot of fast cuing through quiet periods. I think you should listen to them, too. Maybe you'll find details I didn't, something relevant to the forensic side. But I . . . it almost doesn't matter. I think I know what's going on."

They were sitting apart on the couch. Rebecca looked more worried than he had ever seen her, and he couldn't help reaching over and rubbing the knot between her brows, trying to smooth away the anxiety there.

"I was thinking the same thing," he told her. "It'll be interesting to see if we came up with the same answer."

She leaned into his kneading fingers, eyes shut. "You go first."

He had to think about how to say it. The place where Ronald Parker, screaming rabbits, and *puppet-puppet* converged.

"We're not dealing with Pinocchio here," he said finally. "We're dealing with Geppetto."

She opened her eyes and blew out her cheeks. "Someone who *makes* puppets."

"Yeah. This isn't a surviving guinea pig from the Vietnam experiments. This is one of the, what would they be, the doctors or psychologists. The puppet-makers, the puppet-masters—the guys who *created* the killers. He's made several of them. Ronald Parker is just one. There was another, before him, the kills in San Diego. Our copycat killer is a third. Could be five more, lined up and ready to go."

She leaned away to look at him. "You're pretty smart. I'd like to know how you got there without a background in psychology."

"A gut thing. I was obsessing about the ATF broadcasting the screams of rabbits being slaughtered at the Branch Davidians, and I thought, 'You gotta be a sick fuck to even think of that.' And I realized that the guys who were manufacturing these human cruise missiles back then had to be sick fucks. I don't know anything about the terminology here, but they'd have to be screwed up to accept a job like that in the first place. And they'd have to get even more screwed up by spending years twisting people's brains around. It makes sense that some of *them* would have reintegration problems when they came home, too. So that's what we've got here—a puppet-maker. Somebody who manufactures killers."

The idea chilled the room, and they both pulled off into separate places to think about it. Mo had witnessed the terrible swath of suffering cut by even a single, isolated serial killer—not just murdering his victims but wounding the scores of relatives and loved ones who had to live with the loss and the dire knowledge of what had happened. But a *manufacturer* of killers, producing at will that twisted psychopathology, that carnage, again and again—it was almost unthinkably horrible.

Rebecca shivered as if she'd thought the same thing. Her face was expressionless, eyes far away. Wheels turning. After a long time she asked, "When did you figure it out?"

"Tuesday night. But seeing Parker today made me sure. When he was telling us about anger, he was quoting it more than saying it, like a lesson he had learned."

Rebecca nodded. "There's more of that in the tapes. You see this kind of thing often with schizophrenia, when there's been so much delamination of the personality that the patient experiences his own thoughts as messages or instructions from some other source. But Parker is different. These phrases sound like real artifacts from a social transaction, a relationship. The other thing is his scans. There's a lot of damage, it's hard to isolate. But there are suspiciously symmetrical lesions, tiny, on his temporal lobes, a lot like the killer in Oregon. Ronald Parker has been . . . neurosurgically altered and deeply conditioned. Programmed."

Mo got sick of sitting in the dark and reached over to switch on a lamp. *Banish the shadows,* he thought.

"You put it together before we saw Parker, too, didn't you? The way you were zeroing in on the 'daddy' thing."

She didn't answer directly. "Mo, did you ever have a dog?"

"No. Apartment dweller when I was a kid. Why?"

"Because if you ever take a dog to obedience school, the first thing you notice is that it's the human who's training who's learning, just as much as the dog. Obedience school conditions the actions of the masters as much as the dogs. The same is true of parenting psychology—to shape child behavior, the parent does an enormous amount of adapting, learning effective guiding behaviors, cultivating his or her own responses until they become a permanent program. The killers in the experiments had to have been extensively conditioned over a long period of time—and you're absolutely right, their programmers couldn't do that without being affected themselves."

"Sounds right."

"Also, there was another problem for me, aside from Ronald Parker's being too young to have been in Vietnam. For me, the killer's profile always seemed paradoxical. Obsessive, very rigid killing ritual, apparently anchored in past trauma and driven by deep emotions. Right? But I always felt it was too easy for us to pull Ronald Parker in—to get him to target *me*. I would never have thought the Howdy Doody killer was so susceptible to a proactive trap. But Erik insisted he would be, and he was right! Because behind Parker was a deliberate mind, a very intentional personality with a reasoned motive. With an *agenda* that he needed to protect. *That's* who was threatened by me. Ronald Parker and this new one, they're just as much puppets as their victims!"

"Meaning that this Geppetto, this master puppet-maker, programmed Parker to go after you. Retargeted him." And the insider scenario was just Biedermann's contrivance, a way to explain the similarity of the MOs and an excuse to clamp down hard on information. Thinking about it, Mo suddenly remembered Carla's "vision": the dark place with the puppets behind puppets behind puppets. Carolyn Rappaport, Daniel O'Connor, Irene Bushnell: turned into puppets by conditioned killers who were themselves puppets of the master puppeteer.

"But it's not Erik Biedermann," he said.

She looked surprised, and he realized he had a lot more to tell her. So he described Biedermann's late-night visit and his conversation with Zelek at the Zoo.

"And you believe them?" Her eyes had reddened and tears rimmed her lower lid, but now she wiped them away and looked a little stronger.

"Yeah. Biedermann could have killed me, and he chose not to. I think they told me the truth—just not the whole truth."

"Which is that he and Zelek, they're trying to 'clean up' a . . . a Geppetto."

Seeing her rallying, Mo ached to hold her. But he had determined he'd let her lead. And hugs and smooches weren't quite appropriate under the circumstances. Instead he got up and went to the windows. He stared out at the street, drumming his fingers on the sill. The sun was down, the glowing sky casting the shadows across the street, obscuring the pedestrians and car traffic below. Everybody had a furtive, scuttling look from this angle. For all he knew, one of them was the puppeteer, watching the building right now.

"You said the puppet-maker has an agenda," Mo asked her reflection in the glass. "What's the agenda?"

"Don't know. Yet. I'm working on it."

Mo lingered at the window. He was counting the ways they were in danger. Geppetto already knew Rebecca was involved in the case, knew where she lived. He had at least one programmable killer, the one they were calling Pinocchio, out there already. Probably had more than one.

His first thought was that they should tell Biedermann that they knew. But that brought up the other issue. Zelek had called it right, he'd never dealt with anything this serious, this big. Nothing even close. And he had no idea how to fix it, whom to tell or not tell, how to avoid the danger that seemed to be closing in.

Mo switched on some more lights. Rebecca made some coffee, and they each drank a cup as they worked over the problem for another hour.

Yes, Ronald Parker's wrist and ankle scars were the result of past trauma, and, yes, he inflicted that same trauma on his victims. But it wasn't a childhood trauma. It was from his conditioning period, the twenty months between his disappearing from his bank job and his resurfacing as the Howdy Doody killer.

"That's good to note," Rebecca said. "Because it gives us an idea how long the conditioning process takes. Means we can work backwards from the date of this new one's first kill, let's assume for now it's the power station murder, and get a rough idea when he was acquired by Geppetto. Look for someone who went missing about two years before Irene Bushnell's death." She got out her year planner, then rummaged in her briefcase for a legal pad.

Mo just looked at her. She had come back quickly from the dazed and frightened phase. With a little shock, he recognized her state of mind: She had the bloodhound instincts. Part of her roused quickly to the challenge of the hunt.

"Jesus," he said. "You're a lot like a . . . a cop."

"How's that?" She looked up from the pad where she'd begun graphing out a calendar of the puppet-maker's activities.

He gestured at the page. "What you're doing now. You're getting off on the thrill of the chase. This's what . . . what *I* do."

"Should I assume that's a compliment?" She flashed him a sardonic grin. A shrink's comment on his mixed feelings about himself and his job.

They kept at it, turning it over, trying on scenarios. A couple of issues kept coming around.

"Okay," Mo said. "The thing of the repetitive MO. Why do these guys, the killers, do it the same way every time?"

Rebecca bit her upper lip, gave it a moment's thought. "One reason might be that they're recapitulating the trauma of the conditioning process—they're doing to their victims what the puppet-maker did to them. But I don't think that's enough to explain it. I can only assume the MO is part of the programming they've received. They not only experienced that same trauma, they were instructed, *programmed,* to reenact it just so."

"Why?"

She frowned again. "That brings us back to the puppet-maker's agenda."

Which they could only guess at.

By ten o'clock they'd been talking for two hours and had begun going in circles. Soon they'd have to quit, Mo thought, save it for when they were fresh. But there were still a couple of things to discuss.

The first was easy. "I wanted to tell you about the progress we've made on the forensic side," he told her.

"It would be nice to think there was progress somewhere," she acknowledged bleakly.

He caught her up on the day's developments. St. Pierre had gone back to Ossining to interview Irene Bushnell's employer and the Tomlinsons. The Tomlinsons had no idea where she'd gone after she cleaned for them on Monday mornings. Neither did Mrs. Ferrara. But when Mike was leaving Mrs. Ferrara's house, a couple of women had pulled into the drive, other employees of The Gleam Team. He had talked to them for a few minutes, and they'd started giving each other awkward glances. So at last he'd confronted them on it, and they'd reluctantly told him that some of them took clients on the side. A Gleam Team customer who liked your work might say, *You know, my sister needs help with her house, too, perhaps you should give her a call.* They weren't supposed to, all referrals were supposed to go through Mrs. Ferrara. But it was a way to make more money, not have to give a cut to Mrs. Ferrara or Uncle Sam. Neither of them had ever done it, God no, but they'd heard other girls talking about it. Yes, Irene had mentioned a client she had on Monday afternoons. No, they didn't have any idea who or where.

St. Pierre said he believed them. They were frightened enough by that time not to hold anything back: afraid they'd get arrested, afraid they'd get in trouble with Mrs. Ferrara. Afraid one of the local cleaning customers was a killer. Mike had the women's names for further questioning, but he was pretty sure they were mined out.

So Mo had driven to Ossining himself and used the new information when he talked to Byron Bushnell. As before, Byron was half-drunk, miserable, hostile, blaming the world. He insisted he didn't know anything about Irene's activities on Monday afternoons. He didn't know of any outside clients. It was hard to read his red eyes, but Mo thought he saw a lie percolating on that one. So he dropped the bomb: *Mr. Bushnell—to your knowledge, was your wife having an extramarital relationship? An affair?* Bushnell had hit the roof, told him to get the fuck out, fucking insinuating this shit. It almost got physical. But before the explosion, Mo was sure he'd seen a circuit close, a connection getting made for the first time.

Mo finished, "I'm sure Bushnell does know something about an affair, that he had just then put together who his dead wife's lover was. I think he realized it's the mysterious Monday-afternoon client. I tried to push him, but he wouldn't give me any more. I'm not sure how to follow up, but it's definitely something we'll work on."

Rebecca gave an appreciative whistle. "I don't think most people realize how much practical psychology goes into police work."

Mo shrugged. "There's something else we should talk about."

"Which is—?"

"That the puppet-maker and his puppets are only one danger to us. Maybe they're not even the worst."

"What are you talking about?"

"Biedermann. Zelek. No, listen to me, Rebecca. Yeah, they want to protect the public, but more important, they want to keep a lid on the whole problem. We've stumbled onto it, I think Biedermann was serious when he said he'd kill me if that's what it took to keep me quiet. Probably he has license to do so, some national security authorization. Ordinarily I'd say, yeah, he's the guy we go to with this. But I'm thinking, what if Biedermann or Zelek get too worried about us, start feeling too exposed—"

"Oh, come on! You're being paranoid. They'd never . . . do

that!" But she didn't look like she believed herself. He just looked at her, let her think it out. Suddenly she was afraid again, he saw.

She gave it another moment, looking down at her hands, putting her chin in one palm, moving around with a fatigued restlessness. The city outside the windows was dark, and the contrast with the brightness in here gave Mo the sense of being on a island. No, more a sense of defensive enclosure. A sense of siege.

Rebecca fidgeted around a little more, then looked at him seriously. "Funny how the thrill of the chase kind of cools when you're the one being chased, huh?"

35

AN HOUR LATER, Mo reluctantly got up to leave. They kissed each other good-bye. Their first kiss, a solid one. Rebecca was the right height to fit perfectly into his arms, her mouth was sweet, her body an electric contact he felt all the way to his heels. Stunned, he made a brainless, blundering exit, into the sterility of the hallway. The elevator door had just slid open in the lobby when he realized, *Not a chance. Forget about it.* This wasn't working, he couldn't be away from her tonight. He couldn't let her be alone tonight.

When he knocked softly on her door, it opened immediately as if she'd been leaning against it since he'd left. She pulled him inside and the moment the door closed she came against him. Neither said anything until she broke away and started to lead him back into the living room.

"You sure you like police guys?" he asked quietly.

"Are you kidding?" she whispered. "I'm *wild* about police guys." Then she frowned a little. "Some of them, anyway." Then she smiled. "Well. This one, anyway."

When they came into living room, she turned to him again, very serious now, intimacy was serious stuff and he liked that she took it that way. He stood at arm's length from her and touched her face with his fingers, he'd been wanting to touch her face, strong-boned, honest face, good nose with character, red lips accustomed to smiling, the small sorrow in the brow above the watchful eyes now so serious.

And she just stood in the charged half-lit air of her home, letting him do that, letting that be the starting place.

After a while his hand followed a strand of her yellow hair down and accidentally grazed her breast, and the gentle return pressure electrified him. She saw his breathing change, her sober eyes seeing him so clearly, and without saying anything she put an arm around his waist and steered him back into her dark bedroom. She lit a candle. She shivered as she undressed, not from cold. She turned to smile shyly, letting him see all of her, *This is me. This is who I am.* Everything about her was sweet, solid: good rhythms to her limbs and the curves of her strong thighs and the rounded fall of her breasts, and when he drew her close, she smelled like a summer field.

A long time, shy at first and later completely unabashed. At the end she finished just before he did, with a broad smile and a wave that ran up her body until she bent in an endless backward arch. The only words she said were a moment later when she felt him going over the edge, she whispered, "There," speaking of his pleasure, approving and encouraging, "there. Please, yes," welcoming him. And some half-dreaming time later, Mo lay still braided together with her, and the only thing he could consciously think was Mark Twain's story about Adam and Eve, how when Eve died, Adam wrote on her tombstone, *Wheresoever she was,* there *was Eden.* Because this had to be as close to heaven as you could get down here.

Later still, he lay on her bed, half-drowsing and watching her. She had pulled on a T-shirt and some pajama bottoms and was tidying up her bedroom. Just putting things where they were supposed to go, getting clothes ready for tomorrow. He liked watching her. When she was finally done, she dropped her pants again, and when they were around one ankle, she flipped them up with her foot and caught them without bending. Funny. A nice way of moving, graceful and unselfconscious.

This was not how he'd have wanted to begin with her. The

pressure, the fear, the sense of foreboding. He'd rather have met her in a night class, say, had talks with her at the cafeteria, then surprised her with flowers. He'd have time to say the chivalrous things that came to him whenever he looked at her—you walked around with all this heraldry in you, the great longings searching for the right recipient, demanding expression. They'd go dancing at that Puerto Rican place in the Village, what was it called, she'd look great dancing to salsa and she certainly had the spice in her. They'd walk around in SoHo, he'd impress her by talking knowledgeably about architecture. They'd watch movies together and hold hands in the dark. They'd make love without scary shit buzzing around in their heads. They'd talk about serious things they wanted. *All my life. This feeling. I always hoped. What really matters.*

Now Rebecca was in the bathroom, humming a melancholy tune to herself. Her bedroom was pretty. She had more pictures of Rachel in here and some kid and teenage stuff that must be for when Rachel spent the night. On the bureau, Rebecca had set aside a couple of CDs Rache had forgotten on Sunday, she needed them for some-thing tomorrow, *Remind me to take them with me in the morning, Mo.* He liked that she included him in that. As if they'd been together for a longer time. There was something *valiant* about her, he decided, this woman who had done everything wrong for her first twenty years or so and who had shown so much steel when she decided to pull herself together. Single, professional, but not a climber. Dead honest about herself. Completely committed to her daughter. For all her poise and expertise, she was definitely a mother, the way she handled Rachel. There was definitely a family feel to her apartment. To her. That was nice, the family thing.

Jesus, Mo thought, *what's happening to me?*

He lay back on her pillow, still looking over the room, sorting it out. Her pillows smelled good. Family—yeah, it was something to do with that. Rachel's eyes gazed at him, here a seven-year-old, there a ten- or twelve-year-old. Fifteen-year-olds were a pain in the ass, she'd been pretty tough on Sunday. But he'd like to try again, it would be nice if they hit it off. Maybe the kid would like seeing her mother with a guy like him.

What kind of guy was that? Like she said, a guy who chases killers, who has to look at scary, ugly things? A guy who walks around pissed off half the time, who hates his job and lives in the back three rooms of somebody else's house?

No, not that guy. Which guy then?

The guy who really loves your mother, he silently told Rachel's photo. *That's worth something, isn't it?*

That thought sort of shocked him and he just coasted with it, felt around the edges of it, for a long time.

He woke up as the bed sagged. She was kneeling and pulling at the bedclothes. "Come on, sleepyhead," she said. "You've got to get under the covers. I can't get in when you're lying on them. Come on, Mo."

He grunted and sat up blearily. The bedside light was dimmed down. Rebecca had scrubbed her face and her skin shone. She was wearing just the T-shirt, and her bare legs were beautiful as she knelt facing him. She pushed at him until he got off the bed. When she'd pulled back the spread, he fell into the sheets again and let gravity pull him into the mattress.

She cut the light and they lay there in the darkness.

"This is nice," she said after a while.

Mo rolled to face her and laid his arm along her side, the warm, breathing curve of her ribs. He couldn't see her face in the dark, but he knew she was there, just inches away, because he felt the gentle puff of her exhalations against his cheeks. Her breath smelled like toothpaste.

Yes, this was very nice. To have someone to hold on to, some animal company in the dark. To just hold your partner, make sure she's all right, everything's all right. He hoped that by starting off on this weird foot, their time together spent working on such horrible things, they weren't ruining it for later. Setting themselves up for problems. That would be tragic.

"We'll work it out," she said softly. "Don't worry." Sometimes it was like she was reading his mind.

36

M R. SMITH WAS WORKING out on the rowing machine in a gym he favored, a blue-collar dive on the third floor of a run-down building. It was handy to have a place in town to work up a sweat, especially one where no one from the office was likely to show up. Today he was driving himself hard, yanking the cable so that the wheel screamed. Already his sweatshirt was soaked, and a couple of guys on the stationary bikes were eyeing him with curiosity or maybe envy. It was always good to stay in top shape, but more importantly he found he did his best thinking when his heart was maxing out at around 180. All that oxygen flooding his system.

One of the most revered strategies in warfare was to pit your adversaries against each other. There was a tidy elegance to the equation, Mr. Smith felt, but in this case it was probably simply a necessity. Number Four was making great progress but was by no means ready. That left only Number Three to operate as a remote agent to neutralize Mo Ford and Rebecca Ingalls. And if it backfired, if they managed to kill Three instead, that was all right, too. There were only two options for Three: significant conditioning reinforcement, or simple elimination. Or both. The worst-case scenario would be that Three would both fail in his mission and get caught alive, offering clever psychologists or detectives clues to his recent past.

So: If he retasked Three, he'd want to make sure that no one walked away from the encounter alive.

Not that it was always advisable to kill your opponents. Quite the contrary, it was always better to use them if possible. In counter-intelligence work it was sometimes useful to tolerate an enemy mole in your midst, feeding him misinformation and observing him to learn about your enemy's intentions. In this situation, too, you could learn a lot from enemies and lever them in creative ways. That had been the original intent with Rebecca Ingalls, when she first began to deduce what Ronald Parker really was: Listen to her, use her as an ear to anticipate developments.

When he'd retasked Ronald Parker, Number Two, to go to her apartment, it was not with the intent to kill her. No, the goal had been simply to install the listening devices. And fortunately, he had indeed done so before getting his wires crossed, starting the ritual with his hostess, and getting his dumb ass caught.

Not to malign poor Ronald. He had done well—a lot better than Number Three, who was a genuine disaster, both scientifically and logistically. Mr. Smith had thought about that a lot, the mistakes he'd made with Number Three. It was important to learn from your mistakes. The silver lining here was that as a result of errors made with Three, Number Four would be the best of the lot. When he was ready.

Boom, screee, whingggg. The rowing machine was practically shaking loose from the floor.

Mr. Smith thanked God he'd trained himself broadly in various technologies, something the overspecialized lemmings of the younger generation had forgotten the importance of. He'd built the surveillance devices himself. The bugs were nothing special, but the relay was quite clever, a solar-rechargeable sender in a box about the size of a pack of cigarettes. Ronald had attached the relay to the building wall just outside one of her windows and had placed three bugs before losing his mission-specific programming. The bugs in her outlets sent a weak signal to the relay, which amplified it and sent it onward to the receiver in Mr. Smith's Manhattan apartment, only a few blocks south of hers. The tape recorder there was signal-activated, turning itself on only when the relay picked up sound from the apartment. It had recorded her conversations for him to listen to after work or when he came back from Westchester.

After Ronald Parker was apprehended, there hadn't been much to review for four months. With the killer caught, the investigation closing down, her personal relationship inside the investigation ended, she'd distanced herself from the case, didn't talk much about it at home. Mainly when he checked the tapes, he'd hear her phone calls and weekend interactions with her daughter, which did little more than make him angry and miserable, remind him of everything that was denied him. But with Three coming online, the probability that Rebecca would be part of a new task force, he'd known the surveillance setup would come in handy again.

And so it had. That she was now screwing the lead investigator from the State Police was a blessing, overhearing their conversations was invaluable. Priceless. Especially given the progress they'd made.

Geppetto, that was cute. *Hey, kids, trust me, this ain't a cartoon. This ain't a fairy tale.*

The two of them made a rather formidable team, the way they brought together very different talents and experience. Their thoughts seemed to sync. But the worst aspect of their collaboration was that they were both independent thinkers and independent actors. They were both moved by their beliefs and values, not easily deflected. In a way, it would be a shame to kill them.

Mr. Smith realized he'd picked up the tempo of his rowing, and now he deliberately checked himself. His shirt was soaked, the grip was getting slippery. The interest of the other people was more noticeable now as they watched this mature gentleman really killing the ergometer. Better to fade back into the woodwork. He slowed to a warm-down tempo and watched their eyes drift back to the overhead televisions. After another three minutes he called it quits. Best to save some energy for tonight's operation anyway.

★   ★   ★

It was nine-thirty, full dark out, but Number Three wasn't home. Typical. Three had inherited the house along with enough money never to have to work a day in his life, so he didn't have a job schedule that would allow Mr. Smith to reliably intercept him. On the bright side, though, the neighborhood adjoining the Sleepy Hollow Country Club was heavily wooded, the house surrounded by high hedges. Away from prying eyes. Mr. Smith cruised past the house to verify that all the lights were out, then turned back and pulled into the driveway. He cut the headlights and drove in the dark over the lawn to the back of the two-car garage. Neighbors couldn't see the car there, and Three wouldn't see it when he came in. You'd be able to see it from the rear-facing house windows, but Three would never have that chance.

The next step was breaking into the garage. Fortunately, the houses here had been constructed before the era when high-tech security systems were routinely built in. And Number Three, ne'er-do-well, fast-and-loose playboy, styled himself as too tough and negligent to worry about security. The back door of the garage opened easily with a locksmith's pick, and Mr. Smith slipped into the pitch-black interior. He used a penlight to look around the room, finding it just as he'd seen it last: the dusty Bentley in far bay, the empty bay Three used for his Porsche Boxster. The long workbench. The stairwell to the second floor that was once a groundsman's apartment. He positioned himself at the bottom of the stairs and killed his penlight. Now it was just a matter of waiting. Another skill that too few people thought to master nowadays. To their misfortunes. A whole nation of softies, of slackers. People who gave so much away almost deserved what happened to them.

This was good. Got the old reflexes working again. The dark of the garage was charged with the thrill of anticipation. It might be tough to subdue Three at first, he was a big boy, but Mr. Smith had no doubt the conditioning would kick in the moment he had the upper hand. The trick would be the first twenty seconds. If it all went south in a major way, he'd just kill the little prick.

Back in the early days of the Vietnam field trials, Mr. Smith had made a commitment to understand the real conditions under which some of his subjects would have to work. Few of the other psych modelers had such a hands-on approach. They'd spent too much time sheltered in universities and hospitals and labs, they didn't like to put themselves in danger. But Mr. Smith had decided that the success of the conditioning depended upon *specificity*—and this required the psych staff to know the environment, the landscape, the stresses, the physical challenges. So he had volunteered for missions in the jungle.

In enemy territory, you learned things thoroughly and fast, or you didn't survive. He intended to survive. So he worked to master his body and his fear, the art of patience, the craft of killing, the science of silence. On his second mission, he'd killed his first human being, a Vietcong guard at the outskirts of a village. It was night, and the killing had to be done silently, so he had used a knife and felt the hot wash of blood bathe his forearm as he held the guard from behind. The Vietnamese were little people but very strong, and this one had struggled until he had no blood left. Later he killed others who died more easily, but that first one was a lesson he wouldn't forget: Never underestimate the power of a person fighting for his life. It was almost supernatural.

Mr. Smith didn't mind killing. He had seen what the Cong regularly did to U.S. servicemen, and he hated them at a visceral level. His commanding officers knew this about him, and it should have given him more credibility when he began to question the direction the program was taking, some of the assignments. They couldn't doubt his commitment or patriotism. But the brass ignored him anyway, saw his doubts as "going soft." Plus it was all so convoluted, Army Intelligence working with the DIA and CIA and private scientific contractors, the fog of deniability necessary in case an edge of the project should get exposed. You never knew who your real boss was, where the center of the operation lay, whom to persuade or threaten. Everybody was the puppet of some other puppet. At some point he'd realized no one really had control of this thing.

Mr. Smith felt the sweat coming onto his temples and the small of his back. This was not productive. You couldn't let the past come back and throw you off-balance. You had to just wait, empty-headed, ready to act and react. Three could return at any moment. Unless, of course, he was off somewhere doing what was rapidly degenerating into a garden-variety act of psychosexual pathology. He was killing just women now, and he was raping them. For Three, it had turned into something like going out on a goddamned *date*. Sick fart.

A wash of headlights panned through the garage's front window, sending a jolt of high-octane adrenaline through Mr. Smith's body. He listened for the sound of a car coming up the drive but heard nothing. The lights went on by. After another minute he heard the distant chunk of a car door slamming. Just some neighbor. He commanded himself to be calm, consciously slowed his metabolism.

The pisser was that at first Three had seemed like the perfect acquisition. Physically, just the right type: big, athletic, good with his hands. Mentally, an underachiever but very bright. The only child of an older couple, thus limited family connections to interfere. Prep school in Massachusetts, so no close friendships locally. Best of all, he had demonstrated sadistic behavior and impulse-control problems throughout his youth, culminating in his arrest for a violent rape during his senior year in college, which put him in prison for six years.

Mr. Smith had acquired his subjects by scanning back issues of local newspapers, ten or fifteen years old, for the police blotter columns, and noting the names of juvenile arrests. Then he'd track prospects through the psych-treatment or juvenile-justice systems, pilfering files or hacking computers at private and public facilities, looking for evaluations that would identify individuals with the right proclivities. Then locating and observing them in their adult lives, choosing the best. It helped to have a skilled investigative staff at his disposal, who could be duped into doing some of the background work without knowing the real goal.

Number Three's parents had died while he was in prison, leaving him this house and enough money to live on without having to work. *Perfect,* Mr. Smith had thought when he'd chosen Three. Between prep school, college, and prison, the neighbors were used to his long absences from this house, so no one would notice the months spent in conditioning at Mr. Smith's lab. No job meant no co-workers to become curious about his absence on days that killings took place, no paper trail that could prove his whereabouts on any given day.

Yes, Three should have been perfect. But Mr. Smith faulted himself for overlooking the obvious: Impulse-control disorders cut both ways. They gave you a subject capable of violent acts but also one capable of throwing off programming. The sexual nature of his native sociopathology, the resilience of his narcissism. The rich kid's the-world-owes-me attitude of arrogance and disobedience.

Mr. Smith had nobody to blame but himself. He had made the stupidest of mistakes. You wanted sociopathic tendencies that you could amplify and channel, but you didn't want native compulsions so strong they could override programming—that was one of the big mistakes the program had made in Vietnam. Sure enough, Number Three had screwed up on the very first kill, taking that cleaning woman to the old power station, leaving all kinds of loose ends. The little bastard should never have hired a cleaning person in the first place, allowing outside eyes into his home.

Mr. Smith had reclaimed him for a month of intensive conditioning that he'd hoped would get him back on track, and after the

O'Connor kill he thought he'd succeeded. But then, right away, the bungle in the marsh. Again the rape, leaving biological evidence and other anomalies a sharp investigator like Morgan Ford could capitalize upon.

But what was really unacceptable was the proximity of the Rappaport thing to the lab. A couple of lingering questions there. One, *how*—how could Three have found his way back, given that he'd been tied up and blindfolded for the trip in and out? Probably, Mr. Smith guessed, just a matter of deduction: During their work in the old dump, Three would have heard the highway noise, had seen the stream and the nearby hills, could determine direction from the sun and moon. Maybe he had calculated drive time when he was released. A look at topographical maps would have allowed him to identify probable locales.

But then you had to ask *why*—why the *hell* had the little creep come back to the area? It suggested that Three was up to something on his own. Maybe looking for Daddy, a little payback? Or maybe just wanting to emulate Daddy more perfectly, perform his own "conditioning exercises" in the old junkyard?

The more Mr. Smith thought about it, the more it infuriated him. The artery in his neck ballooned against his collar. His heart pounded like a power-hammer, his hands ached for forceful action. But then headlights washed the front of the garage again and this time stayed. Just as he recognized the throaty exhaust note of the Porsche, the electric garage-door opener clunked on and the door began to roll up. A widening stripe of headlight glare lit the garage. Mr. Smith stepped back into the stairwell shadow.

It took a long time for Three to get out of the car. The garage door rolled down behind him, but he just sat in there, lit by the car's dome light, fussing with something on the seat. Then he cracked the door but didn't get out, leaving the key alarm buzzing. *Drunk,* Mr. Smith thought impatiently.

Finally Three swung the Boxster's door open and unfolded from the low car. But the alarm still buzzed, he'd forgotten the key and had to bend back inside to retrieve it. Seizing the moment, Mr. Smith stepped quickly from the stairwell and came up behind him. He grabbed Three's belt and yanked him backward so that his head hit the car roof as he came out. Still, Three was a big boy, strong as an ox, and even drunk he took the hit and managed to half-turn, bringing an elbow around to connect with Mr. Smith's temple. Sparks and flashes, a hard hit.

The pain enraged Mr. Smith, and he kicked Three's legs out from under him with a slashing sideways sweep of his foot. Three went down clutching the Boxster's door frame, and in an instant Mr. Smith twisted his Asp out of its breakaway holster. It was a specialty police tool, a telescoping steel baton that would expand from six inches to sixteen with a flick of the wrist. For this job he left it short. With one knee on the angled back, he hooked his right thumb into Three's ear and drove the Asp's steel tip into the hinge of the jaw, up into the sensitive mastoid region. A little downward jerk and the leverage was wonderful. Three squealed like a pig and slid further down the door frame.

He was mostly on the floor now. Mr. Smith kept the pressure on the Asp as he maneuvered the head into the back corner of the car's door frame, then swung the door shut. Three lay belly-down on the concrete, his head wedged between door and frame, face ground into the door sill. Once he had the head secure, Mr. Smith took away the Asp, sat on Three's rump, and leaned into the door as he pulled the arms up behind and cinched on the nylon handcuffs. He felt some satisfaction, but part of him was angry that it had been so easy. He'd have preferred an excuse to really punish the little shit.

He gave the door some more pressure. Three squealed again, but the big torso didn't budge. The slightest movement would be agony.

Mr. Smith gave it a full two minutes. Then he bent his face close to the corner of the door. "What do we say?" he whispered.

Number Three's voice had a choked sound, his jaw barely able to work in the vise of steel. But he managed wonderfully, considering: "Thank you, Daddy. Thank you, Daddy. Thank you, Daddy."

37

M O SAT IN A storage room in the basement of Ty's precinct building in the Bronx, looking at the wall of cardboard file boxes. More paperwork on the Howdy Doody case—Ty had shown him down here to look over the more peripheral Rosario materials, destined for warehousing or incineration after the trial. The walls were shiny beige like the rest of the station, but the paint was flaking here, and the absence of windows and the dust-fluffed pipes crossing the ceiling made it a depressing place. It was dead quiet except for the occasional flush of a toilet upstairs and the rush of water through the pipes.

Looking at the sagging stacks of boxes, he was tempted to call it quits on this avenue of pursuit. He was feeling an ache, his brain or mind being torqued out of shape by this. Going from the sweetness to the job so hard, so fast. He wondered how she was doing today. Missing him? Morning-after regrets? In any case, anything these files might have to offer had been superseded by developments. There was no insider to look for because the consistent MO resulted not from the killer being a law-enforcement person involved in the case but from consistencies in Geppetto's programming of his killer puppets. Which was derived from whatever agenda he might have.

Still, he figured he might as well finish the job. Deep background, you never knew what would pop up. He put the first of eight boxes up on the table and began pulling out folders. Ah, yes, the glamour of homicide investigation. Whodunits generated a lot of paper, enough to drown in. This box was full of irrelevant memos, the daybooks where Ty's investigators had written up all the dead-end interviews and other useless leads, copies of correspondence with other jurisdictions involved in the first task force. Minutes from meetings, mainly noting attendees and procedural decisions and noticeably lacking discussion of important evidence, no doubt pursuant to Biedermann's gag rules. Copies of letters to and from the Manhattan DA's office, pressuring letters from the mayor's office, pleading or angry letters from the victim's next of kin.

The second box contained reams of printouts from national crime databases that compared MOs, victimology, and path reports with other murders throughout the country. Then a collection of the usual whoopee-nutso confessions and psychic leads called in by attention-starved citizens who had read about the case in the newspapers. On and on. From the materials here, it looked like Ty's investigators had done a damned good job of following down a thousand dead ends.

End of second box. He stuffed the papers back in haphazardly, frustrated. Face it, the real reason he was here: He was stalling. Killing time with busywork while he tried to figure out what to do.

Flannery's secretary had called and ordered another command appearance before the DA this afternoon, but Mo had no idea what to tell him. On the regular forensic front, there was nothing to report. At the same time, there was too much to tell: human cruise missiles, army psych experiments, clandestine government hit units, Geppetto. Without a grip on all that, Mo didn't know what to say or not to say.

Plus, he'd heard the DA was planning to ask the Big Willie grand jury for a second-degree murder indictment against him, the stiffest possible charge under the circumstances. Marsden had given him a heads-up on it this morning. Mo had faced reality and called his rep from the State Police Investigators Association, who had set up a meeting with a union attorney for early next week.

He dumped out the third box on the table, thinking, *Fucking Flannery.*

The thought stopped him. Actually, maybe there was something interesting in that first box. He put away the papers he'd just dumped, set the first box back on the table.

It had to do with the routine correspondence. Here were photo-copied notes from the New Jersey police departments working on the first Howdy Doody kills, before Parker had started up in Manhattan. By the dates, Ty had apparently requested the New Jersey materials after the murder in his precinct, which occurred about six months after the first New Jersey kill. Memos, distribution lists, summaries of early findings. What drew Mo's eye were the CC lists, where Westchester DA Richard K. Flannery's name now stood out like a sore thumb.

Mo opened his notebook to look at the calendar of puppeteer kills. CC'ing Flannery after only the second New Jersey kill, in April of '99? Why so soon? How would Flannery even have heard about a specific murder or two that occurred outside his jurisdiction, across the river in New Jersey?

Mo felt his pulse quickening as other details came to mind. Flannery: bald now but blue-eyed, suggesting he had been blond once. Big, very fit—Geppetto would have to be fit to manipulate his experimental subjects. Flannery, in his late fifties, the right generation to have had a role in Vietnam-era psych projects. Flannery, who, if memory served, had a medical background before going into law— giving him the skills needed for the role of puppet-maker. And, right, Flannery, who personally knew the family of Carolyn Rappaport, murdered in the swamp, a connection no one had even thought to look at twice. Flannery, who hadn't wasted a moment getting Mo Ford under his thumb, thus getting an inside man on the State Police side of the investigation and conceivably a means to subtly deflect the direction of the investigation. Who knew how many others he was manipulating in similar ways?

Mo cautioned himself not to get excited, but his hands were shaking as he reviewed the rest of the papers. You couldn't deny there was a pattern here. Flannery had been copied on Howdy Doody communications starting immediately after the second New Jersey kill. True, the second murder would have suggested it was the start of a serial string and could conceivably have aroused a nearby DA's interest. But why—and how—so soon? And as Mo checked the lists of meeting attendees, he saw that Flannery showed up personally at a surprising number of them. Why had a very busy DA allotted so much time to a single case not yet in his jurisdiction?

By the time he looked up, it was eleven-thirty. He was due to meet Flannery at three o'clock. The thought of facing him after this gave his nerves a jolt.

He tried to calm himself by remembering the mistake he had made with Biedermann. But then he calculated that, allowing for drive time back to White Plains, he had about two hours free. Just enough time for a visit to the New York Public Library, some background research.

The secretary at Flannery's office told him the DA was downstairs, in the fitness center the county maintained for its staff. He was expecting Mo, she said, in one of the racquetball courts. Mo took the elevator to the basement, followed signs through the windowless corridors to the gym area. Three o'clock, a fine day in early June, hardly anyone else was using the facility. Mo turned a corner, heard the echoing *whap-POCK!* of a ball, and followed the sound to Flannery.

He watched for a moment from the corridor. The courts were new, with floor-to-ceiling glass rear walls that allowed observation of games. Flannery was alone in the brightly lit white box of a room, his back to Mo, wearing shorts and a gray T-shirt darkened with sweat. He was knocking a handball against the other wall with sharp sweeps of a gloved palm, moving laterally with quick, wide steps. *Ka-pack! Pa-whack!*

The visit to the library had been productive in a circumstantial way. Mo had said hello to the pollution-stained lions, friends from his youth, and gone inside to the periodicals section. He had decided to begin scanning papers from five years ago, the year before Flannery became Westchester DA. The *Journal News* was there in microfiche, which was a pain, requiring him to mechanically scan frame after frame of newspaper pages. But even so, it didn't take long to find Flannery's name here and there. Most of it was unremarkable, but he did learn a few interesting facts. Flannery had been born and raised in Westchester. He had gone to medical school at Johns Hopkins, but he'd joined the army rather than setting up in private practice after graduating. As a medical officer, he'd served several years at Wainwright Army Hospital in Georgia and a number of shorter stints at hospitals in Vietnam. After the war, he quit medicine, went to law school, and joined the public prosecutor's staff. Why the switch? "For me, medicine and law aren't really so different," the new DA was quoted as saying nobly. "They both stem from a sincere desire to serve my fellow man."

Mo jotted in his notebook: *Family home in Westchester—where?* And: *Wainwright Army Hosp.—What duties?* Was it by any chance where the army ran its monster-making factory?

Another profile from the *Daily News*: WESTCHESTER'S MOST ELIGIBLE BACHELOR LIKES LIMELIGHT BUT GUARDS PRIVATE LIFE. Flannery, though maintaining high visibility at work, jealously protected his personal affairs. Kept an apartment in White Plains and another in Manhattan where he could better escape public scrutiny. Didn't entertain much, kept his love life out of public view. The famously charming, outgoing DA admitted with typical lack of affectation that he had a sensitive, introverted side that was not permitted much expression in his public service career. Touching.

After last night's revelations, Rebecca had started developing a psych profile for Geppetto. Mo wasn't sure what she'd end up with, but surely this had to be close—the two-sided personality, the double life, the lack of close domestic relationships.

The *New York Times* search turned up a number of references to Richard K. Flannery. Again, they were mostly routine, dealing with politics in the Empire State. The most interesting article was a postelection editorial comment that suggested Flannery's meteoric rise owed less to his abilities than to help from powerful outside political influences, the governor's office or maybe even Washington. Connections in the intelligence community? Mo wondered. An old-boy network of former monster-makers helping one of their own? Mo watched the big man pounding the ball, the powerful stoop of the torso and the wicked chop of the right arm, trying to visualize him as the puppet-master.

Yes, he decided, he could see it. *Definitely.*

But there were several problems with the idea, too. Not the least of which was that if Mo Ford could dig up this much suggestive material in two hours, SAC Biedermann would surely have done so long ago. And apparently hadn't thought it worth his while.

On the other hand, maybe they *were* looking at Flannery. Maybe they knew they needed a very solid case against a powerful DA, and it was taking time. Maybe this was one of the "big picture" issues Mo was supposed to turn a blind eye to.

Flannery spotted Mo, snagged the rebounding ball, beckoned him into the court. Mo obediently opened the low door and ducked inside. An air-conditioned gust blew in from ceiling vents, but the room was still full of the musky smell of male sweat.

Flannery's chest was pumping as he came up and chucked Mo on the shoulder. "Thanks for coming. You ever play?"

"A little, back in high school—"

"Hey, there we go!" Flannery grinned. "Let's whack a few. I've got an extra glove."

"No, thanks."

Flannery's smile faded. "You know, you look pretty tense, Ford.

Maybe you ought to try it—work some of it out. Bang that ball, it's very cathartic. Take the edge off some of that tension." He turned to rummage in an athletic bag in one corner of the room, came back with a handball glove. He slapped it into Mo's hand, gave him a baleful look. "I insist. We'll bat it around while you tell me what's bothering you."

Mo held the glove but made no move to put it on. "I hear the grand jury's going to get a request for a second-degree murder indictment against me."

Flannery's face blackened at Mo's refusal to play. He turned away and served the ball hard against the wall so that it leapt back at Mo. A provocation. Mo turned reflexively so that it hit him on the shoulder and bounced away.

Flannery sprang to retrieve it. "I'm doing you a favor with that. I could maybe make manslaughter stick, but the jury'll never go for second degree, they'll have to let you go. Best of both worlds; I make the relatives happy, I get you off the hook. I thought you'd be *grateful* I'd set it up this way. But *no,* that's too much to ask, I guess." Again Flannery smacked the ball so that it came back at Mo. Ready this time, Mo stepped aside.

Flannery caught the ball as it came off the back wall. "What other bug you got up your butt?" He still didn't look at Mo, just whacked the ball so that it came back at Mo's head. This time Mo grabbed it on the fly.

"No bug," Mo lied. "But we haven't made any progress to tell you about. Things are stalled at this point."

"How about your visit to Ronald Parker down at Rikers? Nothing at all useful from that?" Flannery's red face betrayed some pleasure at telling Mo he knew about that. "Your cell phone still work? Because I know for a fact you have my number, and you ain't called me recently, have you?"

Mo decided not to react to the goading, not to ask how he knew. "Parker is incoherent. He's all over the map. If we'd learned anything relevant, I'd tell you."

Flannery bit his lower lip and thought about that. He took another ball out of his pocket, served it at the wall, slapped it back and forth several times. The big torso dominated the small room, moving quickly sideways, apparently oblivious to Mo. Flannery lunged so close Mo could feel the heat emanating from him. And then, without turning his head, Flannery whacked the ball so that it came back at Mo's face again. Mo snapped it out of the air with his left hand and simultaneously fired the other ball at the wall. The move caught Flannery by surprise. The ball came back and hit him squarely in the chest.

For a moment Flannery's face turned scarlet. The veins in his neck stood out. But then his face fell into the big grin, and he chuckled as he turned away, went to his bag, brought out a towel. He rubbed his bald head and face and neck, watching Mo and grinning.

"You're a real piece of work, you know that?" the DA said finally. He shook his head appreciatively. "Seriously. I don't understand why you have such an aversion to playing ball with me—metaphorically speaking, that is. On the other hand, I like your style. The 'last honest man' thing, that's good, you pull it off well. So I'm going to confide in you. Can I trust you, Detective?"

"Depends."

"Right answer! Give Mr. Integrity a *prize*!" Flannery tossed his towel, and then his face got serious again. He lowered his voice. "Okay. Wheels within wheels, right? We've got a stubborn situation with these killings, don't we. Something here doesn't compute. Right?"

"Right."

"So let me tell you a story. Just between you and me." The frown deepened as Flannery sat himself down against the wall and began massaging his legs. "I was in the Army Med Corps during the Vietnam War. Down in Georgia most of the time, some months over there. You know what my job was? I was assigned to treat former POWs, or guys we'd recovered after they'd been lost in the jungle for a while. They had very specific medical problems, which demand both physical and psychological treatment, closely integrated. My specialty. Some of the POWs we treated had been what we used to call 'brainwashed,' but most just got screwed up from a year or two or three in very restrictive captivity. Nowadays they use the term 'post-traumatic stress syndrome,' but the truth is there are many varieties of response to stress or trauma. Imprisonment and prolonged abject subjugation to the will of others produces a unique cluster of problems. You get claustrophobia, depression, rage disorders, what we call 'learned helplessness,' and obsessional stuff around *control*. Control issues, whether it's about being controlled or controlling others, usually both. You see where I'm going with this?"

"The puppet killings are about control."

"Yeah." Flannery grimaced as he worked out a kink in a knotted calf muscle, and when he went on, he spoke quietly. "Okay. So there's a funny coincidence you should know about. When I was over in Vietnam, our unit was primarily concerned with these problems, and we were semisecret because no one back home was supposed to know how bad the war really was, how hard it was on our boys. But we were learning a lot, we were making progress. Other units, both intelligence and combat, would come to us for advice. One individual from an elite black-ops unit came back several times, asked a lot of insightful questions. Coincidentally, that same individual is now deeply involved in investigating the puppets murders."

Holy shit, Mo was thinking.

Flannery caught his expression. "Yes. Biedermann. I'm very interested in Erik Biedermann." He stared hard at Mo.

Before Mo could say anything, a couple of racquetballers appeared at the glass back wall. They smiled, looked at their watches meaningfully, glanced back toward Flannery. When Flannery flashed them two fingers, *two minutes,* they sat against the bench on the other side of the corridor and chatted as they readied their equipment.

Mo asked quietly, "And how're you thinking he might be involved?"

Flannery spoke very quietly and kept his back to the observation wall as he got to his feet and began stuffing his gear into his bag. "Not sure yet. But I'm not a big believer in coincidences. So there're two possibilities that occur to me. One is that Biedermann is on a mission that's pretty important and is related to his past work—bigger than a copycat killer. In which case, the whole scenario is full of opportunities that I find, frankly, rather attractive."

Mo waited, then thought to ask, "What's the other possibility?"

Flannery grinned. "Why don't we just leave it at that for now?"

"And you're telling me all this because—?"

"I'd like you to help me find out more about him. This is going to have to be very delicate. And, you can understand, I'm reluctant to use anyone in my own shop on this."

"Why me? You'd be better off talking to some of the others, NYPD or New Jersey people. They've had more experience with him."

Flannery just chuckled at that. "Because the old killings weren't in my jurisdiction, I don't have as much pull with those guys. Whereas the new ones are, and you—you, I kind of have you under my thumb just now, don't I?"

Mo was thinking of all the angles Flannery was playing, or might be. Maybe just what he said, using Mo as a mole for information he could eventually use to advance himself. Or a trap, a way to catch Mo in some impropriety that Flannery could crucify him for. Better yet, raising the Biedermann red herring at this stage was a perfect way to deflect a suspicious investigator from consideration of Flannery himself. Suddenly he was sick of Flannery, his big smile, his confidence, his machinations.

"What happens if I don't play along?"

"The usual." Flannery zipped his gym bag shut, glanced quickly around the court, scowled at Mo. "Big Willie can go away easily, or he can not go away at all. I might not be able to make anything stick to you, but even having the indictment in your record would put the kibosh on any future promotions. Nah, forget that—a guy like you wouldn't care about that. But with a trial I can surely make your life hell for six months, a year. And I don't think that's something you want right now. It would probably be bad timing for you, wouldn't it, given that rumor has it you're starting something up with that good-looking psychologist. Who, let's not kid ourselves, is a bit of a reach anyway. For a guy in your position." Flannery's eyebrows rose as he drilled his gaze at Mo, like *We both know what I'm talking about.*

Mo was dead beat by the time he made it back to Carla's mom's house. *Mausoleum.* He checked the empty rooms on all three floors, downed a glass of acid-tasting orange juice, took off his jacket. The spot where the handball had hit him still burned on his shoulder, not a physical bruise but the psychic brand of another man's machismo. *Fucking Flannery.* He wanted to call Rebecca, but he was beset with sudden uncertainties, and anyway there was another call to be made first. He dialed the number from memory, got the terse answering machine message.

"Gus, this is Mo Ford. I could use your help. Same problem, different guy. Give me a buzz."

38

M O HAD NEVER THOUGHT of himself as much of a drinker, but Friday nights loomed big when you lived alone in an abandoned house and the one person you wanted to be with was having her night with her daughter, thirty miles away. And the noisy, boozy ambience of a bar sounded like about the right antidote for a growing case of the lonesome scaries. So after leaving the message for Gus he got into his car and let it steer itself through the humid summer streets toward The Edge. A bar that cops knew, a bar that knew cops. Misery loves company.

The Edge occupied the ground floor of a three-story, older brick building. Previously it had styled itself an Irish pub, and though the new owner had changed the name to reflect the postmodern angst of the times and installed a thin veneer of sports mania, the place retained a lot of the dark wood, Guinness signs, Irish flags, and dartboards of its prior incarnation. One section of wall was devoted to photos of celebs and local hero cops. Eight o'clock, maybe twenty people there, half of them in the back room around a pair of pool tables. At the bar, a couple of TV screens beamed sports shows down through a haze of cigarette smoke onto a dozen drinkers arguing about the Knicks' playoff chances.

Mo nodded to a couple of familiar faces, slid into one of the narrow booths, ordered a pint of Bass from the bone-skinny waitress. After the hot day it was good to glug something cold. He'd drunk half of it and was just feeling it hit his bloodstream when a big form blocked the TV light and he looked up to see Erik Biedermann.

"Hey, good buddy," the G-man said. He sat down heavily across from Mo, put his arms on the table, rubbed his meaty hands together expectantly. "What a surprise, seeing you here."

"How'd you know where I was?"

"Vee haff our vays," Biedermann quipped. He grabbed a beer menu, looked it over quickly, tossed it back on the table. "No, seriously, this is a coincidence. I had a meeting up this way, finished up and had a hankering for a drink. Everybody says this is where the law-enforcement community waters, thought I'd check it out."

"In that case, have a seat," Mo said.

Biedermann laughed. "Always the attitude! Love it. Come on, Ford, cut me some slack, huh? Yeah, you think what I do for a living stinks. But I bet you get the same shit from civilians, how can you *do* that shit, wouldn't mind a break once in a while yourself. Right?"

Mo was thinking of Rachel's comment: *I mean, who would do that? Doesn't it gross you out?* Biedermann's grin had gone wry and a little sideways there, Mo could see he meant it, the guy did know that brand of lonely. Okay, Biedermann could have some slack, he decided.

The waitress came, Biedermann ordered a pint of Sam Adams, Mo put in for another Bass.

Biedermann looked appreciatively around the room. He was dressed in jeans and a blue work shirt, cuffs rolled halfway up beefy forearms, cloth tight over his pecs and biceps, and he looked more like a buff suburban hubby after a day of yard work than a covert-ops hit man on his night off. "Nice place," he said. "You drowning your sorrows, or is this just a regular Friday-night gig for you?"

Mo thought about it. "You saw where I live," he said finally.

To his credit, Biedermann just nodded, didn't say anything.

The waitress brought their beers, they slugged some back. Mo felt himself relax a bit. Part of him wanted to broach the subject of

Flannery, bring it out into the open, maybe Biedermann would answer some questions. But really, he had nothing on the DA yet. Certainly nothing he could talk about without revealing that they'd put together the Geppetto scenario. That was the crucial thing, keeping their knowledge from Biedermann.

"I keep feeling that you and I got off on the wrong foot," Biedermann said. "Macho stuff, who's-in-charge crap. But I'd like to get past that. We also have a lot in common. I mean, more than job stuff." He looked at Mo meaningfully.

"You mean Rebecca."

A ghost of wistfulness crossed Biedermann's face. "Well. Yeah. She's, uh, she's quite a gal. Ah, fuck, that sounds sexist. She's a rare person. She's beautiful, she's smart, she's"—Biedermann groped for the word—"she's *genuine*. You know? You're a lucky guy." Suddenly he looked uncomfortable, glanced down into his beer, then finished it with a long guzzle and craned around to catch the waitress's eye.

"I didn't mean to insult your place when I was over there," Biedermann went on. "I know what it's like, I hardly live anywhere myself, no time. But speaking of Rebecca, if you want my advice—"

"I don't."

"Okay, not advice, just an observation. She's *choosy*. You know? Very high standards. And why shouldn't she be? All I'm saying is, you know—a guy in your situation, right, don't take this the wrong way—don't get your hopes up too far? That's all. I'm, uh, kind of speaking from personal experience here." Biedermann looked sadly at his empty glass.

Great, Mo was thinking. Christ, the mismatch was obvious to everyone, even macho lunks like Flannery and Biedermann. How long before Rebecca caught on?

Biedermann's beer came, and he quaffed off a third of it before raising his glass to Mo. "To the gentler sex," he said soberly. They clinked glasses and drank.

An explosion of laughter and applause came from back in the pool room, the slap of a cue stick, and they turned their heads. A young woman in a short skirt was sitting on one of the tables, showing off her long legs as she twisted to take an awkward shot. She knocked the cue ball right off the table, collapsed laughing onto the felt, then slipped down into her boyfriend's arms.

They spent another minute nursing their beers, and then Biedermann said, "Listen, I gotta get going. But I have to tell you something. I lied about this being a coincidence, me finding you here. I was looking for you. I, uh, I wanted to talk to you. Off the record."

Mo felt a tingle of alarm and suddenly wished he hadn't drunk so much. "About?"

Biedermann leaned forward, dropped his voice. "Bad news, Mo. We've been working on the handcuffs? The disposable nylon cuffs on some of the vics. Turns out they *are* traceable, by manufacturing lot, subtle differences in plastic composition. We identified the lot, tracked sales from Flex-Cuf company. The lot in question went to eleven police departments. One of them happens to be—well, it's a little too coincidental for my taste."

Somehow Mo knew instantly where this was going. Abruptly the whole show ramified, elaborated. New depths of complication and confusion.

"Yeah, your friend Ty Boggs. He ordered a couple gross of 'em for his precinct. I know you guys went to college together, hung out some, you're probably fairly close. So I thought I'd give you a heads-up. We've been looking at him."

"He's not the guy," Mo said.

"I wouldn't think so either. But how well do you really know him? We know our perp's an actor, knows how to look unlikely. Ty was in Vietnam, ran some special missions. Has a police and forensic background. Smart, highly organized. Look at what your . . . what Bec has said about the killer's profile. Alienated, probably no real

312

domestic life. Your buddy Ty got divorced eight years ago, right, never remarried, supposedly lives with his sister. Looks to me like an angry man, and you could make a case that the blond, blue-eyed victimology stems from racial hatreds. Physically strong as a tank, martial arts skills, close to the investigation—"

"You must know who your ex–guinea pigs are," Mo countered. "Zelek said you kept a strict record." His head was spinning, trying to figure if this was real or some ploy on Biedermann's part, another deflection for whatever reason. *Ty?*

"There're a thousand ways to lose touch with them over twenty-seven years. A thousand ways to fabricate a new identity. Plus, screw Zelek, the fact is the program's records were so decentralized, so compartmentalized, so hush-hush, we can't be totally sure. Let me ask you this: What's your relationship with him like? Real close, or just . . . more professional? See him much on weekends, evenings? Ever meet his girlfriends?"

"Pretty close. Well, we were until—"

"Until about three years ago, I'd bet. Coincidentally, just about the time the Howdy Doody kills began." Biedermann drilled a look at Mo, obviously seeing his confidence fade.

Mo had to admit that much was true. Ty had seemed to push him out right around then. All he could think of to say was "Why are you telling me this? I thought you wanted me out of the big picture."

Biedermann bobbed his head. "Couple reasons. One, he's your buddy. If it turns out we get very serious about him, we can't have you getting protective here, doing him little favors, turning a blind eye. Getting under our feet deliberately or accidentally. Two, I figured you should know. A professional courtesy, I guess. A gesture of respect. We've decided not to mention progress on the handcuffs to the task force, not just yet, it could get back to him. So do me a favor, keep this just between you and me. Right?"

Biedermann blew air out between his lips, looking resigned and unhappy, then slid sideways and stood out of the booth. "I gotta run.

Sorry to be the bearer of bad tidings. Not easy to think of an old friend as a killer. Hey, maybe we're wrong, maybe it'll all blow over, huh?" His attempt at being reassuring sounded as bogus as they came. He chucked Mo on the shoulder and left the bar.

39

M O WAS FLAT ON HIS back in bed, the Glock in its holster cradled on his chest, when the phone rang. He groped for it in the dark, knocked it off the night table, found it again. The clock radio said 1:02 A.M. He'd only been asleep for six minutes.

"Gus?" he barked.

"Investigator Morgan Ford?" a woman's voice.

"Yeah."

"This is Sergeant Renee Williams, Troop K headquarters. There's a situation in Briarcliff Manor. We've got an armed standoff in a residential neighborhood, a hostage situation, shots have been fired. The suspect has asked for you personally. Can you get out there soon?"

"Who the hell? I mean, why *me*?" Mo couldn't imagine who would be desirous of seeing Morgan Ford, personally, at something like this.

"The officers on the scene say it's apparently a marital problem, a triangle? It's at the home of a Dennis Radcliff?" She paused, and when Mo's silence suggested the name didn't ring a bell, she went on, "The suspect hasn't been positively identified yet, but we're presuming he's the owner of a Toyota pickup truck parked on the lawn of the residence. A Byron Bushnell?"

Driving around the Sleepy Hollow Country Club at one-thirty A.M.: big houses and landscaped yards shadowed by heavy summer foliage.

Mo drove quickly but without a flasher through the quiet streets. He had come fully awake the instant Sgt. Williams had mentioned Byron Bushnell's name. It meant he'd been right when he thought he saw that flash of understanding in Bushnell's face during their last interview. The grieving husband realizing, yes, his dead wife had been having an affair. Yes, it was with one of her cleaning clients. Yes, it was that rich guy she went to on Monday afternoons, the side income Irene kept secret from Mrs. Ferrara. And maybe the rich guy was the bastard who killed Irene.

Mo had been wondering what to do about his hunch ever since the interview, but now Byron Bushnell had solved that problem for him. Byron had obviously decided he wasn't going to leave this to the police, he'd settle things himself.

Deaver Street was spangled with the strobes of a dozen police cars. Sawhorses had been erected to close off the block, and Mo had to show his shield to a State Police uniform to get past. Closer, he saw that the cars had trained their spots on the front of a big brick house set back in manicured lawns, lighting the place up like a movie set. Jagged holes gaped in two front windows of the house. Several police snipers crouched behind cars, rifles mounted with fat nightscopes and trained on an open bay in the attached garage, where the tail end of a sports car was visible. A trio of ambulance vans waited down the street, and there were probably twenty other cops in sight, many of them the serious cowboys from the Mobile Response Team. The night air was alive with flashers, headlights, the electric crackle of radios.

Just past the end of the driveway, a bunch of local and State Police brass were conferring soberly, including State Police captain Max Dresden, whom Mo knew slightly. They gestured him over to their conference, and Mo nodded hello.

"So apparently this guy's some good friend of yours," Dresden said.

"Where is he now?"

"Maybe the garage, maybe the house."

"Is the owner of the house inside?"

"We're not sure. At this point, we're presuming he's being held hostage."

Mo craned his head to look over what he could see of the scene from this angle. Through the hedge he could see Byron Bushnell's battered white Toyota, pulled haphazardly onto the lawn.

Dresden filled him in on how it had gone down. Neighbors had called in a report of shots being fired. The Briarcliff police had come, found the suspect on the front lawn, waving a handgun, shooting at the house windows, yelling something about his wife, about murder. When he saw the Briarcliff car, he took a shot at it and blew out a rear side window. The locals called for reinforcements. By the time the State Police had arrived, the suspect had entered the garage and probably the house. He'd fired at them again from the garage door.

They had sent men into the yards on either side and the golf course in back, cutting off any escape, and a hostage/barricaded-subject specialist from Poughkeepsie had gotten on the bullhorn, trying to talk him down. The suspect was obviously drunk and upset and had responded by saying he hated all cops and he'd kill Dennis Radcliff and himself and anyone and everyone else nearby. He'd taken another shot at the hostage specialist. The MRT shooters were afraid to return the fire, given the hostage possibility. After a while Bushnell had apparently begun feeling scared and overwhelmed. He'd cried and raved and eventually had asked for Investigator Morgan Ford.

After he finished, Dresden waited expectantly for Mo to explain. His look suggested he wasn't one of Mo's fans.

"I interviewed him a couple times on a murder case," Mo said. "I didn't realize we had hit it off so well."

"So how do you think we should do it?"

"You've got to call your men down. It's imperative that we get Byron and the other guy, this Dennis Radcliff, alive." Mo tried the name on his tongue: *Dennis Radcliff*. Very possibly, Pinocchio's real name. At last. If they could take him alive, he'd be the first direct link back to Geppetto. Who was *not* Ty, not not not, couldn't be.

But the circle of cop brass was still looking at him expectantly, so he went on, "Bushnell is the husband of Irene Bushnell, a murder victim. He's grieving, and he probably believes this Radcliff guy is the one who killed his wife. He may be right. In his current condition, yeah, he's capable of anything. I'll try to talk to him. But whatever he does, *do not* kill him. We got to be clear on this, or I can't help here."

Mo drove the point home with his eyes. You didn't usually give orders to captains, but Dresden barely hesitated before relaying the message to his people.

Mo started toward the house but turned back. "Two more things. When we go in there, we've got to secure the whole house. Touch nothing, consider it all evidence. The garage, the basement, the attic, whatever. Your guys have got to know this, no hotdogging in there. Also, get on the phone, get Bushnell's mother-in-law out here—a Mrs. Drysdale, Tarrytown number. If it doesn't work out with me, maybe she can do something."

Mo walked to the end of the driveway and stood in full view of the house. He could feel the tension rise in the cops around him, the visible ones and ones hidden around the yard. The spotlights stretched his shadow along the driveway, stark and solitary.

"Hey, Byron!" he yelled. "It's Mo Ford."

There was no sound from the house.

"Byron, look at me. I'm putting my gun down right here in the driveway. You see it? I'm not armed."

No answer.

"Hey, Byron, come on. This is the pits, man! We got to get you out of there."

After a minute, he heard a muffled voice from inside: "He killed her! He's the one who killed her!" It wasn't clear if the voice came from the open garage bay or the blown-out house window nearest the garage.

"If he did, I want him as much as you do. We're on the same side here. Can I come in and talk to you?"

A long hesitation. Indecision.

Mo took a few steps. "Is he in there with you right now?"

A clunk of something falling over. Swearing. Then Bushnell's voice, choked with grief and frustration: "No! He's not here! Fucker's not here!"

A palpable sense of relief gusted through the police army in the street, but all Mo felt was disappointment: *no Pinocchio*. "Okay. So let me come in, and you can tell me what—"

"They're just gonna kill me, aren't they. Think I don't know how this works? Fucking cops, man, all my life—"

"Nobody's going to kill you. We need you to help us find him. Right? You'll be fine." Mo took a few more measured steps. He was ten paces away from the garage door. He was pretty sure the voice came from there. With somebody as unglued as Bushnell, he knew this could still go either way.

Bushnell didn't answer, just kept up his choked swearing. So Mo kept walking.

When he got to the open garage door, the glare of the spotlights made it hard to see into the shadows. There was the sports car, a Porsche, and to the left a flight of two steps leading to a door into the house. A dark shape crouched behind the open door, gun in hand. From this close, Mo could feel the poor bastard's misery, an aura of suffering.

For a moment they both stood without moving in the light-slashed dark. Finally Mo asked quietly, "You sure he's not in there?"

"Yeah."

"So let's get out of here. First we'll get you out of the hot seat, and then we'll figure out where he is."

"How we gonna go out?"

319

"You put down your gun. Then we go out together."

"They'll *shoot* me. Maybe I'll fucking just kill myself. I don't need this shit! *This* I do *not* need, man." Crying.

"No one's shooting anybody. You come here, you and me will hold on to each other. But first your gun's got to go. Just leave it on the step. Those guys out there, they see the gun and they'll get nervous. Shoot us both."

More indecision. Mo could hear him breathing and swallowing, the wet sound of someone who's crying and scared to death.

It took a few more minutes of back and forth. Finally Bushnell stepped out from behind the door into the half-light.

"All right," Mo said encouragingly. "You're doing fine." He looked to make sure the gun was on the step, then turned his back to Bushnell. "Come up here, hug me from behind. Put your arms around me from either side, but keep your hands up in front of me so the guys out there don't get worried." Not SOP, but he was sure Bushnell wouldn't come without some shelter. "Okay? Byron, you hearing me?"

Bushnell didn't answer, but Mo felt shaking arms come shyly around his sides. They tottered awkwardly out into the doorway like that. Stood in the spotlights.

"We're coming out!" Mo yelled. The lights blinded him. "The suspect is unarmed! I need confirmation you hear me."

An amplified voice: "Confirmed. We hear you. Snipers are standing down."

They shuffled blindly out toward the street. Mo could feel Bushnell's trembling breathing against his back. He was several inches shorter than Mo, so that his head came against Mo's back like a woman's. The guy was holding on for dear life.

Mo Ford, human life-preserver, he thought. And then they were at the street, and the figures of cops were coming around them, and Byron Bushnell was pried loose from his body. Already men were running toward the house.

"Keep it intact!" he yelled after them. "Keep everything intact! It's a lot bigger than it looks!" He meant the whole scenario. He realized suddenly that he was tension-torqued to the fucking moon, and nothing he was saying would make any sense to them at all.

40

I T WAS JUST AFTER noon Saturday by the time Mo got to Rebecca's apartment. His nervous system was doing a shaky tightrope act between the high of coffee mixed with adrenaline and the exhaustion of thirty anxious hours without sleep. He had stayed through the night at Dennis Radcliff's house, searching through the entire structure along with other investigators and forensic technicians, and he'd spent a half hour in a car talking with Byron Bushnell, learning nothing new. Luckily, neither Biedermann nor Flannery had shown up to complicate things.

At eight in the morning, after thinking it through, Mo had called Flannery on his cell phone. Theoretically, it was to act the part of the dutiful slave at last, keeping the DA informed of developments. But it was also a way of avoiding any appearance that he was suspicious of him. Plus he'd casually asked Flannery where he was, did he want to come to the crime scene, how soon could he get here? Didn't mean anything either way, but there'd been no hesitation or awkwardness as Flannery claimed to be at his Manhattan apartment, yeah, he'd take a peek at the scene but it'd be a couple of hours.

Finally, as a grudging afterthought, he'd thought up a pretext and called Ty at the Bronx apartment he shared with his sister. Sister was there, Ty was not. She didn't know where he was, but she'd take a message.

Whoever was Geppetto, there could be no doubt that Radcliff was Pinocchio. In the garage, they'd found a black duffel bag containing a roll of lawn-trimmer line, nylon handcuffs, extra eyelets. They'd also gotten hair from hairbrushes, which he was sure would eventually match DNA evidence from the Carolyn Rappaport scene.

But Radcliff himself was gone. Which meant no easy link back to Geppetto. For now the best Mo had was a tuft of short blond hair, sticky with blood, that he'd found on the bottom corner of the Porsche's driver's-side door. Mo's gut told him that Dennis Radcliff had been reacquired by Geppetto. They had probably only missed him by a matter of hours.

He called Rebecca reluctantly, this being her day with Rachel, but as it turned out they would be able to meet. Rache and some friends were going to go to a matinee. Rebecca explained ruefully that while moms liked to see their teenage daughters as much as possible, teenage daughters weren't as highly motivated to grab quality time with moms, especially since weekends were also when they could hang out with their friends. The call of the wild, Mo said, sometimes you just had to give them their freedom. Rebecca wasn't all that amused.

Rachel and her friends were leaving the building just as Mo arrived. The three of them trouped across the lobby as he came through the door, Rachel and a Goth-dressed girl and a Hispanic girl, all of them with made-up faces and a conspiratorial flash in their eyes. The shine of anticipation. Hitting the streets, fifteen years old, a little cash in your pocket, Manhattan waiting—Mo remembered the feeling. Rachel saw him and her face changed, guardedness concealing the spark like a shade drawn over a window.

"Hey," Mo said.

"Hi," Rachel mumbled. She didn't seem to want some big transaction just now, so Mo didn't slow her down with any other pleasantries. In a second they were past each other. As the girls went out, Mo heard her tell her friends, "He's like my mom's *boyfriend*." An exasperated tone of voice.

That was okay, Mo decided. *Boyfriend* was simplifying things, but it was okay.

The thing about seeing her again, first time after sleeping together, a day later, you've built it up in your mind, your hopes, but you're not sure she's in the same place as you are. Leaving her apartment Friday morning after coffee and kisses, there'd been a lot of smiles. But that was kind of morning-after obligatory, didn't necessarily signify reciprocal feelings.

So now you say hello, and you go in and your heart is pounding because being near her is a thrill, and because you're scared to death she's feeling differently. And there's an awkwardness, she's being formal or cautious or something. And you want to respect that, so you're cautious, too, courteous, hesitant. Trying to respect her needs and wishes, not assume too much or take anything for granted.

For a few minutes you're sure the whole thing has gone down the tubes, you're both watching each other with that high alertness and reserve, and then by accident you bump shoulders and something breaks, the wall falls down. Suddenly you're in each other's arms, full contact. It's the best feeling there could be, coming through the wall, better than the first time because now you know it means something. And it's such a relief for both of you, you can't stop, you just give in and the clothes have to come off and you're in bed and you're *verifying* everything as if you were both afraid it had just been a dream, this is *real,* and there's nothing held back at all.

Some time later, she leaned over him, hair tented around his face, and said, "Hi."

"Hi." They chuckled for no real reason. After another minute, he said, "Listen, you've got to help me get up. I mean it. If I lie here for another minute, I'll pass out."

She heard the seriousness in his voice, *time to get to business,* and reluctantly prodded him out of bed. Once he was upright, she pushed him into the bathroom and started the shower for him. When he came out, she was waiting with a mug of fresh coffee. He drank it scalding hot, using the burn to help wake up.

They got dressed and sat in the living room as he brought her up to date: Byron Bushnell and the scene at Dennis Radcliff's house last night, his belief that Geppetto had reacquired Radcliff.

"It was inevitable," she said. "As a test subject, Pinocchio was falling apart. Geppetto is highly organized, he's got an agenda that shapes his actions just as much as his compulsions do. Radcliff was making too many mistakes. Exposing Geppetto in too many ways."

"Question is, what does he do with Radcliff now?"

"Most likely attempts to refresh his conditioning—reprograms him. Geppetto would be disinclined to waste the time and energy he's invested in him."

"So what's the new program? Just more random kills?"

She didn't answer, but her face told him: No, no more random kills. That wasn't working with Radcliff. Geppetto would use Radcliff strategically, target him to protect his agenda. As he had sent Parker after Rebecca.

"So the question is, who'll be the target?" he asked.

"Does Geppetto have any way of knowing . . . you and I are onto him?" The thought brought fear into her face: She knew too well how it felt to be targeted.

Mo had pondered that, trying to let reason prevail, to get Mudda Raymon's voice out of his head: *De puppet-puppet gon' come after you.* "I don't think so. No more than any other principals in the case—Biedermann, or some of his people, or even Mike St. Pierre, or . . ." He petered out, remembering the other development in his thinking of the last twenty-four hours.

"What just happened? Tell me, Mo." Seeing it in his face.

So he told her about meeting Biedermann at the bar, the handcuffs implicating Ty. Then about Flannery, his suggestive background, the way he was manipulating Mo, the way he seemed to know every-thing Mo did, keeping tabs on him. The right physical type, a number of matches to the emerging psychological profile of Geppetto. The way he'd steered Mo's suspicion to Biedermann. Rebecca listened carefully, no longer so skeptical of Mo's hunches.

"But you're not buying Biedermann's suspicions about Ty."

"I can't see it. I just . . . can't." *Can't or won't?* he asked himself. He wished he felt as certain as his words implied. "Especially not when Flannery is starting to look so likely. I know the material I have on him is completely circumstantial. But I've got a few lines of inquiry out, I should know more in a few days."

"I think you should tell Erik. At least ask him if he's ever considered Flannery."

Mo tipped his head, ambivalent.

"We either trust him or we don't, Mo! Which is it?"

"Not that simple. The more we know about this, the more Biedermann and his 'cleanup crew' have to worry about us. I trust Biedermann to fulfill his brief. I just don't know how far his brief goes."

She didn't agree. They argued about it for a time, ending with a decision to wait a little longer on talking to Biedermann about Flannery.

Then it was her turn. "Let me catch you up on what I've been doing. First, I've been building the profile of Geppetto. The tapes of Ronald Parker's talking to himself in his cell have been a big help. As you heard, he has two primary affective modes, two main 'voices' in his speech. One is rambling, disorganized, dissociated. The other is the lecturing voice, the rote statements and slogans, which I see as an artifact of a conditioning process. From that content I can draw a bead on Geppetto's agenda."

"Which is—?"

Rebecca went to her desk, found a sheaf of notes, flipped through the pages. "I think Geppetto sees himself as a warrior, a guerrilla. His puppet-making is part of a mission that he feels is morally defensible. His actions are statements, almost acts of *protest*. He casts himself and his puppets and their victims as martyrs to a higher cause, because society doesn't acknowledge him. He feels persecuted and outcast."

"That part's pretty typical, with serial killers."

"True. But in his case, the delusion seems to have an unusually powerful internal consistency."

"So what's his statement? What's he protesting?"

She shrugged, and her brows made graceful question marks. "Don't know. Something as simple as his own childhood trauma? Something as complex as some social or political injustice, real or perceived? Whichever, we know it centers on control." For a moment she looked defeated by the mystery, but then she rallied. "I need to go over the tapes again and do some more reading in the medical literature. *But,*" she went on, "I also got a lot from Parker's other voice—his ramblings. I performed a quantitative analysis."

"What's that?"

"In one sense, it's a crude tool, but it can often be very helpful. Basically, you inventory what the patient says when he free-associates. The basic idea is simply that themes that show up frequently are probably significant."

"So what themes cropped up?"

" 'Daddy' is a big one, we saw that right away. In fact, records show Parker was physically abused—violent, not sexual—by his father, but in this case I doubt the daddy theme is directly left over from childhood trauma at his father's hands. I think Geppetto deliberately acted the daddy role, exploited it, to anchor Parker's programming in his childhood. Tie in to archetypes of fear and authority residual from infancy. It's smart conditioning."

"Does that mean Geppetto knew something about Parker's past—knew he'd been abused?"

"If he did, it would suggest that he either knew Parker personally or did background research as part of his procurement process. Parker has a record with social welfare agencies, the juvenile-detention and foster-care systems—Geppetto could have found that out, chosen

327

him on the basis of his past. But not necessarily. Unfortunately, daddies are all too often . . . frightening, authoritarian, controlling figures. Geppetto could just be exploiting that generality."

Mo thought about that, took out his pad and noted it. That was good: Geppetto's procurement techniques could leave a trail back to him. "What else?"

"Let's see. Well, there were a couple of odd ones. 'Dogs' came up a lot. 'Like the dogs.' 'Where the dogs go when they're bad.' Not sure what to make of that . . . Then there's 'the junkyard,' or 'the dump.' It's connected with both punishment and reward. Comes up again and again."

A chill shimmied up Mo's spine. Mudda Raymon said something about a "dump-yard." "Is the junkyard a . . . a real place? Or a symbolic place?"

She did an admiring double take. "God, I love the way you catch these things! I'm not sure. Symbolically, it sounds threatening—a dump is ugly, a place where broken or unneeded things are discarded. If Parker was a 'thing,' maybe 'Daddy' threatened to throw him away if he didn't behave? But I got the sense it might be a real environment. 'Don't make me go to the dump.' 'Daddy loves me, I did good in the junkyard.' "

"So it could be a real place."

"Sure. But not necessarily a real junkyard. Could be a real place that Geppetto gave a symbolically meaningful name. But I have a theory." This was dark stuff, but Rebecca was looking pleased with herself. The bloodhound look. Mo shook his head, amazed at her.

She was getting into it now, pacing and gesturing as she explained, "I thought about how you would conduct conditioning on human beings. Geppetto required about twenty months for each subject, right? We figured that from the time elapsed between when Ronald Parker went missing and his first kill, and it strikes me as about right for the minimum time needed to establish solid conditioning. Okay. You'd have to have a private, secure place to do this stuff. It would be someplace where you could come and go without attracting anyone's attention—maybe a rural location. It'd have to be a place where people couldn't see or hear anything, so it'd be inside, maybe a basement or attic. But if you wanted to create killers who could stay stable in the real world, keep a semblance of normalcy as they went about the killing, you couldn't just turn them loose afterward. Not after twenty months in some dark hole, probably strung up like a puppet a lot of the time. They'd be severely agoraphobic when they first got outside again—cripplingly afraid of open spaces. They might not be in good physical shape. You'd have to acclimate them to the outdoors again by degrees, and you'd want them to get strong. Most important, you'd want to exercise the programming in situations where the subject wasn't under direct physical control. Geppetto would have to be sure his subjects could experience physical freedom and yet still obey commands and implanted compulsions. Parker's remarks are very fragmentary, but I think the dump is where Geppetto took him when he was almost ready to be set loose. The final stage of conditioning. Very strenuous, very scary, yet liberating, too. The site of the most extreme punishments and most extreme rewards."

When Rebecca got into this stuff, she really hummed. She was strikingly beautiful now, animated, eyes alight, and Mo wondered how he'd ever thought anything about her to be plain.

It was getting close to three o'clock. A bright day outside, sun not far past the zenith and just starting to edge the buildings across the street with shadows. The dump or junkyard rearing its head, another tie to Mudda Raymon's vision, had unsettled him badly.

And another concern nagged at him. He'd always had good instincts about how deep shit was getting, and his alarm bells were going off all over the place. It was driving him nuts that Rebecca was at risk. And he was partly responsible—he'd pulled her into this deeper every step of the way, bringing her to the Rappaport scene, asking her to spy on Biedermann, encouraging the visit to Ronald

329

Parker. If Geppetto was Flannery, he'd already demonstrated that he had the resources to know just about everything. Rebecca would be just as prominent on his radar as Mo was.

Which meant that somehow Mo had to protect her. And Rachel. But as with everything else about this case, he had no idea how. Get her away from the case somehow. But it was probably too late for that. Plus her training and talents were crucial at this stage.

Suddenly he felt overwhelmed again, his thoughts fuzzy and chaotic. Rebecca saw it, looked at him with concern. "You're fading, Morgan," she said. Her eyes narrowed suspiciously. "Did you eat anything today?"

Mo tried to remember. He hadn't felt like eating dinner after seeing Flannery yesterday, hadn't had time for breakfast or lunch today. His abdomen had that hollowed-out, charred feeling that came from pouring coffee into an empty stomach. A bite to eat wouldn't be bad. At the same time, he was afraid eating would make him sleepy. But if he was going to crash, it had better be back at Carla's mom's mausoleum, or he might miss Gus's return call. Which was very important just now.

"Gotta get back to White Plains," he mumbled. He lurched upright. "Got a couple of irons in the fire that can't wait."

She frowned, but didn't press for details. "I'm going to make you a sandwich for the drive," she said. She went into the kitchen, and he heard the clink of dishes, the chunk of the refrigerator door. Mo found his jacket, pulled it on, checked the bedroom for his things. In the kitchen, he came up behind her and draped himself around her, burying his face in her hair. She smelled like sun on summer grass. He shut his eyes and just felt her movements as she spread mayo on bread and laid out lettuce and slices of chicken.

"Saw Rachel and her friends as I came in," he said into her hair.

"'The call of the wild,'" she said accusingly.

"She told her friends I was your boyfriend."

Her shoulders dropped in exasperation. "I never used that word!"

"What word did you use?"

"Rachel and I are quite close. But there are . . . areas where I feel entitled to my privacy. I told her you were a professional colleague." She did something to his sandwich and went on primly, "A professional colleague I was quite attracted to."

"How'd she like that? What's her verdict on the cop boyfriend?"

Rebecca turned and presented him with a plastic-wrapped sandwich on the flat of her hand. "She asked if you were going to come bowling with us again tomorrow. Our Sunday ritual. I said if it was all right with her, and you had the time, I would certainly like that. She gave her permission."

"She just wants to chaperone our dates."

"You don't know much about adolescent psychology, do you? Mo, in her language, that's a major thumbs-up! I was very pleased." He hadn't taken the sandwich, so she tucked it into his jacket pocket, then came against him again. "Sometime soon," she said into his shoulder, "can we go to your house? I want to see where you live. I want you to cook something for me, I bet you're a great cook."

Just the thought of her coming to Carla's mom's mausoleum made his stomach clench. But he mumbled, "Yeah, sure. Yeah, sometime that would be good, sure."

She herded him out the door, waved good-bye. He went to the elevator, hit the call button, and waited in a kind of agony. The sweetness with her was so good. The thought of what they were up against, what could happen: so terrible. In his whole life, he couldn't remember ever feeling two simultaneous emotions so opposite and so intense.

41

MR. SMITH SAT IN an aluminum lawn chair, catching his breath and feeling both angry and sorry for himself. Number Four was on the wall in the next room, maybe asleep but probably listening and no doubt very glad to be ignored tonight. Number Three was panting, covered with sweat. It seemed like a good moment to take a break.

Thanks to Three's screwups, Morgan Ford and Rebecca Ingalls were actually doing it, beginning to unravel the whole thing he'd spent these years building. This afternoon, back at his Manhattan apartment, he'd listened to the most recent surveillance tape. He wasn't sure which got to him worse, listening to their sex act with all its tenderness and sensuality—normal, common human intimacies forever denied him!—or their conversations, which showed they'd made startlingly accurate leaps of inference and deduction.

The question was, how to adapt the plan? He'd have preferred more time, at least enough for Number Four to come online. But on the other hand, he'd always intended a major theatrical presentation at the end. Maybe the Dynamic Duo of Ford and Ingalls were precisely the opportunity he needed, and he should just move ahead to the final stage.

His own indecision made him furious. Go for the finale now, or try again to stave off the end? He hated indecision. Indecision caused you to hesitate, made you vulnerable. It took away your control, made you susceptible to the control of others. He'd been down that road before. Never again. He had been successful thus far by cutting the strings. Continued success depended on continued, decisive assertion of freedom.

They were in what had once been the living room of the old house, a spacious room now set up as a conditioning chamber. They needed space to move around, so it was almost empty of furniture. The windows were covered with sturdy plywood boxes built around homey drapes so that from outside, even pretty close up, they'd look like normal windows. A pair of projectors on a table beamed photos of Detective Morgan Ford against one wall, one of them an ID shot lifted from his personnel files and another from a newspaper article. They had worked on Rebecca Ingalls earlier, using slides from her book jacket photos and shots Mr. Smith had taken on the sly.

Number Three huddled on the floor across the room, naked but unfettered. He was well beyond the stage when the strings and other paraphernalia would be of use. His next tasks wouldn't involve the ritual, and anyway he needed to obey commands even when able to move freely: He'd have to be able to act adaptively while still operating on program.

And he was doing great. Always a terrific subject, Three. And that was the problem. With conditioning, it was easy come, easy go. Three programmed easily, but just as easily lost the program. He was too fluid inside, too changeable. Nothing would stick for long with this guy. Maybe that's why the sadness tonight, Mr. Smith thought: Human beings were such fallible creatures. So fickle. Such prisoners of their own weaknesses.

For a while, Mr. Smith had considered trying the radio implant on Three as a way to compensate for his tendency to shed programming. Plus, with the situation as it was, he had to get a lot of mileage out of these weekend sessions, before the workweek began and he had only evenings. The experiment with the golden retriever showed he could do it.

The radio-control idea was nothing new. Even back then, they'd experimented with direct neural stimulation via implants in human subjects. The paranoid fringe had been festering ever since with rumors of implant-controlled assassins, whose every act was governed by somebody at a console somewhere. But the reality was much more crude. In those days, they'd had neither the cranial imaging technology nor the knowledge of human neurology to do anything as sophisticated as dictating specific complex actions. Nowadays, with all the advances in technology, it was probably a different story, even the *New York Times* carried stories on how they were using radio-controlled rats for spying and drug interdiction. But back then all an implant could do was send a shock to the subject's brain, causing disorientation, fear, and pain.

It was, however, *extreme* fear and pain, and as an adjunct to conditioning and hypnotherapy, a remotely activated trigger for activating previously instilled posthypnotic commands, it had some useful applications.

But then he'd worried that with the minimal equipment he had here, he'd screw up the surgery—a hundredth of an inch to the left or right or too deep, and he could kill or paralyze Three. It would be his first human implant in thirty years, he'd be rusty. Or the apparatus would impair Three's fighting skills or decision-making at clutch time. Dogs and rats were one thing, humans another. Vastly more complex brains and behavioral repertoires.

So: Back to traditional methods. With a vengeance. Extreme measures were justified. There wasn't much time, these sessions had to really count. And anyway, Three deserved it.

Mr. Smith tossed a water bottle toward Three, who was taken by surprise but still caught it easily. Reflexes intact, that was good. Excellent physique, too, good muscle mass and little body fat.

"It's important to stay hydrated," Mr. Smith reminded him, mothering a bit. "You should drink at least a pint every fifteen minutes when you're exercising."

Three pulled the nipple valve on the bottle and sucked it down.

"You and me, we've got a tough job, don't we?" Mr. Smith asked commiseratingly. The sadness came over him again, the resignation. All these reminders of human fallibility. Maybe all of life's efforts were in vain. He took a drink from his own water bottle and went on, "No, it's not easy to take on a whole society's ills. We're heroes, but nobody knows it. That's why we've got to stick together. That's why we've got to give it our all."

Three had heard this all before, just one facet of the conditioning process, the "we're a team" angle. You wanted every nerve, every fiber, of the subject's psyche to be allied with the program. Sometimes it meant dominating him utterly. Sometimes it meant confiding, being sympathetic, and even eliciting his sympathy in return. They had just finished two hours of the dominance-relationship routine, so now it was time for the paternal-intimacy thing.

But more than that, Mr. Smith was feeling acutely aware of the night wrapped around the house, pressing against the walls, isolating them and giving the sealed room a secret, urgent, lonesome feel. He felt in need of some semblance of normal human intimacy. So, yes, these confessionals did double duty. The world owed him that much.

"I mean," Mr. Smith went on, "imagine yourself in my shoes. You're young, you're full of idealism, you're patriotic. You study medicine and psychology with the goal of serving mankind, you join the army to help your country in its hour of need. And your country says, *Yes, welcome aboard, do we* ever *need you!*"

He paused and gave Number Three a look.

Three knew that look, knew the drill. "That must have been very gratifying," Three said. His breathing had calmed now, but his voice was raspy. He cleared his throat.

"Oh, let me tell you! It goes straight to your head! You're entrusted with secrets, you're given challenging assignments—very, *very* heady for a young man. When I started, I was young enough to believe they knew what they were doing, that it was necessary, it was *right*. Young enough to be *flattered* I was allowed to be part of it."

Pause. The look. Three quickly cleared his throat again and said, "At first, anyway. Those bastards."

Mr. Smith nodded. "Exactly! I could accept that in wartime normal rules of behavior, ideas about 'right' and 'wrong,' get bent. So I did my job. Our team molded killers, and I could believe in it. The war was going badly, the enemy often operated out of neighboring countries that we couldn't overtly attack. And the Russians and Chinese were helping the North Vietnamese, they were absolutely *loving* the tar baby we were stuck in, but we couldn't strike at them directly. But maybe that's not something your generation can understand—the *frustration*."

"It must have been terrible," Number Three put in. "Can't really blame the armed services for wanting a solution."

Mr. Smith thought that was a little glib, a little too eager. He didn't change his posture or his voice, but internally he went on high alert. Three was tricky as a weasel, maybe he was hoping to lull Daddy, get the jump on him, knowing he often got kind of carried away at this point. Mr. Smith drew his legs under him as he went on.

"So I did what they wanted," he went on. "It was only later that I realized how bad it was. How I'd been deceived. For one thing, our subjects didn't work well. Half of them would go out and we'd never hear from them again, or they'd kill once or twice on target and then drift. Or they'd kill civilians, lots of them, My Lai was only one of *dozens* of disasters. I had a hard time with that. Yes, I had moral aversions. And, hey, just from a practical standpoint, that stuff was making it hard to keep the project hidden. And then, *then,* we began getting reports that some of them were killing *our own guys*. I questioned my superiors about this, they told me to forget about it. I argued that we'd lost our scientific objectivity, maybe it was time we had a moratorium and assessed the real results. But like everything else in that war, bad news was not allowed. 'Do your job,' I was told.

'You don't know the whole story. Trust us.' So I kept on. I was *patriotic*. I was *loyal*. I did my *duty*."

Mr. Smith felt his control slipping despite his wariness of Three. A knot formed in his throat at the unfairness of it. The way he was treated! He glowered at the face of Morgan Ford, the wise-guy good looks, smart-aleck deadpan. The projected image didn't respond, so he turned his glare to Number Three. Time for some normative conversational input from the subject anyway.

Three took the cue. "Those dirty bastards." He almost seemed sincere. "So what happened? When did you realize something had to be done?"

"I'll never forget the day. Never. You have to understand, I hated the Vietnamese, I hated the antiwar movement in the U.S. But I still felt there had to *be limits*. I was still idealistic enough to believe our country's domestic life had to be kept out of it. Our civil government had to be immune from military influence. So one day, I'm in my lab, and I get assigned a new test subject, a big, healthy convict fresh from some penitentiary. Very high secrecy, new program priorities. When I was given my orders about how to structure the conditioning, I realized this guy wasn't being programmed for work in Vietnam. Or anywhere in Southeast Asia."

Mr. Smith remembered it all too well. Reading through his lengthy directive, he'd realized how stupid he'd been, how easily led by the nose. Right there, sitting numbly on one of the steel lab stools, he felt the fabric of his life unraveling. All his commitments and beliefs and loyalties. A long series of compromises, each made in good faith, each with just enough rationalization and justification to continue. But adding up to the insufferable.

Plus the whole program was a scientific and medical disaster! The killers they manufactured were going on the fritz, nobody really knew how to do this! But no one wanted to hear it! And now he was supposed to build a killing machine to be let loose in the United States?

"But I didn't have much leeway, see," Mr. Smith explained. He was tired of worrying about whether Three was going to try something, he didn't care. He got up, took out his Asp, flicked it to full length. He paced up and down, slapping the stainless-steel baton into his left hand. The next part he liked to tell without excess emotion, businesslike, stoical, showing how much he'd endured without complaint: "I knew I couldn't say anything. Because it was *too* big, too secret. Coincidentally, it was right then that my girlfriend got killed in a *very* questionable car wreck back in the States. Lynn, Lynnie—sweetest girl. Murdering her did double duty, for *them*. One, I was heartbroken, my last tie to normal reality was severed, I had nowhere else to go, the program was now my only home. Plus it made it perfectly clear what would happen to *me* if I squawked. So what did I do?"

Number Three had flinched when he'd stood up, that was gratifying. Now he looked up at Mr. Smith, cowering. "Um, you, you didn't have a choice. You went on with it. You had to martyr your moral sensibilities. You had to disregard your scientific skepticism. They controlled you. They manipulated you."

Mr. Smith nodded. Three was good, a bright young man. Too bad he had no *spine* to go with it, no staying power. But at this point, it didn't much matter. His programming would stick long enough for a final mission.

"You got that right!" Mr. Smith went on. The bile was backing up in his throat, thirty years of bitterness, choking him. "I *did* as I was *told. Yes, sir! Right away, sir!* I went into my lab and laid the foundation programming for eight months. Then, at last, they gave me the targeting materials, always the last stage—the photos, tapes, bio materials. This was 1971, the U.S. was in chaos with the antiwar movement, a crisis of national identity, there was this peacenik making presidential noises. George McGovern. He was to be the target. *I was creating a killer to eliminate a United States senator and probable presidential candidate!* At last I was in the inner circle, among the guys doing the dirtiest of the dirty. Five years inside and the sacrifice of the girl I loved were the price of admission." He stamped past Number Three, then whirled on him. "You gotta understand, I *hated* the peace movement! But by then I hated my superiors, too. For killing Lynnie. For what they were doing to my life, to science, to the American principles we were supposed to be fighting for. For fucking *cornering* me, *controlling* me! And when I got the McGovern materials, I started thinking about the last eight years. We were always given secret directives, none of us ever knew what targets the other guys' labs were being assigned. Still, I knew the program had been running for at least ten years before I got there. So I had to wonder about the assassinations, JFK, the other Kennedy, King? I mean, all of a sudden this rash of domestic political hits, in the same few years? It doesn't look fishy? Doesn't look *coordinated*? Give me a fucking *break*! I thought, 'My God, we've taken it on ourselves to decide the future of the United States!' Somebody had, anyway. Some small secret cabal, unelected, unknown. The *arrogance*—that was what did it for me."

Mr. Smith stopped, glared at Three. Through the wall he heard whimpering, which would be Number Four, hearing the rising passion in his voice and feeling the conditioned-in fear mount. That was nice. But Three had been quiet for too long.

"Time for a normative verbal response," Mr. Smith said sweetly.

His tone scared Three, who barked quickly, "So you decided something had to be done! A form of protest that nobody could ignore!" A voice hoarse with fear.

Right answer. Mr. Smith resumed pacing, his shadow briefly eclipsing the huge face of Morgan Ford projected on the wall.

"Correct. Very good," he said. "So I deliberately skewed my new subject's targeting. He was sent off to do his job, fucked up, had to be cleaned up later. And then the Pentagon Papers thing blew up, all the secret bad news of the war came out, there were congressional probes and armed services reviews and news reporters up the wazoo. It got too hot for comfort, our labs were disappeared and the program got vanished. We were all reassigned or sent home. And the war ended about a year later."

Significant pause.

Taking the cue, Number Three said, "But that wasn't the end of the story. That wasn't the end of their manipulation of you."

The right response again. But it was too easy, Three was being facile again and it enraged Mr. Smith. "No, it was not," he said, acting mollified. "No, it was not. There's no happy ending here." He let a benignly paternal expression come over his face, and then without warning, he lunged at Three, whipping the Asp toward his face.

Three dodged with surprising quickness and scrabbled backward across the floor. Mr. Smith swung the Asp again, so fast it whistled in the air. It hit the lawn chair and sent it flying, the tube aluminum crimped at the point of impact. In another instant Three was on his feet, legs wide, ready, chest pumping.

Another whistling swing of the Asp made contact, but only on the forearm, Three had defended himself well. A feint, another hit, partially deflected. Three was wincing from pain, but did a feint himself and then attacked. Mr. Smith anticipated it, sidestepped, clipped the back of his head with the Asp, sending Three sprawling. That must have hurt, too, but Three was up again in no time, face flushed with rage.

This was good. Three was in good form. You always had to keep their reflexes sharp.

"Excellent! Very good," Mr. Smith said. He frowned at Morgan Ford's impassive face on the wall and turned back to Three. "So now let's get back to some serious work."

42

M o picked up the women and they drove into the low-ering sun over to Fort Lee. Rebecca arranged it so Rachel sat in front next to Mo, presumably to let them bond or fight it out or whatever. It was fairly strained.

"So—where'd you guys go yesterday?" he asked casually.

"Movie."

Just out of politeness you could answer with more details, Mo thought. Like even the name of the movie, to give a guy something to go on here. He tried again, "That one friend of yours, she looks kind of Goth—"

"See, Mom? I told you, everybody has this prejudice!" Rachel whirled to face Rebecca accusingly, as if this were part of a continuing discussion. "Cindy wears black and leather, and we all know what that means, don't we? Columbine High School! Kinky sex and murder!"

"Wait a minute," Mo said. "Now you're being prejudiced about me—you know what I'm going to say. How? Because I'm a law-enforcement type?"

Rachel faced him confrontationally. "So what *were* you going to say?"

He actually hadn't been planning to say *anything*, he'd just been randomly tossing off possible starting places. But he improvised, "That she's pretty. That her Goth thing, one of my cousins, in Pittsburgh, is into that. She just graduated high school with honors and got a full scholarship to Smith. Majoring in ecology."

Actually, Mo hardly knew his mother's sister's kids, and the girl wasn't as Goth-identified as Rachel's Cindy looked. He only knew any of this from his aunt's annual family newsletters.

But Rachel took it at face value. She cranked herself around in the seat to say to Rebecca, "See? It's like I was telling you! I mean, the Goths are totally like the smartest, most nonviolent kids I know!"

So now Mo was on her side. In the mirror, Mo saw Rebecca shrug, bemused by this turn of events, keeping her distance.

Then something happened that he would never have expected. Rachel flicked her gaze at him and then frowned critically at her own hands. "You're right. I was being prejudiced. I'm sorry. It's very hard to catch."

So she did take after her mother that way. The honest self-appraisal. Maybe there was hope for the kid.

They got to the bowling alley at six o'clock, parking in the mostly deserted shopping-center parking lot. The fading façade of Star Bowl was lit with watermelon light from the westering sun, bright against the dirty sky of Manhattan beyond. Mo hit the men's room as the women checked in. When he came out and went to the desk to get his shoes, he looked over the lanes and spotted them immediately: two yellow-haired heads above the vinyl back of the booth at their lane. Rebecca's hair was bundled carelessly back, so that strands of it fell onto her face. Rachel seemed to be gabbing away, more kidlike than Mo had ever seen her. So probably there were parts of her she didn't reveal around him. That was instructive.

The old guy at the counter sprayed some Desenex into a pair of shoes that looked like roadkill and handed them over.

Rachel was okay, they had a pretty good time. Mo felt like he was getting the hang of it, handling the ball better. There were only two other lanes in use. It was a beat-up sort of place, the vinyl benches burned by cigarette butts, the wallpaper on the end wall coming loose, tacked at the top but starting to balloon inward. But he could see where you'd like the old-fashioned feel: the long, low room, the waxy smell of the varnished lanes, the out-of-date high tech of the overhead scoring lights and ball returns, all in this rounded, passé futuristic style.

They bowled a game and then took a break and went back into the dimly lit bar and grill. An older woman, maybe the wife of the guy at the front counter, got them Cokes and bags of chips, and they sat in a vinyl booth that smelled of stale cigarette smoke. Rachel tried to teach him how to talk with a Midwestern accent. His attempts were found very amusing. He reminded her they were being ironic here.

Rebecca wasn't saying much, but she looked good even in a place like this, lit only by beer signs. When Rachel went to the bathroom, he reached across the table, took her hands, asked her how she was doing.

"I'm okay. I like seeing you, Mo. Even if our dates are chaperoned. God, you have won Rachel over! It's hard to explain how happy that makes me."

Won over seemed like maybe wishful thinking. The kid was loosening up a little but was still hanging pretty tough.

"But something's on your mind," he said.

"I don't really want to talk business tonight. But, yes, there's something about our basic thesis that's been troubling me. From a psychological perspective."

"Okay—"

Rebecca glanced back toward the bathrooms to make sure Rachel wasn't coming. "Geppetto. Whether it's Flannery or whoever, we believe the puppet-maker got his training during some secret mind-control project in the Vietnam era. Right? And he has some agenda, some statement to make, that has no doubt been conflated seamlessly with a trauma he experienced in his past. But, Mo—the Vietnam War ended, what, twenty-seven years ago!"

"So the problem is—?"

"If the first of Geppetto's subjects was Ronald Parker, or even the one in San Diego that Erik worked on before he was assigned here, in 1995—what took him so long? What was Geppetto doing with his agenda and his bottled-up trauma for twenty-two years? Or, conversely, what happened in 1995 that triggered Geppetto to start up?"

Good question. And good questions were windows into solutions. Mo was holding both her hands in both of his as he thought about it. And then Rachel was there, sliding into the seat next to her mother. "Am I interrupting something?" she said caustically. "Excuse *me*."

Still, they bowled another couple of games, had a pretty good time. They headed out at nine o'clock, the last customers to leave, and the old man locked the door behind them.

They weren't yet at the stage where it was confortable enough for everybody for Mo to drop Rachel at her dad's house. So he drove back across the bridge into Manhattan, not saying anything, feeling the pressure mount again. Rebecca's question had brought it all back. *The dump,* he was thinking. Tomorrow was Monday, he and St. Pierre would begin looking into junkyards, and they'd start digging into Dennis Radcliff's past to see how Geppetto had acquired him. Maybe they'd find a line to Geppetto. But it felt weak. And he wanted to get to work right away, now, tonight.

When they got to Rebecca's building, he said, "Rachel, I'm going to kiss your mother good-night, and I don't care if you like it or not. If it makes you feel better, I'll give you a kiss, too." Rachel looked affronted for only an instant, then said, "Maybe some other time, big boy." A vamping voice that still dripped with disgust, but so well done they all three laughed. When they got out, he waited until they were safely in the lobby before he pulled away.

Into Brooklyn. The thousand strands of the old bridge, the scintillating lights in the looming dark of the cities on either side of the river, then off at Flushing Avenue, down into the dark maze. Brooklyn streets at night. It was 9:48 on Sunday night, not the best time to barge in, but he'd been wanting to do this for almost two weeks. Not that he exactly believed in Mudda Raymon's prophecy ability and all that. But he couldn't deny she had gotten certain things right: the puppet-puppet, the dump. Could have meant nothing or anything—except that both ended up being relevant. Maybe he was being superstitious, but he found it easier to believe in intuition, even magic, than that much coincidence.

And there was another thing he'd realized he needed to do, it seemed like it had to happen soon.

Without Ty there to navigate, it took him a while to find the place again. The streetlight in front was out, leaving the green and yellow door and the blank eyes of plywood-covered windows in shadow. This time there was no bodyguard at the door, but he spotted Carla's red Honda just down the street. A few kids on the sidewalk down the block, otherwise a quiet night in this part of Brooklyn.

He parked, went to the stoop, knocked at the door, waited. For a long time, nothing, just the giant, complicated white noise of the city night. Then a thump and a rattle, and the door opened a crack. He recognized the young woman who had led him upstairs the first time.

"I'd like to talk to Carla Salerno. And Mudda Raymon, if she'll see me. Tell her it's Morgan Ford—she'll know who I am."

The door shut and he heard it locked again. But after another minute it rattled again and then opened wide. Carla came out onto the stoop.

"What are you doing here, Mo?" she asked suspiciously. She was barefoot, wearing a big white shirt open over a gray tank top and skirt. He thought she looked thinner, older, but it could have been the bad light.

"I wanted to see Mudda Raymon again. And you."

"Oh, now you're a big believer?" She shook her head. "Come on, Mo. What—you think that's somehow going to get me back?"

She was so far wrong that it touched him. "You still doing okay? You feel like your life's on track?" Suddenly that mattered a lot to him.

She snorted disdainfully. "This is pretty juvenile, Mo. I mean, I thought you'd be handling this better. I really did."

"No, Carla, listen. I really do want to see Mudda Raymon. She's . . . last time, she said some interesting things, they've kind of come back as significant. I've got this case, I don't know where to go with it, and—"

"And a ninety-year-old Jamaican grandmother is going to help you."

"I'll take any help I can get."

A jet angled slowly overhead, eclipsing the vague stars, drowning them in noise as it slid down toward La Guardia. Carla turned away, wrapping her shirt tighter around her even though it was hot and muggy on the stoop. She looked down the block at the kids. "Well, she can't help you, Mo," she said bitterly. "She died on Thursday. She'd been terminal for years. So your sudden conversion is a little late. I'm just here helping out the family for a few days." Before he could say he was sorry, she whirled around to face him again. "So does that allow you to get real about why you're here? Because I'd really like you to get real about us and stop trying to hang on to something that wasn't working!"

Mo stood there, half pissed at her for the attitude, half wanting to hold her one more time as they straightened this out. Yes, this was partly about her and him. But not how she thought.

"You've got it wrong, Carla. I've been seeing somebody else, it came up really fast and it's really good. It's . . . serious. It's a lot of things I've wanted for a long time."

"And, what, you felt you just had to let me know?" she asked skeptically.

He thought about that. "Yeah, basically. I . . . yeah, I just thought you should know." He shrugged. It sounded lame.

"What do you want—my *permission*?"

"No. Look, I don't know. Closure, maybe." Or some old-fashioned thing, wanting it to be clean and aboveboard and honorable. Like love was a thing that once given was supposed to be willingly relinquished if it was no longer wanted. Like letting it go was important, even when you both were moving on, even when there was someone else. Like it deserved some minimal ceremony.

Now she saw he was serious. "Mo, you give yourself closure on these things."

He nodded reluctantly. "Yeah. You're probably right."

She held her shirt tight around her, arms crossed. That wonderful shape. After another minute she sighed. "Whatever. Okay. You have my permission. You have closure. Okay? And now I'm going back upstairs." She turned, went inside, and shut the door.

Mo drove out of Brooklyn, thinking it was too bad about Mudda Raymon. He'd gotten his hopes up, he'd been serious when he'd said he'd take help from any quarter. Also thinking about how it had gone with Carla, wondering what he'd expected that was any different, and why he didn't feel happier now that it was done.

He didn't get back to the mausoleum until eleven. Carla's mom's big dark house, the oak-shadowed lawns, the echoing front rooms, his semisqualid bachelor domicile in back. He checked the answering machine. No messages. He'd kind of hoped Rebecca might've called in. He sat on the bed, feeling emotionally wrung out. Then the telephone rang and made him jump.

"Who's your new guy?" The flat voice of Gus Grisbach.

"Gus—thanks for calling! Flannery, Richard K. Flannery."

"As in Westchester district attorney Flannery."

"As in, yeah." For an instant Mo thought of adding Tyndale Boggs to the list, but his instincts rebelled. He chided himself for losing objectivity but then gave himself the excuse that Gus wouldn't approve of prying into a fellow PD investigator. Sleazy legal officials and arrogant Feds were more his cup of tea.

Gus didn't say anything for a few seconds. But at last he said,

"Yeah, okay. I'll call you." Another pause, Mo thought he'd hung up. But then Gus spoke one more time: "So tell me, Ford—you some kind of a masochist? Because from where I sit, between this and the last one, you look like a guy who's asking for pain."

43

MONDAY MORNING, first order of business was a conference in Marsden's office, bringing Mike St. Pierre and the senior investigator up-to-date on what they were still calling the Pinocchio murders. The hard part for Mo was getting the others excited about the junkyard initiative while avoiding telling them why he was so hot on it: Yeah, see, a coincidence, this ninety-year-old Jamaican witch, now dead, thought it figured in, and then later it shows up in an analysis of Ronald Parker's free-associating babbling. Nor could he tell them the big picture: programmed human killing machines, the Geppetto scenario. For the first time, it came home to him what Biedermann was up against. This case really was about control of information—who knew what, when. How to survive and move toward a solution knowing as little or as much as you did.

His argument went that with the similar MOs their best bet was to establish a link of contact between Parker and Radcliff. The psychologist thought the junkyard was significant in Parker's babblings and might therefore relate to Radcliff, too. St. Pierre took it at face value, but throughout the exercise Marsden looked at Mo appraisingly, skeptical black, slit eyes over pouches. Marsden finally said, "Yeah. Yeah, you guys go get your junkyard battle plan sketched out. Yeah. And then, Mo, come see me, we got stuff to talk about."

Back out to the main room, going over the leads, looking at maps, taking notes. The plan was for St. Pierre to get the basics on Radcliff's background, then do some legwork in the community to put together a picture of his habits, his hangouts, his associations. From there, Mo could covertly look for a link back to Geppetto. The most important part of the whole thing, and nobody else knew about it.

On that score, Rebecca had assigned herself the job of looking into Radcliff's psychological past. Maybe she was right, Geppetto did tap into social-services and penal systems to acquire subjects with psych profiles appropriate to his needs. If so, they could conceivably track both Parker and Radcliff back, look for the same windows that Geppetto had once climbed through.

St. Pierre's first job, though, was to get maps of solid-waste disposal facilities. In theory, the hypothetical dump could be anywhere, but Mo was certain it would be nearby. All the crimes had occurred within fifty miles, and if Geppetto was Flannery—or even Zelek or, God forbid, Ty—he'd have to have his conditioning "lab" near his office for his double life to be logistically feasible. So St. Pierre would locate disposal sites in southern New York State and adjoining areas of New Jersey and Connecticut. Once they had assembled a master list, Mo and St. Pierre would requisition a few uniforms to help tour dumps in New York State while other task force members checked out New Jersey and Connecticut sites. A total of maybe ten guys looking at a lot of territory, a lot of maps, a lot of trash. But you had to start somewhere.

When St. Pierre was gone, Mo reviewed the minimal information they'd gotten so far: Radcliff's driver's license application and photo. Thirty years old, longish blond hair, fairly handsome face marred by a smug half-smile, a supercilious look in the eyes. Six foot two, 210 pounds—a pretty big guy. They'd made some other inquiries, looking for a criminal record, and Mo expected more shortly.

But there was Marsden in his office doorway, leaning against the door frame and staring daggers, the irritated skin next to his nose like a red warning flag. Mo put on an apologetic face and went in.

Marsden shut the door, went back to the other side of his desk, sat heavily in his chair.

"Okay. Tell me what the fuck's going on." Mo feigned a surprised look, but Marsden wasn't having any. "Oh, look. How dumb am I, huh? I'm too tired to play games here. Let's hear it."

Mo had spent half the night thinking feverishly, *Why not tell it all to Marsden?* Maybe the wily old senior investigator could help find a way out of the maze.

But opening this up would be scary. On the Flannery thing, you didn't even *suggest* you were suspicious of a powerful district attorney unless you had a hell of a lot more to go on than Mo had at this point. Besides which, how much credibility would Mo have, given the guy he was accusing happened to be the very DA currently working up charges against him?

And then, forget Flannery, there really were issues of what you could call "national security" here. This had become a big issue, completely beyond Mo's experience. Maybe it *was* best to keep old government nightmare bungles secret, lay them to rest. And, as Zelek had correctly pointed out, he really didn't want to mess with Biedermann's show: Blowing the Geppetto scenario open now could easily squirrel the SAC's chances of catching the puppet-master.

Most important, spilling to Marsden might set something in motion, increasing the odds that he and Rebecca would become Geppetto's targets. Or Biedermann's.

Marsden was waiting.

"What would you do," Mo hazarded, "if you'd started an investigation and it seemed to lead to, oh, say, some government thing?"

"A government thing." Marsden's head bobbed on his jowly neck, eyes closed, like *Great, here goes another Mo Ford special.*

"Like a . . . maybe an intelligence-community problem. Or national-security-related."

That was it for Marsden. He shook his head, waved his hands, *enough.* "You know, Mo, I was looking forward to reaming your ass this morning. But you know what? I'm too tired. I don't have what it takes. I'm due in for the bypass end of the week, I gotta conserve my strength, I gotta avoid blowing a gasket before Saturday. But I'm gonna tell you two things."

Marsden did look tired, more sad than mad, as if Mo were a big disappointment to him. Mo would have preferred the reaming, this was tragic. Marsden really was a man running out of gas. Now he heaved a sigh, looked back at Mo. "Off the record, as a guy who has some misguided respect for your work, I was gonna tell you something I thought you should know. Which is that Flannery's level of interest in you is very high. Too high, more than called for. He's been talking to me, to everyone in Major Crimes, fishing for shit on you. Also to Dodgson and Paley up in Albany, going over every little glitch in your file, maybe refreshing their memories about you in unflattering ways." He gave Mo a meaningful look with his slits.

That gave Mo a chill. Dodgson and Paley were budding Ken Starrs from Internal Affairs who had conducted previous internal reviews on him. No, not just Ken Starrs, more like Terminator robots, right out of the movies, tireless and unstoppable.

Marsden went on, "Point being, Flannery's acting like he means business on screwing you some big way. If not on Big Willie, something else. I was gonna ask you, A, what'd you do to get Flannery after you like this? It seems almost like something personal. You insult him, call him a jerk, or what? You screwing his girlfriend? Or, B, I was gonna ask, maybe Flannery has good cause to go after you like this, and I don't know what it is? You wanna give me a heads-up on some fuckup you haven't told me about?"

Flannery's extreme hard-on for Mo made sense for only one reason, Mo was thinking. He sensed Mo was getting close to him, he was looking for ways to sabotage Mo's investigation. But all he said to Marsden was "No. Nothing, none of the above. I swear to God."

Marsden looked at him with weary skepticism, a long look obviously intended to allow Mo to change his tune. When he didn't, Marsden bobbed his head again. "Okay. So on the other stuff you mentioned this morning, I'm gonna tell you one more thing. You've got this fucking . . . *impressionistic* way of running an investigation. You intuit this and you suspect that, you see suggestive stuff over *here,* inferences over *there.* And pretty soon, you've come around so your head's up your ass." Marsden had started low but was getting more and more worked up as he went on: "Now, you look to me like a guy up to his neck in hot water. Do I have that right? My point is, you want me to help, you gotta put something in front of me *on this desk!* Some paper, a name, a piece of evidence, a photograph. Something! If you can't do that, you'd better give up the artsy stuff and the national security shit. I can't do anything to protect you unless you show me something worth going out on a limb for."

Marsden had thumped the desk hard with his bunched fingertips, *on this desk,* face swelling red, before getting himself back under control. Calming again, he looked truly ill.

Mo looked at him with concern. "What time are you in surgery Saturday, Frank?" he asked. "I'd like to come keep Dorothea company. She must be worried sick."

With another hour left before he had to leave for the task force meeting, Mo worked the telephone directories, making lists. He looked under disposal services, dumps, garbage, junk, landfills, recycling, refuse, salvage, trash, waste. He also referenced antiques, art, entertainment, restaurants, taverns. In Brooklyn there was a dance club called The Junkyard, in the Village a gallery called Trash Art, and in Yonkers a bar called The Dump. In Greenwich, he found an antique store called Jane's Junkyard, and in Danbury a recycled-goods outlet called Good Junk, Inc. Then he remembered autos and made a list of auto salvage yards and used-parts outlets, then came up with surplus and scrap and listed surplus goods suppliers and scrap-metal reprocessing companies.

A long list, given that their target region included one of the most heavily industrialized areas in the world, a major producer of waste of all kinds.

Dumps or junkyards came in all shapes and sizes. Over the years, Mo had gone to crime scenes in cute, stinking rural landfills covered with thin grass and seagulls, and in urban metals-reclamation yards with mountains of crushed and shredded steel beneath gigantic cranes, processing conveyors, smoking smelter chimneys. What exactly had Geppetto and his puppets done in the "junkyard"? Something for Rebecca to zero in on. They had to draw a bead on that and select only the most promising sites to look at in person. Because there was no way they were going to check out the scores of possibles he had listed here.

Of course, it could all be for nothing. Maybe the "dump" was something else entirely, a code word, a symbolic phrase selected for reasons they couldn't know.

Mo dropped off the lists for St. Pierre to review, then left for the drive to Manhattan. Flannery and Biedermann would both be at the task force meeting, that should be fun, two big macho egos, all that testosterone. Tomorrow they'd put St. Pierre's lists of Sanitary District sites together with Mo's lists, prioritize the sites, and spend their days touring stinking landfills and dumps and salvage yards.

It was shaping up to be a great week.

A good-size crowd, twelve representatives from eight agencies and jurisdictions. Biedermann posed at the head of the conference table with his jacket off, shirtsleeves rolled up over beefy forearms in a workmanlike way. He looked tired, though, overextended, as did everyone else in the room. Flannery had even let a faint haze of white stubble crop up along a male-pattern-baldness line on his shiny dome, confirming Mo's suspicion that he shaved his head. Rebecca looked tired, too, but in a lovely way. When Mo came into the room, she shot a glance at him and then looked quickly away with a tiny, secret smile.

"Okay," Biedermann said. "Lots of ground to cover. I understand we've had some developments over the weekend. Chief Panelli and Detective Ford, maybe you can bring us up to speed on this event in Briarcliff Manor Saturday."

They took turns telling about Byron Bushnell's raid on the house of Dennis Radcliff, Bushnell's claim Radcliff had killed his wife, the puppeteer paraphernalia found in the house. Their theory was that Radcliff had begun a sexual relationship with Irene not long after she'd started cleaning for him and, in early April, had suggested they go for a picnic or tryst near the old power station, where he'd killed her.

The news that they had a probable name for the Pinocchio killer sent a stir through the group. Happy cops, feeling they were closing in.

Flannery had chosen the seat at the end of the table opposite Biedermann and had been absently rubbing his stubble as he listened. Now he asked, "So what do we know about Radcliff?"

Panelli passed around a handout and summarized, "My people tell me he has a history of juvenile problems, vandalism and assault, psych referrals. That's anecdotal in our department—his juvie records are sealed. But we learned he was convicted of aggravated rape in college, spent five years in Massachusetts jails. Released in '97. We don't know what he's been doing since, doesn't leave much of a paper trail. It'll take a while to get more."

"The prior rape's good—ties in with the Bushnell and Rappaport murders," Flannery said. "Between that and the paraphernalia, he looks good to me."

Biedermann: "Leaving us the question, where is he now?"

Nobody had any idea. For all they knew, he'd driven nearby that night, seen the activity in front of his house, and was in Alaska by now. Biedermann asked Rebecca if as a psychologist she could offer any insight into what Radcliff would do, where he'd go.

"Hiding out with relatives or friends? Maybe he's chosen another

355

victim and he's staying at the victim's residence? I'm sorry. I need more background before I could speculate." Rebecca did her act well, gave no indication she had come to other conclusions.

"So why the copycat thing?" Flannery asked. "Why did this guy suddenly decide he's going to not only start killing, but he's going to imitate Ronald Parker?" He narrowed his eyes, directing his question down the table to Biedermann.

Biedermann just shrugged. "He read about it in the papers, got turned on by the idea of tying people up? I don't know. Dr. Ingalls, any ideas on that one?"

"That would be the best guess," Rebecca agreed. "Unless we can prove a link of association between Parker and Radcliff."

"Which so far we haven't," Biedermann hastened to add.

"I want to point something out," Flannery said, "that nobody else here apparently has the balls to say. SAC Biedermann is ducking discussion of an important point here. And as the person who's going to prosecute this guy, I think there's a problem this task force has to have a theory on and a policy about."

Biedermann's face hardened. "And that would be . . . ?"

"A matter of forensic evidence. Okay, Radcliff reads about Ronald Parker's kills in the newspapers and decides he'd get off on that MO, too. Fine. But how'd he know to use the exact same lawn-trimmer line as Ronald Parker? And the knots—I mean, what, just by *coincidence* he also chooses to use a cats-paw and a running-end bight? To me, that cries out for a little reality check here, people."

This was good, Mo decided, these two big guys, each playing his ego theater to the assembled audience. He was interested in how Biedermann would handle the issue.

"Thank you, I'm glad you asked that," Biedermann said. "Because it brings me to the next part of our agenda here today. It's a good question because it suggests Radcliff had inside access to information about the Parker killings. Which to me means two possibilities. One, some participating law enforcement organization's offices or labs or evidence lockups—or *mouths*—are insufficiently secure, and Radcliff had access to them. *Maybe he still does.*" He raised his eyebrows, looking around the table to drive home the seriousness of that possibility. "Two, maybe he had, *or has,* help on the inside, witting or unwitting." Eyebrows: serious also. "In either case, this task force has to have very strict rules about information sharing. And as the federal agency here, my office is the only one with universal jurisdiction. Which means that I'm going to be calling the shots, and—I gotta be frank here—the FBI is going to be watching all of your shops very closely to see how well you abide." And he shot a look down at Flannery; *Your shop too, big guy.*

Flannery just grinned, tossing his head like *Yeah, yeah, heard it before.*

Biedermann went on, outlining the secrecy protocols he expected every participating organization to observe. Mo thought about the exchange. Obviously, Biedermann had to conceal the Geppetto scenario, and the "leaky system" or "inside man" theories were his best excuse. But why would Flannery bring it up? Because he was being a good DA and the point was legitimately important to the case? Or because he was Geppetto and wanted to probe Biedermann's thinking, observe his reactions, look gung ho on this and misdirect any possible suspicions of himself? It went round and round.

Then something hit him, a detail that appeared to have slipped past everybody. Okay, Flannery would know about the lawn-trimmer line, he'd sat in on both task forces, he'd personally looked over O'Connor's corpse. Fine. But the knots—the military knots that Ty had found names for, but no one else had mentioned by name. No meeting, no report, not Biedermann's own photo albums, nothing in Ty's files: *Never* had he heard anyone but Ty give specific names to those knots.

Mo covertly watched Flannery as the meeting went on, wondering if there was anything that marked or distinguished a monster like Geppetto. Yeah, he decided, you could just about see it in Flannery's blunt head, wide face, shrewd eyes. A darkness, a doubleness.

Cats-paw, running-end bight: Maybe Geppetto had just slipped up.

44

M O CONSIDERED TAKING THE clean jobs himself—going to the dance club, the bar, the antique shop—and letting young Mike and the uniforms ruin their shoes slogging around in stinking dumps. But his conscience objected, and they agreed to divide it all by region, save drive time.

Rebecca had done her best to imagine the outside conditioning environment that would best meet Geppetto's needs. It had to be within reasonable travel times of Geppetto's base of operations, because they'd have to get into the outside training by degrees, returning to home base afterward. It would have to allow vigorous physical activity, not be too confined. Most important, it had to be out of view of other people, meaning it was isolated or they worked at night.

Could it be a dance club or bar? Mo asked. Conceivably, Rebecca admitted: teach the subject to interact socially, to obey commands while physically unrestricted. But most likely it was an outdoor environment, rural or suburban. She suggested Mo add graveyards to his list, on the theory that people as "things" would be "discarded" there.

Adding graveyards, Mo and St. Pierre listed eight-two sites, winnowed that list to forty-three, then prioritized the list, most to least likely. They faxed lists to the New Jersey and Connecticut people, recruited a few NYSP uniforms to help, and began visiting the sites.

What to look for? First, the kind of general environment Rebecca described. Second, they'd bring photos of Parker and Radcliff to show site personnel: Ever see this guy around here? Watch the eyes and body language of the person you're talking to, Rebecca said, at the moment you show the photo. If Geppetto was paying somebody for access to the site, and for keeping quiet about it, the micro-momentaries could give it away. Finally, never give up hope of getting lucky: Look for puppet paraphernalia, a dropped disposable handcuff, whatever.

Mo talked to Rebecca briefly on the phone to coordinate. Her plan was to head up to Briarcliff to start probing into Radcliff's past. There were unofficial ways around sealed court records and medical confidentiality issues, and she had a network of colleagues in the right circles. When she asked if maybe they could get together at his place after work, his stomach clenched in panic. Such a reasonable request, so impossible. Again he dodged and changed the subject, and she didn't seem to notice.

Mo and Mike St. Pierre took some sites in Putnam and Westchester counties, while the NYSP troopers headed south to look through some salvage and scrap yards in lower Westchester and New York counties. They'd keep in touch by cell phone.

Mo's first stop was a sanitary landfill near Danbury. A nice, hand-carved wooden sign at the entrance made it look like something classy, a country club maybe, but once you were over the first sloped wall of balding grass, it looked like any other dump. It was a bright day, hot, sun shining down over acres of earth and trash. The offices were a collection of trailers surrounded by gigantic waste containers for controlled materials or valuable reclaimables. A parade of compactor trucks waited to pass the scales and go into the current fill area, where gigantic bulldozers with huge spiked wheels rearranged and compressed the garbage. The stink hit him as he got out of his car, and immediately his lungs rebelled at the mix of diesel exhaust, dust, and garbage smell. He hadn't even made it to the office door before sweat came out on his forehead, and he could feel the grit in the air sticking to him.

The dump personnel were helpful. Mo watched their eyes as he showed them photos of Parker and Radcliff and asked a few questions, and all he saw was interest and pleasure. Having a detective come by was a break from routine, just like TV, made them feel important. They gave him permission to walk around and supplied him with a map of the landfill. He spent some time wandering before he realized he should have put on the rubber boots he'd bought.

He walked over rolling hills of scabby green, penetrated here and there by vent pipes and populated by sated-looking seagulls—the hungry ones were down where the bulldozers were turning over goodies. He decided that the high areas would be too open for Geppetto to use, at least during the day. More likely was the perimeter where the graded slope of the dump came down to the surrounding land, where trees and scrub and some falling-down buildings offered more cover. He circumnavigated the site, looking for signs of activity, finding nothing instructive. Then he spent another half hour around the offices and machinery sheds, again finding nothing. And thát was it. He left his card with the dump manager and left. It was nice to be in the car again, but he could smell himself, the odor that had soaked into his clothes and skin and hair. That's when he realized he should have gone to the antique shop first, while his attire was still fresh.

He worked until five and managed to hit three more sites. Scratch the antique shop, Jane's Junkyard, just a couple of small rooms with a Martha-Stewart-on-steroids ambience. Scratch the others, too. A hot, windy day, he'd slipped and fallen twice, his clothes were stuck to him with a glue of sweat and garbage dust. He checked in with St. Pierre and the others to find they'd enjoyed it as much as he had and had met with comparable success. By the time he got back to Carla's mom's house, he felt like shit and was having strong second thoughts about the value of the dump initiative.

He had locked the car and started up the walk before he noticed Rebecca, sitting on the front steps. Looking at him with a radiant smile.

Mo felt his stomach drop.

"This is a lovely neighborhood," she said chidingly. "Your house is beautiful!"

"What are you doing here?"

Her smile faltered a little, but she told him, "I was in Briarcliff, remember, talking to people about Dennis Radcliff. Since I was up this way, I thought I'd stop by. Surprise you. I thought you'd be . . . glad."

"Yeah, well, I'm surprised," he said gruffly. He was thinking feverishly how to keep her out of the mausoleum.

Her smile was gone, but still she asked, "Are you going to invite me in?"

He stopped ten feet away. "I gotta be honest, this isn't the best time," he said. But she looked hurt, so he explained, "I've been in garbage dumps all day. I stink worse than I ever have in my life. Maybe we could get together in an hour, meet you at a restaurant or something. After I take a shower and burn my clothes."

"How about I come in, you take your shower, then we'll figure out dinner. I don't mind waiting. Besides, I've got a lot to tell you."

The hell with it, Mo thought. *Bite the bullet, face the music.* She might as well see what he really was, it tied in with things he'd been wanting to say anyway. Maybe this was as good a time as any.

He circled her at a good distance, went up the steps, went inside. On a hot day like this the air in the house got stuffy. His garbage stink filled the hall. Rebecca followed him, looking curious and kind of unsettled.

He led her into the front rooms, stood in the middle of the floor with his arms spread to either side. Shiny floors, dust bunnies, bare walls, naked windows.

"Okay? Take a look. This is where I live. This is how I live. This what you wanted to see?"

She looked around. "And you're angry at me because . . . ?"

"How about because this is not a moment when I want you to visit me? That maybe at this precise fucking moment I could use some privacy?" He stepped past her and into his living room, which looked abandoned. Pieces of furniture missing, the absence of anything pretty or tasteful. Standing there with her, he saw it all with professional detachment: It had the sad, squalid look of a crime scene.

"You want to see my bedroom? It's worse, okay? Come on, Dr. Ingalls. This is great. Maybe you can give me a shrink's perspective on somebody who'd live like this." He took her arm and pulled her roughly into the kitchen, then back into the bedroom. Unmade bed, Jockey shorts over the clock radio, shades pulled down, no curtains. Metal clamp-lamp on the radiator for a bedside reading light. Dirty laundry on the floor.

She took her arm away, looking around wide-eyed. "Why—"

"Why do I live this way? Because I'm a fuckup. Because I broke up with my girlfriend and she moved out. Because this isn't my house, I don't even have a lease, it's her mother's house."

"No. Why are we doing what we're doing?"

He didn't answer.

She picked up a book he'd been reading, *The Quark and the Jaguar*, put it back down. Finally she said, "You do smell pretty bad."

"Yeah. I said that."

"I'm sorry if my coming here has upset you, Mo. I had no idea it . . . I had thought . . . Tell you what, I'm going back out to the porch. You can come out with me and talk. If you like. Or not."

She walked back through the rooms. For moment he held back, willing her to go away. And then he quickly followed her, scared to death she'd leave. He found her sitting on the porch railing, arms crossed. She was dressed in her professional clothes, blouse with matching short skirt and vest, and the way she was sitting threw out one hip and showed the beautiful curve of her thigh. The way she looked broke his heart.

"The only thing that's disappointing me," she began, the insightful shrink, "is the way you're acting."

"Hey, it disappoints me, too," he said. "I'm fucked up." She didn't argue, so he blundered on, excuses: "I mean, what, I meet someone I really go for, tell her I live in my ex's mom's house? Tell her my life's a mess?"

She pretended to consider that. "No. But you could be frank that you're in transition, just coming out of a relationship, the ex took half the furniture. You could approach it with some humor and irony and trust her to do the same."

"You caught me at a bad moment, okay? I've been in neck-deep in landfills all day. You second-guess your life when you do that."

"I can imagine." A steady gaze, not backing down at all. She was mad.

He felt like shit. "There are things I've been wanting to say. This just brings it to a head."

"Such as . . .?"

"Such as you're a Ph.D. from Columbia, and I've got a B.A. from City College. Such as you make three, four, I don't know how many times what I make. Such as you've got a nice apartment and I live like this. Such as you're highly regarded in your field and I'm a fucking gumshoe, in trouble in my department, no career mobility—"

"In other words, what am I doing getting involved with a bum like you?" She was nodding, accepting it.

"Yeah." This was murder. The last straw. Mo decided he'd had it, after this he was out, fucking believe it. Move on, try to start up again, clean slate. Seattle maybe. Or somewhere. Surprisingly, at the thought a feeling almost of relief came over him: At least this was a way to get her away from this case. Get her safe from Geppetto.

"Maybe it's just a fling with a handsome cop," she said. "Maybe I like slumming once in a while. Single girl, freethinker, I need to get

364

laid once in while. Preferably with somebody disposable. Until somebody more upwardly mobile comes along."

He'd considered that possibility.

"And I think I know the kind of upwardly mobile men you mean," she went on. "Like the upwardly mobile Chicago city councilman who got statewide political ambitions and dumped me when he thought my unsavory past might soften his downstate polling numbers. Like the upwardly mobile Wrigley exec who positively *doted* on me but had no use for the fact that I had a daughter I loved and was committed to. Or the upwardly mobile FBI man I dated in New York, whose habits we don't need to discuss. I should get a guy like that, right?"

"I don't know."

"You're goddamned *right* you don't know! Don't presume to tell me what I want or need. You want to pigeonhole *me,* you can go take a flying leap." They faced each other, Mo feeling like shit five ways and wanting to find a way out of this. But still she blazed at him: "Silly me, I had thought maybe the right guy for me was more self-inspected, honest. *Real.* Who had come to grips with who he was. Who had no more use for pretentious bullshit than I do. A guy to whom being straight up mattered. Who could sense how much that mattered to me."

He wanted to touch her, but it was out of the question. They just stood facing each other. Finally he said, "I'm going to take a shower. I have to get cleaned up." He turned away, went back into the house, peeling off his shirt.

She followed him inside. How she could breathe, he didn't know. He went into the bathroom and started the water running.

She stood in the bathroom doorway. "A guy who had figured out what he wanted, and it was some of the same things I wanted. Who knew how rare this is."

Mo stripped off the rest of his clothes, tested the spray, warmed it up, got in.

She raised her voice to be heard over the water noise. "Don't ever do this to me again, Mo! That's the one thing I insist on! Don't you ever again impugn me, or our relationship, again."

He let the water run over him. "Just have to get cleaned up," he mumbled into the stream. He realized he'd never met anyone like this before in his life. She was valuable beyond anything. That thought filled him with hope and fear. The water on his face, his head, was like a baptism.

Half an hour later, they took a corner table at Sardolini's, an Italian place that made its own pasta and had a good house Chianti. Tuesday night, not too many other customers.

What you do when you come out of the shower is you stand naked before her and you say how she's completely right. That you'll never let your crap come between you again. She can see how much you mean it. And you're clean now, you can hold her. When you do, the squalid rooms disappear, there's just this clean, bright flame. You try to start from there.

They were both hungry, and they had pressing things to talk about. The house was out of the question. Now, it was nice to sit in candlelight, with clean tablecloths and muted music.

He told her about Flannery looking like he was truly trying to get Mo's ass in a trap, about his slip about the knots, about the dump initiative looking like a dead end. None of it good news.

But Rebecca had progress to report. "I learned a lot about Radcliff. It'll be hard for us to get access to medical files or sealed court records, but the Briarcliff police who dealt with him don't mind talking about him. He was suspended from sixth grade for a violent assault on a girl in his class, for which the court required psychiatric evaluation and therapy. They arrested him twice as a juvenile for starting fires, and then there was an accusation of rape during his first summer home from prep school. That never came to anything, but up in Massachusetts he kept the juvenile justice system fairly busy, and he was required to have therapy at school. Again, I don't have access to these records, but I can see impulse-control disorders and the basics of a sociopathic profile. It's reinforced by his arrest for violent rape as an adult. I'd also guess that he was an abuse victim himself."

Thinking about it, Mo held his glass up to the candle and admired the red light of the wine. "Sounds like the perfect raw material for Geppetto."

"Exactly! And his background closely parallels Ronald Parker's. Geppetto could *not* have acquired two such individuals by chance. No way. Geppetto had to have tracked them, chosen them on the basis of their psychological history."

"So where does that leave us?"

"To me, Geppetto's using this procurement technique, if he did, suggests that he knew the system, knew how to monitor it for information. Perhaps because he'd had personal experience within it himself."

"Meaning he could have a record himself as a juvenile offender or victim."

She nodded. "That—or a job that permitted him access."

Which brought them back to Flannery. As prosecutor, then DA, he'd know the machinery of the system, the channels, the people— he'd easily finesse access to that kind of information. Of course, probably Ty could, too.

Which brought up one more thing. "I need to say something," he began. "And I don't want you to hear it the wrong way."

She got a little wary, but she said, "Okay."

"I'm worried about this. I'm scared shitless. I keep thinking I want to get away from this case, drop it, let somebody else take this on. But right now I'm still a cop, it's my job. I'm a guy, I'm good with a gun. I'm also solo, no family, I don't have a kid to worry about. If something should happen to me." He could tell by her face she understood. "What I'm trying to say is, is there any way I can persuade you to walk away from this? Keep you and Rachel out of it?"

"It has crossed my mind," she admitted. "Actually, I've given it a lot of thought."

A waiter arrived at their table. He set down steaming oval plates, topped off their water glasses, and went away, leaving them staring at the heaps of coiled pasta.

"And?" he prompted.

She was looking very troubled. "You're right about Rachel. I do have a responsibility that takes precedence."

He waited for her to go on.

She fidgeted awhile. "But then I think, you and I together have exactly the combination of skills and attitudes needed to catch Geppetto. We're making great progress. And if Flannery is Geppetto, from the way he's acting it seems as if we're both already, you know, on his screen?"

They both thought about that, staring at the plates of food. Mo realized he had completely lost his appetite.

"Because if we *are* on his screen, isn't our best bet to stick together and try to—I don't know the right vocabulary for this—get him before he gets us? I'm just trying to think strategically." Rebecca paused, also looking at her food with distaste. "I mean," she said, "doesn't it come down to whether it's already too late?"

45

NUMBER THREE WAS LOCKED in the next room, grunting rhythmically as he did sit-ups. In the kitchen, Mr. Smith was getting his equipment ready, clipping the Asp to his belt, checking the charge on the Taser, putting the folding trenching spade into the little backpack.

Mr. Smith had spent the last couple of days assessing the situation, figuring the moves and countermoves. Finally he'd decided to go for the finale now, not try to delay it. Most of the necessary elements were in place anyway.

Making a decision had put him in a determined but melancholy mood. Some of that could be chalked up to the long hours he was putting in between the day job and the project, staying up most of the night to work on Three, reviewing the Dynamic Duo's progress, plotting strategic options. But more, it was the recognition, coming over him by degrees, that the years as a guerrilla army of one were wearing on him. That it was time to wrap this up.

In the last few weeks, he'd alternated between a kind of affection for Rebecca and Mo and a searing hatred. They were actually rather remarkable people: bright, competent. And rebellious, Mo in particular. The very thing that made him dangerous—that he'd always tried to cut the strings that controlled him, resisted stupid procedural limitations and overbearing bosses—also made him admirable. A kindred spirit of sorts. And yet they were also rather innocent, well-meaning, idealistic. So at moments he found their love affair quite touching. But from that sprung immediately a fire of hate, envy, bitterness: They were enjoying the very things he'd been denied. The very thing that had been taken from him. More and more, their happiness seemed inversely connected to his. He'd settled his emotional seesaw by deciding that, all in all, their innocence and sentimentality made them perfect targets for the finale.

In the end, he'd always known, it must bear upon the innocents.

Over the weekend he'd rigged his recording apparatus in Manhattan with a relay that allowed him to live-monitor or review surveillance tapes of Rebecca's apartment from any telephone. He had adapted a remote-activated telephone answering machine to the recorder so that he could dial in and monitor the Dynamic Duo from the office or the lab. Important, given the time crunch.

Not that he'd gotten anything interesting since Saturday. All he'd heard was Rebecca talking with her daughter Sunday night, and then later chatting on the phone to an old friend in Illinois. Morgan Ford figured in her conversations, she was obviously smitten with him. Listening to this stuff infuriated him. She was by nature a sunny person, open as the prairie. Again, the epitome of what life had denied him.

Yes, in the end, it must bear upon the innocents. It had to be *tragic*. And real tragedy was not just catastrophe—another misunderstanding of the current generation—but the obstruction of heroic aspiration by calamitous misfortune.

Mr. Smith had long resigned himself to the protest taking the form of a brutal affront to fundamental values and sentiments. Yeah, it was ironic that he was recapitulating the monstrosities he abhorred. But that's what would receive attention. The program had committed its atrocities in the shadow of secrecy. As a protest, nothing would be more persuasive than to conduct the same horrors in the light, display them in full view. Where people could see them and feel revulsion and do something about them. At the same time, he liked the idea that what he was planning was not a mere atrocity but a *tragedy*. In that sense, it was appropriate because it mirrored his life. The highest aspiration, destroyed.

Tragedy had elements of *beauty*. It would be nice to think his lost, lost life did, too.

Number Four, with conditioning far from complete, would not be of use for the coming weekend's tasks. The question was, let him go, into the wild, as he was? Or kill him? Killing him would be a shame, in that Four was definitely the pick of the litter. But given his truncated conditioning, Mr. Smith really wasn't sure how Four would handle freedom.

As he thought about it, Mr. Smith strapped on a forehead light, cinched it tight against his skull, then tucked several pairs of nylon handcuffs into the backpack. Abruptly, he decided to let Four go. Four on the loose might add an unpredictable chaser, a kicker, a catalyzing postscript to the coming weekend's drama.

One of the basic elements of strategy was to make use of the opponent's routines. Back in the Vietnam era, the program had routinely exploited targets' predictable behaviors to identify where and when to hit them. In this case, Morgan Ford was the harder to anticipate: his bachelor lifestyle, his odd work hours, his sudden changes of tack on the investigation, the occasional nights spent at his new sweetheart's apartment. But Rebecca Ingalls had locked herself into cutesy domestic routines with her daughter: dinner together every Friday night, Saturday-morning errands together, lazy Sunday mornings with the newspaper and pancakes, bowling on Sunday evenings. The bowling alley was looking increasingly like the best point of interception. Its sheer unlikeliness was an asset, they'd never expect it there. And it had other advantages as the stage for the finale, too, in that it was semipublic, a great location for TV news crews. And there'd be other bowlers or staff on hand, other innocents for the slaughter. A grander pageant.

Of course, it also meant more logistical problems and complexities. That brought on a sudden sense of urgency, yanking him back to the job at hand. He snapped the backpack shut and slipped it over his shoulders, suddenly angry at himself. What was the matter with him? Yes, he must be getting tired. This gush of sentimental affection for Mo and Rebecca. More proof it was time to wrap up the show. Thankfully, tonight's exercises in the dump would be a good antidote for this maudlin crap.

He went out to the lab, put on a pair of elbow-length leather gauntlets, and let the big German shepherd out of its cage. Aside from one wicked slash of canines that gouged the leather over his forearms, it went without incident. He snapped the livestock leash onto the dog's harness, tested the clip, and went in to round up Number Three.

They went out through the overgrown yard, down the slope through the heavy forest. Mr. Smith left his forehead light off—that would be for later, for problems and cleanup. Better to adapt the eyes to the dark. And it was a good night for this work, a clear sky pinned with a mostly full moon that chopped the woods into blue light and black shadow. Sounds: in the distance, the highway making a big swooshing noise punctuated by the occasional growl of diesels throttling down an exit ramp. Closer, faint music from some neighbor's invisible house. Closer still, the ticks and whirs of insects. Smells: earth, oak leaves, rotting vegetation, an illicit backyard trash fire.

The shepherd had never met Three, and the proximity of a big stranger had filled the dog with a volatile mix of fear and killing urges, amplified by surgery and conditioning. Frankie alternately bristled and cringed. In the moonlight, Mr. Smith could see the animal's constant alertness to Three, the sharp ears upraised, the wolf muzzle turning, tracking him. When Frankie made little trial lunges at the dark stranger, Mr. Smith could feel the vibrations of the deep-chested body through the taut leash.

Three recoiled at the first lunge but immediately reciprocated, charging at the dog in a display worthy of a gorilla. He drew up just short of contact as Frankie recoiled, too. For now they were even. Afterward, Three paid no attention to the dog's hostility, except to stay outside the radius of the leash.

Got us a couple of real firecrackers here, Mr. Smith thought.

They mustered on into the dark. Leaf-covered junk materialized out of the moonlight and shadow, lumps and bizarre shapes in the forest. Then the ground leveled out and the first humped shape of an old car showed that they were nearing the center of the old dump. A little farther down was the stream that drained this valley. The dog was making a rumble in its chest, getting anxious as the smells recalled prior dump exercises and his hormones began to rev. Three was breathing harder than the walk required, a clue his conditioning was amping him up, too. The dog was getting harder to handle, but still Mr. Smith kept his attention primarily on Three. He used his peripheral vision to keep him continuously in view, knowing he couldn't trust him. Young Dennis had had something in mind when he'd come back this way and killed the Rappaport girl, and Mr. Smith was still not clear what he'd intended. He covertly slipped the Asp out of its holster and kept it in one fist. He had no gun, you never put a firearm within reach of a test subject, but there was the Taser for later, and in his pocket he kept his insurance, a long switchblade honed to surgical sharpness.

They came to the spot Mr. Smith had in mind, a level arena surrounded by kudzu-draped trees. Here the ground was relatively clear of junkyard debris, providing room to move around in. The tree branches parted enough to allow more moonlight to reach the ground, he'd be able to observe.

He slowed to fall behind and stopped when Three was five or six paces across the little clearing. He yanked the shepherd's lead hard, bringing him close to his side. He could actually *hear* the dry sound of the big body vibrating in the dark as he released the harness clip and stepped back.

By the time Three had noticed something amiss and started to turn, the dog was already in the air.

Three's reflexes were good. He got an arm up in front of his face, and though he went down with the impact, he rolled well. For a moment the frenzied thrashing and gargling growls made it seem like the dog had found its grip on Three's throat. Hard to see in the broken moonlight. But then Three used his greater weight effectively, pivoted, came out of it with his legs around Frankie's chest. The dog kept savaging his midsection, his arms, but between Three's heavy denim jacket and his pain conditioning, he didn't seem to notice.

Mr. Smith watched with interest as Three began killing Frankie. Without a weapon, Mr. Smith knew from experience, it was actually quite hard to do. The muffled snapping of the limb joints sounded worse than it was, none would be fatal injuries. Three was clearly frustrated and did some biting himself.

It took a while. Mr. Smith waited, watching critically and feeling better. He had coiled the leash, but as it got close to the end, he let the loops fall again, getting it ready for the next stage of Three's workout.

46

WEDNESDAY NIGHT, Mo called Rebecca and asked if she might want a late visitor. She said she wouldn't mind, so he took a long shower and at nine-thirty locked Carla's mom's house and drove into Manhattan. It seemed like forever since they'd been alone with each other. The scene Tuesday when she'd surprised him on the front steps didn't count, they'd both been off-balance. He wanted to be in a nice room with her, in a bed with her.

Also, Gus had called back. They had things to discuss.

He had spent the day on the junkyard circuit. In all, he and St. Pierre and the others had now toured twenty-seven of thirty-eight priority sites. Tomorrow they'd finish up and call this a dead end. Probably Parker's "junkyard" was something else entirely. The failure of the initiative made Rebecca's work all the more important, especially with what he'd learned from Gus.

Midweek Manhattan at ten-thirty at night. Rebecca in her bathrobe, hair still moist from her shower. You come in and you are literally shaking with longing, you try to pretend you've got any self-control but you don't and she sees it. You can't talk right, you stumble against the arm of the couch, the nearness of her is too much. There's bad business to discuss, you're feeling soiled by this job, but there's no point, you both know it. *Priorities,* she always says, got to keep your priorities. So you come together urgently, desperately, as if good moments like this have to be stolen, fast. Before it's too late.

★　　★　　★

It was midnight before they got down to business. Mo wrapped himself in one of the sheets, she put on her robe again and made a pot of chamomile tea. They got out their notebooks and pens.

"I've learned a few things about Flannery," Mo told her. "First, my . . . source . . . tells me the hospital he worked at in Georgia didn't just deal with wounded and traumatized veterans. It was apparently one of the sites of the MKULTRA experiments, where they did some of the LSD experiments."

Her face showed that this kind of thing grieved Rebecca deeply: the abuse of the sciences of healing. "Was Flannery directly involved?"

"Hard to say. He was there at the time, it's hard to believe he didn't participate or at least know about it. Flannery told me he'd worked there, it's no secret. But according to my source, he understated the amount of time he spent in Vietnam. In fact, he shuttled back and forth pretty frequently for about five years."

"Lab work in the States, fieldwork over there?"

"Could be." Mo looked at his notes, remembering Gus's voice, the acid tinge coming into his monotone as he'd talked about Flannery. Like most former street cops, Gus hated the prosecutors, who too often blew the collars handed them on silver platters by honest cops, losing cases or copping pleas. He hated Flannery's grandstanding, glad-handing style and had been glad to give Mo some dirt.

"The other important info I got concerns his distant past. Flannery did have personal experience of the social-services system as a juvenile. Turns out that's no secret, either. I've got copies of articles about him in which he talks nobly about his own early misfortunes, how his own victimization as a child moved him to go into first medicine and then law, very high-minded of him. Beaten by an alcoholic father, in and out of foster homes from the time he was eight years old. Apparently he had the bad luck to get into an abusive foster home, too. Again, it was the father, the foster father, who beat him. His case made the newspapers back in 1953, caused a lot of public agonizing about the foster care system."

Rebecca was staring into the distance, processing the news. This hurt her, too, Mo saw. After a while she said quietly, "It's funny. So easy to have compassion for a child victim. So hard to have sympathy for an adult who's 'strange' or 'remote' or 'an asshole.' And yet they're the same person! The adult survivor of abuse is just as much the victim." She stared through the wall for another moment, then went on: "Okay. The previous abuse, especially at the hands of a 'daddy,' matches our profile. Did you get any specifics about the form of the abuse?"

"You mean, did it involve bondage, confinement, that stuff? I don't know." Mo made a note to look for those details.

Rebecca was thinking furiously. "Could our junkyard be a place from his past? Maybe he was taken to a dump or junkyard and tormented there?"

Mo shrugged, made another note.

"Also, what about the physical appearance of the abusive fathers?"

"Right—are they by any chance blond, blue-eyed? Don't know." Mo jotted the question. Rebecca was a hot ticket, no question.

Rebecca went on for a while, thinking out loud. She had the mind of a sleuth, thinking of angles, playing them out in her head.

But Mo found himself shifting gears. At this point Ty seemed out of the question, Flannery was looking too good. But how could you catch a guy like Flannery? Positioned at the top of the law-enforcement food chain, cultivating relationships everywhere, Flannery had eyes and ears in every department, every county office. Good connections throughout the New York metropolitan area. Since he was considered a guy who was going places, people liked doing him favors in expectation of some future reward, and outside the DA's office itself Flannery was well liked. The arrangement made it hard to poke into his life without someone noticing and reporting back to him. Gus: For all his uncanny talents, there were basic things he couldn't know, facts that weren't recorded in some file or computer somewhere.

Such as where Flannery went at night after work.

That's where some old-fashioned legwork would do the trick, Mo thought. He looked at Rebecca as she wrote something down and decided that for now he'd avoid mentioning the idea to her.

As Mo had expected, the junkyard idea pooped out. By midday Thursday, St. Pierre and the others had reported in. No employees had recognized the photos of Parker or Radcliff. As far as physical evidence went, dumps were messy places, and short of finding eyelets set into some wall in a star-shaped pattern, it was impossible to tell whether any of the sites had been used as training grounds for killer puppets.

Disappointing, but expected. Long shot. Mo had plenty of other things to do. At four o'clock, he called Flannery on his personal cell phone with the excuse of wanting to report in. He got the DA on the line briefly, related a few details about Radcliff. As soon as he hung up, he left the barracks, got into his car, drove downtown. He parked in a spot with a good view of the county building parking lot and the entrance. At four-thirty, county employees flooded the exit, swarming toward their cars. Mo scanned the crowd with binoculars, watching for Flannery's unmistakable bald dome above the other heads. No sign of him. But that was okay, too: As the cars in the lot thinned out, he spotted the DA's silver-gray BMW. It had been easy to get the DA's registration information from the DMV earlier.

Five-thirty and the BMW was still there in an increasingly empty parking lot. Mo began to feel exposed, sitting here on the street. He started the car, pulled into traffic, took one turn around the block, then another, wondering if maybe Flannery just left the Beemer there for show and used other transportation when he went to his lab or wherever.

But on the third circuit, he came along Martin Luther King Drive to see the big man leaving the building, attended by a couple of suits. The three of them paused on the sidewalk to discuss something. Flannery gave orders, and then they went separate ways. Flannery went on alone, briefcase in hand, the picture of a hurried, harried guy: long strides, tie loosened and jacket unbuttoned, scowling as he went through his keys.

Then Flannery dipped into the BMW, started up, left the lot. Mo held back to let some other cars get in between, then followed the silver car through the city.

For a while Flannery drove through the business district on Mamaroneck, then he pulled over. Mo shrank down in his seat as he drove past, then watched in the rearview as Flannery got out, crossed the sidewalk, and went into a hardware store.

Mo drove up another couple of blocks, pulled a U, drove past the store again. Two blocks farther down, he turned again and pulled over. After a few minutes, Flannery came out with a paper bag that he tossed into the passenger seat before getting in again. Mo experienced a sudden hankering for the contents of that bag. Light-bulbs? Or supplies for his puppet-making hobby?

The BMW pulled out and after a decent interval Mo followed. Flannery was a skillful driver, running just at the speed limit when traffic allowed, his turn signals coming on just before his turns. If it came to Flannery taking evasive maneuvers, Mo knew his Chevy Lumina would never keep up with the agile BMW. But Flannery seemed oblivious—wherever he was going, he wasn't worried about being followed. A turn, another, then onto a residential street. Mo followed for another couple of blocks before realizing with a shock that this was his own neighborhood. And then the DA turned onto the block where Carla's mom's house was.

Mo paused at the end of the tree-shaded block. Six o'clock, sun still well above the horizon, nice neighborhood, a few kids on the lawns. Flannery pulled his BMW into Mo's driveway. He got out, stood looking around the yard for a moment, then sat back against the hood and squinted up at the empty windows of the big house.

Okay, Mo was thinking. *Let's see what you've got in mind.* He pulled up to the curb in front of the house and got out.

"What a surprise," Mo said.

"Nice place you've got here," Flannery said. "Guy almost has to wonder how you can afford a place like this on a detective's salary."

"Looking for something else to charge me with?"

Flannery just frowned at him. "Listen, you got anything cold to drink? It's hot out here."

"Sorry. Nothing. If I'd known I was having visitors, I'd have picked something up."

Flannery took a handkerchief out of his jacket pocket, dabbed his bald head. "Okay, good, we got the pleasantries out of the way. So let's get to business. Why I'm here."

Mo approached the BMW. He could see the bag on the seat, Ace Hardware logo, the bulge that could be just about anything. Then the thought occurred to him: Flannery's wrists. If Rebecca was right, Geppetto might also have scarring on his wrists, bondage might have been part of Flannery's abuse as a child. Thinking back, Mo realized he'd never seen him without his suit jacket on, except on his treadmill or in the racquetball court. And both those times he'd been wearing wide, sweat-absorbent terry wristbands. But Flannery had already put away the handkerchief, put his hands in his pockets so the jacket sleeve covered his wrists.

"I'm here," Flannery went on, "because I wanted a very private conversation with you. Because I need you to do something you have a visceral, instinctive resistance to doing."

"Which is?"

"To trust me." Flannery's eyes were a little wry but very alert as he said it. "To try to help me out."

"Right. Good. Of course."

A little flash of anger, quickly quelled. "Here's the deal. You and I both know what the rules are—what we can and cannot do within the legal constraints of our positions. But the difference between us is, you don't give much of a shit about working within those constraints. You have a well-deserved rep as an independent thinker, a free operative. And at your level, you can just about get away with it. Me, it's a different story. Oh, I can throw my weight around, I can trade favors. But the spotlight's always on me. And I have a career here, I can't jeopardize it with"—Flannery groped for the right euphemism—"marginally acceptable procedure."

"You want me to do something *illegal*? When you're trying to fuck me over? Are you *kidding*?"

"Not illegal, just problematical for me. It has to do with your friend and mine, Erik Biedermann."

"So go for him. You don't need me."

"Sure I do. If Biedermann has any personal connection to this puppet business, it's a big problem. Because he's a highly placed federal agent. Because he has connections with covert intelligence-community operations. Because accusing him, rightly or wrongly, can create big problems for the person doing it."

Mo was thinking, *Tell me about it.* He wanted desperately to see what was in the bag. Flannery's wrists, too. But the DA was still wearing his suit jacket, and now he crossed his arms so that his wrists were out of view. His biceps bulged the fabric of the suit. Definitely one big, fit guy.

Flannery just watched him. Despite his sharp eyes, the DA looked more tired and harried than Mo could remember seeing him.

"Put yourself in my shoes, okay? I'm willing to go after Biedermann. Absolutely. I told you, it's a golden opportunity. But I can't get noticed doing it, I can't have anyone in my investigative unit get noticed, looking suspicious of him, can I? Not until I know I've got something more to justify my suspicions. I can't even explain to any of my own staff what I want or why, a couple of them are former FBI, they'll take it the wrong way. I've got something working in

Washington to look at his background more closely, but that's very subtle and it'll take a while. And in the meantime there's somebody killing people in my town. So I need to get things moving right away."

"Which is where I come in."

"You're the perfect guy! Dammit, I wouldn't be telling you this if I didn't think you had the smarts and the freedom of movement to do this and, frankly, the fundamental honesty to see the necessity of it. You won't make problems for me if it turns out to be wrong, because you're not that kind of guy, it's not worth your time to play those games."

Flannery was turning on the charm, staring straight at Mo, looking absolutely the honest-but-desperate guy asking for a reasonable favor.

"Also so you don't take any heat if Biedermann notices and gets offended. But you can still take major credit if you're right."

Flannery looked pleased that Mo had understood. "Sure, taking credit is an issue," he admitted easily. "Hey, Mo, look, it's no secret I'm thinking of bigger and better things. Are *you*? Look at yourself— we both know this kind of thing isn't your game. You're no climber. You wouldn't want what comes with this, you wouldn't know what to do with the opportunities this presents. But me—I'm hungry for this, I'm in position for the next step. Whether this means blowing the lid off an old government secret or maybe nailing a prolific killer who turns out to be employed by one or more federal agencies, either way, it's a news story of national importance. A springboard. A launchpad. And PR aside, the fact is I've given you a potentially big lead here. So if and when we nail this bastard, it was *my* operation. So I thought I'd offer you a little carrot-and-stick thing here."

"What's the carrot?"

"Well, let's see. The stick is the grief I can give you. But figuring out the carrot for a guy like you, that's hard. So in this case I guess the carrot is the simple absence of grief. Standard Pavlovian conditioning." Flannery gave him a conspiratorial wink as if they both thought that was funny.

382

Conditioning: Mo felt ice in his spine. But he just blew out his cheeks and looked away with a thoughtful frown. "What did you have in mind?"

Flannery unfolded his arms, pulled back his left jacket sleeve to check his watch. The move goosed Mo's adrenaline, the chance of a peek at the wrists. But the DA wore a rugged, outdoorsy watch with the wide "sports" band. Just part of the athletic image he liked to project, or a way to conceal his wrist? Mo hoped Flannery hadn't noticed his quickened interest.

"It's simple," Flannery went on. "And it's not illegal, but it does require some time. I want you to figure out where Biedermann goes after work. What he does with his free time. You do the legwork here, I'll take care of the Washington connection, keep that ball rolling. We'll make a good team."

"You mean, like what—tail him?"

"Exactly! If he's got extracurricular activities, I'd like to know about them. Where he goes. When. With whom."

Mo was thinking, *Is this ironic or what?*

Flannery went on, not at all cutesy conspiratorial now: "You know—kind of like what you were doing today. When you were tailing *me*." Mo's expression must have shown his surprise, because the deadly nasty look on Flannery's face showed a hint of satisfaction.

47

Friday afternoon, Mo left the barracks and headed out to the baking parking lot. A lousy week. Slogging around junk-yards, really severing it with Carla, fighting with Rebecca. The shadow of Geppetto. The fun meetings with Flannery. Maybe the worst thing was that Flannery was now aware that Mo was suspicious of him. Mo had denied tailing him, said he'd just been driving home, but the DA looked anything but convinced. Just before he'd driven away, he'd told Mo, "The clock is ticking, Detective. I don't know what you're doing, exactly. But you play ball with me or I fuck over your life so it stays fucked, so help me."

The dump initiative had fallen flat but for one last gasp, Rebecca's suggestion that the junkyard might be a relic from Geppetto's past, the site of his own childhood torment. Dumps and junkyards eventually closed up, got covered over, abandoned. In fact, with the advent of stricter controls on waste disposal, there had been a period in the seventies and eighties when large numbers of old dumps were shut down and new landfills built to more hygienic standards. So Mo had asked St. Pierre to call the county land records offices. He found that, yes, they retained older maps, and, yes, the maps would show most disposal sites active from, say, 1945 to 1970. St. Pierre hadn't made it back with the materials by the time Mo left, but Mo planned to give the matter some time over the weekend. It was almost certainly a dead end, one he'd pursue only because his bulldog instincts demanded exhausting a line of inquiry before abandoning it.

That and the continued resonance of Mudda Raymon's "vision."

He had to look into it over the weekend, because next week was shit-hitting-the-fan week. On Monday, he'd have meetings with the union rep and attorney, and then on Tuesday the grand jury hearing. And after that, who knew? The relatives of Big Willie were waiting to hear the results of the grand jury hearing and would decide whether or not to file a civil suit. And in the background, always: Geppetto, no doubt working overtime to reprogram Dennis Radcliff. If it was Flannery, he would have to be feeling some pressure, and since he'd caught Mo following him, he'd be seriously considering countermeasures. Mo wasn't kidding himself anymore about who his targets would be.

There'd been another suggestive development on Flannery. A piece of chuckle gossip had been going around the uniform side of the barracks this morning when Mo got to work. A young trooper named Galliston had pulled over a speeding BMW on Friday evening, and when he got to the window, who should it be but Westchester district attorney Flannery. A tough moment for any rookie, but he dutifully wrote out a ticket. So Mo made a point of dropping casually by Galliston's desk. Heard you pulled over the DA, Jesus, doing eighty in a fifty-five zone. This was northbound on 684? Wonder where he was going—hurrying home for a hot date? Galliston didn't know, but it wasn't home, because Flannery's legal address was an apartment only five blocks from the county building in downtown, and it probably wasn't a hot date because everybody knew his pied-à-terre was an apartment he kept in Manhattan, straight south. Galliston said he'd made the stop only about ten minutes after Flannery had left Mo's house.

Everybody got a laugh out of it but Mo. He was thinking that having to maintain a day job would put a crimp in your private time with your puppets, especially during the workweek. Especially now, when you were maybe beginning to feel things unraveling. If you were in a hurry to get back to your lab in northern Westchester, you might slip up and get caught speeding.

*   *   *

Thinking about it, Mo had crossed the parking lot and pulled out his keys before he noticed the big black car idling next to his Chevy. He could barely make out the interior through the tinted glass, but it seemed there were more heads in there this time. When the window slid down, it was Erik Biedermann's face that emerged.

"Hey, buddy," Biedermann said amiably. "Hop in. Enjoy some government air-conditioning. Cool your heels."

The heat was rising from the asphalt in waves, oven-dry air that singed the nostrils. Biedermann moved over and Mo got inside, and, yeah, it was cool and dark. Zelek was also there in back, and this time there were two guys in the front seat.

"What're we feeding today?" Mo asked. "The hyenas?"

Zelek didn't think that was funny. In fact, his alien face looked downright sour, the mouth a small wound at the bottom of the triangle. The car pulled out, the locks snicked. Nobody said anything until they were on the Cross Westchester Expressway.

"Mo," Biedermann said, "you want to do me a favor and take off your jacket?"

"Not particularly."

Zelek looked at him, ice in the tilted eyes. "Take it off or we'll take it off for you."

"Go ahead," Mo told him.

Biedermann's big shoulders slumped and he looked exasperated. Then without warning he pitched a vicious left hook that smashed Mo's cheek hard and drove his head against the side window. It almost knocked him out. Before he could recover, Biedermann had swung a leg over and was straddling him, pinning his arms with his hands. Zelek began feeling in his pockets, around his waist, the small of his back, the clever fingers searching expertly. He pulled Mo's Glock and pocketed it, then looked through Mo's briefcase. It took only a moment. When he was done, Biedermann got off. The guys in front never looked back.

"Why d'you always have to be a dickhead, Ford?" Biedermann

was puffing from anger as much as from exertion. "I mean, here I thought you and I had established, you know, a fucking *rapport,* a little camaraderie. But, no. Why can't anything be easy with you? Why can't you get into the team spirit here? We need to talk, you've been getting very crafty recently, so it's in our interest to see that you're not carrying a recording device. But you can't just cooperate, can you? Prick. What, you think we're kidding around here? Is that what you think?"

"Calm down," Zelek ordered.

Mo put up a hand to probe his cheek. Biedermann's fist had hit like a plank of wood. No teeth seemed to be loose, but the jaw was already swelling and could easily be broken. "What're we doing?" he asked finally. "What's the agenda today?" Talking hurt.

Zelek took the lead: "I thought, I really did, that we had an understanding. That you would honor your word to me. But you and the psychologist *continue* to pursue avenues that jeopardize the integrity of our mission."

"Like what?"

"Oh, like what, like what." Biedermann snarled, as if Mo were playing stupid.

"This isn't about recriminations," Zelek interrupted. "This is about putting things in order again. Since I saw you last, you and the psychologist have interviewed Ronald Parker. You took video- and audiotapes and brain scans of him, given to you by Dr. Iberson in complete disregard of our instructions to him. We also understand that Dr. Ingalls contacted several colleagues to discuss the issue, and, *and,* has now personally requested some FOA documents related to the programs. It suggests that you two are actively engaged in pursuing the larger issues you were instructed to leave alone."

"Didn't you *tell* Rebecca about our discussions?" Biedermann asked. "Didn't you *tell* her it was time to cool it on this line of inquiry?"

The car veered off at an exit, Mo didn't see which one, went around the ramp, and pulled to the shoulder under the viaduct. Between the shadow of the bridge and the tinted windows, it was dark as night in the car. Rush-hour traffic blew past close by, rocking the suspension, and they were smothered in the muffled roar of traffic above.

Mo thought about it, decided he didn't have too many options. "Let's cut to the chase. Are we doing something drastic today? If not, what would you have me do to atone for my sins?"

"Asshole," Biedermann said. "I mean, it's this fucking *attitude* that—"

"We're not recriminating," Zelek said. "And we're not threatening. We're well beyond that. We're in the home stretch here, Detective. We can't afford any problems at this stage. So what we're doing is giving you instructions that *you will follow to the letter*. What you do is, you turn over the observation tapes and brain scans to Erik, along with Dr. Ingalls's interview tapes, her transcriptions, and your notes on the case. You instruct Dr. Ingalls that the behavioral-modification-projects angle is no longer part of the investigation. Then you go back to walking around in landfills, or digging in old files, or whatever else you like to do."

"Fine," Mo said sincerely. "How should I—"

"We'll expect all the materials by Monday noon." Zelek took out a blank business card and jotted a telephone number on it before handing it to Mo. "This is Erik's cell phone number, you can call him at any time day or night, and we'll find you. Sometime this coming week we'll also require a thorough debriefing of you and your signature on a legal document that swears you to secrecy." Zelek's little mouth turned down as he checked his watch. He took Mo's Glock out of his jacket pocket, slipped it into the briefcase, and handed the briefcase back.

Biedermann had been looking out the window, and now he seemed to have gotten control of himself. "I gotta be frank here," he said. "This is one of those times when a guy needs to make the right decision, Mo. It's a biggie for you and Rebecca. Fork-in-the-road time. Don't blow it." His tone was calm, almost regretful, and far more intimidating than his earlier heat.

"And that's all for now," Zelek said. "You can get out of the car."

That took Mo by surprise. But the locks snicked open, and Biedermann reached across him to lever the handle. So he got out and stood under the howling highway overpass, holding the business card in one hand and his briefcase in the other as the car pulled away.

He recognized the exit now, about ten miles from barracks. Calling State Police dispatch to ask for a lift back would require too much explanation. His jaw was killing him. And shit week hadn't even started yet.

48

M O ROLLED OUT OF bed Saturday morning with his head pounding as if he'd gotten stinking drunk last night. In fact, all he'd done was come home and put ice on his jaw. Getting home had been a heroic effort all by itself, given that he'd walked maybe three miles before he'd thought to call a White Plains cab to take him back to the barracks and his car. Once he'd gotten an ice pack on, he'd called Rebecca to let her know the latest developments. But, Friday night, Rachel was right there, they couldn't really discuss what to do. He'd taken four ibuprofen tablets and tried to think, then lay down and tried to sleep. Neither effort had been successful.

The bathroom mirror showed that the left side of his face was swollen and discolored. The jaw was too sore to touch. It was bad enough to get hit when you were expecting it, but getting cold-cocked while sitting down, your body absorbed all the energy at the point of impact. Plus Biedermann was a big guy.

As he got dressed, he reluctantly faced the reality that he'd have to go to the hospital to get the jaw x-rayed. Thinking of the hospital reminded him abruptly that this was Frank Marsden's bypass day, he'd wanted to be there when the old man went in, give Dorothea some support.

So he splashed water on his face, did his best to brush his teeth, and made it downtown to Cornell Medical Center in time to be there when Marsden and his wife arrived. Mo saw them before they saw him: a tired, worried, older couple coming in alone and looking as if they'd been having a fight or something. But they seemed relieved when they saw him, and suddenly he was glad he'd come. *Priorities,* Mo thought.

So he stayed through the morning as Frank was prepped, making small talk with Dorothea. Dorothea was a barrel-shaped woman with dyed dark-brown hair. She was a drinker, which was sometimes a problem for the marriage, but today she was just a scared aging lady trying hard to keep it together. For a while after Frank was strapped into a bed and waiting for the operating room, they stood with him in a corridor and tried to be peppy and upbeat. It was nobody's best performance. Frank had severe clogging, mild diabetes, and redline hypertension. Not a heart surgeon's dream patient.

At one point when Dorothea went to the bathroom, Marsden said, "So, you pissed because I made Paderewski acting unit coordinator?"

Mo shook his head. "What do you think?"

"I think you've got other things on your mind right now, you're preoccupied. What happened to your face?"

Mo lightly fingered the new bruises. "My preoccupations caught up with me. I'm fine."

Then they stood there in silence. Frank's face looked yellow and old, there against the crisp white sheets. After a while Dorothea came back, and then a green-suited crowd rolled Frank away. Mo stayed with Dorothea for four more hours until the surgeon came out to say it had gone great, couldn't have been better.

While waiting, Mo had tried several times to call Rebecca, but he hadn't reached her. He tried to tell himself not to worry, she often spent Saturday out and around with Rachel. She'd said something earlier about both of them needing new bathing suits. Probably shopping. But after a while he couldn't control his anxiety, so he found the card Zelek had given him and called Biedermann's number.

The familiar G.I. Joe voice answered, "Yeah."

"It's Ford."

"That was quick."

"No, I'm just checking in. Calling to let you know we're working on it, I'll call again as soon as we've got the materials together. Tomorrow, Monday at the latest. So you don't have to . . . get worried about anything."

"The only one should be worried is you." Biedermann chuckled humorlessly. "Shit, Mo, if I'd known it would change your attitude so profoundly, I'd have clopped you sooner."

Once Frank was in the clear, Mo left Dorothea and checked himself into Emergency. He waited some more in a different lobby, got x-rayed. They told him that he had a hairline crack in the left mandible, but that all he had to do for it was take it easy, keep the swelling down, eat soft foods. When he was done at the medical center, he swung by the barracks to pick up the parcel of old disposal-site maps St. Pierre had left and drove back to the mausoleum. Took four ibuprofens. Called Rebecca's answering machine. Lay down with the Glock on his chest and fell asleep.

It was eleven o'clock when she finally called back. He woke up in the dark, fumbled the receiver, mumbled hello.

"I'm calling late so we'd have some privacy. Rache is in bed, we can talk."

He gave her the details about his encounter with Biedermann and Zelek, the urgent need to return the materials and get away from the Geppetto side of the case.

She was quiet for a while, thinking about it. Then she asked, "And you feel all right about that? Just . . . turning away?"

"I feel great about it. I feel terrific."

"It doesn't bother you that this program, this whole situation, is horrible? A . . . a betrayal of human principles that maybe somebody should *do* something about? I mean, maybe these awful things happen because people like us keep *letting* them happen."

"Bugs the shit out of me. But so does global warming and

sweatshop labor. It's not something I feel I can do much about. But more than that . . ." He petered out, his vocabulary failing him again.

"What?"

"I don't want to take the chance of anything happening. To you, to Rachel. To this thing that's just started up. With you and me. A month ago Biedermann and his guys, or Geppetto, they could have taken me out, I wouldn't have given a shit. But now it's—"

"You're kind of mumbling, Mo, I can hardly understand you." He realized he hadn't told her about the broken jaw. She went on, "I think I got the gist, though. Thank you. I feel the same way. And I know you're right, I just . . . you know. It doesn't go down easy." She was quiet for another moment. "I guess I'm willing to quit, but I can't get them the materials tomorrow. I was sweating about this, too, worried about the evidentiary value of the tapes and scans if . . . well, after Ronald Parker, I can't pretend this apartment is secure. So I took everything to a safe-deposit box. I can't get them until Monday. But they said Monday was okay, right?"

The prospect of a delay didn't make Mo happy, but there wasn't any choice. "Yeah. I'll call Biedermann, let him know. Just so they don't start thinking we're being uncooperative if we don't get in touch tomorrow."

They talked for a while more. Nothing about the case, it was as if once they'd made up their minds, it was gone. He'd been right, she and Rachel had gone out to pick up bathing suits and other hot-weather clothes. Bowling tomorrow night, she reminded him, and then she suggested that maybe Mo could spend the night afterward. Mo told her that sounded very, very good.

It was midnight by the time they got off the phone, but Mo called Biedermann anyway. Answered on the first ring, sounded wide awake. Thought it was amusing, Mo's keeping him so well informed.

★ ★ ★

It wasn't until two o'clock Sunday that he got around to looking at the old maps St. Pierre had dug up. Most dated from the fifties and sixties. Looking at them, Mo realized how much the area had changed in fifty years. There were fewer roads back then, no corporate headquarters, no interstates. The yard-square photocopies St. Pierre had provided were good, but the original maps had obviously seen better days, and the copies had reproduced all the creases, rips, discolorations, and penciled notations.

Sure enough, dumps and junkyards were noted. Mo marked the locations with a yellow highlighter, then tried to find the equivalent places on a new Hagstrom road atlas. Given that road names had changed, new developments had sprung up, the scales of the maps were vastly different, it wasn't easy to correlate old with new. In fact it was tedious. It was also almost certainly a dead end. On the other hand, sitting at the kitchen table looking at maps, a cup of coffee in one hand, an ice pack in the other, was about Mo's speed for today. It was a lousy day outside anyway, overcast but not giving forth with the needed rain.

Plus, shit week began tomorrow, he'd need to be rested if he wanted to cope with everything that was coming at him.

It was one thing to say you weren't going to pursue the Geppetto scenario, another to stop thinking about it. As Mo worked, a question kept returning to him, something Rebecca had mentioned: What had triggered Geppetto to start his puppet factory in 1995, twenty-two years after the end of his involvement with the military psych projects? The hypothetical trigger was important because its nature would reveal something about Geppetto's "statement," his agenda. And knowing more about Geppetto's agenda could tell them what he was likely to do next. It might also throw some light on some of the troubling undercurrents of the Biedermann and Zelek thing.

Mo reminded himself that this was no longer his concern. He shook off the thoughts, unfolded another map, began marking off the dumps with the highlighter. He had just marked the third one when he startled and almost choked on a swig of coffee. He checked the location again: the hard curve of the road, then the stream.

Stupid, stupid, stupid fuck, he chided himself.

The old map showed that the road had been called Dump Road back in the early fifties. A dirt road in a rural district then, but now paved and called Eldridge Estates Road. Between the interstate and an upscale residential area. The same road that less than a mile below the old dump crossed the bridge over the marshy stream where Carolyn Rappaport was killed.

He should have remembered it the moment they started thinking of old dumps. The wringer washer he'd encountered. The odd debris in the muck—an old toaster, a rusted chrome side mirror from some old car—probably washed downstream over the last fifty years.

Mo tried to tell himself it could be nothing, coincidence, irrelevant. The longest of long shots that it had any bearing. But he stood up feeling hot all over, suddenly in a hurry. It was three-thirty, a little late in the day but still enough time for a reconnaissance before dark, before going to meet Rebecca. He strapped on his shoulder holster, checked the Glock's magazine, then dug the Ruger out of the mattress and put on the ankle holster. He was thinking about the marsh, the deep forest uphill on either side: a big area, a job for more than one guy. Wondering what Mike St. Pierre had planned for his Sunday evening.

Mo parked at the bridge and pulled on the rubber boots as he waited for St. Pierre to show. Sunday afternoon, not much traffic. He kept trying to tell himself that there was probably nothing to this, it was another dead end. But there was a thrill in his nerves, that breathless pressure at the center of his chest, that told him this *clicked*. Yeah, as Carla had said: his radar, his gut. Whatever, his instinct told him this was something important.

Four-thirty. It would probably take the two of them a couple of hours, even if they found nothing of interest. So he called Rebecca on the cell phone.

"Hi, it's me," he said. "Listen, I'm going to be a little late for bowling. Or if I get something going here, I might have to skip it this week. You guys should probably go over to Star Bowl on your own, I'll meet you."

When he told her where he was, she sounded skeptical: "I thought Erik and his people looked over the marsh area pretty well. Whatever else Erik isn't, he *is* thorough."

"The old dump is farther up. I don't think they went up that far."

"And you don't think it's coincidence?"

"Could very well be," he agreed. No way to explain the prescient buzz he felt.

"What about Erik and Zelek—won't they frown on this initiative?"

"I don't think so. I don't know if I care. If this gives us a chance to find Geppetto, to get to him before he . . . If we get to him fast, it may make the whole problem moot."

And then St. Pierre was pulling over, getting out with a grin, and it was time to go. Mo told Rebecca good-bye, gathered up the maps, and got out of his car. It was good to have Mike there, Mo thought. Rough and ready, big, lanky eager beaver, anxious to prove his worth.

"Sorry to take you away from the family on a Sunday," Mo said.

"Hey, Lilly doesn't mind the overtime pay either." Mike was dressed in jeans and a loose short-sleeved sweatshirt and had put on rubber boots, too. He locked his car, took his gun out of a waistband holster, checked it, tucked it away again. Then he confessed shyly, "And, you know . . . I mean, I love my kids, but there are times when, you know? When you don't mind getting out of the house. It gets crazy with three of them, plus their friends." He looked over the marsh, the foliage grown greener and thicker since they'd last been here, and he squinted at the clotted sky. "You really think this could be something?"

Mo shrugged, *maybe*. They stepped over the guardrail and headed down the embankment.

49

FLEXIBILITY WAS THE KEY, Mr. Smith had always known. Being able to adapt to changing conditions was crucial to success in any endeavor, and he had developed contingency plans in the event that Three's mistake with the Rappaport girl could lead someone to the old junkyard. In fact, if he did this right, he could turn Mo Ford's imminent pilgrimage to his advantage.

On Saturday, he had taped Number Four's eyes and driven him out to his former hometown. Letting him go was a touching moment. It signified the end of the Mr. Smith era, tangible acknowledgment that these were the closing moves, this was the end game. It was like releasing a captive bird: ordering him out of the van, leaving him standing there tugging at his blindfold and then blinking in the daylight, stunned by his sudden freedom. No way to know how he'd adapt. Four had become like a message in a bottle, thrown into the sea. Or a time bomb, depending on how you looked at it.

After releasing Four, he had spent a good part of Saturday at the Star Bowl, bowling a few sets, exploring the grill area and the bathrooms. He'd memorized the regular faces at the counter, and at one point when the old man had gone into the bathroom, he'd wandered innocently into the service rooms at the far end of the lanes. He had familiarized himself with the layout of the pinsetting corridor and located the emergency exits and electrical breaker boxes. When he'd left, he toured the outside of the building just as carefully: the front and rear entrances, the alley behind, the vacant store next door, lines of sight to the rest of the shopping center. It was kind of a dive, a commercial district drifting into extinction. All things considered, not bad for this operation.

Operation was a good term for what he planned, Mr. Smith thought dourly. Among the other equipment he'd packed in the duffel were surgical tools, including his electric Stryker saw and scalpels. You never knew what might come in handy.

He had intended to arrive at the alley ahead of Mo and Rebecca, so by four-thirty everything was ready to go: van packed, guns loaded, Three dressed in athletic clothes and revved to a high emotional idle. Then, just before leaving, he'd dialed out for one last check on the surveillance setup. He had been just in time to overhear the phone call from Mo Ford.

Fine, he thought. *So be it. Let's boogie.* Adapt. Hit Ford here, at the old dump. It made tactical sense to eliminate the unpredictable variable of having such a capable opponent at the bowling alley, so he'd task Three to Ford while he went on to the Star Bowl alone. If Three lived through the encounter, he could take the other car and join the party later. But if he didn't live, if Mo was the one who walked out, that was okay, too. Either outcome would work. Having Ford there for the finale would provide an opportunity to personally inflict some comeuppance on the arrogant bastard.

All in all, he told himself, *it's a win-win situation.*

He was still unwilling to trust Three with a firearm, but he gave him a switchblade. They had spent some weeks working with the weapon in the first phase of Three's conditioning, he was pretty good with it. Hopefully, despite his hyped-up mood, Three's likable face and social engineering skills would allow him to get close enough to use it.

He told Three about the switch to plan B, worked him up into a frenzy of hate and fear. It wasn't hard to do. Mr. Smith himself was good and sick of Mo and his bulldog style, his relentless pressure, his attitude. Really, he was *controlling* them, forcing Mr. Smith's hand, always tightening the noose. Put that together with his sickeningly sweet feelings and tendernesses, all the romantic crap with Rebecca, his undeserved good luck, and it was easy to hate the son of a bitch.

Mr. Smith torqued Three up to a high pitch, then brought him to the back door. Clipped off his nylon handcuffs and shoved him outside.

"Sic 'em," he said drily.

Three went loping off across the backyard with big springy strides, down the hill and into the woods. In his colorful nylon windbreaker, he looked like a jogger, out for an afternoon run.

Mr. Smith locked up the house, got into the van. Forty-minute leisurely drive to the bowling alley. Bowl a game or two until Rebecca and her daughter arrived, he thought, then let the real fun begin.

But it didn't really feel fun. It felt bitter and sad. He was bloated with bile and envy and misery. Plus he was exhausted, he was running on fumes here. He'd made the right choice in deciding to go for the finale. When he'd first started, it pained him to think of the victims—the collateral damage. But over the last two years, he'd had to acknowledge there was a dire pleasure in it for him: the game, the power, the pain. That pleasure marked his final and complete transformation into a monster, the culmination of his abuse at the hands of the program.

As he thought about it, Mr. Smith's teeth creaked with pressure, the vein coiled in his neck. Here was his last chance to make someone pay, and to show it all to the world, and he was by God going to make a good job of it.

50

THEY STOOD ON THE culvert and looked at the maps, which showed the old dump spread on both sides of the creek starting about another half mile upstream. From the culvert, they could see the forest close over the marsh about a quarter-mile away. The newer maps showed a residential area beginning on the right slope about half a mile up, the big houses Mo had glimpsed through the trees the other night. To the left, the forest and former dump stretched to the interstate corridor, which was bordered along this stretch by a high wooden noise barrier. Without going over the berm or through someone's yard, this was the best route in.

It was a lot of ground to cover, an area a mile or so square, most of it densely grown over, so they decided to divide it up. They'd each walk a loose grid pattern, St. Pierre taking the left side of the stream all the way to the highway berm, Mo the right side up to the backs of the yards and estates. They'd make contact by cell phone if either found anything interesting. Otherwise, they'd give it until seven, rendezvous back here at the culvert, quit before the light got bad.

"Got a question for you," St. Pierre said. "Don't take this the wrong way. But what're we really looking for here? Given there's no one to show photos to."

"Indications of human activity you wouldn't expect in a lousy place like this, like disturbances in the soil or vegetation. Um, abandoned puppeteer paraphernalia. Something of Carolyn Rappaport's? Maybe we'll be lucky and find indications that someone has been tied up or suspended." Mo was thinking, *And maybe dogs, something with dogs, what was Parker's thing with dogs?*

Mike was grinning as he caught Mo's eye. "Sounds thin to me."

"It is."

"Sounds like there's something else percolating here. Personally, I think it's that ol' black magic. The famous Mo Ford intuition."

Mo just looked at him. There was a lot he'd have liked to tell him, St. Pierre deserved the truth. But more, he deserved to be protected from it. After it was all over, maybe.

Mike held up his hands. "Hey, it's all right. I like seeing it in action, that's all. It's impressive, what do they call it—fuzzy logic. Definitely not something we learn at the academy!" He sobered and squinted upstream at the flat of muck and scrub. "We're not thinking we'll run into Radcliff himself?"

"No." Actually, Mo had given that some thought. It might be that Geppetto's lab was nearby, but he thought it unlikely that the puppeteer would risk using the dump after the Rappaport murder. And there was no way Geppetto could know they were coming— the only other person who knew where they were was Rebecca.

They squelched upstream together. The water level had dropped since last time, exposing areas of the marsh floor and covering the muck with a layer of drying skin. The bugs had come out now, and blackflies dive-bombed their eyes.

"You saw Marsden, huh?" St. Pierre called conversationally. "How's he doing?"

"He's okay."

"Think he'll be back?"

"My guess is no. I think he needs a less stressful line of work."

"Any chance you'll take over as senior?" Mike was drifting away, moving to the left, eyes scanning the ground. A tall, young, affable guy, looking in his rubber boots more like a Maine clam-digger than a specialist in major crimes. "Nah," he answered himself. "Not with the bullshit they're trying to hang on you. Which is too bad. You'd be the best, Mo." He looked up with an admiring, open-faced grin, thirty feet away now, and Mo felt an irrational stab of concern. Something about St. Pierre framed against the backdrop of sumac trees, the artificial-seeming milky light of the overcast. A cameo look.

"Hey, Mike," Mo called. "Keep your eyes open in there, huh?"

St. Pierre nodded, waved. After a few more minutes they were a hundred yards apart, and then Mo lost sight of him among the trees.

After passing the wringer-washer, Mo moved on another quarter mile to the point where the houses began to be visible through the foliage off to the right. Five o'clock and the light was still good, but the leaves were thicker and cast more shadow now, the kudzu vines cut forward visibility. He left the stream bank, glad to move onto drier ground. More and more indications of the dump were cropping up around him: a rusting barrel, an old tire, mysterious machine parts, all half-buried in leafy soil. From the map he figured he should be just approaching the perimeter of the old junkyard, and he began walking a long zigzag pattern.

There was a curiously lifeless quality to the place despite the early-summer vegetation. The narrow, wandering avenues between trees and junk and humped boulders seemed unnaturally uninhabited. The interstate made a quiet white noise that smothered the landscape, tricked the ears into mishearing the occasional distant noises of human activity. Among the moist forest smells were foreign odors, stale and somewhat chemical, faintly overlaid with exhaust from the highway. No signs of activity disturbed the blanket of last year's dead leaves, which seemed smoothed as if pressed flat by the bright milky overcast.

The dead land, the in-between land.

After a while, Mo folded the map and stuffed it into his pocket. Judging by the amount of debris, there was no question he was in the old dump now. Still there was no sign of activity, animal or human, not even birds or bird calls. No wind. Just the odd, lifeless maze, motionless beneath the low sky as if waiting for something. He peered into the interiors of several rotting, round-backed cars, examined closely some rusted farm equipment, pushed over the remains of a fifty-gallon drum. Nothing of interest. He called St. Pierre on the cell phone, felt a flash of relief when the chipper voice answered and reported nada at his end, too. They agreed that this was a hellhole and probably another dead end.

An hour later, beginning to feel tired and frustrated, Mo moved up the slope to get a closer look at the residential end of things. The lots varied from two or three acres to much bigger estates, and from semiwild woods to groomed, parklike lawns and gardens. From what he could see of the houses, a few were older, smaller, weathered-in, but most were more recent, massive, gigantically ostentatious. *Every goddamned house in Westchester is the size of St. Peter's*, he thought. *Where the hell does anybody get this kind of money?* Then he decided the harrying flies and mosquitoes were making him cranky. All he needed was to catch West Nile virus on top of everything else. He headed back downslope into the denser jungle.

Another hour. By a quarter to seven, he'd had about enough and began to wend his way back toward the culvert. It was darker beneath the trees now, the dull sun almost gone over the far ridge. The cooling air began to move, full of moist scents. He had gotten about to the center of the old dump when he caught a whiff of something familiar that made his stomach tighten. Something dead nearby.

He followed his nose downhill until the odor surrounded him. He turned in a circle as he looked for what had to be a fairly sizable dead . . . something. But aside from humps of leaf-mounded junk, nothing was visible. Suddenly he was struck by its similarity to that roadkill carrion dump he and Carla had stumbled into. Maybe this was the place she had seen in her vision. The shadowed, vine-choked trees, the apertures of evening light in the gaps between. Something dead in the soil.

He circled for a few minutes longer, finding nothing. This was definitely the epicenter of the odor, but the ground here was undisturbed. He pushed over another rusted barrel, found only a mesh of flattened white roots, some bugs that quickly burrowed out of view. It wasn't until he pulled aside a heavy, rotted car door that he was rewarded with a gush of stench. The soil beneath was looser, not root-matted, and seemed to swarm or scintillate with white things. In the bad light, it took him a moment to see they were maggots.

He found a branch and probed at the pulsating layer, digging down and lifting. A clot fell away to reveal the dirty skull of an animal, only partially decomposed. Long muzzle, sharp teeth. Dog.

Mo reared back, sickened. A shock wave of anxiety hit him, and he pulled out the cell phone, called St. Pierre. Five rings, then the robotic voice of the relay service: "The person you are calling is not responding or is out of the service area . . ." Or his batteries were dead. Or he'd dropped it in a puddle and shorted it out. Or—

The dead dog didn't necessarily mean anything, Mo told himself, Ronald Parker's ramblings or no. This was probably nothing. And Mike was no doubt waiting at the culvert by now. Suddenly pouring sweat, he left the skull exposed and began to run back through the jungle.

He came out into the broader marshy area, saw the culvert side-on, squelched toward it. As he came along the curve of the stream, his angle changed and he was relieved to see Mike, sitting in the box end, waiting. He was leaning into the corner of two concrete walls, long legs out in front of him, hands relaxed in his lap, head tipped back and a little to one side as if taking a moment to savor the evening air.

Closer, Mo called, "Hey, Mike." No answer, no movement, and Mo felt the bottom drop out, the well of heartbreak. Four steps away now and he could see that Mike's eyes were open.

Mo's hands found the Glock and he was bringing it out of the holster when Dennis Radcliff leapt around the culvert wall. Big, wearing a red-and-white nylon Windbreaker, lunging forward as Mo brought the gun up. The muscular forearms drove up under Mo's chin, knocking him off his feet. Radcliff followed him over, landed on top of him, crushed him into the curdling mud.

Mo twisted to the side, trying to avoid Radcliff's full weight. He hadn't lost the gun, but he couldn't bring it around. Radcliff was trying to pin his gun hand. With his free hand, Mo slugged him in the Adam's apple, heard a cough choked off in his throat. Then Radcliff swung back and hit the broken jaw. A big shadow rose inside Mo's head as the pain detonated. He went blind for an instant, then swam back. Radcliff had felt his muscles slacken and had dived onto the gun hand with both his hands.

Mo bent his left leg, brought it under him to try to roll Radcliff over, but he was too big, too heavy, the mud was too slippery. Radcliff had one hand on Mo's right wrist, the other working to pry the gun out of Mo's grip. Mo flailed uselessly with his free hand, then reached down along his own muck-coated thigh. To the Ruger in its ankle holster. Too far, couldn't bring the leg up enough. Radcliff was prying his fingers off the Glock.

Mo's right forefinger snapped suddenly backward off the gun and still Radcliff levered it agonizingly.

"Let go of Daddy's hand!" Mo screamed. *"Do what Daddy tells you!"*

Mo felt Radcliff's hesitation, just an instant as his body processed its conditioned-in reaction. Mo arched with all his strength. It didn't shake off Radcliff, but gave Mo's left leg another couple of inches of movement. His hand found the Ruger. For another moment the gun seemed tangled in the holster, in his cuff, in the mud, and then suddenly it was free. He brought it up under Radcliff's armpit just as he felt the Glock wrenched out of his grip. Then he fired up into the big body.

The shot was muffled, surprisingly small. Radcliff didn't show any response, just turned the Glock in his own fist, and Mo thought he'd missed. He fired again and this time a tremor shook the big torso.

Another two quick shots, *pam-pam*, and the bastard dropped like a side of beef falling off a butcher truck's tailgate. The full weight hit Mo, crushing the breath out of him. Lay inert.

Mo stared at the gray sky for a moment, then rolled the body off and hoisted himself up. He made sure Radcliff was dead, then leapt to Mike St. Pierre and felt the side of his neck. No carotid pulse. Up close, he could see the stain in Mike's shirt, just below and to the left of the breastbone. Three narrow stab wounds, not much blood at the sites. More pooled in the waistband of his pants, but Mike had died fast, his good heart pierced and quitting before it could pump out much.

Mo felt weak and fell next to Mike on the slab, hating this. Hating death. Hating Geppetto. The abyss of wrongs and pains that had swallowed Mike was dark and bottomless, and Mo felt himself tumbling into it. He remembered the special light that had seemed to surround St. Pierre as they'd headed into the marsh, only a couple of hours ago, the sense of warning. The sense of it being a last sight, that's what it had been. The guilt choked him.

One thing he knew: Dennis Radcliff hadn't been hanging out in the dump for the last nine days, waiting on the off chance that Mo and St. Pierre would show up to be killed. He had come for them, he'd hunted them.

Somehow Geppetto had known they'd be in this spot, at this time, and had sent Radcliff to intercept them. Mo had only decided to come here three hours ago. He'd made exactly two phone calls, one to St. Pierre, one to Rebecca. Which meant that Geppetto was monitoring them somehow. Which meant that Geppetto knew everything.

Mo lurched back to Radcliff, lying on his side in the mud, one arm beneath his body. He felt in the bloody windbreaker pockets, found a folded switchblade. In the right rear pocket of his pants, he found a wallet that he opened desperately, thinking, *Geppetto, something to lead me to Geppetto. Which house? What next?* But it was just an ordinary brown leather wallet. Some credit cards, driver's license, maybe eighty bucks in cash. He dug into the right front pants pocket: car keys. Rolled the body and dug through the mud to the left pocket, found a folded piece of paper. Opened it, held it to the sky to see it better.

The penciled note read, *Star Bowl, 8511 Commercial Way, Fort Lee.*

51

H E GAVE HIMSELF TWO minutes to decide what to do as he ran back toward the car. Geppetto would be at the Star Bowl. Geppetto knew Rebecca and Rachel would be there. No doubt Geppetto had put the note there not just to make sure Radcliff knew where to go after he'd completed his task, but so that if Mo lived, *he'd* know, too. An invitation. A challenge.

Decision time. Who to trust? Who could handle somebody as sophisticated as Geppetto? He could vaguely see the lines of probability heading forward from this moment, but the pain in his jaw throbbed like a drum and he couldn't think, couldn't take the time to follow them out. Mo vaulted the bridge railing, got out his cell phone, tried to catch his breath as he dialed Biedermann's number. Nothing. The phone was soaked in muddy water and defunct. He tossed it away, unlocked the car, flung himself inside, and tried Biedermann again using the car unit.

"Yeah." First ring.

"This is Ford. I've got Radcliff, he's dead. I know what he is, I know you're after the puppet-maker. He's going after Rebecca and her daughter. Right now."

"Where are you?"

"The Rappaport murder scene—the swamp. Radcliff found us. He killed Mike St. Pierre. Geppetto's got a place, a lab, near here. He's going to this bowling alley, called the Star Bowl, in Fort Lee, just south of the GW Bridge. Probably there already. Got something complicated planned." He could hardly talk. He caught a flash of his own face in the mirror, covered with muck and blood.

" 'Geppetto,' huh? Okay, Mo you've done great work. Fort Lee—we can be there in ten minutes." Biedermann was suddenly absolutely focused, on full alert, competent-sounding. Something of a relief there.

"You want me to call the New Jersey State Police?"

"No. It'll have to be my team that goes after him. The States aren't going to know shit about this, way over their heads. Bunch of sirens and flashing lights and this'll turn south in a hurry." Mo was thinking, *Yeah, and people will know about it*—even now, keeping this under wraps was a high priority for SAC Biedermann. "But we'll definitely need some backup, logistical support, crowd control," Biedermann went on. "Let me call them, I'll need to establish our tactical command and give them instructions. You just worry about getting your ass down there. If he's there, Rebecca's going to need you."

"Yeah. Listen—it can't be Ty. I think it's Flannery. It's got to be Flannery."

Biedermann didn't sound surprised in the least. "It's the total shits, isn't it. Okay. I'm gone. Hey, Mo—you've done the right thing here. Calling me first. We'll fix this. This isn't the first time for us, you know what I'm saying?" And the line disconnected.

Mo tried to call Rebecca on her cell phone, got her service, tried to tell himself it meant nothing, she always turned the thing off when she was taking personal time. Then he laid stripes in the gravel as he peeled out.

Sunday night, light traffic, flasher blazing, knuckles white. Mo made the forty-minute drive in twenty-five, barely aware of the pounding ache in his jaw, the screaming pain and unresponsiveness of his index finger, the mud stiffening on his clothes. The highway landscape rushed toward him like a sucking whirlpool, surreal. Here was the rearing bridge, the rooftops of Fort Lee, the exit ramp, and the distant

STAR BOWL sign glowing pink and blue neon against a darkening eastern sky. Mo took the curves of the ramp at highway speed, the Chevy's wheels squealing. Then a couple of agonizing minutes of tangled New Jersey streets and the STAR BOWL sign again. The shopping center, mostly dark now, stores closed, parking lots almost empty. He shut down his lights as he approached the front of the alley.

He'd expected more activity, a couple of MRT vans, perimeter patrol, something. But there were just a handful of civilian cars in front of the Star Bowl. One was Rebecca's Acura.

He got out, trying to figure whether everything was completely wrong or completely all right. The lights were still on in the glass entry of the Star Bowl, nothing had changed since he'd last seen the place. Just a quiet Sunday night in Fort Lee. Maybe Biedermann's guys had parked around back or arrived in civilian cars, part of keeping the profile low. Maybe the whole thing had played out and they'd already taken Geppetto away. Maybe Geppetto hadn't shown up, the horrors Mo had imagined weren't part of the plan after all.

He got out of the car with his Glock in his hands, but put it away as he approached the door. Bad enough he was coming in here covered with blood and filth, no need to put a gun in the picture. He opened the glass doors, went through the second set and up three steps to the lobby.

The lanes were brightly lit, no sign of trouble.

He paused at the front desk. The old man wasn't at the register, but a quick scan of the alley showed five or six people sitting at one of the lane booths on the left side. And two blond heads, over on the right at lane nine. Rebecca and Rachel, side by side, huddled close. A warmth of relief poured over Mo. Rachel's head was shaking as if they were laughing or goofing around together. But where was Biedermann?

He started down the short flight of steps and was halfway to

411

Rebecca's booth when it clicked that something wasn't right. The lanes were silent. Nobody was walking around.

"Rebecca?" he called.

Her head whirled in surprise. "Mo! Don't come over here! He's cuffed our hands to the table! He's going to—"

Before she could finish, the lights went out with a *chunk!* The alley became a pitch-black cavern. An instant later the emergency lights went on over the exit doors, a glow that barely made it to the center of the room.

Mo dove to the floor behind a rack of bowling balls. He rolled to the right, froze, listened, then cautiously lifted his head. A dim, low-ceilinged cave, lit only by the insufficient emergency spots, red exit signs, a faint glow from the entry area.

He could make out Rebecca's head over the back of her booth, and though she was craning to look behind her, she was immobile, hunched awkwardly forward. Then the sound of whimpering drew his eye down the left side of the alley, where he could dimly see the cluster of people at lane three also hunched over. Mo groped for his cell phone and remembered it was dead and gone.

And then something slashed out of the dark, hit his temple, sent him sprawling across the waxed boards. A dark shape loomed over him and eclipsed the emergency lights as another blow bounced off the back of his head. The explosion shut the world down, everything shuddered and went small and far away. It was Biedermann, swinging a telescoping steel baton. Mo rolled onto his back and put up his hands to intercept it, but instead of a sharp crack he felt Biedermann's knee plunge down on the center of his chest. The baton came across his throat. Mo's empty lungs labored, but the baton was a crushing bar cutting off all air. No blood to his brain. He dipped just under a roiling surface of darkness. He vaguely felt his Glock being ripped away. He heard it clatter on the boards and then Biedermann's voice: "And that tricky little Ruger, let's not forget that." A tug at his ankle and another skittering noise. *Biedermann bowling with guns*, he thought. The instant the pressure left his throat, he gulped burning air and clawed back from his confusion. In slow motion, he raised his hands to strike at Biedermann's face, but instead of contact he vaguely felt his arm gripped hard and then a sharp bite as a band came tight around one wrist. Then the other. The weight came off his chest and he felt his arms drawn up over his head.

"To complete Rebecca's informative comment," Biedermann panted, "what I'm planning to do is appeal to your consciences in a dramatic fashion."

He dragged Mo by his wrists past Rebecca and Rachel to one of the ball-return carousels at the head of the lanes. Mo pulled his knees up, waited, and when Biedermann knelt to fix the cuffs to the ball return, he straightened his legs hard. Both feet hit Biedermann in the chest. Knocked him upright, put a surprised expression on his face, but nothing more.

Biedermann jammed his booted foot up under Mo's chin so hard he was afraid the jaw would come off. "Always the attitude," he snarled. "Always. Cocksucker. Okay, one more like that and I'm going to fuck you up badly. But first I'll fuck up your girlfriends, right in front of you. So act nice. *Talk* nice. I mean it, Mo."

Biedermann yanked his arms and cinched the cuffs to a flange on the underside of the ball return. He tested their hold and stood up again. "Much better," he said.

He gave Mo a halfhearted boot to the ribs, then stepped into the lane to kick the guns away. The Glock skated almost all the way to the pin box, the Ruger spun into the gutter twenty feet down.

Beidermann rubbed his chest. "You know, that one *hurt*. Rebecca, would *you* tell him to try to be more cooperative? He has such a hard time doing what I ask. It's this fucking attitude problem, maybe he needs some counseling . . .?"

"Mo, please do as he asks. Please." Rebecca's voice had an edge he'd never heard.

"I made some calls on my way down here," Mo gasped. "I knew it was you. I called the State Police, they'll be here any minute. This is a hopeless situation for you. If you need a hostage, take me, let the others go. You don't need to hurt anyone else."

Biedermann was crossing behind Mo and didn't answer immediately. Mo twisted his head to see that the big man had gone to the booth where Rebecca and Rachel were tied. He slid onto the seat next to Rachel and put an arm around her shoulders. Muffled weeping continued at the other booth.

"Nah, you didn't call them. I've been monitoring my scanner, and the only trade those boys're seeing tonight is speeders on the Garden State Parkway. And you're wrong about the other thing, too. I *do* need to hurt people tonight."

"What do you want, Erik?" Rebecca asked. "What is it you need from us?"

"Oh, ho! What I really need, what I *needed* anyway, was a *life*. What I need *now* is to tell a very sad story."

"We'll listen. We'll gladly listen. You don't have to—"

She was cut off as Biedermann reached across the table and drove his fist into her face. The smack of impact echoed in the room. Rachel began squealing quietly.

"Save the sensitivity and compassion. It's a little late."

Mo scanned the dark room, looking for opportunities, resources. His vision had adapted enough to see a still figure down in one of the lanes at the far end. Down at the booth at lane three, he could just make out a tight half-circle of heads, six of them, one just a kid. All bent hard over the central table.

The booths were plump vinyl horseshoes, wrapped around small tables that held built-in electronic pin displays and scoring materials. Biedermann sat at one end of the horseshoe of booth nine, wearing a black turtleneck and a pair of shoulder holsters. His right arm was draped around Rachel's shoulders. Rebecca sat across from them on the opposite arm of the U and like Rachel was leaning awkwardly forward against the edge of the metal table, hands and lower arms out of view beneath. Biedermann had cuffed their wrists to the table's pedestal with the same convenient, disposable Flex-Cufs that he'd used on Mo.

Mo tested the straps, then groped at the underside of the ball return. It was hard to feel anything there, with fingers numbing from the cuffs and the useless right index finger Radcliff had broken. He turned to sit awkwardly facing Rebecca, leaving his hands pulled to one side against the ball return. Fifteen feet away from her, and he could do nothing to help.

"Down at lane three," Biedermann called, "we have six good citizens of Fort Lee. There were seven, but one of them was uncooperative and had to be put down. But I won't kill you, Mo. Counting you and the girls, we got nine people here. The plan is that two or three of you will walk out of here alive because I need living witnesses. I need messengers to the world at large. If you're nice, it'll be you and Rebecca and Rachel."

When the people at the far booth heard him, the weeping intensified and a chorus of pleading broke out. It subsided quickly as Biedermann half stood and shined a flashlight in their direction. He sat back down and stroked Rachel's hair. Rachel leaned away, still making the grinding squeal in her throat.

"He means it," Rebecca said. "Survivors are central to his agenda."

"No! He's bullshitting!" Mo called. "He just wants us to be submissive. He—"

Rachel shrieked as Biedermann did something up near her face. A second later something small fell to the floor and rolled unevenly near Mo. In the dim light he could just make out its shape against the floorboards: Rachel's nose ring. Rachel was crying now, snuffling through the blood in her torn nostril.

"Attitude, Mo. Attitude." A glower deepened the shadows on Biedermann's face. "You, too, Rache—stop that racket. There comes a time to acknowledge when you can't fight it. I think you're there now."

Rachel went quiet. She looked out of her mind, pale and frozen, eyes wide with fear, blood running from her nose down her chin. But even in the bad light, Mo could see there was something very different in Rebecca's face, something he'd never seen there before. An emotion her sunny face wasn't well suited to: absolutely unmoving, lips flat and thin, brows level, eyes—what?

And Mo thought, *Jesus. Better not make any mistakes, Biedermann. Not one. Or you'll have to deal with that.*

52

"Now," BIEDERMANN SAID, "we've got a lot of ground to cover. So don't go away. I'll be right back." He leapt up, came quickly over, checked Mo's handcuffs again, snugged the bands hard. When he was satisfied, he jogged off in the direction of the front door, up the four steps, and into the lobby area.

Mo bent to inspect the underside of the ball return. Too dark to see much. The cuffs were nylon bands, three eighths of an inch wide, about a sixteenth of an inch thick. Easy to cut with the right tool, but with a tensile strength of 375 pounds, breaking them would require more force than even the biggest prison-muscled con could exert. Each of Mo's hands had about eight inches of movement. He gave a couple of powerful jerks to test the steel flange. Nothing budged.

Rachel was moaning, her head hanging toward the table.

"Rache, it's going to be okay," Rebecca whispered. "Just hang on. Hang on."

Mo said, "How're your hands, Rebecca? Any movement at all?"

From where he sat on the floor, Mo could see that her wrists were tied hard against the foot-thick steel pedestal. She worked at them for a moment, gave up.

"No," she said. "But listen—"

But Biedermann was coming back, springing down the steps, carrying a big duffel bag. He dropped it halfway between the occupied booths, went to check the people at lane three, came back.

"Doors locked," Biedermann said, "sign says *Closed*, nothing happening in the parking lot. Answering machine at the desk turned on. I think we're ready to go."

"Erik, we know who you are," Rebecca said. "We know about the psych projects, we know you manufactured killers during the Vietnam War. That you programmed Ronald Parker and Dennis Radcliff to do the puppet murders. We don't know exactly why, or what you want. I know you've got a statement to make, but—"

"But you don't know what it is. Well, it's simple. It's that no one should do these things to other human beings. It's that governments shouldn't make people into monsters." He turned toward lane three and raised his voice. "I worked with a special branch of Army Intelligence from 1964 to 1973. My job was to destroy the part of people that made them human. To turn men into killing machines. I had primary responsibility for making fourteen of them. And I was only one of half a dozen doing that job."

Biedermann's voice had risen, affronted, appalled. Now he stared over toward lane three as if expecting more of a response. "Do you give a shit? Does it matter to you? Well, you're gonna give a shit tonight! You're gonna know exactly what it means."

When nobody said anything, he charged down there, leaned into the half-circle of frightened faces. A moment later, a wrenching scream echoed in the room. It was a man's voice that peaked high and ended in a guttural, choking noise. Mo could see one of the heads at the far booth bobbing and bucking. Another scream rose and subsided, and then there was just the sound of weeping.

Mo tried sawing the handcuffs against the flange, but it was too smooth, no abrasion. He glanced over at Rebecca. Beneath the table, he could see that her hand had found Rachel's hand and was caressing it with her fingers. She was also doing something funny with her hips, lifting slightly and arching them forward and back against the seat.

Biedermann came back to the center of the alley and stooped to unzip the big duffel. He started taking out equipment and ordering it on the floor.

418

"When the program shut down, it left all kinds of lingering problems. All these guys with their circuits screwed up. We'd operated on their brains, we'd severed the little wires that gave them the nice feelings most people take for granted. We'd conditioned them to take orders absolutely and to fear and hate things. What that really means is, I'll tell you, there are parts of your brain and mind that go way back. That still have the instincts of reptiles, the program to kill prey and rivals. You just have to let those monsters out of their little soft boxes in the brain. We've all got 'em, they're always right there, I fucking guarantee it." Biedermann's voice was smug yet grieving, choked with sorrow. "But our experimental subjects, our robots, they didn't work very well. They went fritzy five ways come Sunday. Oh, well—psychology is an inexact science. Right, Bec?"

She responded immediately. "And you're recapitulating these atrocities, even though you abhor them, because, what, you wanted the public to know?"

"Ah—dawn breaks over Marblehead! Yeah. To know and *to experience revulsion*. Hey—anybody experiencing revulsion yet? If not, believe me, I'm gonna fix that." Still digging in the duffel.

Rebecca continued to move her lower body, that odd sideways sidle and forward slide. "And you wanted revenge. Because you felt controlled—they turned you into something you never wanted to become. Somebody deserved to pay, and you deserved some catharsis. But you also experienced something in your own childhood, didn't you? What they did to you fit right into the lifelong pattern. That's part of why you submitted to it in the first place, why it was easy for them to convince you to go along. Was it your father?"

Biedermann stopped, looked over to Mo. "God, she's good. So good. A good lay, too, huh, Mo? Sometimes when they've had a kid, they're not as tight, but this gal . . . Nice attitude about it, too. But that's right, Bec. You know, for moments there I almost thought we had a chance —you and me, maybe there was another way, a sweet, *normal* way out of it. But when you got me up close, you didn't like me so much, did you."

"Erik . . ." she began. Real sadness in her voice. But still the movement of her lower body.

"Oh, Bec. What chance was there I could be 'normal'?" A voice of misery. "I don't even know what that means. You gotta understand, they'd killed my fiancée, back in '71. They did surgery on my *life,* trying to cut out the parts of me that would rebel. But I always felt the strings on me. Thirty years, it always hurt, I always resisted."

"Which is why you chose the puppet motif," Mo said. "You wanted to re-create the injustice you experienced. To demonstrate how horrible it was."

Biedermann stopped his unpacking again to look across at him with shadowed eyes. "You guys are great together, you know that? Sharp as tacks. Bec, what Mo just said, remember to explain it to the press tomorrow. But, see, it didn't end there, when the program shut down. I felt bad about what I'd done. They'd ignored my protests, but they gave me a chance to help remedy it, to some small degree. I was given the *delightful* job of cleaning up the domestic messes back here. Because so many of them came home and started doing awful things. And I took that job. I even had to clean up some of the guys I'd made. You know, really, it wasn't a lot of fun. The only good thing about this was that by doing it I stayed above suspicion myself, I wouldn't get cleaned up myself. And by staying on the inside I was still on the grapevine, I could still hear things."

Biedermann had taken out a roll of plastic line and was pulling off lengths, clipping sections with a wire cutter, setting them aside.

"One of the items in this duffel is a manila envelope. It's got photos, it's got tapes, it's got lists of names and dates. It isn't all that much, but it details what I know of the program. It tells how I personally made a puppet to kill Senator George McGovern and gives information on four other domestic political hits. Sirhan Sirhan will be the easiest to prove was one of ours. I mean, Jesus, do you

420

know what the *weight* of this does to you? The weight of knowing this?"

"You want us to take the materials to someone?" Mo asked.

"We're going to have a lot of media coverage here in"— Biedermann checked his watch —"about twelve hours. The proverbial eyes of the world will be on this building, and the person who walks out of here will present this file to the newspeople. It won't be me, because I'll still be in here with whoever's still alive. I'll be in here with the TV and radio on, making sure the information gets circulated properly. If it doesn't, the body count goes up."

Rebecca sneezed explosively, and Biedermann glanced over at her. Mo did, too. From his position on the floor, he saw that a dark lump had appeared near her feet. Hard to see, the light was no good. It looked shapeless, a bag. A purse. It had been on the seat, and she'd been working it toward the edge with the movement of her hips.

Thirty feet away, Biedermann went back to unspooling line, clipping it, laying it out.

"Bec, you're not going to like this much, but you're gonna have to be the messenger. You've got the credibility, God knows Ford doesn't. Plus you're photogenic."

"Send Rachel out. Please."

"Um, no. No, unfortunately Rachel is central to this pageant. So is your boyfriend. They'll be used to help light a fire under your fanny, I need you to go out of here in high gear. The maternal-grief thing— that'll play persuasively on TV, right? It's awful, I know. But they're not walking out, and you're going to have to watch the—"

"*Erik. Don't. You. Dare.*" Rebecca's voice curdled Mo's blood.

"*Don't tell me what to do, Bec!* You *know* better than that! You're gonna go out of here as hurting as I am. You're gonna be *motivated*. To make sure the information gets play." Biedermann's voice was a snarl. He took out a small black case, opened it, sorted inside. From what Mo could see, it looked like a medical tool-kit. "Plus, you know, I fucking *hate* Ford. The fucking attitude, the bulldog thing, always weaseling in closer. You know, you can blame him for your situation right now. If he'd ever let go. If he'd ever take an order. He's the one who forced my hand. And I have a lot of resentment around control issues, don't I." Biedermann was starting to lose it, the feeling taking over. He took out a rechargeable electric drill, looked it over in the dim light, revved the motor.

"You're thinking I'm some kind of freak, huh, Mo? You think you're so different? Well, take a look at yourself. How you hate the strings on you. If you'd seen what I did, how far would you go to do something about it? How well would you do with that demon riding you? Think about it!"

That echoed uncomfortably in Mo's thoughts. He was glad that Rebecca didn't seem to be listening. She had her eyes shut and was taking deep, slow breaths. Beneath the table, her feet were moving, sliding the bag to the end of the booth. Yes—her purse. When Mo looked up again, he found her staring at him. Eye to eye in the dim light, no movement, just the message in the eyes.

This would need some covering noise, some distraction. Mo began talking: "So you were the cleanup man for over twenty years. Why did you start . . . this? Why didn't you just finish, get the last of them, close the book? After so many years?"

Biedermann reared up, eyes shut in mock ecstasy. "Yes! I knew you guys would do it! I knew you'd zero in on the fundamental question. Tell you why, fuckhead. Tell you about how your tax dollars are spent."

He stood up and went down to lane three, leaned on the table with both hands, his face lowered to the circle of heads.

"Why did I start making puppets myself, going freelance, in 1995? Twenty-two years after the original puppet-masters had seen the error of their ways? Any guesses? No? Well, you couldn't know. Because that's when I had to kill a guy, another cruise missile gone out of control. This was a serious screwball, not only hurting other people but doing this autosurgery routine, too? And after I kill him I

422

see that he's only in his late twenties. Six months later, *whoops,* had to do another one, same age. So I made some discreet inquiries. And found out that the program *hadn't ended* in 1973. It had never closed down, just got put on the back burner until things cooled off! *It's going on right now!*"

Biedermann stopped and shined his flashlight into the faces of the people at the far booth and then across the room into Mo's eyes and Rebecca's. "Time for some normative conversational input," he said in a flat voice. "Time for some expression of outrage, people. Or are you too far gone? Too used to this shit?"

A paralyzed silence from the other booth.

"It's horrible, Erik!" Rebecca called. "But why did they—"

"Thank you. Why did they do such a terrible thing? Because with the Vietnam War over, we still had the Shining Path to kill, we had Commander Marcos and his Mayans, we needed agents in communal movements all over. And we had to have contingency plans for troublemakers here at home—radical environmentalists, socially conscious rock stars, that type. Manufactured assassins and provocateurs are so politically convenient, see. No overt action needed. And they'll do *anything,* they don't make moral judgments about assignments, they'll take on suicide missions, they'll kill our own people so the powers that be can pin the blame on someone else. If they're caught alive, they're impenetrable under questioning. For a decade or so it was still the commies, anything faintly Red, had to nip it in the bud. But then the truck bomb went off in the World Trade Center, and good morning America! Suddenly everybody's worried about the Middle East. Islamic fundamentalists, America-haters, Arab terrorists. Don't think it's a real concern? Fact is, our guys who know about this shit, all the Defense Department spooks, they all know it's only a matter of time before we see some major terror damage here in the U.S. But how do we fight these guys, how do we manage what they call an 'asymmetrical conflict'? The Arab fanatics, they're more than happy to die for their cause, plus they're decentralized, they're in enclaves and cells scattered all over the world. Can't hit them with our big weapons, we need a more precise, delicate tool. But our normal soldiers don't seem to have sufficient commitment or desperation just now, do they? So how do we get at all those nasty guys?"

Biedermann paused expectantly, but again got only frightened silence from the other booth.

"The program," Rebecca called.

Yes! We manufacture operatives that are their equivalent. Programmed androids without scruples, who'll go in and do unspeakable things. Who won't care who they kill or if they live through their missions. We build ourselves some pet monsters, terrorists to fight terrorists. But the funny thing is, all the advances in the neurosciences, and the psych boys still can't do it right! These puppets still go screwy on their handlers. You wonder why we've seen twenty years of rising statistics in serial murder and rampage killing? You see now? You see how heavy this is? You see why we've got to go through with this?"

With Biedermann looming over them, cranking himself up, the people at the other booth were crying more loudly. Rebecca positioned the bag with her feet. Biedermann was only about fifty feet away, there'd be only one chance.

She deftly booted the purse toward Mo across the smooth boards. It skated straight but stopped short, a black mound appearing in the middle of the floor, obvious even in the half darkness. Mo flung out his legs until he was out full length, hanging by his cuffed hands from the ball-return carousel. He managed to snare the purse with his feet, then drew his legs in. The weight of it told him some bad news: not heavy enough to contain Rebecca's .38 as he'd hoped. Of course not—Biedermann would've checked. Then what? He had slid it up below his arms before he realized he couldn't pick it up. The cuffs stopped his hands several inches short.

He threw himself prone again, got his teeth on the bag, raised his

424

head, got his hands on it. Hard to open with the cuffs on, the dead finger. But now Biedermann had straightened from the other booth and was looking back. Mo froze, hoping the purse wasn't visible. Biedermann looked back for a moment, motionless. Mo's heart pounded so loud he was afraid the G-man would hear it.

But then Biedermann bent back to his cowering audience. He was obviously coming more than a little unglued. "See? Look at your own skepticism! I mean, you wonder why I had to do this whole big production, look at your own fucking response—'Guy's a real fruitcake, all this paranoid conspiracy shit.'"

Mo loosened the drawstring and got his hand into the bag. Rebecca was still staring at him as if beaming a transmission from her brain to his. His fingers felt her wallet. Computer diskette. Key ring. Tampon. A roll of breath mints or something. The broken finger was getting in the way, stiff and fat as a frozen hot dog, the purse a tangle of invisible objects.

"Give me a fucking break!" Biedermann was saying. "Didn't anyone notice how every goddamned assassin is this total loony, driven by weird compulsions, voices in his head? With mysterious chunks missing from his past? I mean, Oswald, Sirhan Sirhan, Hinckley, Mark David Chapman, the whole gang—you got super-powers and terrorists up the wazoo wishing they could bump off our leaders, and their best agents, their James Bond types, *can't* do it, but these guys *can*? Guys who can hardly wipe their asses they're so fucked up, but suddenly they can get past the Secret Service? You think about that! I mean how *obvious* can it get? I finally decided somebody had to say, *Wake up and smell the coffee, America!*"

Lipstick. Fountain pen. Soft pack of Kleenex. And then Mo found what she must have intended: a clipper. Just a fingernail clipper, but a fairly heavy-duty one. A little lever that swiveled out, biting razor jaws. He got his fingers around it, shook it free of the bag, used his knee to shove the bag out of Biedermann's view. Turned the clipper awkwardly, felt along his left wrist to the strap there. Couldn't get the angle right. Followed the band up to the flange, found the loop there, fitted the jaws to the strap.

Biedermann was facing this way again, coming back to his duffel. Mo froze. Then Rebecca was starting to sneeze, *Ah—ah—*and at her explosive *ka-CHOO!* Mo snipped the band.

The click was lost in her sneeze, but when he felt the cut he realized it had only gotten halfway through. Another painstaking fit of clippers to nylon, another sneeze from Rebecca, and he felt the tension go off the band.

Crouched over his duffel, Biedermann looked over at her. "What the hell, Bec. You coming down with a cold? Allergies, maybe?" He stood up and started toward her.

She sneezed again and Mo clipped through the second Flex-Cuf. Biedermann striding quickly now. "You up to something, Bec? You being a bad girl?"

"You ever have to sneeze when your hands are tied?" Rebecca asked acidly.

Biedermann's big body was moving with that scary heavy agility, coming toward her. He passed Mo. The instant he bent over Rebecca, Mo slipped the bands free of the flange and got up with one long strand of Flex-Cuf trailing. Biedermann had Rebecca's golden hair in a big handful and was wrenching her neck back over the booth seat, and that's when Mo hit him from behind, hands clenched in a double hammer blow, knocking the bigger man's head to the side.

Biedermann went to his knees and Mo leapt onto his back. The advantage lasted only an instant. Abruptly Biedermann flung his weight into a roll and struck out with an elbow all in one move. Mo hit the floor next to him, two feet from the booth. He tried to get his hands under him, but Biedermann was too fast. He kneed Mo between the legs and then was on top of him, whaling at his face with fists like wrecking balls. Mo felt his jaw snapping, the grind of bone ends.

And then Rebecca's foot whipped up and caught Biedermann square under the chin with a *chock!* and Biedermann tottered sideways. Mo got an arm around him, found the trailing end of the handcuff, pulled it against the bull neck.

Twenty-two inches of nylon band, just enough. One end was still cinched around his wrist, the other he wrapped in his broken hand. Pulled with every ounce of strength. Rebecca pounded Biedermann's temple with her heel. Biedermann's face turned scarlet with rage. Mo felt his grip start to fail, his strength giving out, but then Rebecca raised her leg and put her whole weight into a second heel to the purpling forehead.

And then it was Big Willie all over again. The bucking, grappling, fading. The slackening back muscles. The torpid dead-meat half-roll.

Mo gave it a full minute. Then slipped the band, got unsteadily to his feet. Limped down the lane to retrieve his guns. Came back to the booth, stepped over Biedermann's body.

Rachel was in shock, head tilted and mouth half-open, and Mo crossed quickly to her. "Rache. *Rachel.* Try to look at me." She didn't lift her head, so he did it for her, trying to be gentle as he turned her face to him. Her nose bled freely down her chin and throat. "Are you hurt badly somewhere?"

She seemed to think about it. "No." And all Mo could think was *Not the parts you can see, anyway.*

"It's all right now." Mo's face felt paralyzed, he could hardly talk at all, but he made the jaw move: "He's not going to hurt us anymore. Do you hear me?"

Again, she thought about that. "Yeah."

Mo squeezed her shoulders hard, caught Rebecca's eye. He went to get the clipper, came back, cut their hands loose. Rachel fell into her mother's arms. Then he needed to sit down in a hurry, the pain in his jaw so intense he couldn't see, he felt like he was going to throw up. Ringing in his ears, sweat on his temples. He closed his eyes to get a grip on the pain.

Only an instant, he thought, but when he opened his eyes, Rebecca was just sliding back into the seat. She wrapped her arms around Rachel. She had gone down to lane three and cut the others loose. Mo could see them lurching out of the booth. One of them stood and immediately lay down on the boards. Probably the old man, having a heart attack.

On the floor Biedermann suddenly sighed and rolled his head.

Mo had put the Glock in its holster, but still held the Ruger, and now his hand flicked like a snake and the gun seemed to fire itself. Once through the throat, point-blank. Only a .22, but the shot was loud in here, the muzzle flash blinding. When he regained his vision, he saw a small hole just to the right of the Adam's apple.

Biedermann's eyes rolled, focused. "Well," he gurgled. "You get the idea anyway. Some idea of the hurt, huh." He blew some blood out of his mouth. "Should have taken the purse away, huh. Should have known how resourceful. Gotta admire you guys." On the floor, a pool was spreading away from his head, black as an oil slick in the dim light.

Rebecca's face had that look that gave Mo chills. She reached over, took the gun from him. Put it into Rachel's hand, wrapped her fingers around it. "Rachel. I want you to focus. *No one has the right to do what he did to you.* If you want to, shoot him."

Rachel tilted her head to look at Biedermann's face, almost curious.

"Rachel, you understand, *you don't ever have to be subject to him again.* Him or anyone! If you need to kill him to prove that to yourself, do it."

"You don't have to talk so loud. I'm not retarded," Rachel mustered.

She angled the wobbly Ruger at Biedermann's face, still watching him curiously. Held it for a few seconds. Then set it on the table.

"You think you're free now?" Biedermann asked in a wet whisper. "Dream on. You'll know what I mean when you walk out of here. Even after you've gotten the materials out, you'll be afraid. I'm dead, but Zelek isn't. They won't like it that you know things. They'll wonder how much more I told you. They'll need to protect the program. Not just a dirty secret from the past. A very *now* kind of secret. It's worth your life. To even know about it."

Rebecca gave Mo a wide-eyed questioning look, *What do we do?* The black cape of blood widened around Biedermann's head like a poisoned soul taking its leave. After another moment he turned his cheek into the wet and closed his eyes. He looked relieved to be shut of the problem.

53

M O DIDN'T UNDERSTAND ALL of it, but Rebecca explained at length and gave him a couple of books to read. Post-traumatic stress, on top of the regular stuff between mother and daughter and Mo the new rival for Mom's intimacy, very complex psychology. But a couple of months had passed, Rachel was beginning to come around. It helped to have someone as insightful as Rebecca working with her. And Rebecca had been very strategic about the three of them being together, almost always outdoor stuff, where conversation was not central to the activity. No bowling.

Today it was Rollerblading in Central Park. Sunday, mid-August, the foliage was thick and full, everybody was out in the steamy heat, a great weekend. Mo was fine on the skates until he had to stop—braking was tricky. But that was okay, it gave Rache something to laugh about.

With all the residual anxiety, concern about her daughter, Rebecca had lost weight since that night, but it made her look even more terrific in shorts, knee- and elbow-pads, T-shirt. God have mercy, Mo thought, what skates did to an already long-legged woman.

They got to the area around the zoo and pulled over for a rest. It was nice beneath the big trees, rocks and lawns all around, the bustle of activity, the smell of hot dogs and roasting pretzels. Rebecca went to one of the carts and got lemonade. They watched the passing parade for a few minutes, then Rachel met a trio of friends and they skated off with promises to rendezvous in an hour.

Rebecca picked up a discarded *Times* from the bench, and they scanned it together. She pointed out an inside article featuring a photo of a familiar face: bald head, big grin, eyes that didn't smile as much as the mouth.

She shook her head. "You called this right, all the way, Mo. Did I tell you I think you're a genius?"

"I think you might've, but you're welcome to tell me again."

The article was about Westchester DA Richard K. Flannery, who was quitting his job to take over as deputy-something-or-other in the Defense Intelligence Agency. A nice fat Washington posting with a title that told nothing about the new job. His meteoric rise from a county-level position to a national-security role was attributed to his prosecutorial skills and his shrewd political networking. Also his apprehension of the deranged FBI agent who had flipped out and killed a couple of people at a bowling alley, a demonstration of investigative cunning and bravery that had gotten him national press only two months ago.

It was still uncomfortably fresh in Mo's memory. Biedermann lay dead, there was one man dead in the middle of a lane and another, it turned out, with his throat cut in the other booth. Rachel was in shock, the old man was lying on the floor, the others down at lane three were trying to console each other. And once the threat to her daughter was gone, Rebecca had kind of gone into shock herself. Mo got his bearings again and went to the front desk and picked up the phone. But Biedermann's last words stopped him before he dialed. *You think you're free now? Dream on. It's worth your life just to know about this.* This fucking thing would be controlling their lives long after Biedermann was in his grave.

With the pain in his head he couldn't think straight, but still it occurred to him that there was another call he could make first.

When he got Flannery on the line, he said, "I've got something for you to take credit for. A real springboard. But it's only yours if you get here within twenty minutes."

Sunday, Flannery was at his bachelor's pad Manhattan apartment. He made it in eighteen minutes. Mo unlocked the Star Bowl's front door to let him in.

"You were right about Biedermann," Mo mumbled, trying to ignore the crushed bones grating in his jaw. "There's a file containing materials that blow the whistle on secret U.S. military programs. I don't know any details, but I can guess it'll make the national news for weeks. You're also right that I'm not in a position to use this, I wouldn't know how. I don't need the headache. But somebody like you—"

"Gotcha," Flannery said, oblivious to Mo's less than flattering intent. They paused at the top of the steps down into the alley. Mo had deliberately left the lights off, so it was still dark, but they had a pretty good view of the scene: Rebecca holding Rachel close and stroking her hair, the bodies on the floor, the others huddled and just holding on. "Great God Almighty," Flannery said appreciatively. He practically licked his chops. For a moment his eyes went click-click, the wheels turning, calculating odds and angles. Then he turned to Mo. "Okay. Deal. So here's how we're going to play it."

Mo had made good use of the minutes before Flannery arrived, and Rebecca and Rachel already knew what to say and not to say: It was about jealousy, Biedermann going off the deep end after she'd ended their relationship, thank God Flannery had seen it coming and had charged to the rescue.

Flannery went to work on the survivors at lane three, finessing their recollection of events. Their memory of what the perpetrator had said was jumbled anyway, the old man and his wife couldn't hear very well, the young woman and her husband had been injured, the kid traumatized, everybody preoccupied. In the bad light, they hadn't gotten a good look at the guy Biedermann had handcuffed to the ball return down near the other end. Rebecca and Flannery would both say it was the courageous DA himself, who came when he put together the scenario and rushed to the Star Bowl at the very last minute. By the time more of the DA's people arrived, only a few minutes later and just in front of the ambulances Mo had called, Mo was gone.

In fact, he'd never been there.

But that still left a loose thread in the whole scheme, one that could threaten them if he didn't act immediately. So before leaving, Mo had stopped at Biedermann's corpse and rummaged in his pockets until he found his keys. He couldn't quite remember the address Gus had given him for Biedermann, but of course Rebecca knew it. Then he drove across the George Washington Bridge and into the Upper West Side. Flannery would cover the bowling alley scene, they could maybe just manage to fudge that, but Biedermann had to have been listening in on Rebecca's phone calls and probably live conversations at her apartment. Which meant that Biedermann kept monitoring equipment somewhere. He couldn't have been able to listen at all times, so most likely he'd rigged it to make tapes that he could review when time permitted.

If there were any such tapes, they were dangerous. Mo's whole plan hinged on Zelek and company not realizing how much he and Rebecca knew. If Zelek got the tapes, he'd hear the two of them piecing it together.

At the three-flat brownstone he checked the windows of nearby buildings, then gimped up the stoop steps and unlocked the outer door. Good luck so far, Sunday night, people winding down early, nobody on the street. He put on latex gloves and went up to Biedermann's third-floor apartment. Nicer furniture than Mo's own hellhole, but dimly lit, musty, not a place where anyone really lived. Taking a turn through the rooms, he saw only the meagerest tokens of domestic life. Most interesting were the handful of photos: some hard-faced men in camo outfits and face paint, standing in front of a ruined-looking patch of jungle. A busty, matronly old gal in out-of-date clothes. A dog. And a blond kid standing between a meek-looking woman and a man Mo first took to be Erik Biedermann until he noticed the fender of the station wagon just behind the group. Had to be a late-1940s vintage. So the man would be Biedermann's father, and the boy with the locked-in face Biedermann himself. The son's head was tilted slightly away from the man, signifying some aversion or resentment. Or fear.

Rebecca would love this, he thought: a clue to the original trauma suffered at the hands of a tyrannical and very blond, blue-eyed father.

But there was no time to delve further. The pain from his shattered jaw rose in blinding flashes, Mo kept feeling himself slipping toward unconsciousness. And the moment Zelek heard about the bowling alley fiasco, his guys'd be all over this place, sanitizing it, discovering more about Biedermann's secret life. Mo had to find the surveillance setup. But what if it wasn't here? Maybe Biedermann kept the gear at another place, maybe at the secret lab that must be somewhere near the old dump.

But then he opened a louvered closet and found a set of rack-mounted electronics, including two reel-to-reel tape recorders, a cassette dubbing setup, some heavily customized telephone equipment sprouting wires like Medusa's head. He took the two reels from the machines, then looked around until he found a stash of half a dozen others and a bunch of cassettes. He stowed them in a paper grocery bag from under the kitchen sink and then found a couple of fresh reels in unopened boxes, broke the seals, replaced them on the machines. Checked the telephone answering machine for messages. None. He pushed ERASE five or six times anyway.

Not perfect, but it would have to do. He locked up and left with the bag full of tapes.

The next day, jaw wired and finger splinted, Mo searched carefully through his house and Rebecca's apartment, looking for surveillance devices. The three bugs and the relay box ended up in the river that night. The tapes they burned in the barbecue pit behind Carla's mom's house.

The scenario he'd crafted with Flannery would just about play.

Especially, Mo figured, with some help from interested parties behind the scenes.

Mo and Rebecca had played dumb for Flannery, but Flannery would have learned all the details about the program from the evidence in Biedermann's duffel. And he'd done with the information just what Mo had anticipated. Mo and Rebecca, had they showed interest in whistle-blowing, were small fry, the kind you shut down, got rid of. Flannery, though, he was big enough to bargain, sufficiently lacking in conscience, and very smart with people and deals. He was in position to use his knowledge to his advancement and more than willing to make himself useful. Hey, he wasn't selling out, he was buying in.

The FBI put a tight lid on the whole case, one of those demonstrations of press obfuscation and spin control only "national security" warranted. Later, Mo heard though the grapevine that the FBI had located Biedermann's secret Westchester place. Nobody knew any details, but the consensus was that Biedermann had flipped while working on the Howdy Doody case and had started playing puppet games himself. Another example of job stress, too damn bad. The house had apparently belonged to his mother's sister, Eleanor Smith, who'd left it to him when she died. All he'd had to do to keep it secret was finesse keeping the Smith name on the tax rolls.

As a psychologist, Rebecca was dying to learn more about the original abuse that Biedermann had experienced, and if the old junkyard really had a role. She was also curious as to how many puppets Biedermann had been working with, whether the house contained evidence that there'd been others. But she resigned herself to not knowing. Showing any curiosity at all would have been a very bad plan.

Rebecca brought Mo out of his thoughts and back to the heat and bustle of Central Park by slapping the newspaper on her lap. "Of course," she said, "we still have a problem."

He looked around at the happy activity, the swaying high foliage. "That he never gave Biedermann's materials to the press. That he traded it all for his next step up. That the program goes on and nobody's doing anything about it."

"It kills me, Mo. I can't stand that somewhere they're still . . . doing it. Betraying basic human—God, I can't even—" Her eyebrows drew together and she glanced quickly over to the people on the nearby benches. But no one was interested.

"It screws me up, too," Mo whispered. "I never saw this as a permanent solution. More just buying us some time."

"How much time?" she asked. "And how much do we pay for it?"

As always, she'd seen to the heart of the issue. Their cover wasn't perfect. Realistically, it couldn't last. Maybe Zelek would think Mo was too dumb to figure things out, but no way he'd believe it about Rebecca. And maybe Flannery could give them some shelter, for a while, but Flannery had to have guessed what they knew. So the question was, *when* would it come back to bite them? And in what form? Not an outright whack, Mo figured, at least not for a while, that'd raise too many eyebrows. But at the very least, if Flannery was giving them shelter, it would be in exchange for something. Mo could easily imagine a future visit or call from him: *Hey, I've got a little project I need your special expertise on. Nothing illegal, just marginal procedure. A little carrot-and-stick thing. You guys help me out, I'll help you out, everybody stays happy.*

"I don't know," he told Rebecca. "Hopefully enough time to figure out what we should do. To maybe decide something about . . ." He stalled out, hesitant to mention it: *About us. About our own priorities.*

But of course she understood. It shut them both up for a few minutes. After that night at the Star Bowl, Rebecca had pulled back. She said things had gone too fast, she'd been impulsive again, Rachel needed a lot of her time. And Mo was deeply associated in Rachel's mind with the trauma of the bowling alley, she needed to build a basis of trust of him before she accepted her mother with him. Also, Rebecca needed some time to think through being with a guy whose job involved what they had just been through. The goddamned job.

They all needed some recovery time, Mo had to admit. After something like this there were a lot of hurts inside you. At first you were numb, just glad to be alive, in a state of shock that protected you. Then you began realizing how it had changed you. What was it, Biedermann's agony? The program, what it implied about the United States government, or about human beings in general? All the corpses, the puppets? You couldn't look at other people the same way. Couldn't read the newspaper headlines without a crawly feeling, that sense of things working behind the scenes, it seemed as if every time Mo opened the *Times* he saw another item like DEFENSE STRATEGISTS REASSESS RESPONSE TO TERRORIST THREAT. Sometimes you woke in the night in a sudden sweat.

No, you couldn't blame Rebecca for pulling back a bit.

Okay, so Mo was rolling with that. He could understand that. He had his own stuff to deal with anyway. He'd taken a two-week leave to get his jaw and finger rebuilt. He'd found an apartment, a three-room on the south end of White Plains, and had gone into his credit cards to make it nice: a couple of neo-Navajo rugs, a decent audio system, a few framed prints for the walls. A vacuum cleaner to keep things up. Not a palace, but it was getting there, almost the kind of place where you could have somebody over.

The grand jury hearing about Big Willie had been delayed during Mo's recovery. By the time the jury convened, Flannery was a media darling and was feeling grateful for Mo's gift, so he hadn't pressed the case. The hearing was a formality, the county's case perfunctory, and the jury had determined against probable cause. No charges would be brought.

So things were getting sorted out.

But there was still the big hurt, the real killer: the aftermath of Mike St. Pierre's death. Racing to the Star Bowl, Mo had called in to report the incident in the marsh, officer down, perpetrator dead. Later, when asked where he'd gone, he told his colleagues that he'd been badly injured and in pain, had rushed off to get medical treatment, and had passed out in his car in the hospital parking lot. Came to hours later and hauled himself into Emergency. All true—he just omitted telling anyone about the detour he'd made between the marsh and the emergency ward.

But none of that helped him with Lilly St. Pierre. Lil and three kids, it was too fucking sad and it was all Mo's fault. He shouldn't have called Mike that Sunday, or they should have stayed doubled up. Something. Anything. Marsden, Rebecca, everybody argued that there was no way Mo could have anticipated the attack. But it didn't wash. He *had* known, he'd just ignored that shrilling nerve of warning that day.

Mo felt like it should have been him to bring the news to Lilly, but Paderewski and Valsangiacomo had done it that night while Mo was at the hospital. They said Lil had dropped in her tracks, fell right down in the doorway. Then the kids had come in and seen her and started crying. This was the hell part. Whenever Mo had called, Lil had hung up as soon as she'd recognized his voice. He'd sent flowers and cards, but at the funeral Lil couldn't give him so much as a glance, just stood across the grave from him with her raw, red face averted. She looked so damaged. So different from the proud, strong Madonna with the sunlight halo, the mother of the happy mammal pile.

And there was nothing anybody, least of all Morgan Ford, could do about it.

On the brighter side, lying around recovering had given him time to chew on a lot of stuff. Hadn't discussed it all with Rebecca, but at last he was feeling a little more ready if and when she brought it up. Starting with Biedermann's comment: *You think you and I are so different? Take a look at yourself.* That jab had slipped under his guard and up between his ribs. He couldn't deny that, yeah, he would go to just about any length to be free of the feeling of strings on him. That somehow both his and Biedermann's life commitments seemed to require bending rules, working outside the system to defend what they believed in, and, too often, killing people. Yeah, and that neither ever quite managed to have a normal, regular domestic life or lasting relationships. *Touché, you bastard,* he acknowledged.

But ultimately he'd decided, no, that's not who he was. Biedermann's response was to control others in return, but Mo had an instinct to relinquish control once in a while. In the long run, your best bet for slipping free of the control of the system or bosses or your personal demons was to relax and let your own humanity happen. Surely Rebecca would see that: He'd never tried to force their relationship, her sense of timing, he'd accepted Rachel's presence in everything, he didn't have to be in the driver's seat all the time.

The biggest thing would be the job, how she could be with a guy whose profession brought him into situations like the Star Bowl and Big Willie. And she was right, it was the thing dead center in whatever he didn't like about himself, his day, his thoughts. But, he'd decided, it was also central to what he *did* like. Paradoxical, but that was life, you had to stake out your commitments somewhere and stick with them.

He wouldn't blame her at all if she brought it to a choice between her or his work. He just didn't know what he would do if she did.

Rebecca brought him out of his thoughts again by taking his hand. "There's something I've been wanting to say, and I keep not getting to it. But I think I need to tell you."

"Okay—" Mo felt a wave of uneasiness come over him. She was telepathic, she'd been thinking down the same avenues.

"There's something you did that drives me crazy—no, Mo, in a good way—when I think about it. That night. The first thing you did when you got loose was to come to Rachel. To see if she was all right, to comfort her."

"Well, she—"

"That means a lot to me. I'm having a hard time telling you this—how much that means to me. I think it says a lot about who you are."

Mo felt the relief of a near miss, the balm of her praise. "And what's that?"

"Mm, a lot of things. Nice things." Rebecca turned toward him on the park bench, sun-dappled hair, blue eyes straight into his. Those long, good thighs, driving him crazy.

"So what're you going to do about it?" he asked.

"I'm working on that. Giving it a lot of thought." She squeezed his hand meaningfully.

Mo liked the way she said it. Funny and serious at the same time, full of promise.

She had folded the paper and set it on her lap. Mo was feeling pretty good, but suddenly the half of the headline he could see jumped out at him and gave him a jolt: KILLER . . . The subhead began NINE DEAD IN . . . and reflexively he reached and twitched the paper open.

He was relieved to see the rest: KILLER HEAT WAVE SWEEPS MID-WEST. NINE DEAD IN OHIO, INDIANA.

Just forces of nature, he reassured himself quickly. *Not mankind's little propensity. Not something to get all existential about. Get a grip.*

Still, a smaller heading gave him an unpleasant buzz, NEW YORK AREA BRACES FOR MORE OF SAME. *Tell me about it,* he thought, suddenly feeling the jittery sweat on his body. Christ, it was scorching already.

When he looked over at Rebecca, she gave him a small, rueful grin that said she had observed his reaction and knew where it was coming from.

But for now, neither of them wanted to say any more about it. So they both just turned their faces to the sun. A moment in the sun. This was nice. Whatever the future held, you had to grab a moment like this, give it its due. Priorities.

ACKNOWLEDGMENTS

For helping me with this book, I owe sincerest gratitude to:

Major Tim McAuliffe (ret.), of the New York State Police, my friend and ally, a man who truly does know it all and gives most generously of his wisdom; Senior Investigator Nelson Howe, New York State Police Bureau of Criminal Investigation, who set me straight on many a detail; Joseph Becerra, NYSP BCI investigator extraordinaire who, for all that he gave generously of his time for this book and is a definitely cool guy, you wouldn't want after you (miscreants be warned); FBI media liaison James Margolin, of the FBI Manhattan field office, for generously giving of his time, expertise, and sense of humor.

You're the greatest, and the people of New York sleep better at night knowing you're on watch. May you forgive me for my inaccuracies, exaggerations, and rampaging literary license.

Thanks are also due to Vernon Geberth, homicide investigator and educator; to Dorothy Otnow Lewis, M.D., for elucidating the psychology of violence and daring to expose covert mind-control projects; to Betty Sue Hertz, my wise guide to Brooklyn; to Mudda whose name be not mentioned here, but who appears in this book and deserves much praise for her insight and generosity of spirit. Special thanks to Geoff Williams, chief among Mo Ford's fans, for demanding his resurrection. And of course to Nicole Aragi.

A NOTE ON THE AUTHOR

Daniel Hecht was a professional guitarist for twenty years. In 1989, he retired from musical performance to take up writing, and he received his M.F.A. from the Iowa Writers' Workshop in 1992. He is the author of four other novels: the best-selling *Skull Session,* which features some of the same characters as *Puppets; The Babel Effect;* and two novels in the Cree Black series, *City of Masks* and *Land of Echoes.* Visit Daniel Hecht's Web site at danielhecht.com for more about his books.

A NOTE ON THE TYPE

The text of this book is set in Bembo. This type was first used in 1495 by the Venetian printer Aldus Manutius for Cardinal Bembo's *De Aetna*, and was cut for Manutius by Francesco Griffo. It was one of the types used by Claude Garamond (1480–1561) as a model for his Romain de L'Université, and so it was the forerunner of what became standard European type for the following two centuries. Its modern form follows the original types and was designed for Monotype in 1929.